BOOKS 10-12

WORLDS OF THE FAE

MELISSA A. CRAVEN

M. LYNN

Edited by Caitlin Haines
Cover by Maria Spada

For the Love of Ham...
And Gullie

MYRKUR
NORTHERN
VATLANDS
FARGELSI
LOCH VILLANDI
ELDUR
SOUTHERN
VATLANDS
TEOTANN
OASIS
DESERT
ELDUR
DRAGUR
FOREST
VINDUR
CITY
LOCH LANGT
Queens of the Fae

NORTH EASTERN VATLANDS

KALT

HUNTING LODGE

VALE OF STORMS

EASTERN VATLANDS

THE FIRE PLAINS

LENYA

THE BURNING SEA

CRYSTAL MINES

VONDUR

GRIMA

ROCKY SEA OF LENYA

GRIMA SHOALS

Queens of the Fae book Ten

FAE'S ENVOY

MELISSA A. CRAVEN
M. LYNN

Chapter One
GULLIVER

Cold. Freezing cold air seeped into the throne room at the Iskalt palace. Despite the multiple hearths blazing. Despite thick velvet rugs covering the stone floors. Despite the warmth that normally enveloped the people sitting around the circular table.

Because none of them knew why they were here, except Gullie. Darn Tia for bringing him into this mess. All he'd been able to convince her of was that they had to consult the other royals when they arrived and couldn't just act unilaterally to fix the problem. And a big freaking problem it was.

A gathering of all the ruling royals of the now five kingdoms didn't happen often. There were only two circumstances that could make one of them call on their peers in any official capacity.

An imminent death. Or war.

Gulliver didn't want them to think Tia was dying. Magic, he

hoped they didn't assume that. New fear imagined, he paced along the rear of the throne room where all the other plebeians stood. Each had been invited into this meeting for one reason or another. None had royal blood. Well, none except his parents.

"Why am I here?" he mumbled to himself. He understood why his father and mother were told to come. King Hector of Myrkur rarely made any decisions without consulting them first. Sure, Gulliver was a friend of Queen Tierney's—he still couldn't get used to that crown on her head—but that didn't make him one of them. Tia wanted him involved in this, but he didn't see what he could do.

He didn't belong among the lawmakers, the magic wielders, those with the power to hold the kingdoms together or break them apart. Never before had there been a time where they were more united. Yet, a chilling foreboding filled the air.

"Will you stand still?" Griff hissed. "You're putting your mother on edge."

Riona scowled at him. "Speak for yourself. If I were Gullie, I'd be pacing too. Why was he summoned with the rest of us, Griff?"

"Exactly." Gulliver pointed at his mother. "I should be safe in my room here at the palace. It's my right as the queen's best friend."

"It's the middle of the afternoon." Griff did not look amused.

"And?" Gulliver didn't care what time it was. He wanted to curl up and sleep. They had arrived only yesterday and Tia had forced him into her rooms almost immediately to tell him of the news from her father. Before that, he'd been in Lenya as an emissary to oversee the delivery of the newest shipment of crystals. Without one of the O'Shea's, it was a long journey back.

Gulliver caught sight of one such O'Shea as Toby slouched in and leaned against the wall nearest the exit, trying not to be seen. Gulliver hadn't seen Toby much since his boyfriend, Prince Logan, died in a terrible accident in the fire plains. In fact, it would be six months ago tomorrow. They'd both been busy.

He skirted along the wall to reach the prince. "Tobes."

"Quiet." Toby looked at his feet.

Gulliver glanced toward the table, where the rulers of Eldur, Fargelsi, Myrkur, and Lenya chatted amongst themselves, tension thick in the air.

"No one is paying attention to the likes of us." He leaned beside him. "Do you know what this is about?"

"No." So, Tia hadn't even confided in Toby? Were Kier and Gulliver the only ones she trusted now?

"Do you know why I'm here?"

"Not everything is about you."

Gulliver's tail smacked Toby in the face. The prince didn't even flinch. "Don't be rude. I just want to know why the summons my parents received demanded my presence as well."

"I don't know. Maybe you ran afoul of my sister and everyone is here to watch her hang you by your tail."

Gulliver twisted to look at his tail. It flicked like it had a mind of its own. "Don't listen to him. Tia would never hurt you." His cat-like eyes narrowed. He opened his mouth to say something to the prince he knew he probably shouldn't but stopped when the ornate double doors, carved with intricate scenes from Iskaltian history, opened, revealing Queen Tierney in all her regal finery.

For a girl who never wanted to be queen, she sure took to the role magnificently in her ice-blue gown trimmed in silver. Her collar sat high on her neck, clasped at her throat with a silver brooch encrusted with fire opals, matching the one nestled in her strawberry blond hair.

Next to her, Keir Dagnan wore a jacket that matched her dress. They looked like a perfect set, but Gulliver saw it for what it was. A performance. This was the first time in her reign Tierney would host the other rulers, some of whom were her aunts and uncles, and she sure knew how to make an entrance.

For a moment, she met Gulliver's gaze and winked.

"Hello." She reached the long table and released Keir's arm. They took two of the many open seats at the table, leaving their thrones vacant on the dais behind them. "Thank you all for coming." Lifting her eyes to those along the far wall, she smiled. "Please, everyone, come sit. I have called you all here for a reason, and it affects more than just those who sit on thrones."

Thrones Tia continued to refuse to sit on. The last time Gulliver was here, she'd said she still thought of it as her father's seat. Brea and Lochlan were suspiciously absent. They had taken the youngest children to the human realm for some traveling, only returning occasionally to deliver news of the other world.

The only members of Tia's family that remained in Iskalt were Toby and their sister Kayleigh.

Gulliver didn't hesitate, walking forward and collapsing into a chair next to the king consort of Fargelsi.

Myles looked at him out of the corner of his eye. "You could at least pretend to be graceful."

A grin spread across Gulliver's face. "And what fun would that be, Oh great and mighty King Consort Myles?"

Myles rolled his eyes, but Gulliver caught the hint of a smile coming to his face.

Griff and Riona took their seats, as did Toby and a few other dignitaries Gulliver couldn't place. Once they were all seated, there were no more empty chairs. Tierney definitely knew how to plan. And she also knew not a single person would decline the invitation.

Gulliver raised his hand.

Finn, King Consort of Eldur, laughed, as did a few others. King Keir sighed and whispered something to Tia.

She shook her head and snapped back. "What is it, Gullie?"

"I don't think I should be here. Your summons must have been a mistake."

She looked straight at him, her eyes glinting with a danger he knew all too well. "A mistake?"

"Um, yes?" He swallowed. There were few people in this life he feared, but his best friend was one of them.

"Care to withdraw that statement?"

"Leave him alone, Tia." Queen Alona to the rescue.

Tia lifted an eyebrow, glaring at her aunt for only a moment before a laugh echoed out of her. "I'm sorry, Gullie. You're just so easy. Of course you need to be here. We have to discuss an imminent danger, one I already spoke to you of. That's why you're here. Plus, I've decided you are to move to Iskalt and become one of my council members." She cocked her head. "Did I forget to tell you? Oops." Her mouth quirked into a half-smile and Gulliver vowed to wring her neck the next time they were alone. Could he be faulted for committing regicide if the queen in question technically wasn't his?

Tia didn't forget anything. She had a mind like no other, and she knew Gulliver would have declined with a big old 'over my dead body'. Unless she asked him to do it in public. Then, he'd have no choice. His jaw tightened. Guess he was becoming a politician. "It would be my honor, your Majesty." He gave a curt bow and hit her with his best 'you're going to get an earful later' glare.

"Wonderful." She turned to the others. "Again, thank you all for coming. I am sorry for the short notice and for the necessity of sending Prince Tobias to fetch you through his portal rather than allowing you to travel by more ... comfortable means."

"I hate portals," Myles grumbled.

"They're so disorienting." Finn shook his head.

"That is not the point." Tia stood, placing both hands on the table. "I'm afraid we face a problem that affects all fae. We're receiving reports of attacks on both fae and humans accused of cooperating with fae in the human realm."

Silence followed her words, but it only lasted a moment before shouted questions volleyed around the room.

"How is this possible?"

"Who is perpetrating the attacks?"

"How many Fae could there even be in the human realm?"

"How do we stop them?"

Griff leaned back. "Did my brother bring you this news?"

Tia lifted one brow. "Yes. The *King* of Iskalt is still watching out for us, as always." She put a special emphasis on the title her father no longer held. Since he basically forced the crown on her, Tia's reverence for her father had gone up a few notches. She'd told Gulliver she understood him better now that she felt the weight of this kingdom on her own shoulders. He wondered if she regretted all those youthful rebellions, but who was he kidding. It was Tia. Probably not.

Tia held up a hand, magic sparking and crackling from her fingertips. Everyone quieted down.

"Wow," she breathed. "Even works on royalty."

"Tia ..." Neeve, Queen of Fargelsi, prodded.

"Right." Tia leaned forward. Her eyes flicked to Gulliver with a look he didn't understand, but then they moved around the table to each royal in turn. "My father believes the attacks are organized, and from what he's told me, I agree with him."

Griff shook his head. He knew more about the human realm than most fae. "But our features appear human there as long as we use glamours. How do they even know where to find the few fae who've managed to reach the human realm?"

"We haven't figured that out yet. My father believes there are more fae and half-fae there than we ever knew. Their non-human features are more subtle than ours, probably because their blood has been mixed with humans over many generations. And we all know the Dark Fae don't even need glamours to appear human. Their defensive magic does the trick. It seems before any of us were born, there have been fae and half-fae living among humans. It's quite a success story, actually. They must have escaped generations of war here, either via Aghadoon or led into the human realm by an O'Shea ancestor. Then, they bred with the humans and created their own communities. I'd love to study it someday and—"

"Tia ..." Neeve shook her head, steering her back on track.

"Fine, no history lesson. What you need to know is there are likely dozens—maybe even a few hundred—fae descendants in the human realm and they're currently being hunted and murdered. It is our duty to help them."

No one spoke for a long moment before Alona, one of the only humans in the group, sighed. "I do not know the human realm as I should. It is where I was born, but I have never lived there. Yet, I have read as much as I can, and it seems to me that wars are as commonplace there as ice storms in Iskalt. Are we sure these are targeted attacks and not just their usual human violence?"

Tia paused, and Gulliver could see it on her face. She wasn't sure of that at all. "I think it's—"

"Don't think, Tia," Neeve said. "For us to act, you have to know."

"But it's ..." She sighed and slid down in her chair. Movement caught Gulliver's eyes. Keir taking Tierney's hand under the table. "One community has already been targeted. What if it happens to another one?"

"And what if it doesn't?" Alona scrubbed a hand over her

face. "Tia, you're young, but I believed in your father when he gave you the crown. You are ready, and yet, you still have much to learn. I hope you will let us all teach you because one day, you will make the best queen Iskalt has ever known."

The words were honest, but even Gulliver knew it wasn't the right time for a public teachable moment. Here, in Tia's own throne room, with all other royals in attendance.

"She is already a great queen," Queen Bronagh of Lenya came to her defense. "She has always shown great care for all fae, even those not of her world. Lenya would have died if it wasn't for her. I wouldn't turn my back on other fae experiencing the same fate. But perhaps we should proceed with caution? We need more information before we can act."

A few others nodded. Across the table, King Hector sat perfectly still. Many had wondered if he was the right man to rule Myrkur when Riona named him king. Of all those present, he knew how it felt to suddenly have a crown thrust upon his head. Neeve should understand that too, but she had always been a leader, even before her father abdicated his throne.

Gulliver kicked Myles to get him to stand up for the niece he'd always adored. Myles sat up straighter and kicked Gulliver back. 'You do it', he was saying. Myles was right. As a reluctant part of her council now, it was up to Gulliver to take her side.

"I think we should send a group into the human realm after these as—fools." He cleared his throat, trying not to lose his cool in front of the most important fae in the realm. "We have to do something to help them."

"No." That was Hector. "Sending anyone who isn't familiar with the human realm risks further discovery. We must protect what we have here. Those fae chose to live among humans. They are out of our reach now."

Gulliver would show Hector out of his reach when he jumped across the table and strangled him.

"Are we all agreed, then?" Griff rapped his knuckles on the table. "We wait for more information from Loch?"

Heads bobbed around the table, and Gulliver vibrated with anger, this time directed at his father. How could he abandon those fae? It didn't matter that they chose to live with humans or that they had forsaken their heritage. They were fae, and they were in trouble. It was their responsibility to care for *all* fae. It was their *only* job. Even when the fae in question lived across the veil.

Everyone stood except for Tia. She sat stone-still in her high-backed wooden chair, her face a mask of the perfect queen. Calm. Confident. But Gulliver knew what brewed behind it because it reflected in him.

"Tia." Alona stopped beside her chair. "Since we're all here, I'm hoping to engage in some trade talks before we go home."

Tia nodded. "Sure, Aunt A."

Alona moved along the table and put a hand on Toby's shoulder. He ripped away from her and fled the room. Her shoulders sagged, and Gulliver couldn't hold on to his anger toward her. Not when she still mourned Logan's death. He was her only son.

They filed out of the room, but Gulliver stayed. He hadn't seen Tia in months before last night and just wanted to hold her and tell her to forget about the rest of them. She was already a great queen. When he, Keir, and Tia were the only ones who remained, he walked up beside her and bent down for a hug. Her head rested on his shoulder.

"I can't believe you'd betray me like that." Gullie patted her shoulder.

"What?" She sniffled and lifted her head. Tears dampened her cheeks, and Gulliver hated them all for making her cry.

"Council member, really?"

"Oh, that." She wiped her eyes. "I just really wanted you here after ..."

"After what?"

"I need you to risk your life for me again, Gul. I have no one else."

Chapter Two
GULLIVER

Gulliver followed Tierney from the throne room into the hall. Keir brought up the rear, stern and silent. None of them talked, but Gulliver had so many questions. He couldn't have heard her right.

They wound through the palace to the royal residence and into the grand sitting room where Princess Kayleigh was with Niamh and Nora, Gulliver's six- and eight-year-old sisters.

They all lay on their stomachs, the Myrkurian girls' wings fluttering behind them. There was way too much giggling coming from that corner. That usually meant they were plotting pranks on Gulliver. He loved his sisters very much, but they were trouble.

"Sis." Tierney flopped onto a couch. "Can you take the girls outside?"

Kayleigh pushed to her feet. "It's freezing out there. Ice storm, remember?"

"Right." Tierney looked tired as she rubbed her eyes. "Just go bug Myles then."

Her sister grinned. "Now, that is something we can do. Come on girls."

As they walked by, Gulliver ruffled their dark braids. Niamh pulled his tail and ran from the room, cackling.

Keir sat beside Tierney and wrapped an arm around her. She melted against his chest, her entire body sagging. "I don't like this," she said. "Any of this. I'm supposed to rule over a time of peace. My father, my grandfather ... they were meant to end the strife."

"But there is peace." Gulliver approached the hearth and held his hands out, needing the heat for this conversation. He didn't have a good feeling about whatever came next.

"Between the kingdoms, yes. But this danger in the human realm is big. I can feel it. We can't just ignore it and shut our eyes like the others wish to do."

"They aren't ignoring it," Keir said. "They want to wait and see."

"Do I look like a wait-and-see kind of queen to you?" She glared at her husband. "My father did not hand me his kingdom so I could sit back and let our people—however distant—suffer. If they are in the human realm, they must have been brought there by an O'Shea at some point. I have to trust my ancestors."

"All of them?" Gulliver turned to face her, one eyebrow raised.

She sighed. Her mother's aunt almost destroyed three kingdoms and imprisoned another. Not to mention the atrocious things that aunt's grandmother did to the dark fae. "Don't look at me like I'm nuts, Gullie. Not you. People have been doing that my entire life. I heard the whispers at my coronation. *She's too young, too impetuous, headstrong, and quick to anger.* And they're right about all of it. Maybe it should have been Toby born first, but here I am, and there's no changing it now. So, the question is, are you willing to face danger for me once again?"

"I—" The door slammed open, cutting him off. Griff stormed in, and Gulliver turned to block him from Tia in case he wanted to stop whatever ridiculous scheme she'd thought up.

"So, what's the plan?" Griff stopped right in front of him.

"I don't understand." He eyed his father from his auburn hair to the simple cut of his doublet. He was born a prince, raised to be the king of a foreign nation, and then finally became who he was meant to be in the prison realm. Now, he was protector of the rift in Myrkur but also just a fae living a simple life, who occasionally happened to get drawn into a queen's schemes.

"Let him join us, Gullie." Once Griff sat, she leaned forward to study him. "You made everyone agree to wait and watch for what happened in the human realm. You put a lot of lives in danger."

He sighed. "No, that's what they would have decided, regardless. I only sped them along to a conclusion. No one would have changed their minds. Alona, Neeve, Bronagh, and Hector have to do what's right for their people. Their kingdoms have seen a lot of struggles over the years, and possibly creating another wouldn't have been accepted in their cities. They're cautious now. Conscious of how every choice in this matter could lead to another war."

"And you?"

"I've seen more than they have. I know what it's like to be the one no one wants to fight for. We cannot let those fae down. Plus, I trust Lochlan."

Gulliver had never loved his father more than at that moment.

The doors opened again, and Riona froze in the doorway, her eyes landing on Griff. "What are you doing here?"

He stood. "What are you doing here?"

She straightened, her wings stretching out behind her. "I was looking for Tia and Gulliver, knowing they'd have a plan. As someone who fits in nowhere," she looked behind her, "I know how scared those fae must be."

"And you just weren't going to tell me you wanted to plot with Tia?" Griff crossed his arms.

Riona's look could have cut glass. "As if you'd have told me."

"Guys." Gulliver walked toward his mom and pulled her into the room, kicking the door shut. "Stop being idiots just because you're upset you both had the same idea." He knew them too well to think it was anything other than that. No matter how much they loved each other, they were always competing.

Tia looked between them. "So ... you both want in?"

"Depends on what it is." Riona sat on the arm of the settee.

"Well, I sort of want to send your son into the human realm to find out more about the group targeting fae. He'll have to act human, of course, and it's wicked dangerous. If they find out what you are ..." She met Gulliver's gaze as her words sank into him.

She wanted to send him on a mission to save the fae of the human realm. It was ridiculous.

"What makes you think I'm capable—"

She reached for his hand, holding it between both of hers. "Because you're the only one I trust enough to send. And your defensive magic will protect you more than a simple glamour. To everyone there, you will be no different from any other human."

Why did she have to put it like that? "Tia ..." He couldn't get the words out, couldn't voice what he really thought. Sure, his father sent him places all the time, but the human realm? Alone?

She stood, facing him, and put a hand on each shoulder. "You fought in the war for Myrkur," she started. "The battle of Eldur. You survived the Vondurian dungeon and sailing the Vale of Storms. I don't think there's anything you can't do."

"All of those were with you by my side."

"Isn't there anyone else?" Griff asked, putting a hand on Gulliver's back.

She shook her head. "Not anyone who could pass as human. Gulliver knows their customs well enough—the way they speak and dress. I can't send anyone who hasn't spent time there, and that list is very short. Plus, don't underestimate your son, Griff. He's the best of us. He just hasn't realized it."

Griff's hand slid up to the back of Gulliver's neck. "I could never underestimate this fae. I'm just worried."

Riona pulled him away. "Griff, something brought you to Tia tonight. Someone needs to protect those in the human realm. If Gulliver can do it, we have to let it be his choice. We cannot do the right thing only when it is convenient."

Gulliver could barely hear any of them as he pictured the farmhouse in Ohio. He loved it there, loved the peace. But this wouldn't be that. He'd have to assimilate with humans, talk to them. And yet ... he remembered spending every day in Vondur scared for his life, taken advantage of by those in power. If he could prevent other fae from ever experiencing that, he would. "What do I have to do?"

Tia smiled, but there were tears in her eyes. She wiped them away, and her ice queen face returned. "We have intel on the leader of a group we think is responsible for most of the crimes against a community of fae living in a place called New Orleans. Many in the human realm think the deaths are just part of organized crime related to the local gang violence. But we aren't so sure. His name is Claude Devereaux, and his power comes from the number of people throughout the city following him. He has what humans call a militia. Do you know what that is?"

Gulliver shook his head.

Tia continued. "It's when humans prepare for a war they

think is coming by waving around weapons and spreading dangerous information."

"So, you want me to what ... kill him?"

She shared a look with Griff. "No. Your first mission is just to find enough information that I can bring to the other royals so we can force a more active response from them. We can't have any further overabundance of caution like we saw from them today. However you can get the information, do it."

Tia laid out her plan for them to go over and change as they saw fit. The entire time, Gulliver caught his father casting sad glances at him. His mother was right, though. Others risked their lives to do good all the time. He had before. So, why not again?

He could never say no to Tia.

When they finished, Keir escorted Griff and Riona out, but Gulliver and Tia hung back, not ready to leave each other just yet. Tia turned into him, wrapping her arms around his waist and burying her head in his chest. His tail twisted around her.

"I hate that I have to ask this of you. I tried to find another way, anything else that could help those fae, but I kept coming back to you."

He rested his chin on top of her head. "You're the queen now. The decisions you have to make will be hard sometimes. But I trust you more than I trust myself. If you think this needs to be done and I'm the one to do it, I know that's right." He sighed. "But Tia ... what are we going to do about the others who sat around that table and told you to do nothing?"

She leaned back and looked up at him. "We can't tell them. Not until we have something more concrete. Your parents won't discuss it further for the moment, though Uncle Griff is likely going to make a quick trip to see my father tonight. He'll want the information from the source."

"Eh, he'll probably corner your mother first."

She laughed. "True." Her face sobered. "There is one part I

didn't tell Uncle Griff because I don't want it getting back to my parents."

"What? You want me to start a war or something?"

She bit her lip and sighed. "Kind of? Just with one person." She stepped out of his arms and turned away from him. "I'm sending Toby with you."

He froze. "Wait, I think I heard you wrong. Who are you sending?"

She whirled on her heel to face him again. "He's broken, Gullie. I have tried for so long to piece him back together, but it's almost like there's nothing left to heal. He isn't there, and I'm scared for my brother."

"And you think sending him to the human realm, where humans are hunting fae, is the answer?"

"He needs a mission, a purpose. He needs to do something, go somewhere that doesn't remind him of everything he's lost. Moping around this palace and pretending to be fine isn't doing him any good."

"This is insane."

"I know." Her voice rose. "But I don't know what else to do. The truth is, I may have been able to find someone else to go to the human realm, but you are the only fae in the five kingdoms I trust with my brother's welfare."

The idea of not going alone definitely held some appeal, but Toby? He'd seen him today at the meeting. The guy didn't meet a single fae's eyes.

"This could get us both killed."

She shook her head. "I don't believe that. No matter how torn apart Toby is, he'd never put your life in jeopardy. You two can protect each other. He needs you, Gul, just like I always have. Since I was a kid, I had you by my side. Toby deserves a little of that magic too."

"I'm not magic, Tia." He didn't even have magic other than

the defensive kind that would protect his identity in the human world.

She gave him her I-get-whatever-I-want smile, knowing she'd already won. "You have no idea how special you are." She reached up on her toes to press a kiss to his cheek. "I know you won't let me down."

Chapter Three
SOPHIE-ANN

"Are we ever going to get our order, miss?" the annoyed customer called to Sophie as she hustled past his table to deliver coffee and fresh beignets to the people that arrived two tables before Mr. Impatient and his nasty friends.

Sophie-Ann Devereaux hated waiting tables on days like this.

"Your order will be out as soon as it's ready." She rushed back to the kitchen, clutching an empty tray over her chest, as if it would protect her from the stares of all her customers. Sophie hated crowds, and the small cafe near Jackson Square in the French Quarter was always crowded. Pulse pounding in her ears, she ducked into the waitress prep station to get her social anxiety under control and catch her breath. Working was getting harder by the day. Some days, it seemed nearly impossible just to put on her uniform.

Her head ached, and she waited a moment to see if it would get worse or if it was just a result of the intense afternoon heat.

Each ache, each roll of her stomach, could mean something dire for her.

"Sophie, we're too busy for breaks! Get your butt in here and deliver these orders!" Vicky, the head waitress sent to Earth just to torture Sophie, shouted at her. Rather than helping out, she stood at the counter, slamming her hand down on the buzzer to tell the waitstaff orders were up. Like they didn't already know they were a table or more behind the demand for fresh beignets, chicory coffee, and all the French pastries the tourists could demand.

Sucking in a breath, Sophie gathered up her wits, pasted a smile on her face, and slid five plates of piping hot beignets onto a tray. She grabbed a pitcher of iced coffee and a sampling of all the best sauces to dip their treats in, and rushed back into the fray.

"Sorry about the wait," Sophie murmured as she set the dishes onto the white linen-covered table at the best booth in the house. Or the worst, depending on who you were. The oversized booth sat in the window overlooking Jackson Square and the streets filled with tourists, artists, and street performers. For those who didn't want to miss a thing, the booth was a prime spot. For those like Sophie, it felt like sitting in a fishbowl, where the world could see every flaw on display.

"Watch it!" one of the ladies at the table shrieked. In her rush to get past the window, Sophie had dropped a plate of beignets all over the pristine tablecloth, where the oil from the fryer immediately spotted the linen. She'd probably have to pay for that.

"I'm so sorry!" Sophie snatched up the hot pastries with her bare hands, wincing at the sting. "I'll get you another order right away."

"It's fine." The young woman sighed, rolling her eyes as she brushed the scattered powdered sugar into a neat pile. "Kind of on par with my day of bridal fittings." Tears swam in her eyes, and Sophie started to panic. Standing here with her head pulsing, she wasn't sure she could handle a crying customer. A bride no less. Sophie was one of those people who cried whenever other people cried. It wasn't sympathy so much as a nervous reaction to not knowing how to handle it.

The woman's companion reached out and patted the girl's hand. "It's been just awful." She shook her head, her eyes full of sadness, like someone had died. "The seamstress stabbed her with a needle and got blood on her beautiful white dress."

"And now, I'll probably die of tetanus." The bride scowled. "And don't expect me to pay for those." She pointed at Sophie's hands.

"Right." The beignets were turning to mush in her hands. "Uh ... I'll be right back."

Sophie ran into the kitchen and tossed the mess into the trash. Her shoulders slumped as she furiously wiped the sticky sugar from her hands. Between the tablecloth and the fifteen-dollar plate of cheap fried dough, she'd probably end up working for free today. Not that she needed the paycheck for anything specific.

She still lived at home with her dad, and she was a low maintenance kind of girl with bigger problems than a less than a perfect afternoon of shopping with her non-existent friends.

Sophie went out to grab the tray she'd left perched on one of the waitress stands. She could never keep track of that stupid thing.

"Seriously, girl, where's our order?" The jerk from earlier gave her a murderous look. "We're starving here."

"Sorry! Be right back." She ran past the table to the safety of the kitchen again. The dining room was like a gauntlet she never seemed to get through unscathed.

"This is the worst job ever." She stood at the pastry chef's counter, tapping her foot and waiting for the jerks' order. Her father thought working at the cafe was exactly what she needed to prepare her for following in his footsteps. He'd even gone so far as to fill out the application for her and called in a favor with the owner—a fact Vicky liked to remind her of at least once a shift.

He thought getting her out of the house would somehow magically make her the daughter he wanted.

Still muttering to herself, Sophie slammed the artfully plated tiramisu onto her tray and marched out to the dining room to deliver the desserts and refill their coffee before the silly boys perished right before her eyes.

"Worst waitress ever," one of the boys said loud enough for the whole restaurant to hear.

Sophie's face flushed beet red, and for once, she found her words. "I'm sorry, but as you can see, we're a bit busy."

"We shouldn't have to pay for this." The meanest of the group pinned her with his stare, and Sophie stammered an inarticulate response.

"Seriously, sweetheart, you might want to consider another line of work because you really suck at this job."

And just like that, she lost her words, turning on her heel, she ran for the kitchen, itching to take her apron off and scream her resignation so everyone in Jackson Square could hear it. But she'd almost made it through her shift. She could last another twenty minutes, and then she'd have two blissful days off where she could stay at home, reading under her favorite old tree in the backyard ... and attend her father's meetings.

"Stupid fae freaks have to ruin everything." She slammed an empty coffee carafe into the machine and punched a series of buttons to set it brewing again. She used to spend all her free time with her dad, hunting through the city's oldest bookstores for treasures and talking about their favorite fantasy books. And her mom ... before she died, they used to cook together on the weekends, making a huge batch of the best gumbo she'd ever tasted. They only used the freshest ingredients they could find at the French Market. They even bought their crawfish from a local fisherman who lived down the street. Thanks to the fae and their dark magic, that idyllic life was over.

"What was that, Sophie?" Vicky came up behind her to add the coffee grounds she'd forgotten before she ruined it ... again. "You know this makes better coffee when you do it right."

"Sorry. I'm a little scattered today."

"Busy days will do that. You just have to take it one task at a time and not let it overwhelm you."

"I'll try that." Sophie wondered why she was being so nice and understanding. Two qualities Vicky sorely lacked.

"Your bridal party just left. Go bus the table and change the linens. The dry cleaning will come out of your paycheck."

Now that was more like the Vicky she knew.

"Yes, ma'am." Sophie grabbed a bin and headed back into the dining room. Truth be told, she'd rather be a bus girl than a waitress. She didn't mind bussing tables since she didn't have to talk to people. Dumping the half-eaten plate of beignets into the bin, she focused on the mindless task. She didn't see the person staring at her through the window until it was too late. As she lifted the bin that was almost too heavy for her, she blew a short strand of blue hair from her face to find the handsome man staring at her.

"Gabe," she muttered under her breath. He was too beautiful standing there watching her with a bemused expression on his face. Too bad the ugly showed through whenever he opened his mouth to speak. She turned away, hurrying for the kitchen to dump off the dishes and buy herself a minute before she had to face her father's second in command.

"I'll finish your last table," Vicky said as Sophie set the heavy bin of dishes on the stainless steel counter for the dishwashers to handle. "I'll see if I can salvage our reputation. Those guys are furious with you."

"They didn't like waiting, but I swear, I didn't make them wait long."

"You have to balance your time better or I'll have to put you on the slower shifts where you won't make as much."

"I understand." Sophie was quick to respond, thinking it wouldn't be so bad. She'd probably still make enough to fund her book-buying habit.

"Go clock out."

"Yes, ma'am."

"And don't call me ma'am. I'm only a few years older than you."

More like a decade or two.

"Yes, ma'am ... er, sorry, Vicky." She headed for the back room to clock out before she grabbed her clutch purse from the office and darted out the door to avoid Gabe. She made it halfway down the alley before she ran into him.

"I guess I should have seen that coming." Her shoulders drooped in defeat. "What do you want?"

His eyes said he wanted her, but as far as she was concerned, that was never going to happen. He just wanted her for the connections she could bring.

"Your father's called a meeting." He ushered her onto the sidewalk.

"We just had one." Sophie quickened her steps. If her father sent Gabe after her, she couldn't escape the summons. He was the most trusted of her father's followers.

"Not a regular meeting. This one's an emergency." Gabe's southern drawl was an odd mix of his father's old creole and his mother's Cajun roots. The leadership was a handful of her dad's most trusted soldiers–his very own militia.

Gabe seemed to vibrate with nervous energy as they walked along Chartres Street toward Esplanade Avenue and the French Market.

"What's the meeting about this time? Have the fae attacked?" Her heart thudded in her chest at the thought. "Is anyone hurt?"

"No. You'll see when we get there." They walked in silence along the busy streets, the hot summer sun beating down on their shoulders, sweat making Sophie's clothes stick to her skin. It was always hot in the Quarter during summer, but today was sweltering.

"Keep up," Gabe called over his shoulder as she fell behind, unable to match his long stride. Sophie was a petite girl—all of five feet and an inch or two to spare, depending on which shoes she wore. She had to take nearly three steps for each of his, and her heart was flying in her chest by the time they reached the corner of Decatur and Esplanade.

The market was packed today, and the sidewalks swelled with too many people. A panic attack rose up within her as they crossed the street.

Finally, they stepped through the wide gates of her little slice of heaven in the middle of the Quarter. The old Spanish chapel had been converted to a residential home ages before she was born, but when her father moved them here many years ago, it became her oasis. Huge cypress trees shaded the small chapel, and Spanish moss hung from the branches. A high brick wall skirted the property, and as they closed the wrought-iron gates behind them, the noise of the streets faded and Sophie took a deep breath, slowly letting it out.

She left the budding panic attack behind her on the sidewalk. It would be there for her when she left for her shift on Saturday. The courtyard garden blossomed with fragrant flowers and spicy herbs, and the sun shone through the stained glass windows that illuminated the interior of the house in a riot of warm colors.

"Where's Dad?" She frowned at Gabe. Her father spent most of his time working in the garden or sitting in his favorite patio chair, working on his laptop.

"The warehouse." Gabe nodded to his car. "I'm to take you there in an hour." Sophie turned wide eyes on Gabe, who nodded. "We finally got one, Soph."

Chapter Four
GULLIVER

"Are you sure about this, Tia?" Gulliver shoved an old pair of human jeans into the backpack Griffin had bought him on his first trip to the human realm when he was just a kid. Somehow, he'd been braver then than he was now. Back then, a trip to the human realm seemed like a great adventure. Now that he was the adult in charge of this mission, it seemed like a really bad idea.

"You've been to the human realm so many times, Gullie. You're the best man for the job." Tia took the jeans out of the bag and folded them properly. "Why are you so anxious?"

"Every other time I've visited the human realm I had adult supervision or we just stayed at the farmhouse. I know how to order takeout and get around okay in small towns. I know how to use their weird plastic money, but that's about it. I'm not even allowed to use the microwave because I've blown up three of your mom's applences."

"Appliances."

"See, I don't even know the right names for their magic boxes."

"Electric."

"Tia," Gullie growled.

"Has it occurred to you that I *am* sending an adult? This time, you're the adult, Gullie."

"And that doesn't terrify you?" His eyes grew wide with alarm. "Because it's got me off my food and that never happens."

"You're going to be great." Tia sat down on the edge of his bed, her pale blue dress fanning out around her. "I wouldn't send you if I didn't think you could do it. This is too important. I have a bad feeling about this, Gul. I think there are more fae in the human realm than any of us ever realized, and someone is targeting them. I need you to find out what's happening. That's literally what you do, Gulliver O'Shea. You always know more about what's going on in Myrkur than Uncle Griff or even King Hector. And it's because you're good with people."

"I'm good with Myrkurians." Gulliver gathered up his stone carving kit and a few small pieces of marble with veins of blue cobalt and stuffed them into his pack. He'd make something for his sisters while he was away. No doubt they'd expect something human upon his return. "Myrkurians love me because I am dark fae. Outside of Myrkur, things are a bit difficult for my kind."

Tia laid a sympathetic hand on his arm. "And I hate that. One day it will be a better world where all fae are accepted as equals. But remember, you're going somewhere where everyone around you will see you as a regular person. To them, you'll be human."

"True." Gulliver sank to the bed beside her. "I just hope I don't let you down."

She leaned into him and rested her head on his shoulder. "Well, that would be impossible. You could never let me down."

They sat there for a minute in silence.

"Gullie?"

"Yeah?"

"Why does your duffle bag smell like ham?"

"In case we can't find food where we're going, I, uh ... brought some provisions. The humans' plastic money always seems iffy to me. I always feel like it can't possibly work."

"Mom uses the money cards all the time. It'll be fine." Tierney reached for his duffle bag.

"Wait, don't do that!" But it was too late. Tia had already unzipped it, and she just looked at him like he'd lost his mind. "Do you even know how long it took me to get that bag zipped?"

"Do you really need a ham, a string of sausages, what looks to be two pies, and three loaves of bread?"

"And a pudding." Gulliver's tail whipped irritably behind him.

"Gullie. They have all your favorite foods in the human realm."

"I don't know about where we're going. I found a book on New Orleans in the library, and they have strange food there."

"I'm sure you're going to like it just fine, and based on my own travels in the human world, you can get pizza and hamburgers practically anywhere, anytime."

Gulliver felt a bit better knowing that. "I just ... If I run into trouble, there's no one to ask, Tia."

"Of course there will be. Did you think I wouldn't ask Dad and Uncle Griff to check up on you now and then? Mom and Dad are visiting Montana right now. Mom said they were glamping. I don't know what that means, but it's a marvelous human word, isn't it? They want to keep the kids away from what's going on over there. So I think they're pretty far away from where you'll be, but you should expect a visit from at least one of them after you get settled. They'll let me know if you need anything."

Gulliver let out a sigh. "Okay, but you have to help me zip this back up. I'm still taking it with me."

"I wouldn't expect otherwise." Tia slipped down onto the floor beside the bulging bag, and together they fought with it until it closed. "Did you bring any more clothes with you? I saw exactly one pair of jeans that probably don't fit you anymore."

"There's a shirt in the bottom of my pack. They fit. Sort of. I'm going to need some new stuff once I get there. I'll go to that big scary marketplace in Grafton. You think Myles' mom would take me?"

"Walmart?" Tia shuddered. "I've never seen a marketplace like that anywhere else. It's terrifying, Gullie; don't go there alone. Just call Mrs. Merrick from the farmhouse, and she'll help you with anything you need. You might find some of Toby's human clothes that would fit you now."

"Speaking of Toby, I haven't seen him since the meeting."

"He's probably in his room. We should go check on him. It's almost moonrise." Tierney stood up and tried to lift Gulliver's food bag onto her shoulder, but it wouldn't budge. "Want me to put a weightless spell on this before you go?"

"Better not. If humans are attacking fae, the last thing I need is something magic I can't explain."

"Good point." She kicked the bag. "You lift it, then."

"Tia, watch my pies; you'll crush them!"

"Let's go find Tobes."

He was in his room, but he hadn't packed. It looked as though he hadn't gotten out of bed yet, and the day was almost gone.

"Toby." Tia sent balls of light into all the lamps in the room. "What are you doing? You're supposed to leave in less than an hour." She flung back the curtains, letting in the moonlight.

"Go away." Toby groaned from somewhere under the furs on his bed.

"No." Tierney tugged the furs aside, leaving him to shiver in the chill of the room. "And don't complain to me that you're cold. You're the one who let the fire die out."

"Dóiteán," she murmured under her breath, and flames leaped to life in the fireplace. "Now, get up. That's an order from your queen."

"I don't care. I'm not going." Toby sat up and reached for the wineskin that sat by his bed, cursing when he found it empty.

"Are you drunk, Tobias O'Shea?"

"Very." Toby got up and went in search of a chamber pot.

"You stink." Tia covered her nose, turning her back on the screen in the corner.

"Go away." Toby stumbled across the room to collapse on the big leather chair in front of the fireplace.

"You're leaving for the human realm. Right now." She lifted her hands, murmuring a few Gelsi spells under her breath, and clothes and supplies started packing themselves into a bag she'd magicked from under the bed. "Don't make me chase you down the hall with my magic, because you know I'll do it." She stood with her hands on her hips, panting with the effort of packing and yelling at the same time.

"Fine." Toby grabbed a tunic from the corner of his room, gave it a sniff, and shoved it over his head. "At least I won't have to listen to you shrieking at me to do something with my life." He snatched his pack and stalked from the room. "Gullie, we're going now. Keep up."

Gulliver and Tia darted down the hall after him. "And just where were you when I spent half the morning packing my belongings? The best friend who is willingly—if not silently—doing as you asked?"

"While you were pilfering food, I was running a kingdom."

"Right." They came to a stop in the moonlit courtyard just outside Tia's study. She still called it her father's study, even after so many months of being queen. Gulliver wasn't sure she'd ever get used to it.

"Oh no, he's already opening the portal, Gullie. Hurry!"

"Wait a minute, Toby. At least let me say goodbye."

But the air around Toby shimmered for a moment before an opening split the atmosphere. "If we're going, let's go already." He swayed on unsteady feet.

"I'm not getting into that thing." Gulliver shook his head. "He is not sober enough to be taking people through portals." He backed up against the stone walls that surrounded the courtyard, his arms over his chest and a stubborn glint in his eye. "Not doing it, Tia. Don't even give me that look. You know what happened last time I went through a wonky portal."

"But that was *my* wonky portal." She pushed him toward the blue glowing light beside her brother. "Toby is better than me. It's not like he'll send you to a foreign world we don't know anything about."

"It's not, is it?" He resisted her pushing, but she was freakishly strong for a pampered queen, and she had him facing the portal far too easily.

"You two mean everything to me," Tia said. "I'm grateful for your help. Just be careful please. And ..." But Toby didn't stick around to let her finish. Without a backward glance, he stepped into the portal, disappearing in an instant.

"Go, Gullie!" Tia shoved him. "Before he leaves you behind."

"Wait, Tia."

"There's no time." With a final shove, she pushed him into the portal. "I'm sorry!" she called after him. "I love you. Take care of Tobes!"

Gulliver didn't get a chance to reply. The portal took him and whirled him around upside down, bouncing him from side to side before it spit him out.

Thudding onto the ground in a spray of dust and gravel, Gulliver groaned, covering his face with his arms, too afraid to look at his surroundings. "Please don't be the middle of a battle. Please don't be the middle of a battle." He peeked through his arms, and the familiar sight of the farmhouse came into view.

"Oh, good." He sighed, lying down flat in the driveway. "It's just Ohio."

Gathering his wits about him, Gulliver stood up, looking around for Toby. He found him under the old oak tree where Tia's sisters had begged their dad for a tire swing. It looked like a death trap to him.

"Toby?" he called out softly, but the prince didn't move. "You okay, Tobes?" He toed him with the tip of his boot. "Please don't be dead."

The prince let out a snore, and Gulliver was both relieved and irritated. "I should leave you here to sleep it off, but I'm scared of the human house. It's too easy to break things." Grunting, Gulliver managed to get Toby to his feet long enough to drape him over his shoulder and get him into the house. They made it as far as the living room, and then Gulliver went back out for their bags.

While Toby slept on the couch, Gulliver searched the rooms upstairs for human clothes that might fit him and lucked out with a few of Toby's things and some of the former king's t-shirts. They were a bit large on him, but Toby's were too small, and he wasn't sure he should try wearing any of Brea's clothes. Humans were funny about things like that.

Finally, he made a plate of ham and a slice of pie from his stash and went to call Mrs. Merrick. Gulliver hated using human phones. He never remembered how to work them. Most of the time it was just easier to go visit the Merrick farm than take the time to work the phone. But Gulliver didn't want to leave Toby alone.

He finally found the number and hit send.

"Hello?" a lady answered the phone.

"Um, hello." Gulliver held the contraption up to his face. "Mrs. Merrick?"

"Yes, dear. Is this a friend of my son's?"

"Er, yes. How did you know that?"

"Caller ID. It tells me someone is calling from the O'Shea farm."

"Oh. Okay, yes, this is Gulliver. I've visited before."

"The boy with the tail, right? Though, you've never shown it in front of me."

"Yes, ma'am, that's me. It's not visible to humans here. Um …"

"Do you need some help?"

"Yes, please. I have to go to a place … um, hold on a second. I have the name here." He searched through his pack and fished out a notebook Tierney had given him. "It's called New Orleans. Is that nearby?"

"No, it's quite some distance from Ohio."

"Thank you so much!" Gulliver shouted into the phone.

"No need to shout. Cell phones have excellent connections."

"Sorry!"

"New Orleans is in a state called Louisiana. It's about a thousand miles from here."

"Is that as far as Ireland? I went there once and didn't care for it." Gulliver didn't want to fly in one of the humans' metal birds. It was one of the worst experiences of his life.

"No, much closer. "Have you ever flown before?"

"Yes, though, I'd rather not. My mother and sisters have wings, but I was born with two feet, and I'd rather keep them on the ground if possible."

Myles' mom chuckled and said, "Well, the next best thing is a bus."

"What's that?"

"It's like a big car that carries a bunch of people to the same place."

"That sounds like a good plan."

"All right, I can order you a bus ticket and drive you to the station if that helps."

"I have plastic money."

"Is it one of Brea's cards?"

"Um, yes, Tia gave it to me."

"Perfect. I have the numbers right here on my fridge. I'll use that to buy your ticket. When do you need to leave?"

"As soon as possible."

"Okay, I'm looking at the bus schedule now. There's a bus that will take you nearly all the way there leaving at six a.m. tomorrow. Does that work for you?"

"Yes, ma'am, thank you ... Oh, when is six?"

"It's very early. I can call you to let you know when I'm on my way. We'll have to leave by five to make it to the station on time."

"That would be wonderful if it's not too much of a bother." He didn't want to take advantage of her time.

"Not at all. You can tell me all the news you have about my son's family on the way."

"I can do that."

"Is anyone with you, Gulliver?" She sounded worried about letting him loose in the human world without a guide. A reasonable worry considering it freaked him out too.

"Oh, Toby is with me. I guess he'll need a ticket as well."

"Poor darling. It's a shame what happened to his Logan."

"He's not doing so well. That's why Tia sent him with me—to get him out of the palace for a while."

"That will be good for him. The best thing for a broken heart is activity. Do you need help with anything else? You have human clothes? We can take a quick trip to Walmart if you need to."

"No!" Gulliver panicked at the thought. "Thank you, but no, we have clothes."

"All right, try to get some rest tonight, and I'll see you bright and early in the morning."

"Thank you, Mrs. Merrick." Gulliver ended the call, feeling slightly better about his situation. Once they arrived in New Orleans, that might prove to be a different matter.

Chapter Five
SOPHIE-ANN

Sophie-Ann had conflicting feelings about her father's plans and the organization he'd started to help set them in motion. Yet, here she was in a drafty old warehouse near Lake Pontchartrain. Officially, the building was used by an industrial laundry service, and the whir of constantly running machines filled the air with a familiar vibration.

Unofficially, it was also the headquarters for HAFS, the Human Alliance For Survival. As if they were in any real danger of extinction because a handful of stinking fae decided to make a home in the human world.

She didn't like the fae. They didn't belong here with their unnatural abilities, but even so, most HAFS meetings left Sophie feeling a bit sorry for them.

Her father made her stand at his left while his followers filed in. She'd thought only the leadership group would be here tonight, but more and more people entered. They came from all walks of life. Old, young, all ethnicities, and political affiliations.

White supremacists standing side by side with those who'd spent their entire lives fighting for equality.

For humans. That was the point of HAFS. This world belonged to humans. Some of these people should hate each other, but her father brought them together. She should be proud, and she was ... mostly. Before her mother died, he was just another guy working too hard to afford a living in the increasingly expensive city.

Now, he was an icon.

And at the same time, she wasn't sure she recognized him anymore.

The chatter grew as more people entered the room to see what their leaders had called them in for. A captured fae. One of the bad guys.

Only, the man just looked like a frightened human to Sophie. He was on his knees, his shoulders shaking in the dirty and torn shirt he wore. There was a rope around his neck, and Sophie flinched when he moved and it shifted, revealing the red burns on his pale skin.

Sweat-soaked hair clung to his forehead as he lifted his eyes, finding Sophie. "Please. I don't know why I'm here."

The rope jerked, and he tumbled onto his stomach with a groan. Gabe stepped forward, holding the other end. He leaned down. "You don't get to speak to her."

The man's entire body trembled as he sobbed. "Why are you doing this? I haven't done anything."

Gabe kicked him, sending him onto his back. "Fae don't speak here."

"Gabe." Sophie's father put out a hand, calling for calmness. "He's right. He has not been tried for a crime. Yet. We are a just group. Don't touch him again."

Relief bloomed in Sophie's chest, but it didn't last because she'd been around long enough to know exactly what her father's words meant.

The crowd quieted, waiting, anticipating. They came for a show, to witness their work done. There were dangerous people here, but Sophie was protected, untouchable. Alone.

"Welcome, friends," her father said, lifting his hands with a smile. He should have been a preacher with the way he could influence people with his words, his voice. But then, he'd have to believe in something good, and she wasn't sure what he believed in anymore.

"We are here today to do our grave duty." He bowed his head, and the others followed suit. "Let us bring justice to the human race this day. We fight for our wives, our husbands, and our children. We fight for those who do not even know the battle facing them. You see, friends, we are blessed. Our eyes have been opened to the existence of these otherworldly beings. They don't belong here, among us, deceiving us. Our trials will be rewarded."

Each meeting began with a similar opening—one to remind the people that every action they took, no matter the guilt they felt, was entirely right. They were justified in their indignation.

There was a word for groups like this, but it had taken Sophie too long to see it for what it was.

A cult.

Her father was a cult leader, and her mother would be so ashamed.

A smile spread across her father's face. "Now, shall we begin?"

A light above the scared prisoner flickered on, shining directly down on his beaten form. Those nearest to them closed in, making the circle smaller, and others pushed from behind to see the captive, to witness his pain.

Sophie couldn't stop casting glances his way. He looked

maybe a decade older than her twenty-one years. Someone who was probably loved, whether he was fae or not. As much as Sophie hated the creatures, as much as she wanted them gone, she couldn't help wondering what this all meant. Fae looked no different from anyone else she'd met. From what they knew, the fae kept families, had culture. These weren't wild animals.

"Who accuses this man of a heritage not of this world?" Her father's question rang in the empty rafters of the room, sweeping over the curious crowd. "Come forward."

A moment of stillness passed before commotion sounded at the back of the group, and a woman pushed her way through. She had blond hair pulled severely back from her scowling face and a very pregnant belly.

"I am the accuser." Her voice was rough, a smoker's voice. As she drew near, tobacco wafted off her.

Sophie's father approached the woman and took both of her hands, speaking gently. "Your care for the human race is a precious thing. We thank you for your bravery. Please take your time and tell us your truth."

Murmured thank yous came from the others. Sophie kept her lips clamped shut.

A tear streamed down the woman's face. "My name is Annette Colewell." She sniffed. "My ... my husband, Henry, I thought our marriage was based on trust. But the entire time, he was pretending to be something he was not."

"How long were you married?" Sophie's father asked.

"Six years."

"Annette," Henry croaked. "Don't do this."

Annette turned her back on him. "He—I didn't know. I thought I loved him, but I never would have—" She devolved into sobs.

Sophie's father put an arm around her shoulders. "We know. You are a brave and loyal woman."

She wiped her eyes and nodded. "I am. The fae have no place in our world."

"When did you suspect your husband?"

She bit her lip. "Well, he started to sneak out of the house a lot. Sometimes, he claimed to be at work, but I'd call and he wasn't in the office."

Sounded like an affair to Sophie.

Annette went on. "I've known about fae my whole life. My father used to tell me stories, but when I was old enough, he told me the truth. He'd befriended one such creature in his younger years. He didn't know what he was doing."

"He is forgiven for his ignorance," Sophie's father whispered, though the point of that was lost on her since he wore a microphone that broadcast the whisper.

"Thank you," she said. "When I grew suspicious, I followed Henry."

"And what did you find?"

"He had bewitched my sister." Her hand tapped nervously on the top of her belly, probably itching for a cigarette.

"How so?" The calming tone of Sophie's father could draw the deepest secrets out of anyone. It was why he was so good at this. He knew which buttons to press, how to make people trust him.

Another tear raced down the woman's cheek. "They were in bed together. His magic led her to betray me."

"Annette." Henry tried to crawl toward her, but Gabe jerked the rope, and he fell back. "Honey, what have you done? What magic? It isn't real. There's no such thing as that kind of power. Please believe me. Celeste and I were a mistake."

Sophie wanted to tell her father to stop this farce, that this man wasn't one they were hunting, but she knew how it went from here. One accusation was all it took, one person with a story.

"Dad," she whispered. "I don't think he's fae."

Her father sent her a scathing look and covered the mic on his shirt with his hand. "That is not for you to say. A wife knows her husband, and we can't take any chances."

It was then she realized how much her father had truly changed. He'd rather kill humans than spare fae. All she could do was nod and take a step back.

"This man is guilty, Soph." Gabe's fingers grazed her arm, and she froze, not wanting to make a scene in front of all these people. He was respected in HAFS, a man on high, with only her father more highly thought of. "Accept it."

Her jaw clenched, but she didn't respond. To her, Gabe was nothing more than a young tyrant, one who wouldn't leave her alone.

Her father paced in front of the crowd, arms clasped behind his back and head bowed as if in thought or prayer. But if it was the latter, something told her God wanted no part in what happened inside these walls.

Annette bent down, saying something to Henry none of them could hear. Then, she disappeared into the restless crowd.

They waited for her father to stop, to speak to them again and tell them what to do. He took his time as Henry yelled, "I'm sorry. I'm sorry. I'm sorry. I won't ever do it again."

Seeing a grown man cry wasn't something a person forgot. The fear, the pain. Also, the hope. He still believed there was a way out of this, that he might be released, battered but alive.

Sophie pitied him.

Her father stopped moving, his face sure. He'd made his decision and uttered a single word. "Guilty."

The crowd of followers roared their approval, and Henry jerked his eyes from Sophie to her father to those cheering on his verdict. He still didn't understand.

Closing her eyes for a brief moment, Sophie tried to breathe, to calm her racing heart. When she opened them again, she was the perfect image of her father's daughter. Cold, ambitious. Also, frail. These people didn't know her. She didn't let them. So, they couldn't see the doubt clouding her mind.

Couldn't see that she held in tears as her father approached his captive, or that her body was only ramrod straight because she couldn't move, despite the wave of dizziness sweeping over her.

Her father looked down at Henry. "Henry Colewell, you have been found guilty of fae heritage."

"You're all out of your minds," Henry yelled. "Fae ... they're just fantasy." He tried to scramble back, but the rope pulled tighter around his neck, cutting off his air. He gasped for breath, his face turning red.

"I was speaking," Sophie's father growled. "Now, as I was saying. Henry Colewell, you do not belong in this world with your fae blood. God put humans on Earth, and you are an abomination. Your magic is a danger to our survival. On behalf of the Human Alliance For Survival, I sentence you to death."

Henry gripped the rope, trying to loosen it with every bit of energy he had left. Gabe let it go just enough for him to breathe. There was a protocol here.

Her father held out a hand, and Gabe placed a Glock in his palm. He only waited a beat before pulling back the slide and firing a single shot.

Henry Colewell jerked, his head slamming into the concrete floor as blood pooled beneath it.

Sophie hadn't been prepared; she wasn't ready to see the coldness with which her father executed a man on the word of his scorned wife. She stared down into his face, still with shock. His wide-open eyes held no life. Gabe bent to remove the rope.

"Can't lose a good rope." He shrugged with a smile before walking away.

Angry red burns marked where it had tightened around his neck.

Lifting her eyes, Sophie caught sight of Annette leaving through a rear door.

Her father lifted his hands to quell the crowd. "Friends, today we have protected everyone we hold dear. Remember that." What he really meant was that any of those present could find themselves accused if they told others outside HAFS of what happened here tonight. "Go home to your families knowing there is one less creature out there waiting to destroy us."

As the crowd dissipated, her father turned to one of his men. "Have that cleaned up." He didn't point or gesture, but everyone knew what he meant.

When he faced Sophie, all tension faded from his face. "I'm starving. How about you, kiddo? Or do you need to rest? I know this was a lot of activity for you."

She stared at him, trying to see the father she knew. The one who held her when her mother died, the man who cried when Sophie got her diagnosis. What would happen to him once she was gone?

Because that wouldn't be long now. Sophie was sick, and she'd never recover. A part of her still wanted to see if she could save her father before she died.

Chapter Six
GULLIVER

Five in the morning came long before Gulliver was ready for it, but here they were. It had taken too long waking Toby up, too long making him get dressed and eat the delicious thing called a Pop-Tart that Brea stocked. And longer still to get him to glamour himself so the humans couldn't see his fae features. They couldn't just rely on a hat or hood this time.

And now, they were late to the bus station.

"The bus leaves in five minutes and we still haven't found it yet." He tugged on Toby's arm, trying to get him to speed up from the sluggish pace he'd had all morning.

"If we miss this one, there'll be another." Toby shrugged.

"We aren't missing this one." Not for the first time, he wished Tia hadn't saddled him both with figuring out who was killing fae and dealing with Toby. Grief was tricky. It had been months, but there was no timetable for moving on, for returning to a life the person one lost wasn't able to live.

But Gulliver couldn't let it derail the mission Tia defied the other sovereigns for. The mission his father thought he could handle. He pictured his parents' faces, how they'd had so much trust in him. It was time to have trust in himself.

Only getting there might be harder than he'd thought. Gullie stopped when he saw a line of identical busses taking on passengers. "Which one is the bus that goes to New Orleans?" Gullie asked a station employee at the gate.

"First one." She pointed to the shiny silver bus. "Better hurry."

"Thanks." He handed over both tickets and took off running for the bus that was about to leave, yanking Toby behind him.

"Ow, let me go."

"Not until we're on that bus." They waded through the crowd and finally made it to the funny sliding door and the steps leading into the huge human car. "Come on." There were only a few open rows in the back, so Gulliver led Toby toward them, shoving both of their bags under the seats and dropping into one.

"Squishy." He wiggled his butt, trying to decide if he liked the seat or not. He better. It would be his for a while. He'd never seen so many humans so close together, and it sent a thrill through him.

An older couple was sitting across from them, staring. Gulliver averted his eyes to the woman a few rows in front of them. She held a baby in her arms.

"Have you ever seen a human baby?" he whispered to Toby.

Toby only acknowledged the words with a shrug, but Gulliver couldn't help wanting to get closer, to see if that baby was just like his sisters had been—without the wings, of course.

The woman turned in her seat and smiled at him. "Hello." She had thick, dark hair pulled into tight braids, not unlike his mother's.

"Toby." He elbowed him. "A human is talking to me."

"Good for you." Toby pulled the hood of his shirt up over his head. "I'm going to sleep. Don't bother me."

Gulliver returned the woman's smile. "Your baby is cute."

She laughed. "It's a good thing because this creature is a little terror."

"Creature?" He crawled over Toby to reach the aisle and slid into the seat behind her, peeking over the back. "What kind of creature? Does he have wings?" He straightened as he felt his tail twitch. "A tail?"

Her laughter confused him. "You're funny." Her eyelashes brushed down across her cheeks. "Why are you headed to New Orleans?"

"Oh." He rubbed the back of his neck. Tia had prepared him for nosey human questions. "Work."

She smiled. "And taking the bus? How odd."

He shrugged. "Oh, I take the bus all the time. I quite like the ... smell." Smell? Really, Gulliver?

Her nose wrinkled. "You mean body odor and trapped farts?"

"Of course." He hadn't meant to say that. Now, she thought he was an odd man who enjoyed smelling farts. Why didn't Tia tell him that was what humans smelled like after a while? He didn't smell it yet, but something told him he would.

She clutched her baby closer, probably trying to keep it from the stranger behind her. "You're cute."

His face heated. "Um, I, um. What?"

"Gullie," Toby called. "I need you."

Understanding dawned in her eyes, but Gulliver wasn't sure why. He smiled in farewell before rejoining Toby.

"What?" He slumped in his seat.

"Nothing." Toby didn't open his eyes. "It's just ... that girl was flirting with you, and you were acting like a fool."

"Huh?" Flirting? No way. With his feline eyes and tail,

Gulliver wasn't quite marriage material to most fae outside Myrkur, where he spent most of his time. He was different and had always been okay with that. Okay with the stares and the whispers. It had gotten better over the years as Iskaltians, Eldurians, and Fargelsians grew used to the Dark Fae, but it was never normal.

Toby shook his head. "You're hopeless. The humans can't see your Dark Fae side, remember? To them, you look just like any other bland chap. Don't worry, though, now she thinks you're dating me."

The bus lurched forward, and he gripped the seat in front of them. "You? I would never in my life ... That would be like dating my sister. Gross."

"I'm not a girl, Gullie."

"No, but you're Tia's twin." Revulsion curled in his gut. The twins were family. He didn't want the humans thinking anything else.

"Why do you care what some random human thinks?" Toby sighed.

"I don't ... I don't know."

"I do. It's because you always need to be liked. Well, Gullie, you're not Tia's goofy sidekick anymore. Now, you're the main character of this humantale. Sometimes, you're going to have to be as unlovable as the rest of us."

The smell hit Gulliver then. It hadn't taken long for him to realize that the woman described it perfectly. Humans smelled, but when trapped in a metal box together, it amplified their stench.

Gulliver choked on it, trying to picture the open fields of Fargelsi that smelled of Gelsi berries or the clean frozen air of Iskalt. *Breathe in. Breathe out. Don't use your nose.*

Tonight they'd reach their destination and escape.

* * *

"Gullie." Toby shoved his shoulder. "Wake up. Come on, you Dark Fae fool."

Gulliver groaned as he lifted his head. There was a pain in his neck that hadn't been there before he fell asleep, but they weren't moving. "Another stop?" he asked.

Toby shook his head, peering out the window. "I think we're there."

"Thank the magic," he whispered, reaching down to zip up his bag. "Mrs. Merrick told me to look for a yellow car when we got here. Apparently, they'll let us use plastic money and take us to the address Tia gave us."

Toby didn't respond as he looped his bag over his shoulder and started toward the door. After so many hours cooped up with these humans, they didn't want to stay any longer than they had to.

Outside, there were more buses than they'd even seen in Ohio. Some coming, others going. It was a mess of traffic that sent Gulliver's nerves into overdrive.

Why did humans insist on such loud, smelly machines? There was something to be said for a good steed and a quiet mountain pass. Even the Eldurian desert was better than this.

Gulliver dodged people who didn't seem to be watching where they were going. He slammed into someone and bounced back against Toby.

The man scowled, yelling a word Gulliver had never heard before, and shoved past them.

"Rude." Toby glared after him.

"Let's just find a yellow car and get out of here." He didn't particularly relish the thought of getting into another one of their metal contraptions, but he didn't know how far of a walk it would be to the address they had.

"There." Toby pointed to a small car that was, in fact, bright yellow.

At least it would get them out of this mess. They hurried toward it, yanking open the back door and piling inside before shutting the door. Shoving the slip of paper with the address to the older woman sitting in front, Gulliver said, "Go here."

She hit the gas, jumping the car forward, and it bounced down the road, weaving in and out of cars at a slightly terrifying speed.

Gulliver cracked his knuckles and then tilted his head to the side, just trying to loosen up his body after so long on that bus. Toby stared out the window with a menacing look, like he wanted to tear down the entire city. Maybe he did. It was whatever was going on here that forced his presence, after all.

"Do you think I'm going to get to hurt anyone?" Toby asked suddenly.

Gulliver caught the woman looking at them in the rearview mirror, her eyes wide. "Why would you ask that?" he whispered.

He shrugged. "I just ... I think it might help."

Gulliver rubbed his eyes. This was why Tia kept Toby locked up in the palace for so long. She was afraid of letting him out. How much courage had it taken from her to let him go this time?

He wanted a fight, to take out his anger on someone.

"Please don't hurt me," the woman said, her knuckles going white where she gripped the steering wheel. "I have grandchildren. Eleven of them. And four children. A husband. People who will look for me if I go missing. My husband is probably already wondering where I am since I wasn't there to get him at the bus station."

Nothing she said made sense. Gulliver leaned forward between the seats, and she shied away from him. "Why would we hurt you? Is this about money?" He pulled the card out of his pocket. "You can take as much from this as you want."

"Money?" A tear slipped down her cheek. "I don't need money. I just want to return to my family."

Gulliver and Toby shared a confused look.

"Is there something keeping you from your family?" Whatever Toby had been lately, he was still himself, still a protector, someone who always did what was right. He yanked Gulliver back so he could talk to the woman. "Do you need us to help you? Has someone hurt you?"

"Why are you doing this?" She used her shoulder to wipe her cheek. "You don't have to."

Gulliver stared at his hands, a realization hitting him. "Um, this is one of those taxi things, right?"

"No," she practically shouted. "This is my car! You got in and ordered me to go somewhere. I had no choice. I just wanted to pick up my husband. He's been gone for a month, visiting our son in Alabama, and I miss him."

"But ... but your car is yellow." Mrs. Merrick said to look for a yellow car.

"So?"

Oh, for magic's sake. They just abducted a woman from the bus station.

"What do we do?" Toby hissed.

"We have to let her go."

"Before we get there? Can't we just let her keep going?"

Gulliver punched his shoulder. "Absolutely not."

"No, you're right. Um, my lady, you can let us out anywhere."

She wasted no time swerving to a stop along the curb of an open-air market. Gulliver and Toby jumped out onto the sidewalk, grabbing their bags.

Gulliver stuck his head back in. "We're sorry for the trouble, lady. Please tell your husband he's lucky his wife has a yellow car that can drive him where he needs to go." He slammed the door, and she sped off so fast he had to jump out of the way.

"I don't think she liked us." He turned to Toby, who was inching away from two men.

"I bet I can tell you where you got your shoes," one of them said, waving a filthy rag in the air.

Gulliver looked down at the shoes Brea called sneakers. He didn't have a clue where Brea bought them. "You can?" he asked as the other man bent down to spray his feet with something shiny.

"I sure can." The other guy beamed a friendly smile. "Let me take a guess while my man here shines your shoes."

"Shines my shoes?" Gulliver looked down at his feet again. They might look better shiny, though he'd never considered that as something he looked for in shoes.

"We just need directions," Toby said, his voice gruff.

"Sure, sure." The friendly man bobbed his head. "I bet I can tell you where you got your shoes too."

"That doesn't seem necess—" Toby tried to move away from the shoe shiner man coming after him next.

"They're on your feet, bro." The man threw his head back and laughed.

"Now, that'll be twenty dollars for the shine and twenty for the line ... each," the second man said with a heavy accent.

Gulliver looked around them for some kind of line they wanted him to stand in. He shrugged. "Sounds reasonable." His eyes found a disapproving Toby. "If they say it's worth paying for, I believe them. Why would they lie? Let me ask you, sirs, does it look more ... normal to have shiny shoes?"

One grinned. "It does, young man. Now, you owe us eighty bucks."

Gulliver wondered what a buck was, hoping it was similar to

a human dollar. "Do you take plastic money?" He reached for the card in his wallet.

A hand pushed his down, and he found himself looking into the eyes of someone who was very much not human. "Don't give them your credit card, you idiot." He turned to the men. "Get out of here before I call the cops." He shooed them away, and the two went running across the street toward some other tourists new to the city.

"Who are you?" Toby folded his arms across his chest, looking at the newcomer with suspicion.

The young man looked him over from head to toe, and Gulliver took that time to study him, from his umber-brown skin to the short-cropped black hair and golden haze in his eyes.

"My name is Xavier." He looked around, as if to make sure they were away from eavesdroppers. "Come with me." He took off toward an alleyway to the side of the marketplace, only stopping when the shadows hid them.

He blew out a breath and leaned against the brick wall. "Could you two scream fae any louder?" He shook his head. "There are people hunting us." His gaze found Gulliver's tail and sparked with curiosity, but he didn't ask questions. "You must be new to this city, but right now, it is the most dangerous place for fae. You should leave."

Toby shook his head. "We're here because it's dangerous."

Xavier stared at him for a moment before sighing. "I don't know you, so you're not my responsibility. Do whatever you'd like." He ripped the address out of Gulliver's hands. "Take this road here until it dead ends, turn left, and then make your first right. That's the street." He handed it back and started toward the parking lot, stopping at the mouth of the alley. "Try not to get yourselves killed."

Chapter Seven
SOPHIE-ANN

Hey Dad,

I picked up an extra shift today, so I won't be home till late. Don't wait up for me.

Sophie.

Coward. Sophie hung her head as she crept out of the house at an ungodly hour to avoid her father. She couldn't face him after what he'd done. The word execution had echoed through her mind all night long. That was what she'd witnessed. The execution of a man whose only crime was cheating on his wife. If he was fae, Sophie would eat her hat.

She pulled the brim of her baseball cap down low over her eyes. At this early hour, the Quarter was not a pleasant place to be. It stank of last night's revelry, and she avoided Bourbon Street altogether. For the moment, she shared the empty streets with the early workers, clean-up crews, and the last of the drunken tourists shuffling back to their hotels and B&Bs,

wearing stupid grins and Mardi Gras beads when it wasn't even Mardi Gras.

She headed up to the city park on Decatur Street. It was her favorite place to sit on a blanket, soak up the sun, and read. She'd missed the sun when it went dark, and she wasn't alone. People had flocked to the city parks in droves, more than they ever had before.

But today, Sophie was restless, unable to get lost in the pages of her newest fantasy obsession. The fantasy worlds of her books had gotten all too real in recent years.

Ever since the world went dark when she was only eleven years old, her life had taken a drastic turn with her mother's death and the birth of her father's group, the Human Alliance For Survival.

It started in a few central locations across the world. The sun rose in the sky as it always did, but darkness seeped into the world, drowning out the sun's rays. Scientists attributed it to Global Warming, and others speculated that the sun was dying.

In the months after, the darkness continued to spread and daylight faded almost completely. All the major cities fell into chaos and anarchy. People thought it was the end of the world and quit their jobs to stay home with their families. Supplies were scarce and looters warred in the streets.

Sophie didn't remember much of the violence from that time because she'd stayed home with her mother, behind the safety of their walled property.

But the sun hadn't died. It was still warm and still hung like a black orb in the sky for all to see, but the light couldn't penetrate the perpetual night. The darkness had an effect on the mental health of the general population. Humans weren't meant to live without light. It wasn't natural.

That was when the first murmurings of otherworldly creatures began to arise. Some attributed the phenomenon to aliens, and others spoke of the fae. Creatures who lived in another realm that bordered the human world.

It became a witch hunt after that. So many were accused of being fae and were killed because of it. But they were out there. Sophie had seen it with her own eyes. Things that couldn't be explained. Her own mother died because of the fae and whatever they'd done to weaken the veil between the worlds.

Sophie's father knew more about them than anyone she'd ever known. He said their magic was responsible for the darkness seeping into the human world. It all started in a small town in Ohio. Then, other places fell into darkness. Like here in the Quarter, Central Park in New York, and a rural village in Ireland. From there, the darkness spread across the globe.

As the sun rose higher and the temperature became unbearable, Sophie picked up her blanket and her books and headed for the trolley stop on Saint Charles Avenue. The streetcars were Sophie's favorite thing about living in the city. Sometimes, she rode the them all day, letting the breeze cool her as she read her favorite books. From Esplanade Avenue all the way to the Garden District and back again, and again. At least until they kicked her off, and she moved to the Canal car or the Riverfront route.

Eventually, Sophie found herself on Canal heading toward the cemeteries, a huge draw for the tourists. She had to admit, the old cemeteries were interesting, with their above-ground mausoleums dating back centuries. The cities of the dead, the locals called them.

Sophie left her seat on the streetcar and made her way from Canal back to Saint Charles and, eventually, the Garden District and Lafayette Cemetery. Her feet moved along the familiar path through the gates and into the maze of tombs, avoiding the tourists and keeping her head down.

It was eerily quiet in the city of the dead. Like the noise of the Quarter couldn't reach past the iron gates to disturb those who were laid to rest here. But Sophie wasn't so sure her mother was at rest. Not considering how she died.

Sophie came to a stop at the Devereaux family tomb. Most of her family were entombed here, thanks to her great-grandparents, who had it built a few generations ago. Grandma Devereaux was the only one she'd actually known other than her mother. She liked to think they kept each other company so her mom wouldn't be lonely buried among her husband's people.

"Hi, Mama," Sophie whispered, laying her hand against the rough stone of the tomb. "I hope Gran is talking your ear off wherever you two are." A sad smile tugged at her mouth. "I miss you both." She set a bouquet of fresh flowers she'd picked from her mom's garden at the base of the tomb, tossing the old ones aside.

Standing, she plucked the ferns sprouting between the gray bricks and smoothed a hand over the crumbling facade. One day, she wanted to fix it up, but for the moment, it was enough that her grandmother's and mother's names were chiseled into the marble stone, just below the names of relatives she'd only heard of.

Sophie didn't remember much about her mother's funeral. Only the endless march through the Quarter and the music. She vividly remembered standing right here with her father, but she had no memory of what was said over her mother's grave. She'd been too lost inside her own grief and confusion to pay attention to mere words that didn't mean anything. Pretty words wouldn't bring her mom back.

"I don't know what to do, Mama." She closed her eyes, trying to remember the sound of her mother's voice, hoping she might recall some words of advice that would help her now. But nothing came to her. She'd forgotten too much about the woman who gave her life.

Forgotten too much about how she died.

All Sophie remembered was an otherworldly scream and a blast of power. Then, her mother lay dead on the ground beside her.

Sophie's father blamed the fae, and that was good enough for her. She hated the fae and everything they represented. Magic tore her family apart. Magic sent her world into darkness for months. And then, one day, the sun rose, the darkness faded, and everything went back to normal. On the surface.

But for Sophie Devereaux and those like her, everything had changed. Those who belonged to HAFS wanted revenge. They wanted to rid the human world of the fae and send them back to wherever they came from.

The only problem was they were really difficult to identify because they looked just like humans. To capture a fae, one had to see them use their magic. Magic they hid well.

People like Henry ... just didn't seem like fae to Sophie.

"I think Dad's carried it too far, Mama. And I don't know how to stop him. I won't be with him much longer. Soon, I'll be with you and Gran. I'm afraid of what Dad will do once I'm gone." Sophie bowed her head, murmuring a trite prayer for the departed, hoping her passing would be a peaceful one that would end with her in the loving arms of her family.

She hated the fae. Hated everything they took from her, but she wasn't so sure she hated them so much she wanted to see them executed right in front of her. Not when she couldn't be sure they actually were guilty of harming humans with their magic.

"See you soon, Devereaux clan." She traced her fingertips over the column of names chiseled into the marble façade, letting her touch linger on the blank place where her name would soon join theirs before she turned to go.

It was time she stopped avoiding her father. The sun was

high in the sky, and she'd wasted as much of the day as she could. If she was going to have to leave him behind, the least she could do was help him get past the vendetta he felt he owed his wife. Sophie wanted a better future for her father. He wasn't an old man, with the best years behind him. He deserved more than the early grave HAFS would give him.

Leaving Lafayette Cemetery and the Garden District behind, Sophie made her way home. She was too tired to stay out for the remainder of the day. And she had to face her father at some point.

The gunshot echoed in her mind as she walked down Esplanade Avenue toward the iron gates of her sanctuary. She wasn't sure she could ever get the image of her father pulling the trigger out of her mind. He'd never even hesitated or shown any remorse. This all started because a monster had taken her mother from them, but in the end, had her father turned into a different kind of monster?

"Sophie-Ann!" Claude Devereaux greeted her with a smile as she entered the courtyard. "Didn't expect you back so soon."

"I got off early." She hated herself for lying to her father. "They just needed some help with the morning rush." She refused to meet his gaze, shuffling over to the patio table to drop her pack and help him with the weeding.

"Thank you, honey. You sure you aren't too tired?" Concern filled his voice, and she hated it. Hated that she worried him so much.

She was tired from her jaunt through the city, but not too tired to help out. "I can do a little weeding." She knelt down on a knee pad and went to work on the box of lavender, sorting through the new growth for invasive weeds. Her mother had started the garden after they first moved into the house when Sophie was small. It was still hers. They just tended it for her. It was like having a living connection to her. As long as her herbs and flowers lived, a bit of her lived on too.

"We'll have leftover gumbo for dinner." He groaned as he got to his feet.

"Sounds good. I'll make some dirty rice to go with it." Sophie kept pulling weeds, moving on to the rest of the herb garden while her father chattered endlessly about HAFS news and plans for their next gathering.

Sophie offered up a second prayer for her dad, hoping he didn't have another meeting planned like the last one.

Chapter Eight
GULLIVER

"This city is kind of strange, even for humans." Gulliver peeked through the odd slatted blinds covering the windows into the streets below, where humans wandered around with bags, drinks, and gaudy-looking jewelry they wore around their necks. "We should go out this afternoon and explore. Tia said we'd have to search for fae in the area to get the story about what's happening to them."

"Have fun with that." Toby rolled over on the bed in the strange room to stare at the corner.

The room had two beds, and it reminded Gulliver of the inn he'd once stayed in with his father in the human realm. That was in a place called Ireland. But this building looked nothing like an inn. And the room was larger, with a couch and a television, along with something in the corner that looked a lot like a very small human kitchen with appliances he would likely break if he tried to use.

"You know, for a city that's supposed to be new, this place

looks kind of grubby." Gulliver dropped the blinds and went to sit on his bed right beside Toby's. "I'd hate to see Old Orleans."

Toby continued to ignore him. After they arrived in the city the previous afternoon—once the nice lady they accidentally abducted let them out of her car—neither were up for any further excitement. But Toby still hadn't gotten out of bed, and the day was well underway. Dressed in his best human clothes, Gulliver was exceedingly aware of his role in this mission. There was no one to ask what they should do next. It was up to him. And he had no idea how to go about searching for fae villages within human cities.

"Want to go get some lunch?" Gulliver tried to tempt the sad prince with food as his own stomach growled. The innkeeper in the main house said something about a continent breakfast included with their stay, but nothing ever showed up at their door this morning, and Gulliver was starting to feel faint from lack of food. Most of what he'd brought with him was already gone after the long bus ride and the boring evening of watching Toby sleep.

"Bring me something when you return," Toby muttered, throwing a pillow over his head. "Wine. Bring me wine."

"When I return? Where am I going?"

"Go explore. Get the lay of the land. Just get out."

"You want me to go out there? By myself?" Gulliver's tail tried to flick out of his human jeans, but he'd bound it securely under his clothes so it didn't call any undue attention to them. Not that humans would see his tail either way, but he didn't want to take any chances. Humans were out there killing fae, and Gulliver had spent a lifetime defending his Dark Fae features to those who didn't understand them.

"Yeah, Gullie. Go find food, wine, and the fae villages, and then come back tonight with a plan. I'll be ready for action when you do."

"Really? Okay. I guess I could do some exploring just to get a feel for the city. You get some rest, Tobes." Gulliver gathered up his pack and checked his reflection in the mirror before he grabbed the room key that wasn't a key but a piece of plastic that looked too much like the plastic money Tia gave him. He was almost certain he would mix them up at the worst possible moment. "I hope you feel better soon." Gulliver glanced over his shoulder at his friend rolled up in the blankets like it was a freezing Iskalt morning. "I'm really going to need your help on this mission."

"Just bring me some wine, Gullie." Toby sighed. "That will help. For a while anyway."

Gulliver closed the door carefully behind him, flinching when the locks clicked with human magic. Stepping into the courtyard outside their room, he glanced around, unsure how to access the street. A pool of blue water sat at the center of the courtyard, and green ferns grew everywhere. A fountain tinkled at the edge of the walkway, and squashy moss grew all over the brick surrounding the fountain, where small orange fish swam around big green leaves that grew on top of the water.

An iron gate sat just beside the fountain, and the sounds of the city seemed to come from that direction.

"I sure hope you sent the right fae, Tia." Gulliver took a deep breath, tugged his hat down low over his eyes, and ducked through the gate onto the sidewalk. Tall trees with knobby trunks and weird, hair-like plants hanging from the branches towered over the street, casting the sidewalk in shadow.

Before he left, Tia taught him how to use the map on the human telephone she'd told him to take from the farmhouse. Her instructions were vague, though, and he still wasn't sure how to work it. Staring at the screen, everything he knew about human technology seemed to fall right out of his mind. But he started walking, hoping he could find his way back to the inn. He looked over his shoulder at the sign hanging over the iron gate he'd just stepped through. The Lamothe House. He committed it to memory, along with the street sign for Esplanade Avenue.

As he walked, Gulliver felt reasonably certain he'd never see the inn or Toby ever again. The city was vast, with street after street filled with similar-looking buildings and so many people. They were everywhere. Choosing at random, Gulliver headed down Royal Street, thinking he could easily remember that since he was here on a mission for his royal best friend.

"Royal Street to Esplanade Avenue," he muttered to himself. "Got it." He walked on for a long time, searching the faces of the people who passed him, wondering how he was supposed to find the fae.

Something very exciting seemed to be happening one street over. There was loud music, shouting, and general merriment, even at this early afternoon hour. And the people walking from that direction seemed to be about as drunk as anyone he'd ever seen. He wondered if this Bourbon Street might be a fae area. It would explain the strange behavior that seemed to be contained in just that location.

But today was about studying the city. Perhaps he would observe Bourbon Street later in the evening on his way back to the inn.

A strange building caught his attention, and Gulliver wandered across the narrow street, avoiding the honking cars that seemed like they didn't quite fit on the streets. Like the streets weren't built to accommodate them.

The old building wasn't any more intriguing than all the others, but the sign outside proclaimed it as the New Orleans Historic Voodoo Museum. A shrunken head hung from the sign, and all manner of odd things were on display in the windows.

"Excuse me?" Gulliver asked a lady in bright floral skirts standing outside the museum. "What is voodoo?"

"That is a loaded question, young sir." Her dark brown skin shimmered in the sunlight as she took a seat at the front of the museum. "Voodoo is part religion, part mysticism," she said in an oddly slow accented English Gulliver had never heard.

He took a step forward. "Mysticism?" That sounded like magic.

"The spirit world, boy. It is all around us." She waved her hands in the air. "We must keep the spirits happy, or bad things will happen." She leaned forward. "Come in for a tour and I'll show you all about the voodoo magic."

"Magic?" Gulliver smiled. "I'll return tomorrow with my friend. He'll want to see your shop too."

"Don't keep the spirits waiting too long, boy," she warned.

"I won't." Gulliver went on his way, down Royal Street, feeling a little better about this mission.

The day was growing hot, his clothes were sticking to his skin, and he was beyond hungry. Brea once said when Gulliver got good and hungry, he got grumpy as well. She said that was when he was hangry, which he was right this minute. And something wonderful caught his attention. A sweet fragrance that sent him down a side street to a place called the Vieux Carré Cafe.

"What deliciousness will you provide?" Gulliver took a seat at the outside patio under a canopy of shade trees, facing a big park and a cathedral. At the center of the park was a large statue of a man on a horse. In Gulliver's limited experience with humans, they didn't often ride horses. But even now, as he impatiently waited for someone to come bring him food, people rode by in horse-drawn carriages. It was such a familiar sight it made him a little homesick.

"Hi there, what can I get you?" A pretty girl with a shy smile came up to the table with a glass of ice water and a menu.

Gulliver stared at her lovely blue hair for a moment, forgetting how to speak.

"Do you want a minute to look at the menu?" she asked.

"Hi. Um. Yes, what's that smell? I want whatever that is."

"Beignets?" She smiled. "First time in NOLA?" She scribbled something on a pad of paper.

"Um, yes." Gulliver wasn't sure what a nola was, but if the question was about his first time doing something human here, then it was an automatic yes.

"Would you like an iced coffee? It's a slightly sweet and creamy chicory blend we're famous for." She refused to look him in the eye, and her cheeks flushed pink under the scattering of freckles on her nose.

"Sure. Sounds good. But what's a Benny-ya?"

She laughed, the sound clear and sweet, like something she didn't do very often. "Beignets are like doughnuts dusted in powdered sugar. It's kind of the one thing about New Orleans that lives up to all the hype." She leaned in closer. "Just don't tell anyone I said that."

"I won't." Gulliver grinned. "I don't know anyone here." He shrugged. "What else is good?" He looked at the menu, but none of the words made much sense. "What's a Po Boy?"

"It's a street food thing with fried shrimp or oysters and coleslaw. It's probably the best thing on the menu, other than the beignets."

"Sounds good. I'll have the large."

"That's pretty big. You sure you don't want a half?"

"I'm pretty hangry."

The girl laughed again, her feet shuffling nervously as she scribbled on her pad. "Shrimp or oysters?"

"Uhhh, shrimp." Gulliver made a guess because he didn't know what either of those things were. The one thing he did know about human food was that if it was fried, it was probably delicious.

After the waitress left him with an awkward wave, he sat back and checked out his surroundings. Tugging on his hat, he shrank into his seat, trying not to look too conspicuous. He was used to getting odd looks wherever he went outside of Myrkur.

But no one gave him a second glance. They couldn't see his strange features. To all the other people dining outside the Vieux Carré Cafe, he was just another human having a late lunch.

Gulliver sat a little taller, lifting his chin. It was an odd feeling, blending into the crowd like everyone else. Even at home in Myrkur, he was the great Griffin O'Shea's adopted son. But when the other Dark Fae looked at him, it was with reverence and distance. He commanded respect he didn't feel like he'd earned, but few got close enough to really get to know him.

And everywhere else in the five kingdoms, Gulliver O'Shea was Queen Tierney's most trusted friend—and Dark Fae. He didn't know what it was like to just be himself among strangers

"I have your beignets." The waitress stumbled, and his food went flying across the table. "Oh no!" She set the basket down. Half of the little triangle pastries sat at the bottom of the basket and the other half lay in a scatter of white powder on the tablecloth in front of him. "I'm so sorry! I really have to stop doing that." She stomped her foot as nervous hands fluttered up to her face, and she cast a glance over her shoulder at a rather sour-looking blond woman watching from inside the restaurant. "I'll get you more." She reached for the beignets on the table.

"It's fine." Gulliver was quick to snatch them up and dump them back in the basket. "No harm done to the food." He stuck a finger in his mouth, and a burst of sweetness hit his tongue from the powdered sugar. It looked like Iskalt snow dusting the pastries.

"What's going on here?" The sour-looking woman came up to stand beside the flustered waitress.

"Nothing at all." Gulliver smiled. "I was just about to dive head first into these sweets."

"You spilled them everywhere ... again? Sophie, what am I going to do with you?" She shook her head, reaching for the basket. "Please let me get you a fresh batch."

Gulliver clutched it to his chest. "I'm starving, and this food is perfectly fine, thank you."

"Well, at least let us bring you another batch. For the trouble."

"It's really no trouble." Gulliver stuffed a triangle into his mouth. "But if you want to bring me more of these, I'll eat them."

"Sophie." The woman snapped her fingers, and the girl all but ran back into the safety of the kitchen. "She's a bit of a klutz; I'm so sorry." The woman gathered up the tablecloth and moved his iced coffee and plates to another table.

"I don't know what a klutz is, but she's very kind and knowledgeable about the food. This is the best thing I've ever eaten, and that's saying something." Gulliver moved to the new table with the clean tablecloth, wondering what was wrong with the first one.

"I'll send over a new waitress to take care of you." She fussed over him like the poor girl had set him on fire.

"That's not necessary. I like Sophie just fine."

The girl in question rushed out with a fresh basket of sweets and whatever a Po Boy was.

"Sophie, you serve the sandwiches before the beignets," the insufferable woman groaned irritably. "I'm so sorry, sir." She took the sandwich from the tray. "Please take your time with your lunch, and then when you're ready, we'll bring out your beignets."

"No, don't bother." Gulliver took the platter with the huge

sandwich and set it in front of him, nodding for Sophie to set the second basket of sweet things he couldn't pronounce right beside his plate. "I'm good here." He smiled at Sophie. "Honest."

"Thanks for your help, Vicky," the waitress said. "I think I've got it now."

"All right." She scowled at the girl. "I'm watching you," she mouthed as she walked away.

"Well, she's pleasant." Gulliver tucked a linen napkin into his shirt collar and went to work on the sandwich.

"I'm really sorry about all that." Sophie blushed, taking a step back. "Just, um, let me know if you need anything else."

"Thanks, Sophie." Gulliver gave her a shy smile. It was a rare thing when a pretty girl looked at him the way Sophie was staring at him right now. Like he was a handsome guy she wanted to impress.

"Enjoy your meal." She smiled again and shuffled away to check on her other customers.

As he tucked into his food, Gulliver thought he could get used to this. Sitting in a nice restaurant, blending in with the crowd, and flirting with cute waitresses who didn't think he was repulsive. Maybe spending some time in the human realm wouldn't be so bad.

Chapter Nine
SOPHIE-ANN

“Is that boy here again?” Vicky stepped up beside Sophie in the kitchen doorway to peer into the dining room. The man sat inside today.

“He’s not a boy.” Sophie saw a kind man who treated her like she mattered, even though she was only serving him food. Not to mention how completely adorable he was with soft brown hair that sat messily on his head and hung down into deep amber eyes. He had the build of a runner, long and lean, but not without muscle. So much different from the gym rat junkies that surrounded her in HAFS.

“Order up!” came from behind her.

She turned to grab the plate of beignets, a double order, and walked past Vicky.

The man smiled up at her. “Thank you.”

She set the plate in front of him, unable to take her eyes from his. She didn’t know anyone else who came in daily for beignets, let alone twice a day like yesterday. He didn't order anything else like that first day, except for a glass of water.

"You're welcome," she squeaked. Smooth, Sophie-Ann.

The door opened, and Gabe walked in. Her entire body tensed as he sat in her section, always hers, and waved her over. She stood frozen in place.

"Are you going to do your job?" Vicky called, nodding toward the newcomers.

Stiffly, she walked toward Gabe and pulled out her ordering pad. "What can I get you?"

"What?" He grinned up at her. "No hello? I thought we were friends, Soph."

"We are whatever my father decides," she muttered. It wasn't meant to be an acknowledgment, but he nodded.

"Good girl." He leaned in. "Your father wants to know if you've seen any suspicious customers in here this week. We're doing our typical rounds to New Orleans businesses, and I had the pleasure of being assigned to your lovely establishment."

"Don't you think I'd report something like that directly to my father?" HAFS kept an eye on the entire city, intimidating people into turning in anyone who rubbed them the wrong way.

Gabe lifted one brow. "Your father isn't so sure."

"You mean, you aren't. My father trusts me. Can you say the same?" Ever since her mother's death, her father refused to put his faith in anyone except his daughter.

Gabe's smile dropped. "You listen to me, you little—"

"Is there a problem here?" Her only other customer now stood behind her, drawn to his full height. In a fight, he'd be no match for Gabe, but having the stranger on her side calmed her.

"No." Gabe looked him up and down. "Not that it's any of your business, but I'm just having a chat with my girl here."

"She doesn't look like she's enjoying the chat."

"And?"

The man crossed his arms over his chest. "And that's a problem. I suggest you go get your pastries someplace else."

"Pastries." He narrowed his eyes. "You must be a tourist. Well, let me fill you in on how New Orleans works. I work for a group that runs this town. We don't appreciate tourists coming in and messing with our business. Stick to Bourbon Street."

Gabe stood. "I've lost my appetite, but Soph, you'll make this up to me." He stormed out, and she released a pent up breath.

She was watching the swinging door he'd disappeared through and didn't realize the man was still behind her until he spoke.

"Are you okay?"

A soft laugh escaped her. "I'm used to him." Pushing a hand through her short, blue-streaked hair, she turned and put on her best fake smile. "You shouldn't have stepped in like that." She walked past him toward the kitchen.

He followed. "Why not? You looked like you needed help."

"And you just help any stranger? That could get you killed, sir. Or at least hurt. I don't know where you're from, but this city is not what it appears on the surface. It's not just a fun jaunt to drink and party."

"I'm from Ohio."

That explained his naïveté. "Well, it's probably better for your health if you let people fight their own battles."

"Battles don't scare me. I've seen many of them in my lifetime."

She turned to face him, studying the earnestness in his expression. "What's your name?"

"Gulliver."

"What an odd name."

"Is that bad?"

One side of her mouth lifted into a half-smile. "No. It's just odd. I like it."

"You can call me Gullie."

There was something so honest, so rare in this man she couldn't help wanting to dive inside his mind, to see the world through his eyes. "How long are you in New Orleans?"

"I'm not sure. I'm here for work, and it could take a while."

"Then, you're going to want to stay clear of men like Gabe." She glanced toward the door. "And if you're going to eat beignets every day, I have two tips for you."

He leaned in. "I want to hear these ... tips."

He did. She could see it in his curious eyes. Gullie wanted to listen to her, to take in her words. It was so rare in her world that she couldn't help smiling. "First, take up running."

"Will they give me extra running speed?"

She laughed. "You're funny."

Confusion flashed across his face, but he shook it off. "And the second?"

She pulled a napkin out of her apron, stepping closer to wipe his cheek. "Learn to clean the powdered sugar off your face."

It was only when his breath hitched that she realized just how much she'd invaded his space and retreated, handing him the napkin. "I should get back to work."

He continued cleaning his face. "Yes, I should go get my roommate out of bed." He gave her a small bow. "It was a pleasure seeing you today, Sophie."

She was still smiling long after he was gone. There was only one thing she knew about this strange man. He'd return tomorrow. She was sure of it.

* * *

The cafe was packed by the time Sophie clocked in.

"You're late." Vicky held a tray with one hand, brushing past Sophie to set plates on a nearby table before returning.

"I know. I'm sorry. Today was another lecture from my dad about wasting my potential." That was the line she gave everyone. In truth, it had taken her too long to dress, to make it down the stairs. The days were getting worse. Soon, she wondered if she'd even be able to get out of bed. Dying was strange. At first, the news was a shock. Then, it just became another part of life. The weakness normalized until she could hardly remember a time before.

Sophie's vision swam as she looked out at the full tables. Vicky thought she was the biggest klutz on the planet when in reality, dizziness hit her at random times.

If her father wasn't so insistent that she was fine and the job was good practice for her future, she wouldn't be working now.

Trying to hide her ragged breathing, she headed into the dining room to where two tables of hers had just seated themselves. Vicky took the outdoor tables today, and for that, she was grateful. The sun was not a welcome sensation on her skin right now.

The first table was a family of four, with two adorable kids who were probably bored on a family trip to New Orleans. Sure, there were some things for kids to do, but it was more of an adult vacation spot. "Hi, I'm Sophie, and I'll be your waitress today. Can I start you with something to drink?"

The tiny red-headed girl couldn't have been more than five. She waved up at Sophie, a giant smile on her face. Her brother, looking equally as young, gave her a shy smile and said, "You're pretty. I like your hair."

Sophie laughed. "Why thank you, sir. I hope you're enjoying your stay here in New Orleans."

"Oh, yes," the mother gushed. "This city is beautiful. So much culture and history. It must be amazing to live here."

Sophie didn't know any different from this city, with its pothole-filled streets in front of incredible multi-million-dollar homes with more charm than many places had in their entire towns. Not to mention the melding of cultures, the mysticism. She wanted to see more of the world, but this was home. "It is."

She pictured this family returning to their suburban lives, where the kids played soccer and came home to a house that looked just like all the others. They were probably happy, all their problems small.

The father leaned in, dropping his voice. "We're actually here for a reason. Renauld over at the daiquiri place told us we might be able to find the information here."

"Sure." Tourists asking questions about where to find things in the city wasn't anything new. "Are you looking for some kind of tour? There's a great one that'll take you out to where The Battle of New Orleans took place, and—"

"Actually, have you heard of the Human Alliance For Survival?"

Her heart sank, and she suddenly saw the family through new eyes. Kids who'd grow up with the same kind of hate their parents harbored, parents so obsessed with finding the "others" that they'd let horrible injustices slide right on by. "Never heard of it," she lied.

"Really?" The mother's smile dropped. "That's disappointing. We come from the Dallas chapter and were hoping to attend a meeting while we're here."

The meetings didn't happen on a regular schedule. Members usually received a coded text only hours before they had to be there. So, even if Sophie wanted this family to get into a local meeting, she wouldn't have the information they needed. "I'm sorry. I can't help you."

The father nodded. "Well, in that case, we'll take four orders of beignets, two coffees, and two apple juices."

Sophie nodded, her movements rigid.

She turned to head back toward the kitchen when someone

else caught her eye. A wave of dizziness came over her, tilting the world on its side. She dropped the order pad, the pen bouncing off the tile. Strong hands gripped her, holding her upright.

"Sophie." Gulliver sounded panicked. "Are you okay?"

She shook herself, the spinning fading away as she regained her strength. "Yes. I'm fine." Righting herself, she stepped away. "I think I just need some water."

"I have some. I haven't touched it yet." He led her to his table and forced her to sit, sliding the cold, sweating glass across to her. It left a slick of water behind.

"I should really be working." She sipped the water, wishing this wasn't so difficult.

"No. Drink more."

"Sophie." Vicky stomped toward them, making a scene. Customers turned to stare. "What do you think you're doing?"

"She needed a moment." Gulliver's brows drew together.

"She has work to do. Have you put your last table's order in?"

"I'll do it." Gulliver stood, bending to pick up the order pad. He didn't wait for permission before marching to the kitchen, where he slapped the ticket on the counter. When he returned a moment later, he offered Vicky a smile. "They said the order will be right up. I'm not sure how high up it will be, but I assumed you could figure it out."

Sophie hid a laugh behind her hand. She'd never met anyone who could make a joke out of pretty much anything and not sound like they were trying too hard. For Gullie, the lightness came naturally, like he was born to it.

Vicky stared hard at them both. "The trash needs taken out." She stormed away, leaving Sophie and Gullie staring at each other. Neither could help laughing.

"I should go before she murders me." She stood.

Gulliver's eyes widened. "That seems like an extreme punishment."

She suppressed a laugh, trying to play along. "There are worse ones."

Worry lined his face, and for a moment, she thought it might be real. But he had to know she was joking, right?

Heading back to the kitchen, she lifted the half-full trash bag out of the can. It didn't need to be taken out, but whatever Vicky wanted, Vicky got. She tied it shut and pushed through the door to the alleyway out back.

The moment it shut behind her, two hands grabbed her, shoving her face-first against the wall. The bag hit the ground and split, sending waste across the pavement.

"Ow, let me go. Do you know who my father is?"

Abduction was a constant risk when her father was enemy number one of the fae, but she knew how to protect herself. Kicking a foot out, all she felt was air.

Someone laughed. "I know all your tricks, princess." Gabe turned her around to face him. "Don't worry, honey. Your father is the one who wants to see you." He pressed a rough kiss to her lips, and she bit him.

He leaned away with a smile, his finger gingerly touching where she'd drawn blood. "I so very much enjoy when he sends us to retrieve you."

"And one day, I will very much enjoy wringing your neck."

More laughter and she realized just how many of her father's men were there. Whatever he wanted couldn't be good.

Chapter Ten
GULLIVER

Toby wasn't there. The one time Gulliver needed him was the one time he'd decided to go into the city alone.

He hadn't seen Sophie in days. She'd left to take the garbage out and never returned. When he'd gone to look for her, the trash lay scattered in the alley and there was no sign of the waitress.

He didn't know this city, didn't know this girl or what she could possibly be involved in, but he wanted to find her, to help her if he could. It was what his father would do.

"I wish you were here right now, Dad." He sat on his bed and rested his head in his hands. They'd been in the city for a week now and had no signs of this supposed fae-hunting group or even the fae they were after.

Well, except for the one who threatened them their first day. He'd never felt more alone in his life, and yet, he wasn't alone here.

"Toby," he growled. "You blasted idiot. You better be easy to find." He was done with Toby's moping. Done with his grief. Yes, the man he loved was dead, but a lot more fae could die if the two of them didn't get their act together.

He had to find him.

Tearing from the room, he thundered down the stairs and out into the courtyard. Once he reached the street, he tried to think where Toby would go. "Think, Gullie," he whispered to himself. Somewhere that reminded him of home. That could be a lot of places. There were so many magic shops in this city, and none of them were for real magic. At least, the kind of magic he was used to.

Like him, Toby didn't have much magic. Except for the portals. He wouldn't have left, would he? The old Toby wouldn't, but he wasn't the same fae.

No. Gulliver had to believe he was still here. He wandered the streets near the inn for a while before it hit him. Magic. Turning around, he headed toward the voodoo shop he'd come across on his first day of exploring. He still wasn't sure what voodoo was, but the owner claimed it was mystical, a kind of magic. Maybe it really was.

He was almost there when he saw him. Toby sat on the curb, his knees bent and elbows resting on his thighs. His head hung between his hands. He looked defeated.

"Are you drunk?" Gulliver asked, wishing he could take it back the moment the words left his mouth.

Toby lifted his head and glared up at him. "I should be."

Gulliver hesitated a moment before sitting next to him. "No, you shouldn't. It's time to face the world, Tobes."

"I know." He rubbed a hand across his face. "What did Tia think sending the two of us on such an important mission?"

"Probably that we'd never failed her, and we aren't about to start now."

"I've failed her for months."

"Can we stop with the pity party?" Normally, Gulliver had endless patience. It came from being Tierney's best friend. Sort of a requirement of the job. But right now, he was too worried about where a certain waitress could be.

"I went looking for the fae, thinking it would make me feel like I was home. The locals say this place is magic." He gestured back at the voodoo shop. "But I didn't feel any."

"Maybe it's their kind of magic."

He shrugged. "Doesn't help us."

They fell into silence for a long moment before Gulliver sighed. "I lost my waitress."

"You ... what? Your waitress?"

"Not mine, exactly. But she's been serving me pastries all week, and now she's not. I thought humans went to their jobs every day. They live for them. But I keep going back and she's not there."

"Maybe she—" His words cut off as the ground below them shook and fire rent the air only a few blocks away.

Both fae jumped to their feet.

"Was that ..." Toby started.

"An explosion." Gulliver tugged on his arm. "Come on." They sprinted down the street, where humans rushed out of buildings to see the smoke blackening the sky for themselves.

They followed the flow of the crowd until they reached a blazing row of buildings right in the heart of New Orleans.

"What do you think happened?" Gulliver overhead a human ask another.

The other shrugged. "Most likely witches."

"It wasn't witches," a low voice said as Xavier stepped up between Gulliver and Toby. "Do nothing sudden. Come with me." They'd only met the fae once when he issued a warning to them, yet he was one of them, and Gulliver followed him without question.

"How do you know it wasn't witches?" Toby asked.

"Because human witches do not have what you or I think of as magic. They are more spiritual than actually magical. Keep up." He increased his pace until they reached the rear of the crowd and kept going onto an empty street.

"Humans did this." Xavier looked behind them to make sure they weren't followed.

"What?" Gulliver didn't know if he could believe that. "Why would humans blow up their own buildings?"

"You obviously know nothing of human history." He turned sharply to climb up three steps and knocked twice on the door of a narrow blue house. "It's Xavier."

An elderly woman opened the door. "It was the tourist center, wasn't it?" She stepped away from the door to let them in.

Xavier nodded, removing his hat. "Found two strays there and figured I should get them away from the crowd." He gestured to Toby and Gulliver. "Take your shoes off and come in."

Once inside, Gulliver looked around the small house. The door led straight into a bedroom and then a long sitting room. Beyond that was a tiny kitchen at the back. It was a strange house with barely any furniture.

"You're safe here," Xavier said. "We use this house when any of us need to escape from the city. May is a human friend."

May must have been the woman who let them in.

"There are humans who befriend the fae here?" Gulliver asked.

"Of course there are. Not all humans want to see us eradicated." He dropped onto the settee.

Toby stayed in the doorway. "You mentioned a tourist center."

"The fae run many businesses in this town. One of them was a place for tourists to get information about activities. We used it to connect visiting fae with our communities. Secrecy is important here, so we must be careful."

May walked in with three mugs. "Tea?"

"Thank you." Xavier took one, so the others followed suit. He took a sip before setting it on the table next to him. "Now, tell me why you're both here."

Gulliver and Toby shared a look, neither wanting to answer. Would this man laugh in their faces if he knew the truth? Try to stop them from investigating?

Xavier sighed. "I know you're not from New Orleans. No fae lives in this city without us knowing about it. Are you from the New York community?" He paused, dark fingers running along his solid jaw. "No. Midwest."

"I don't know where that is," Gulliver said. "But what are we doing here? Shouldn't we be out there helping?"

"How? By alerting HAFS to your presence? No." He cocked his head. "You really don't know anything about us, do you?"

Toby grunted. "You already decided we aren't from here. How would we?"

"Interesting." He leaned back, reached for what Brea called a remote, and turned on the television. A human appeared in front of the explosion site with the same claim they'd heard.

Witches.

"We suspect the recent bombings are from the same forces that turned our world dark so many years ago. It may all be happening again."

"The mainstream media always blames witches or science." Xavier kicked his feet up onto the table. "Before the darkness, no one would have said witches even existed. But now, it's a convenient way to get out of blaming their own. Many of the humans agree with what this terrorist group is doing; they just won't say it."

He pointed at the screen. "Do you see why you shouldn't be here if you do not know this city? These humans may not be able to see your eyes or that tail you're trying to hide—something I've never seen before—but they will sniff you out with their dying breath."

"Why do they care so much?" Gulliver didn't know many humans. There was Myles and Alona, though she was raised as fae. A few people in Ohio. Each of them was kind, welcoming.

Xavier sighed. "Because they fear us, what we can do. Most of us don't ..." He stopped, clamping his lips shut.

"Don't what?"

"Nothing. It's not important. Just know, to stay alive here, you must fit in."

The door banged open and two women walked in. They were tall, taller than any man here. The first had raging emerald eyes, pointed ears, and an untouchable aura. The second was more delicate. Gulliver's gaze traveled from her long, lithe limbs with her umber skin, beautiful hazel eyes, and bright white wings stretching out behind her.

The first one kicked the door shut and shoved Toby out of the way to walk into the room, her eyes finding Xavier.

He stood. "How many?"

"Four." The second folded her wings around her like a shield, but her tears were still visibly sparkling on her smooth cheeks. "Including Tina and Mathew."

Xavier cursed. "They weren't even fae." He kicked the table, and it overturned, sending his tea spilling across the floor as the mug shattered. A roar escaped his throat. "Why didn't we have a warning?"

"We did," the winged woman said. "That's why it wasn't

worse. There was a meeting going on, some of our elders gathering to discuss possibly leaving New Orleans."

"No." Xavier pinned her with a glare. "We will not abandon this city. It belongs to us as much as them." He pinched the bridge of his nose. "At least most of the fae got out."

Gulliver couldn't hold his questions in any longer. "Are there more Dark Fae living in the human realm?"

The woman wiped the tears from her face. "Dark Fae?"

"You know … from Myrkur …"

"I don't know what you're talking about. I'm from Louisiana. My family has been here for generations. And now, they're trying to drive us out."

"But the wings …"

"Gullie," Toby hissed. "Not the time."

There were so many things he wanted to know. How big was this community they spoke of? Did none of them know anything of the fae realm? And just how many communities of fae were there?

"We have to find a way to fight back." Xavier bent to where May had started cleaning up his mess and took the towel from her to do it himself, absently wiping up the tea.

As he watched Xavier, Gulliver couldn't help thinking about the waitress who spilled food every time he was at the cafe. "There's a girl," he blurted. "Maybe you all can help me find her."

"Not this again," Toby groaned.

All three of the other fae looked at Gulliver.

The first one spoke, her eyes returning to a natural green. "Who are you?"

"Strays." Xavier waved off the question. "Can't have idiots getting themselves killed in our city."

She pursed her lips. "I'm Sasha. This is Amandine." She gestured to the winged fae.

"Gulliver and Toby." He pointed to himself then to Toby.

Sasha nodded. "Now, what's this about a missing girl?"

He went into the story, much to Toby's chagrin, of meeting her and returning to the cafe. They listened, and he appreciated that because he knew they'd just lost friends, that there were more important things going on than a single missing woman.

He didn't notice the suspicion clouding Amandine's face until she asked, "And the waitress's name?"

"Sophie."

"And she works at the Vieux Carré Cafe?"

"Yes! You know her? If you could please—" His words were cut off when each woman grabbed an arm and dragged him toward the front door. "What's going on?"

Amandine opened the door, shoving him down the steps. He hit the cracked sidewalk and pain shot through his shoulder. Toby landed beside him.

When Gulliver looked up, only Xavier stood in the doorway. "Sophie-Ann Devereaux is not a woman you want to find." He tossed their shoes down and slammed the door.

Pedestrians stepped over them as more continued down the road toward the fire. Gulliver pushed himself up, trying to catch his breath. "You okay, Tobes?"

Toby lay on his back, staring up at the gray sky. "That was kind of fun."

Gulliver extended a hand down and pulled him to his feet. "You're deranged."

He shrugged. "At least we gained a valuable piece of information."

"And what's that?" Gulliver slipped his shoes back onto his feet.

"Your waitress. If they hate her so much they'd abandon their own, she might be the key."

"The key to what?"

"Finishing this mission and returning home."

He looked sideways at Toby, glad he wasn't in this alone. Tia had known what she was doing sending the both of them. He clapped a hand on Toby's shoulder. "So, we find her?"

"Absolutely. Then, we come up with a plan."

Chapter Eleven
SOPHIE-ANN

"I'm sorry, Dad." Sophie lifted a trembling hand to her clammy brow, ignoring Gabe and his idiot friends standing in the living room behind her. "I'm not feeling very well."

Her father rushed to her side, despite the full house of HAFS members in a seemingly celebratory mood. "You look tired." He studied her face, frowning at the dark circles under her eyes. "Go upstairs and have a lie down. We'll call you back for the meeting in a bit."

"She's fine, Claude," Gabe was quick to add. "She's still mad we picked her up from work early."

"Dragged me away from my job in the middle of a shift is more like it," Sophie snapped, feeling lightheaded. "And then kept me practically locked up here for days to supposedly keep me safe. From what, I still don't know. I'll be lucky if I even have a job when I go back."

"I'll put in a call to Ben and have him smooth things over

with Vicky. You shouldn't let her push you around anyway. She's just the manager."

"And my boss."

"But Ben signs your paychecks. Remember that."

"Whatever." Her dad was never going to get what it was like working with Vicky. Every time he went to Ben about things like this, Vicky made her life miserable. More miserable than usual. "Just let me handle things with my boss."

"All right." He gave her a gentle shove toward the stairs that led to her bedroom. "Get some rest, sweetheart."

The stairs up to her bedroom might as well have been a mountain, but she took each one slowly, hauling herself up using the rail for support. Sophie's bedroom had once been used as a choir loft when the house was a chapel. The long, narrow room was now closed off and housed her bedroom, bathroom, and walk-in closet.

By the time she reached the safety of her bedroom, Sophie was sweating and shaking.

She collapsed onto her bed, the room spinning as she closed her eyes to the dulcet tones of Gabe's annoying voice.

"You coddle her too much, Claude," Gabe said, not bothering to lower his voice. If she could hear him, then everyone in the house could. Just what she needed, everyone knowing her business. "She's never going to be ready to lead the cause until someone rips her out of that shell she hides in."

Sophie rolled over, trying to shut out the din of too many people stuffed into the small house.

"You don't know what you're talking about, Gabe." Her father's deep voice was as soothing as it had always been. "You leave my daughter to me." Only her dad knew the truth. She wouldn't be around long enough to lead anyone.

"Score one for Dad." Sophie sighed as she pulled a blanket over her, kicked off her shoes, and fell asleep in an instant.

Being chronically ill and trying to act like everyone else was the most exhausting thing Sophie-Ann Devereux had ever done.

* * *

"Wake up, Sleeping Beauty." A gentle voice pulled Sophie from a deep sleep filled with dreams of warm amber eyes and a kind smile covered in powdered sugar.

"Mmm?" she groaned, eager to get back to her dreams. Dreams were the one place where she was never tired or in pain.

"Come on, Soph, we've got people waiting for us downstairs." Warm breath brushed against her ear, and her eyes snapped open.

"You better not be in my bed." She wanted to roll away from him the second she realized Gabe was the one breathing on her, but it would take her a few minutes to get out of bed and on her feet.

"We're having a celebration, and you've been up here for hours being lazy." Gabe moved to sit on the edge of the bed. "Go put on your best dress."

"My best—and only—dress is for funerals, which we'll all be going to if you don't get out of my room right now." Sophie dragged herself to the opposite side of the bed. "And if you knew me at all, you'd know I don't do dresses."

"Well, put on something decent at least and come down. Everyone's waiting for you. And do something with your hair. You know I prefer it when you wear it down."

"Get out now and I might think about leaving this room." She settled her feet on the floor and moved to sit up, the room spinning like a top, leaving her nauseated. She reached out to clutch the edge of her dresser for support. The last thing she wanted to do was socialize with HAFS. Not after what happened at the last meeting.

She'd supported her father in the beginning when he first created this sector of HAFS. Too many people had chosen to ignore the unnatural darkness the fae brought to their world, choosing to believe the fake news that claimed it was witches or some solar flare phenomenon that could be explained away with science. With fae creatures hiding among the humans, and no way to identify them until it was too late, someone had to do something to spread awareness. That was where she thought HAFS was the most beneficial. But sometimes, she wondered if her father had taken things too far from the group's roots.

After witnessing an execution, where she'd done nothing to help that poor man, she hated herself for her involvement.

"Make it quick, and do something about the shadows under your eyes too. You're too young to be looking so rough after half a shift waiting tables." Gabe moved to stand by the door. "We might need to get you a gym membership to work on your stamina."

"Get out," Sophie said, her voice cracking on the words. "There is no *we* here."

"Don't be like that, Soph." He turned to her with a wide grin. "Especially not when your father has just given his permission for us to marry." He leaned against the doorframe, his grin widening into a leer.

"Not possible." Sophie shook her head. There was no way her father would agree to that. What was the point in her marrying anyone when she was dying? "He wouldn't do that to me." Not when he knew how much she loathed Gabe.

"It's a done deal." Gabe crossed the room to her closet, rummaging through her things, pulling out blouses and pants she hadn't worn in ages. "The recent attack on the fae in the Quarter was my doing. I led a team of HAFS on your father's orders. It was my win." He tossed the clothes onto the bed where she sat, unable to speak. "You're my prize."

"You're disgusting," Sophie croaked, the words lodging in her throat.

Gabe just laughed at her. "Come down. Now. We're celebrating our success, and Claude wants to announce our engagement as soon as you make an entrance." He turned to go. "Oh, and just so you know, once we're married, I won't tolerate this nonsense. You're a grown woman, Soph. You shouldn't be taking naps in the middle of the day. Claude coddles you, but I won't."

"Get out!" Sophie threw a pillow at him.

The door closed behind him, but his laughter echoed down the stairs.

Sophie sat shaking on the edge of her bed. How could her father even discuss such a thing without her? Let alone agree to it. She moved woodenly, pulling on a pair of dark jeans and a clean t-shirt. Running a brush through her hair, she twisted it up into a neat bun. No way was she wearing it down for Gabe.

As she made her way downstairs, her movements went from wooden and slow to deliberate and fueled by rage. The revelry below had reached top volume in celebration over the deaths of many. She paused on the stairs. They were offering up congratulatory toasts to the demise of the fae. A tragedy that had likely killed more humans than non.

Sophie would be the first to say the fae needed to be dealt with. Too many people had died from their magic. People like her mother. But this ... She couldn't celebrate when innocent humans were hurt. She wanted no part of HAFS if that was the direction they were going.

"Sophie-Ann!" her father called above the noisy din of the crowd. The largest part of their home, the living room, used to be the sanctuary when the building once served as a chapel. The ceiling towered overhead, with exposed beams and trusses. A huge wall of windows and French doors stood open, overlooking the courtyard and letting in the evening light and a cool breeze.

She stepped into the room, and there were HAFS members standing shoulder to shoulder, spilling out into the courtyard.

"Dad, we need to talk." She wound through the crowd to where he was holding court at the dining room table, a large slab of natural wood still edged with the bark from the tree it came from. Her father had made it himself when she was young. Back when he had a successful woodworking business that had failed in the years after her mother's death. Now, he worked construction to pay the bills.

"We're celebrating, sweetheart." His smile hit a chord in her heart. He was clearly drunk, but that was a real smile. One she rarely saw anymore. "Grab a beer from the fridge."

"You know I can't drink." She moved to sit beside him after one of his men stood to offer her the seat. "It interferes with my medication."

"Right." He nodded, giving her that look that said he didn't want to talk about her illness. He'd worked hard to keep her condition from the HAFS community. She was supposed to be the one to take over for him when he retired, but they both knew she wouldn't be here for that. He would have to choose a successor from among his loyal followers.

"What are we celebrating?" she asked, though she knew.

"To the success of HAFS and our most recent victory over the fae."

"And what of the human deaths?" She gave her father a kick under the table. "What of them?"

"Unfortunate casualties of war," Gabe answered, coming to stand behind her.

"Should we not be mourning the loss of our own? Perhaps discuss ways we can avoid such tragedies in the future?"

"Don't bring us down, Soph." Gabe brushed a hand down her shoulder, squeezing harder than necessary. Hard enough to leave a bruise, though she tended to bruise easily because of her illness.

She was getting strange looks from those across the room, and she realized she was never going to get through to them. They were hungry for blood. Fae blood. And they didn't care who got in the way.

A chair scraped against the floor, and all the color drained from her face as her father stood up raising his beer for a toast. "I have an announcement to make." He turned to his daughter. "Sophie-Ann, this includes you. Come stand with me, sweetheart."

She shook her head. "We have to talk. Now." She stared down at her lap, unable to meet her father's eyes. He couldn't be doing this. He couldn't be so callous.

Gabe took her by the arm and pulled her up from the chair. "Come on, Soph. Don't ruin this," he whispered in her ear as he shoved something onto her finger, the thin metal scraping her skin.

There was nothing she could do. She glared at her father as he addressed his people.

"Ladies and gents." He tapped his bottle against the edge of the table to get everyone's attention. "I have a happy announcement to make."

"You can't do this," Sophie hissed under her breath.

Her father ignored her, refusing to meet her gaze as he lifted his beer bottle, the light shining through the amber glass. "I'm pleased to announce that Gabe came to me earlier tonight and asked for my daughter's hand in marriage." He paused for the applause and cheers that swept through the room.

Gabe grinned and laughed as those closest to him slapped him on the back.

"It was a difficult decision." Her father sighed. "Sophie-Ann is precious to me. But Gabe has been the son I never had, so it does my heart proud to be able to say I have given them my blessing."

More cheers and catcalls echoed around her, and no one seemed to notice the horrified, betrayed look on her face as she watched her father make decisions for her.

"To the engagement of my daughter, Sophie-Ann Deveraux, to my right-hand man, Gabriel Christoph—the man of the hour." Her father beamed a smile as Gabe wrapped an arm around her shoulders. "Congratulations. I wish you both great happiness in your lives together."

"Hear, hear!"

"Try to look happy, Soph." Gabe leaned in to press his head against hers as people started taking pictures and asking to see the ring.

Sophie stood, stunned in a sea of smiling faces, everyone celebrating her engagement when no one had even bothered to ask her if it was what she wanted.

"No," she whispered, shaking her head. "No!" she shouted louder and louder still, until the room grew silent. "I'm *dying*! I can't get married. Certainly not to you." She tugged the cheap ring off her finger and threw it at Gabe before she turned to her father. "How could you?" She shoved her way through the crowd, desperate for a moment alone and a breath of fresh air. She ran across the courtyard and through the iron gates onto the sidewalk, and she didn't stop running until she couldn't take another step. She collapsed onto a park bench near the trolley station, letting the tears break free.

Chapter Twelve
GULLIVER

Sophie set the basket of pastries in front of Gulliver, and he saw the bruises along a finger of her left hand. Without thinking, he grabbed her hand, startling her.

"Sorry, I um ..." He fumbled over his words. "Didn't mean to scare you. What happened to your hand?" His eyes traveled up the length of her arm, where another bruise peeked out from under her t-shirt sleeve. It looked suspiciously like a thumbprint. Gulliver couldn't imagine why anyone would want to hurt Sophie. She was so nice. And pretty. And a thousand other things he liked about her.

"I hope the other guy looks worse." He tried to pull a smile out of her. He loved it when she smiled at him for no reason other than she thought he'd said something funny. But Sophie had seemed odd over the last few days. She'd come back to work like she hadn't been abducted from the alley behind the café and refused to give any sort of explanation, only retreating into herself if Gulliver tried to ask.

The light had gone out of her eyes. and she moved lifelessly from one table to the next, giving little notice to the people who came and went throughout her shift. All except him. She still seemed to take notice whenever Gulliver sat down at his regular table.

"Oh, it's nothing." Her hands fluttered awkwardly as she fumbled with the notepad she used to take orders. "I bruise easily." She brushed a short lock of her odd blue hair out of her face.

Gulliver stared at her hair. He never knew humans could have such things as blue hair, but he really liked it.

"Can I get you anything else?" She refused to meet his gaze.

"I saw him. That man who was bothering you the other day. He was on the feletision."

A smile tugged at her mouth, and Gulliver eagerly awaited seeing it light her eyes. No doubt he'd said something stupid again.

"You mean the television?"

"Oh, right. I always say stuff wrong by accident." Gulliver dropped his gaze down to the basket of heavenly sweets that awaited him. But for once, he was more interested in the girl than the food she'd brought him. "He doesn't seem like a very nice guy."

"He's not." She sighed. "But I can handle him. My father's another matter."

"Sophie! Stop flirting with customers and get back to work!" Vicky rang the buzzer that let the servers know orders were backed up.

Sophie's pale face flushed a delicate shade of pink. "Gotta get back to work." She shuffled away, looking both weary and embarrassed at the same time.

Gulliver went back to his beignets and iced coffee, but he kept an eye on Sophie as she moved around the restaurant. The cafe was busier today than usual, and he didn't get a chance to talk to her again before he finished his snack. But something caught his eye on a nearby table after the group of humans left talking loudly.

"That attack was the first of many." A thin man with a weak chin tossed a bundle of paper onto the table. "I just hope that the HAFS group takes them all out. The fae don't belong in our world."

"They don't, but I just don't like to see any humans getting hurt. Those boys from HAFS could have been more careful with human lives." A petite woman with dark hair and kind eyes followed the man from the cafe.

"What's a HAFS?" Gulliver muttered as he slipped out of his seat and retrieved the rolled-up papers from the empty table and took it back to his own. Sinking down in his seat, Gulliver stared at the familiar face on the cover of what he believed was a human thing called a newspaper. The picture staring back at him was the same one he'd seen on the big screen thing Tia called a TV. Toby had figured out how to turn it on, but they didn't know how to look for Netflix like they had at the farmhouse, so it stayed on the same channel. It was always the news. Boring and tedious. Why anyone wanted to watch that was beyond him.

"Gabriel Christoph," he read the name under the picture. Hadn't Sophie called him Gabe?

Gulliver bent to read the article.

Gabriel Christoph and several unknown members of the local New Orleans sector of HAFS, the Human Alliance For Survival, were suspects in the explosion that left the French Quarter reeling only days ago.

The explosion, thought to be an act of terrorism against the suspected fae colonies within the human realm, left dozens injured and eighteen dead. HAFS members across the country believe magical creatures known as fae are responsible for the darkness that threatened our world over a decade ago, yet there is little evidence to corroborate that myth.

The local HAFS leader, Claude Devereaux, made the following statement just after the explosion:

"It is regrettable that human lives were lost in such a terrible tragedy. Rather than focusing the investigation against the innocent young men of HAFS, we strongly urge the New Orleans Police Department to search for evidence against the fae who continue to prey on human life. We can no longer turn a blind eye to those who tried to send our world into the blackness of eternal night. Fae creatures with evil magic live among us, and those in HAFS will stand for it no longer."

"He sounds like a lunatic, doesn't he?" Sophie returned to bring Gulliver his check, nodding at the paper clutched in his hands.

"Yeah. The whole thing is kind of unbelievable." Gulliver wasn't sure what to say. That a human newspaper would even mention fae was cause for alarm. Gulliver needed to speak to his father about what they should do next. Fae were being targeted—likely by this HAFS group—and it was up to those of the five kingdoms to bring an end to such suffering. If that meant they could no longer visit the human realm, then that was a price they would have to pay. It was time for the fae living among the humans to come home. It was much too dangerous here.

"Mind if I take this?" Gulliver asked, holding the newspaper up in question.

"Go for it. Customers leave their papers here all the time. There'll be ten more laying around by this afternoon."

"Thanks." Gulliver stood, eager to get back to Toby with this news.

"See you next time," Sophie said in an absent voice.

"Hey, Sophie." Gulliver reached for her hand to stop her. "Take care of yourself." He glanced down at the bruises on her finger. They looked painful and swollen, like someone had touched her in anger. "No one should ever leave marks on you. For any reason." He started to walk away. "Whether you bruise easily or not," he added with a gentle smile. "You are far too kind to deserve that."

He thought he saw her eyes shine with tears before she dropped her head.

"Thanks for the superior snacks," he called over his shoulder as he walked out of the cafe and headed back toward the Lamothe House at a brisk pace.

* * *

"Hey, Tobes, you're not going to believe this!" Gulliver burst into their hotel room, expecting to find Toby still in bed or well on his way to getting drunk in the middle of the day. Instead, he found his roommate showered and wearing clean clothes, sitting on the small sofa with Xavier. "Oh, sorry. I didn't realize we had a guest."

"It's just Xavier." Toby shrugged, sipping a cup of hot tea. Gulliver hadn't seen him drink anything other than wine since they arrived, so this was an improvement.

"Have you seen this in the human news?" Gulliver tossed the paper onto the coffee table and sat down on the edge of his bed. "I've seen that man. He was giving Sophie a hard time the other day."

"How do you know Sophie?" Xavier asked. "I wanted to ask the..." He paused, seeming to remember how he'd treated them. "I just couldn't around other people. Sophie, she's..."

"She's a waitress he has a crush on." Toby yawned, looking very uninterested in the conversation. "You'd have known that if you didn't kick us out of your safety house just for mentioning her name."

"I go there for the pastries," Gulliver insisted.

"The beignets at Cafe du Monde are a thousand times better," Toby said.

"Since when do you go out for snacks?"

"Since Xavier made me." They were friends now? Something about that didn't make sense.

Gulliver tried to ignore the warning bells going off in his head, tried to forget this man kicked him and Toby out of their house of safety after the bombing. "Well, I like the ones at Sophie's place, and you would too if you had them fresh."

"Listen to him. Sophie's place," Toby mocked.

"I can't pronounce the Vew Kar-y Caffy."

"It's the Vieux Carré Cafe," Xavier said. "Okay, so you know Sophie. Which means you need to tell me anything she's said about Gabe Christoph?"

"Just that he's a bully, and I'm pretty sure he's the one that kidnapped Sophie in the alley last week. And he's probably the one responsible for her bruises today."

Xavier pulled his feet off the coffee table and placed them on the floor before he leaned toward Gulliver. "Bruises?" he growled. "Are you sure they're from Gabe?"

"Um. I don't know. Honestly, I don't really know anything about her other than that she's nice." A small smile played on his face. "She's really nice to me."

"Her father is dangerous," Xavier said, but there was something off in his words, something he wasn't telling them. "And Gabe is his right-hand man. He's the one responsible for that explosion. The fae communities live in fear of the HAFS groups across the country. But we have ways of hiding and tracking HAFS activities. It could have been a lot worse than it was. The humans don't know how to identify us, so they end up killing their own. Still, we lost six fae in that attack. It has to stop."

Xavier sat with his hands clenched in fists as he stared at the image of Gabe in the newspaper.

"Did you say communities? As in more than one?" Gulliver asked. "Across the country?"

"Many more," Xavier said. "Across the world. Most of us fae have been here for generations."

"How?" Gulliver thought they were here to save one small group of fae. He wasn't sure he could handle more than that.

"You two really aren't from around here, are you?"

"Isn't it obvious?" Toby spoke for the first time, still sipping his tea. "We're from the fae home world. I thought I told you I was Prince of Iskalt."

"And I thought you were just drunk and in need of sobering up." Xavier shrugged. "It doesn't really matter where any of us are from. We're here. This is our world too, and we aren't leaving."

"Even if you could go back to the fae realm, where you could live in peace?" Gulliver leaned forward, his elbows propped on his knees. "I can't imagine how much easier that would be for everyone."

"This is our home. It's all we know, and we aren't leaving."

Chapter Thirteen
SOPHIE-ANN

She shouldn't be here. At work. Out in the world. In fact, all Sophie wanted was to curl up in bed and pretend she was a kid with all her hope for the future still intact.

A coughing fit overtook her, sending a shock of pain through her chest and making it hard to breathe. She bent over, trying to catch her breath. The symptoms were getting worse, and no amount of treatment had helped her much in the last year. The breathing treatments never lasted. The chemo had only made her want to die more quickly.

"Go in the kitchen if you insist on looking so sick." Vicky put a hand on her back, urging her through the swinging door. "Why'd you come in today if you can barely stand?"

Sophie gripped the edge of the metal counter for support. The noisy kitchen was a welcome distraction, but the cooks ignored the intruders. "I need the money."

That was a lie. She'd never needed the income from this job

and she hated waiting tables. But what this job truly provided her was an escape. Even if she'd love to wrap up in a heated blanket in bed, that was too close to her father, to the men and women constantly stopping by.

She could barely look at any of them after the bombing, after their cold disregard for life. And the surprise engagement.

Lucky for her, she'd never have to see the marriage through. Not unless her father forced the matter soon. The announcement was nothing more than politics. Gabe setting himself up as the successor to her father's role in HAFS, and her father desperate to believe she'd still be here when it all came to pass.

He had a toxic optimism, but she was a realist.

Another cough wracked her body. Vicky scowled and walked back into the dining room, leaving Sophie to try to remain standing by herself. Her legs wobbled beneath her, but the weakness was nothing new for her. Both her mind and body lacked the strength this world demanded of her.

"I have to get some air." No one was listening to her, so she edged toward the door to the alleyway, her hands skimming along countertops and walls for support.

When she finally pushed out into the fresh air, she drew a cleansing breath into her burning lungs. Her throat was raw from days of coughing. She was tired of it all. For the last two years, she'd fought. And fought.

There was nothing left in her.

Sliding down the wall, she sat next to the overstuffed trash cans. They didn't smell particularly pleasant, but she couldn't have moved right then if she tried. Pulling her knees in, she rested her forehead against them and closed her eyes, trying to forget where she was, who she was.

Her mother used to tell her she was too good for this world. It was something only someone blinded by love could claim, but she held on to it now, trying to make herself believe that was why she'd be leaving it so soon.

Sweetheart, the good things in this life hide away. You have to go searching for them while the bad try to make you believe you've seen all there is to see.

Her mother's voice was once so clear in her mind, so present. Over the years, it faded until only the words remained. What would her mom think of her now? She may not have set off the bombs, but that didn't mean she was innocent in the recent tragedy.

Most of the world thought HAFS was insane for believing in the fae. To them, the group performed terrorist acts. Now, Gabe was a watched man.

"Fancy seeing you in an alley that smells no better than Bourbon Street." The familiar voice had her lifting her eyes to the man leaning against the wall opposite her.

"Xavier." His name came out on a sob. "What are you doing here?"

"I could ask you the same question?" He pushed off the wall to approach her.

She lifted a shoulder in utter patheticness. "I..." She sighed. "I can't get up."

His face softened. Xavier was one of the only people in the world, other than doctors and family, who knew of her condition. It wasn't by choice. She'd called him after one of her treatments when she could hardly stand. He wouldn't rest until she'd told him everything.

He sat beside her, not saying a word.

Leaning her head on his shoulder, she drew in a deep breath. "Do you ever think about what kind of people we'd be if we'd grown up in a different city? If our parents were still around?"

Both of Xavier's parents were gone. He only had a brother he never mentioned, who he hated, and a grandmother.

He didn't answer her question. "Sometimes, I wonder what this city would be like if we didn't live here. Maybe there'd be peace."

She heard what he wasn't saying. If her father didn't lead HAFS in their attacks, New Orleans might not be the dangerous city it had become. Leaning away from him, she tried to push to her feet. He jumped up to steady her, but she shook her head.

"Why are you here, Xavier? It's been a year." He'd once been her only friend, but over the years, distance grew between them, and it was his doing, his choice. He'd wanted her to fight against HAFS from the inside, but she'd been scared. Terrified, really. Her father was all she had left.

Doing nothing is almost worse than doing wrong, he'd said back then.

Xavier clasped his hands behind his back. "The bombing—"

"No." She couldn't talk about this with him. "I didn't even know it was happening. They abducted me from work and kept me locked up until it was over."

"It was bad, Soph."

"You were there?" Why was she asking? She already knew the answer. Xavier had made a habit of tracking HAFS movements and trying to save as many people as he could. He didn't care if he saved fae along with the humans.

"If you'd seen it, you'd know this war your father is waging needs to be stopped."

"It can't. He can't." She hugged her arms across her chest. "And soon ..." She couldn't voice her biggest fear. When she died, would her father lose it? Would he seek healing through violence?

"Evil can always be stopped."

"He's not ..." Evil? Maybe he was, and she just didn't want to think it.

"I need to know what's next. If there's another target already."

She shook her head. "You don't understand. I'm the gem of HAFS, a stone to be protected, shown off. That's it. They don't involve me in their plans. I didn't hear about the bombing in the French Quarter until after it happened."

He pushed a hand through his hair, clear agitation on his face. "I don't know what to do next. How to stop this from happening."

"Maybe you can't."

His shoulders drooped like the weight of all the future lives he'd lose pulled them toward the ground. Would she have to bury Xavier before she died?

"You should go." She straightened, slivers of her strength returning. "Before someone sees you." She was forbidden from associating with Xavier, and she didn't know what her father or his bulldogs would do if they caught them together.

He didn't move. "There's something else." His lips tugged down. "Gabe ..."

"I didn't have a choice." Tears sprang to her eyes.

"You're engaged to my brother."

All she could do was nod, letting tears flow freely down her cheeks. Gabe and Xavier hated each other for reasons they'd never told her. She was the only person who knew about their relation. They shared a mother but had different fathers and personalities like day and night.

Xavier was so sure, so steady. He wasn't necessarily a happy, smiley man, but there was a gentleness to him that was completely absent in his older brother.

"I tried to say no. My father won't hear it. It's okay," she whispered, forcing a smile. "We all know I'll never have to go through with it."

Xavier pulled her against his chest, wrapping strong arms

around her. "Do you need help? I have people ... We can get you out. You'll be safe with us."

She pressed her face into his shirt. He always smelled good, familiar. A mixture of honey and pine. Ignoring his words, she sighed. "A year is too long to go without seeing you."

That was her answer, and she knew he'd understand. She couldn't leave her father, even if what he was doing was so wrong. The mission of the group—pushing fae from their world—was righteous. She didn't agree with their violent methods, but the simple truth was that fae creatures did not belong in this world.

The back door opened, and Sophie expected Vicky to come out and make her get back to work, but a large frame filled the doorway.

"Hello, brother." Gabe grinned, stepping into the alley. "I'd appreciate it if you took your hands off my fiancée."

Sophie didn't want to leave the safety of Xavier, but she pushed him away and wiped the tears from her face.

"You shouldn't be here, Gabe." She attempted a look of concern. "Your face is all over the news."

He scowled. "I couldn't hide out in your father's garden shed any longer. Come here." He gripped her arm, fingertips pressing into the bruises, and yanked her against him.

Peppermint breath hit her moments before his lips touched hers, rough and vindictive. A show for his brother.

Sophie let him kiss her, her body frozen in place.

When he finally yanked himself away, he smiled at Xavier. "I just came for that. Now that we're engaged, I expect a lot more." He slapped her butt, making her jump and yelp in surprise.

Sophie wiped her mouth in disgust, too angry to use her words.

Xavier's eyes narrowed in fury. "If you so much as hurt one

hair on her head, I will come for you. Brother or not, I will kill you."

"I prefer the not part of that."

A commotion sounded at the end of the alley as a group of tourists walked by. Gabe pressed himself up against the building.

"You have to go." Sophie shoved him. "And don't you ever touch me like that again."

"This will blow over when your father gives them another fall guy."

She pushed him again. "That day is not today."

Gabe looked from Xavier to Sophie and back before a growl ripped from his throat and he yanked open the door, disappearing inside.

"I should get back to work." She brushed dirt off her butt and the front of her apron.

Xavier's gaze connected with hers. "If you ever decide you want to live the rest of your limited time outside a murderous cult, you know how to reach me. I will do anything to help you, Sophie-Ann. You just have to let me."

"Noted." Her shoulders slumped, and she wondered if anyone would ever get how tired she was of it all. Too tired to fight back.

"And seriously, don't marry that guy, Soph. You're way too good for him." He gave her one last look before heading down the alley toward the main road.

Sophie pushed out a breath, his words running back in her mind. Limited time. She could feel the clock ticking inside her, a time bomb just waiting to hit zero.

And it was closer than anyone else realized.

When she went back to work, she attempted a smile, but it felt as fragile as every other part of her. She reached the dining room and slid into a chair at an empty table, leaning her head on the solid wood. It was all she could do with the meager energy she had left.

"Go home." Vicky sighed. "Come back tomorrow or not at all."

One day soon, it would be not at all.

Chapter Fourteen
GULLIVER

"What do you mean you can't tell me where we're going?" Gulliver stopped Toby on the shaded sidewalk of Esplanade Avenue near their hotel. "I'm not just going to trust Xavier. I've only met him a few times. What do we even know about him?"

Toby stiffened. "It's been more than a few times." He'd grown distant over the last days but differently than before. He wasn't drinking or mooning over Logan. It was like he had too much on his mind.

"That's where you've been?" While Gulliver was at the library combing through articles on bombings and murders, connecting various ones to HAFS so he could send Tia a full report whenever his dad or Loch showed up to check on them, Toby was off making friends. "Tobes, he threw us out of his house."

Gulliver wouldn't forgive that. The mere mention of Sophie got them tossed onto the street by their own kind. And he wanted to know why. Now, sitting in the room at the inn was a folder detailing every piece of information he could find on Claude Devereaux. Next, Gulliver needed to tackle the internet, but that was a scary place, and he didn't know where to start.

"He had his reasons, I'm sure." Toby turned to Gulliver with a sigh. "He says he can take us to one of the local fae communities."

Gulliver drew up straight. "How many are there just in this city?"

"I don't know. He's slow with the information, but this particular group wants to meet us."

If Tia were here, she'd jump at this chance. Maybe this community would have more information on HAFS. "Fine."

Toby grinned. "Thought you'd see it my way."

They turned onto Bourbon Street, where a white car waited at the curb with a yellow stripe and the word Taxi on it.

"I thought Taxis were supposed to be all yellow," Gulliver whispered, remembering the poor woman they'd abducted at the bus station.

Xavier opened the passenger door. "Get in."

A pale woman with wild black curls sat behind the steering thing. She had a metal ring piercing her lip and a bar in her eyebrow.

"Good day." Gulliver leaned forward to offer her his hand. "I'm Lord Gulliver O'Shea."

She and Xavier shared a look, both hiding their smiles.

"Lane." She shook her head. "And there ain't no fae lords in this world, Your Highness."

"Oh, I'm not a prince." Gulliver's face reddened. "But Toby here is."

Toby elbowed him. "Will you shut up?"

Lane hit the gas, and they sped forward at a too-fast clip. She narrowly missed hitting a woman in a bright outfit covered in some kind of shiny material. Gulliver didn't stop gripping the edge of the seat until they were out of the city.

The roads were crowded with cars, and the landscape was marred by giant metal structures. He wondered if the cities of the human realm had ever held the beauty of Fargelsi or Iskalt.

Music blared from the box built into the car. Gulliver had never been particularly fond of human music, and this made his ears hurt with its screeching voice and a thumping he felt all the way to his bones.

Toby didn't seem to mind as his head bobbed to the beat.

"Where are we going?" Gulliver yelled over the awful sound.

Xavier looked back, studying him. "A place called Chalmette. Our communities keep a low profile, sticking mostly to the nondescript suburbs where we can blend in."

Gulliver didn't know what a suburb was, but if that's where the fae lived, it must be a beautiful place. They passed old houses with boards in place of windows. Walls leaned in like they'd cave at any moment, and some had missing chunks of their roofs.

Any moment now, they'd get to the wide-open spaces fae loved. The rolling hills and greenery. There'd be horizons as fine as paintings and fresh fruit ripe on the trees.

But that never came. Instead, they drove through neighborhoods of squashed together homes, cracked roads, and so many of those shops humans loved.

Disappointment hit him when they pulled up to a small house with peeling brown paint, a sinking porch, and a faded red door.

"This is ... it?" Gulliver tried to get Toby to meet his gaze, but his eyes were firmly fixed on Xavier.

"It's where we meet." Xavier stepped out of the car.

"Meet for what?" Something about this didn't feel right, but Gulliver couldn't quite put his tail on it.

"Stop with the questions, Gullie." Toby frowned. "I'm sure we'll find out."

Gulliver had never known Toby to lack curiosity or common caution. He was Tia O'Shea's twin, after all. Sure, she never backed down and barged into places she shouldn't, but she also recognized when something was wrong.

Xavier seemed trustworthy, but Gulliver didn't trust anyone who wasn't part of his family. He'd learned that the hard way. From growing up in the prison realm to suffering in the Vondurian dungeons, his experiences taught him even the right reasons could cause evil.

"Why'd we take a cab here?" Gulliver wouldn't stop asking questions. It wasn't in him.

"Because cabs go mostly unnoticed." Lane stepped through the door. "We're back!"

Heads popped out of doorways, fae appearing like those white-faced people with colorful hair Tia once made him watch pile out of a small car.

"You brought friends." A broad man lumbered forward, wings sprawling out behind him. At his side was a small older woman, her eyes flashing pale green. Was she using magic, or was that a trick of his imagination?

The door slammed behind them, and Gulliver did his best not to jump. Magic didn't scare him, not anymore. He didn't grow up around it, but since the prison magic broke, he'd spent more time than he'd admit with the most powerful magic wielder of all the fae.

Xavier dropped a bag on a beat-up settee with a tear across one cushion. Shiny gray stuff covered it. "This is Gulliver and Toby. They're from ... there." That's all he said to describe the vast world beyond this one, but the fae crowding the living room nodded as if they understood. "They came to investigate what's happening with HAFS."

"And what have you learned?" The big man crossed his arms.

Gulliver rubbed the back of his neck. "They're killing fae and any humans accused of being fae."

Silence. And then, laughter wound through the group.

"Astute observation." Lane lifted one brow. "Tell me, how did you come by such top secret information?"

"All right." Xavier held up a hand. "Leave them alone. They're trying to help." He looked at Gulliver and Toby. "You are, right?"

Both men nodded.

"Perfect. Well, you're just in time." He sat on the back of the settee.

"Time for what?" Gulliver looked from gleeful face to gleeful face.

"We've watched our fae die for too long. Our human allies have sacrificed their lives. We can't keep sitting still and doing nothing. We have to fight back."

A cheer wound through the room, fae high fiving and smiling.

Despite the muggy air, a chill settled into Gulliver.

Toby grinned along with the rest. "What are we planning?"

We. That didn't take long.

Lane clapped him on the shoulder. "Just know, if you betray us, we will kill you, fae or not."

"I'd never betray the fae." Toby clenched his fists. "The humans have to be held to account."

There it was. His reason. He needed to take his revenge on anyone he could blame for fae pain. Logan died at the hands of the fire plains. There was no vindication to be had there. But here there was an enemy he could fight.

Xavier jumped off the back of the couch and walked toward a smaller room, where a table sat with maps spread out before it. "We've chosen our targets. We have our supplies." He pressed the map flat as it started to curl up. "Here." He pointed to something directly in the center of the city. "We can get word to the nearby fae communities and our human allies to avoid this area. Then, we take out an entire block."

Many sets of eyes flashed different colors, and Gulliver knew exactly what they were thinking. That this would show them. The fae had been pushed too far.

"What about the other humans?" Gulliver asked. "The ones who know nothing of fae and don't believe in the mission of HAFS?"

Lane shrugged. "We can't let collateral damage hold us back. The only way to preserve our fae is to fight."

This wasn't okay. Gulliver shook his head, backing up. "I have been to war. Twice. I've seen the true damage it can do when unleashed."

They all stared at him like he was some kind of creature who didn't belong. He guessed he was. "I've been to war too." Toby's voice was soft. "I've lost people I love. But it's taught me that short-term violence is sometimes necessary for long-term peace."

"You can't believe that." The only time war was justifiable was to fight back against evil. This would only antagonize it, embolden it. It wasn't a fight. It was suicide.

"So, the two sides are just going to keep killing those who have nothing to do with this waiting for the other to give in?" Gulliver's back hit the wall. "This isn't what our queen sent us here for, Toby."

"My sister wants HAFS dealt with."

"We're gathering information. That's our role."

"She sent me with you to get me out of her hair. You can continue your mission, but I will choose one for myself."

Gulliver turned and ducked through the doorway, not looking back as he headed across the house. He could hardly breathe until he reached the front stoop.

A raindrop hit his cheek, and he peered up into an angry sky. With no way to get home, all he could do was wait. Wait for Toby to come to his senses, for the fae here to realize attacking humans was not the way to gain their freedom. Too many people were going to die.

He sat on the stone step and buried his face in his hands. His tail curled around him, as if trying to comfort him. He'd learned long ago he couldn't stop those bent on destruction.

"Tia," Gulliver whispered, "I wish you were here." He'd thought he and Toby were in this together, that they'd do their duty and then report to the queen so she could decide what actions needed to be taken. But he was wrong.

Gulliver was very much alone.

The door opened behind him, and he didn't lift his head when Xavier took a seat at his side. Neither spoke at first, and the rain came down harder. The small overhang protected them to an extent, but Gulliver could still feel spritzes of water dampening his clothes.

"You don't want to be here, do you?" Xavier peered into the rain, looking for answers.

It took Gulliver a moment to answer. "My queen sent me."

"That doesn't answer my question."

"Someone needed to come. Why not me?" Gulliver had asked himself that question his entire life. As a child, when he entered Lord Kvek's fortress to steal food. Why shouldn't it be Gulliver keeping his village fed? In the war of the four kingdoms, he was a ten-year-old who did impossible things, and why shouldn't he? When Tia wanted to save the kingdom that held her prisoner as the fire plains expanded, he'd stood at her side. There was no reason not to.

He was Gulliver, an orphan turned son of a prince, best friend of a queen. A dark fae with no offensive magic. It didn't take someone who was born "special," someone with an obvious fate, to do the right thing.

Xavier rubbed his chin. "I don't understand you."

"Few fae do." Only Tia. She would know what he was trying to say without him having to explain it. One must always fight for good, fight to protect as many lives as possible. It was the harder choice, the unpopular one, but to fae like him or Tia and her parents, it was the only choice there was.

"Sophie." Xavier breathed out her name like it was sacred to him.

Gulliver's gaze snapped to his. "You mean the woman whose very name made you and your friends throw me out onto the street?"

Xavier closed his eyes for a fraction of a second, and when he opened them, there was a softness that hadn't existed as he'd instructed his fae on how to make war with the unsuspecting humans. "Let's just say I've known her for a long time, and I have very personal reasons for wanting to destroy HAFS. You want another way? I'm giving you one."

"What are you talking about?"

"She is the key. Her father leads the New Orleans sector of HAFS, and if circumstances were different, she'd be the obvious successor."

No. Gulliver couldn't think, couldn't feel. The waitress who entranced him the moment he saw her, the one with bright smiles and sad eyes ... she was part of this? Part of the group who hated his kind?

"We watch her, watch who she talks to. You've been at the diner nearly every day since your arrival. There's no use denying the connection between you two. This war is coming to New

Orleans. We are fighting back. The only way to stop us is to destroy HAFS. From the inside."

Gulliver jerked back, his cat eyes widening and his tail going completely still. "You want me to get closer to her."

He nodded reluctantly.

"Become one of them."

Again, a nod was the only answer.

"And what then?"

"We help you kill Claude Devereaux and his lieutenants."

Kill? Sophie's father? "Will that prevent fae attacks?"

Xavier's brows drew together. "The humans must pay for what they've done, but it will bring a swifter end to this war if we can cut off one of their leaders."

Gulliver stood, looking down at Xavier. This man wanted him to become an assassin surrounded by those who hated him, an island in an angry storm. And doing so wouldn't even prevent the deaths from coming. "That's not my mission. I am loyal to my queen."

He started off down the driveway.

"Think about it, Gullie," Xavier called after him.

He wouldn't. His answer was the one his conscience could handle. Yet, there was so much to what Xavier said that his heart couldn't.

Sophie was one of them. HAFS. The humans wanted to survive, but didn't they see so many more of them would die because of their hatred?

Good, sweet Sophie. Was the abduction from her diner a ruse?

An ache rested inside his chest as he walked down the road. Cars passed, some pulling into a lane next to a strange building that sold something called a daiquiri from a window. There was an acrid, dense smell to the air that couldn't be erased by the rain falling from the heavy clouds above. Water dripped into his eyes, and he didn't bother wiping it away.

How far was it back to the city? All he wanted was to go home to the green fields of Myrkur or the icy shores of Iskalt, where the air froze a fae's eyelashes to their cheeks while also cleansing them with the scent of the sea.

A car pulled up to the curb in front of him. "Need a ride?" the driver called.

"A taxi," Gulliver whispered. A real one this time. It said it right on the side, but then so had Xavier and Lane's car. Walking to the city wasn't an option, so he threw himself into the backseat.

A blast of cold air hit him, and he hugged his arms across his chest for warmth.

"Oh, sorry, kid," the man said. "Had the AC on full blast, but you must be freezing your knickers off."

"I'm not sure what knickers are, sir, but I'm sure I still have them. Just a little wet."

He let out a bellowing laugh.

"Is this a real taxi? I don't want to make you drive anywhere you do not wish to. Please know I do not plan to abduct you."

The man pulled onto the road, chuckling to himself. "Good to know. Didn't you read the side? Taxi. That's me. I'll take you to the moon if you can pay."

Gulliver pulled the damp plastic card from his pocket. "Does this still work when it's wet?"

"You're a hoot. Yes, it'll work. Just remember you want to give Jerry here a fat tip. Where am I taking you?"

Gulliver gave the name of Sophie's cafe without a second thought. He had to see her, had to look into her eyes and search for the hate that must reside there.

The old man up front prattled on about traffic, yelling at other cars and raising a finger at them. It was all very strange. By the time they reached the Vieux Carré Cafe, Gulliver almost needed to throw up. He pushed the card through the machine and hit the button for tips, selecting the biggest one. With a quick thank you, he stepped out.

The taxi sped off, leaving Gulliver alone on the sidewalk. He peered into the wide windows, looking for her. There were no patrons around the tables, and he assumed the rain scared them off.

And then, she was there. Sophie breezed out of the kitchen like a Fargelsian summer, light and airy. She worked to clear tables, a slowness to her movements. He suspected she was in no hurry without any customers to serve. A small smile tilted the corners of her mouth, and her lips moved. It took a moment for Gullie to realize she was singing to herself.

How could this woman be a member of a group bent on killing and destruction? He'd known a lot of evil people, and one thing he'd learned was that there were clues. Long before they ever did wrong, their behaviors predicted the future.

But not her. In his weeks coming here, Gulliver sensed two strong things in her. Kindness and a strange sadness. Not ill intent, not even a mean word spoken.

The bell over the door made a soft jingling sound as he entered, and she looked up from where she stacked dishes on her tray, her smile finally reaching her eyes. "Gulliver."

"Hi." He wasn't sure what else to say, how to talk to a woman who hated everything he represented.

"If you have a seat, I'll be right with you." She walked toward the kitchen with her tray. There was something even more fragile to her than normal today. Each step looked like a conscious move instead of the habit of walking humans and fae alike developed.

Could Gulliver do it? Could he get close to this woman simply to reach her father? Even if Tia gave him that exact order, he wasn't sure. Lying to her felt like lying to himself, to his soul.

Sophie returned, pulling paper and a pen from her apron. "Just beignets today? Or are you here for dinner? The rain kind of kept the dinner rush away, so I'm hoping you'll be here a while."

Gulliver's face flushed with warmth. "I'll be here as long as you want me to be." Until he went back to the world she'd destroy if she had the chance.

Her eyes met his, and he did it. He searched for any clues he'd missed, any way he'd misread her. There was nothing. Only a softness he'd grown to appreciate. Also, a hidden strength, the kind that only came about after extreme trials. He recognized it because Tia wore the same look in her eyes. Like every day they woke up, it was in defiance of the very world.

"So," she coughed, her breath wheezing in her chest. "Dinner?"

"You don't look so well." He stood, reaching for her arm to guide her into a chair.

"I'm fine. It's just been a long day." Her eyes clouded over, a film keeping her secrets inside.

Her entire body slumped in the chair, and she whispered, "I'm okay," before falling sideways onto the cold tile floor.

Chapter Fifteen
SOPHIE-ANN

Am I dead?

That was the first thought rolling through Sophie's mind before she opened her eyes. Maybe she dreaded it, or maybe she hoped it was true this time, but whatever her circumstances were, she'd learned long ago that she had to accept them.

Dying wasn't easy for anyone, let alone someone who should have their entire life ahead of them. She used to sit high up in her room, watching people out her double-paned window. They laughed and smiled, making plans for their futures.

She'd spent so long forced only to live in the present. But had she truly been alive?

"Sophie," a soft voice called to her. For a moment, she thought it was her mother welcoming her home. A hand gripped hers, and she smiled.

"I think she's waking up." This voice held less care, less

regard for her. She didn't need to see the speaker to know that. "You can leave now."

"Not a chance."

They were still arguing when her eyelids fluttered open, so they didn't see her stir. Two men stood above her bed, both tall. One was broader, but the other was a sea of calm in the middle of her storm.

She wasn't with her mom, didn't get to see her quite yet, but Gulliver quelled the panic inside. It wasn't over, as much as she wished it were. Being dead would be an upgrade over dying, and yet, she wanted to hear his voice again.

"Gullie," she whispered, unable to get more volume into her voice.

Gabe pushed Gulliver out of the way. "Sophie-Ann, you scared us." She knew what really scared him. That she'd die before he could formally entrench himself in her family as Claude's prized son-in-law. He touched her arm, and she flinched away.

"Where's my dad?" she managed. Whatever he'd done, whoever he was, the one thing she knew was he'd be by her side until the end.

Gulliver opened his mouth to speak, but Gabe cut him off.

"The hospital called your house, but he wasn't there. One of the guys answered and got a message to me."

It was her house, but it really belonged to them. The people of HAFS. They came and went at all hours, and she couldn't even die in the presence of only her father because others would hear about it.

Gulliver rounded the bed to the opposite side of Gabe. He didn't touch her, something she was grateful for. "He's coming."

She nodded, trying to swallow. Her tongue stuck to the roof of her mouth. It was so dry. More than anything, she just wanted water and peace, but neither seemed possible at the moment. An

IV in her arm kept her from reaching too far, and the drugs they pumped into her turned her brain to mush.

At this point in her illness, nurses and doctors no longer pretended there were treatment options to look into. Every time she ended up in the hospital, all they could do was load her up with pain medications and wait to see if that was it for her.

It never was. At least, not yet. One day soon, she'd finally get her painless sleep.

Her head pounded, and she squinted against the bright white fluorescents they seemed determined to torture patients with in every hospital she'd seen. "Gabe." She turned her gaze on him, making her voice quiver on the way out. "Can you find him? Please."

Gabe took her hand in his. "I will. And then, you and I need to talk. I love you, Soph. I don't want to wait to marry you because then I may never get the chance. All those times I called you lazy ... I didn't know. I swear."

She'd have said anything to get him out of the room. "Tomorrow." She wouldn't have to go through with it if she died before then.

Gabe leaned down, pressing a kiss to her lips, and she did her best not to gag. When he left, shutting the door behind him, her shoulders relaxed and she released a breath.

Gulliver was silent for a long moment. "You're going to marry him?"

"No." She tried to lift her head, but she didn't have the strength. "I don't know if it'll get that far."

The heavy meaning of her words sat between them, the silence stifling. She didn't really know if today was the day she never went home again. Episodes like this over the last few months weren't rare, but they'd gotten exponentially worse each time. Her doctors forbid her from working, from taxing herself, but the alternative was to die an unremarkable death in the house that sometimes felt more like a prison.

She'd wanted to be out in the world, to see people and remind herself life would go on without her. It was a strange sort of comfort. Not even Vicky knew how sick she was. There were other terms she'd used to describe her.

Clumsy. Lazy. Incompetent.

From her constant need to sit down to the frequent falls, it was all true. And yet, it wasn't her truth.

Gulliver crossed the room and pulled a heavy recliner toward the bed. It scraped against the tile floor. Once he'd positioned it, he reached for the tray near her bed, picking up the giant cup. It had a lid and a straw, but there was no way she had the strength to hold it.

He didn't ask her to. Instead, he positioned the straw against her lips. She tried to draw water into it, but when none came, tears welled in her eyes. She was helpless, and that was a feeling she'd sought to avoid at all costs.

Sensing her distress, Gulliver took off the lid and tilted the cup against her lips, letting a tiny trickle enter her parched mouth. More, she needed more.

"Careful," he cautioned, setting the cup back down. "You should only have a little at a time."

"Why ..." She drew in a breath, trying to gather the strength to speak. "You're here."

He sat in the recliner, crossing one leg over the other. A soft smile tilted his lips when he looked at her. She'd never gotten the chance to study him this closely before, to look into his clear eyes and find out what was behind the mystery that seemed to follow him.

Now, they were here, and all she could do was stare at him. At the way his smile was slightly crooked, his irises larger than normal. They were like a window into his soul. The look he gave her infused warmth into her chilled limbs.

"I'm the one who brought you here. I got one of those helper cars."

"A taxi?"

He nodded. "Do you remember what happened?"

She nodded. The restaurant. Falling. Darkness. "But you stayed."

"You needed me to." He shrugged like it wasn't a big deal, but to her, it was. Other than her parents, she'd never had anyone do anything for her without wanting something in return. Even Gabe... He wanted to marry her to become her father's successor, the son he never had. And when she was gone, he'd be the only child of Claude Devereaux left. No one would care if it was by blood or marriage.

"Thank you." She attempted a smile, but her face felt numb, like it was frozen in place.

Gulliver leaned forward, elbows on his knees. "I still don't understand what happened. The healer who stopped by seemed to know you, but she wouldn't tell me anything." There was anxiety in his voice, a true worry. Sophie barely knew this man as anything more than her favorite customer, but something inside of her screamed to trust him.

That maybe he was the only one she *could* trust.

"I'm sick."

"I see that." Gulliver's brow furrowed. "But places like this give you herbs, right? And tonics that can make you better?"

Her eyelids were heavy, but she struggled to keep them open. "Not for me. No medicine can cure cancer once it's spread into as many organs as it has in me."

"Cancer." Confusion clouded his face, as if he'd never heard the word. "Like a plague?"

"You're right. It is a plague. One I won't survive."

His eyes glassed over, and she wished she could take her words back, that she could return his smile with one of her own. "No. You're young. Even humans don't die this young. It's a lie."

In her drug-addled mind, a warning signal told her there was something off in his words, but she didn't have the energy to consider them more closely. "No lies." She sighed, and it felt like her entire chest caved in, squeezing her lungs. The heart monitor to her left started beeping, a familiar rhythm to her life.

Darkness enveloped her before she blinked her tired eyes open again. Doctors rushed into the room, yelling at Gulliver to get out of the way. She vaguely remembered the panic on his face, the redness in his eyes.

Don't cry for me, she wanted to say. *I'll be okay*.

Her throat seized up, and her entire body jerked as pain seared into her chest.

"Again," a doctor shouted.

"Charge to two hundred." One of the nurses pressed the cool paddles against her chest once again. "Clear!"

This time, when the world faded away, she sank into the darkness, welcoming its cold embrace.

Still not dead.

Wasn't that a shame?

Her father refused to let her sign a DNR, to let her die in peace. And every single person in this hospital knew enough to fear him.

"You saved my daughter," she heard him say. "Young man, I don't know you, but if there's anything you need in this city, all you have to do is ask."

"Thank you, sir." Gulliver's voice was soft yet strong. "But I really just want to stay to make sure she's okay."

"She is. Thanks to you."

Sophie forced her eyes open. Every part of her hurt, and she wondered how many more times she'd have to wake like this. Feeling a familiar button in her hand, she hit it twice, waiting for the morphine to take over.

"Honey." Her dad stood when he saw her awake and rushed to the bed. "We've been so worried."

Tears crusted in the corners of her eyes, and if she had more in her, they'd probably stream down her face. Instead, all she had was a barely audible, scratchy voice. "Why can't you let me go?"

His mask fell, and she realized how exhausted he looked. His suit, normally pressed to within an inch of its life, sat wrinkled on his frame. Even his hair refused to behave. The last time she'd seen him so destroyed was after her mother died. "You're my baby girl."

"I know." She flipped her hand over, palm up. It was all the movement she could make. He slid his hand into hers. "I can't keep doing this."

"But you were fine. Working, coming to HAFS meetings. Only days ago."

He didn't get it. "I wasn't fine." Those in pain, the sick, hid in plain sight. They didn't let others see how much they struggled, how much they needed. She'd tried for too long not to be the sick girl, the dying girl. Yet, one cannot escape their fate. "Let me go to her, Dad. Please."

She'd never seen the man cry, not even at her mom's funeral. But there were tears in his eyes now. "I can't."

"You mean you won't."

He bent over her hand, his tears warm against her skin. "You're all I have left."

"You'll still have me even after I'm gone." Like she had her mother. Always and forever.

Gulliver cleared his throat, but it wasn't to interrupt. She could tell by the way the man was openly weeping. "I'll ..." sniff, "... give you two some time." Despite the tears, there was a purpose in his eyes she didn't understand, some knowledge that kept him from completely breaking down.

She wondered if she'd ever get to learn what it was.

Chapter Sixteen
GULLIVER

Tia would say this city sucked. It was one of those human phrases she thought was hilarious. She'd complain about the dirty streets that smelled like bodily fluids he didn't want to think about. She wouldn't like the uneven sidewalks, which was odd because sidewalks were a very human creation. Yet, the O'Shea in her would say, if you're going to do something, do it well.

Still, Gulliver had loved it here. The buildings looked like they were straight out of a humantale of the best kind. Bright colors and people from so many places. It was a melding of human cultures he'd found beautiful. That kind of thing didn't happen in the fae realms. Even in Myrkur, where there were fae of all types, one tended to stick to their own.

For someone like Gullie, who had no one else like him, it could be lonely.

But now, this beautiful city had turned sour in his stomach. When he went home, he wouldn't think of all the ways it amazed him. Instead, he'd see a girl, with the most beautiful blue hair, lying in bed, looking as if death called her name. Looking as if she wanted to answer.

Maybe it was despair. She knew this was the end, so she hoped it came quickly. Maybe it was the impending marriage she didn't want, one that couldn't last but would ensure her legacy lived on within a terrorist organization, a group he still couldn't believe she had any part in.

It was raining by the time he reached the inn after wandering the streets for longer than he'd intended. He hadn't seen Toby since the meeting Xavier had taken them to, and he couldn't face him when the only thing he wanted was to take away Sophie's pain.

He stood in the courtyard, contemplating heading back out for another wet stroll, but he couldn't put this off forever. If he could only talk to Tia, he'd let her know what was happening and she'd have the answers. He was sure of it.

But she wasn't here, so it was up to him.

"I am the hero of this story," he whispered to himself as he approached the stairs. He'd never felt like a hero. He was the sidekick, the loyal friend of those who were meant to save the day.

For Sophie, he had to change the story.

There was one conclusion he'd come to since leaving the healers. He could save her, but he wasn't sure she would ever forgive him for what it would take to accomplish such a feat.

When he opened the door to his room, he found Toby and Xavier huddled together near the window. They broke apart when they noticed his presence. Gulliver didn't know what to say, or how to ask Toby for something he wasn't sure he had a right to ask.

"How is she?" Worry etched into every line of Xavier's face. Toby had contacted him after he heard from Gullie. He clearly loved Sophie too, despite the drastic actions he wanted to take against her people.

"Not good." Gulliver stripped off his wet shirt and threw it in a heap in the corner. "I need a hot shower." The air conditioning pushed the damp chill from the rain right into his bones. He needed to gather his strength before entering into the argument with Toby.

Because that was what it would be. A fight. A duel. Their wills pushing against each other until one of them broke.

He kicked off the rest of his clothes on his way to the bathroom. Once the shower heated, he stepped under the hot spray. His tail quivered with pleasure, even as his eyes filled with the tears he thought himself empty of.

"I need guidance, Tia." He rested his forehead against the cold tile wall. The mission was to stay in the human realm to gather intelligence. That was all. Now, Toby was involved in some kind of plot, and Gulliver was considering breaking a sacred rule of the fae. Bringing a human through the portal.

It was more of an unspoken rule than anything else, but there was a reason Myles always had to visit his parents and not the other way around. Other than Myles, the last time a fae brought a human into the fae realm was when Brea was swapped with a human baby. Alona.

"Gullie." Toby's uncertain voice reached him through the pattering of the shower.

"I need a few minutes." He couldn't face him until he scrubbed the desperation from his face. The tears couldn't leave this shower.

"I'm ..." He paused. "I'm sorry about your friend."

For a moment, he sounded like the old Toby. The one who was never far from his sister's side, who was quick to smile but slow to speak. He'd grown up in a magical world and possessed little magic of his own. Like Gulliver, he was different.

Gulliver pushed his anger aside and opened the shower curtain enough to stick his head out. "Thanks for saying that."

Toby shifted from one foot to the other. "Tia never should have sent me with you."

Gulliver reached behind him to shut off the shower and then grabbed a towel. He wrapped it around his waist and stepped out. "Your sister always knows what she's doing." Would even she hate him for what he wanted to do?

"I guess." Toby rubbed the back of his neck.

Hesitating for a moment, Gulliver put a hand on his shoulder and squeezed. He walked past him into their room, where Xavier sat on Toby's bed with a book on his lap.

Xavier looked up and whistled. "Didn't know you were hiding all that behind the tail, Gullie."

He looked down at his chest, not sure what Xavier meant. "Do fae in the human realm have different skin?"

Behind him, Toby laughed. "He's not going to understand you, Xav. Leave him alone."

Xav? Toby already used a nickname for him. Gulliver wasn't sure how he felt about the new closeness between his friend and a fae who knew nothing of their world, one that sought revenge.

As Gulliver dressed, Toby and Xavier spoke in hurried whispers. When he'd had enough of their secrecy, Gulliver turned. "Sophie is going to die."

That stopped both of them.

Xavier hung his head. "She's been sick a long time." He closed his eyes for only a moment. "I wish there was something we could do to help her."

"There is." Gulliver crossed his arms over his chest, his gaze locking with Toby's. "I'm taking her to Lenya."

* * *

"No." With that single word, Toby walked from the room. He didn't stop when he reached the pouring rain in the courtyard.

"Seriously, Toby?" Gulliver shouted after him. "You're not even going to talk about it?" He'd just warmed up from his last jaunt in the rain, but that didn't stop him from running to catch up with Toby before he reached the gate to the street.

Grabbing Toby's arm, he forced him to turn.

Toby wouldn't meet his eyes. "You know it's not possible, Gullie."

"You're wrong. Just because something isn't acceptable doesn't mean it's impossible."

"Fine, then I'll just say I won't do it."

"Why not?"

"Oh, I don't know. How about the fact that not a single royal would sanction such an act? Not even my sister, and we both know she loves wild ideas."

"There's one who would, and you know it." Gulliver released Toby and stepped back.

Toby's jaw clenched. "Then, it's a good thing my mother is no longer in power." Tia may have been a little wild, she may have loved human phrases and food, but only Brea was truly connected to them. Only she was nuts enough to try something like this.

Well, the only royal. Gulliver knew who it was he really needed, but Griff had no power in the courts.

Toby pushed a hand through his sopping wet hair and blew water from his lips. "What do you expect our healers to do for her that hers cannot?"

Thunder crashed overhead, and Xavier yelled from the balcony. "You two idiots ready to come inside yet?"

They both ran toward the winding staircase and didn't stop until they were inside, puddles forming at their feet. Gulliver's chest heaved, and he struggled to catch his breath.

Xavier threw a towel at him, and it smacked him in the face before he caught it. Despite the muggy air outside, he was freezing. Again. He dreamed of crawling into his bed in the small house he'd built near his parents' in Myrkur. Of having his sisters sneak in to curl up against him, their wings wrapping around them in a cocoon.

But he couldn't go back when he knew there was a girl here who deserved to be saved. "I wasn't planning on taking her to a healer."

"Then, what—" Toby's eyes narrowed. "You can't be serious."

"Like a bear attack."

Xavier suppressed a smile. "The phrase is 'like a heart attack'."

Gulliver frowned. "And why is your heart attacking you?" He shook his head. "No, you must be wrong. That doesn't make any sense." Heart attacks? How ridiculous.

Toby growled. "No one cares! What I care about is the fact that Gulliver wants to take Sophie to a place most fae aren't even supposed to know about. It probably wouldn't even work on a human."

"You don't know that."

"What I do know is Eavha and Declan are guarding it for a reason. If others found out what we possessed ..."

Xavier looked from one to the other. "I'm missing something."

Toby turned to him, fire in his eyes. "Xav, I think it's time you went home." He shoved him toward the door. "I'll be at the meeting tomorrow."

"But—" Xavier's protest was cut off by the door slamming in his face.

Toby whirled to face Gulliver again. "You can't take her to the healing pools." Fully restored to its original glory, the healing pools of Lenya were now the most powerful magic in all the fae realms, able to bring back fae from the brink of death. Since allying with Lenya, the council of royals decided not to publicly share knowledge of the pools until they knew how to handle the demand for such unknown magic. Magic with equally unknown consequences.

If they weren't cautious, Lenya would be overrun with those who wanted to control it.

This was all Gulliver had, his only plan. If he could get Sophie there in time, she might stand a chance. "Please, Toby."

"She's human. They live shorter lives than us for a reason. They hold less value. I am—"

"Less value? Do you even hear yourself right now?" Gulliver gave him a horrified look. This was not the Toby he'd known since they were kids.

"I am sorry for you, Gullie. I really am, but death cannot be defeated." He was thinking of Logan. Gulliver could see it in his eyes.

"What if it can this time?" They wouldn't know if they didn't try.

"It doesn't matter if it can." He sighed. "She's human and therefore not our responsibility."

Gulliver stepped back, the chill no longer from his wet clothes. "How did I not see it before?"

"What are you talking about?"

"You hate them. The humans. You wonder why they get to live while Logan, a fae, had to die. Don't you see? You're just as bad as them, as HAFS. They despise us because we're a threat to them. They don't understand us. That's how you feel about them."

"If you love them so much, Gul, then you should stay here and live where none of them can see the features that make you so much better than them. You'd love that, wouldn't you? To never have to be different again?"

"Careful what you say next." Gulliver's fists clenched at his sides. "I have forgiven a lot, we all have, as you moped around Iskalt. You're treading dangerously close to the point where I give up on you entirely."

Toby stepped closer, dropping his voice. "What do you think happens when she goes through the portal? When you're no longer just the cute human guy she's been flirting with at the cafe? Do you think she'll rejoice when she sees the tail growing from your backside?"

"I don't know."

"Yes, you do. She hates us simply for who we are. Don't forget who she is and what she has been raised to believe. Make no mistake, Gulliver, that girl is not our ally."

"You don't know her." Gulliver refused to give up on her just because of who her father was. He'd seen something in Sophie, a desire to escape the trap she'd found herself in.

"No, you're right. But I know you. You're different. You will always be different. Everyone in the fae realm sees it, and if you take her there, so will she."

Gulliver lunged, knocking Toby back onto the bed. His fist connected to Toby's cheek, but Toby didn't fight back. "Hit me again, Gullie. I deserve it."

Gulliver froze, staring down into the face of a man who used to be one of his greatest friends, one who wanted to feel pain. Maybe it would be the first thing he felt in many months.

"No." He rolled off him. "If you want to get yourself killed, Toby, you'll have to find someone else to do it."

Toby sat up. "I won't open a portal for you." He pushed to his feet. "Let the human die. You'll get over it." He didn't say another word as he yanked open the door and left Gulliver in the silence of their room.

Toby was reckless, just looking for a fight. Gulliver wanted to go after him, to make sure he didn't do anything stupid, but he didn't because Toby's words echoed in his mind.

You're different. You will always be different.

The words Gulliver feared. The ones that defined his life.

And yet, words that bolstered him now. Yes, he was different, and that meant he wouldn't give up on Sophie, not until she took her last breath.

Chapter Seventeen
SOPHIE-ANN

"Relax, Sophie," the nurse crooned as he stuck her with another syringe full of chemicals. "This will help you feel better."

"I'd rather just go home without the drugs." She winced as the needle left her tender arm. "And let nature take its course." Sophie glanced down at her arm covered in bruises from the treatments her father insisted on.

"Honey." The nurse moved to sit on the edge of the bed, taking Sophie's hand in his. "Your leukemia is at an advanced stage, and your father fought hard to get you into this clinical trial. You and I both know the time you have left is short. This treatment will probably give you a few more weeks. Maybe a month. Your dad wants you to have that time."

"Why prolong the inevitable?" Sophie stared into the young man's eyes. He was the only one who had met her gaze all day. And she hadn't even bothered to learn his name.

"If you want to stop the treatment, you're old enough to speak for yourself."

Sophie turned her head away from the nurse, looking out the window at the hazy clouds in the blue sky. "I can't tell him no." Tears filled her eyes. She'd never been able to tell her father no when it came to what he wanted for her. That was how she'd ended up working at the cafe in the first place. It was how she'd found herself engaged to a man she despised even after she'd said no at first. There was no acknowledgement of her refusal, just the acceptance that she'd do as told eventually.

"Then, you're going to suffer through some horrible weeks ahead if you can't be honest with him. This treatment will buy you more time, and you'll probably have some good days, but the bad days are going to be bad." The nurse brushed the short strands of her blue hair away from her face, and she half wondered if it would all fall out again. She didn't want to be on display at the funeral home with her bald head shining under the lights. She'd never worn a wig before when her hair had fallen out after chemotherapy. She'd made bald work for her. She just didn't want to die like that.

"I can help you talk to him if you want. It's nearly time to talk to you both about hospice care, so you can at least go home."

"Thank you." Sophie squeezed his hand. "I appreciate it, but I've got to be the one to do it." She moved to sit up, trying to get comfortable, but it was just too much work. Sophie wanted to die in her own bed. Not in a hospital surrounded by her father's people who insisted on visiting around the clock.

Even now, several HAFS members lingered in the hall with her father after the nurse had chased them out of her room for her treatment. They'd come flocking back in as soon as he left.

"I can give you something to help you sleep and keep you comfortable." The nurse stood and punched some numbers into his rolling cart, and a drawer popped open with the magic drugs that would send her back to oblivion.

"Thank you." Sophie lay back on the bed, completely exhausted from the treatment that was only going to make her feel worse.

"Hey, champ." Her father peeked into the room with Gabe on his heels. "Up for some company?" He gestured over his shoulder. "Half the leadership is waiting to hear how your treatment went."

"It's just like all the others, Dad," she said, her voice a weak rasp in her throat. "It leaves bruises, burns up my veins, and makes me sicker than I already am."

"But it's going to make you better. You'll see." He sat in the chair beside her bed and took her hand.

"I'm not up for visitors." She glared at Gabe. "I need to talk to my dad. Alone."

"Anything you say to him, you can say to me, Soph. I'm your fiancé."

She wanted to laugh, but it hurt too much. "I seem to recall throwing this ring back in your face." She lifted her hand and clawed the ring off her finger again, tossing it on the table beside her bed. She could just imagine how Gabe slid it back onto her hand when she was unconscious, especially after she'd promised an imminent wedding. "You're deluded if you think I'm going to make it to a wedding."

"Give the treatment a chance to work." Gabe moved to sit on the edge of the bed. "You'll be back on your feet soon. People go into remission with this stuff all the time."

"You just found out I have leukemia, Gabe." Her tone was rude, but she didn't care. Dying just might finally give her the strength to say what she needed to say. "But I've been dying for a very long time. Now, I said I wanted to speak to my father alone." She lifted her hand and pointed to the door. "Get out."

"What about today like you said? I can find a priest and..."

"Give us a minute, son," her father said, putting a hand on Gabe's chest.

She waited for the door to close behind Gabe before she spoke. "That's what all this is about, isn't it? You want to be able to call him your son. To train him up to be the leader you wanted me to be. So when I'm gone, you won't be alone."

"Is it such a bad thing for a father to want to see his daughter get a happy ending? I'd like to see you settled with a husband who loves you. I think it will help to give you something good to look forward to. So you can get better."

"A happy ending?" She snorted a laugh. "Dad, this is no one's idea of a happy ending. I'm twenty-one, and I'll never see twenty-two. No matter how many chemicals you have the doctors pump into my body. It's too late. I want to go home and die in my own bed. I don't want to spend whatever time I have left inside a hospital room with strangers coming and going all day and night.

"And there is zero chance I will ever marry Gabe, whether I somehow survive this disease or not. You picked the wrong son-in-law. I can't stand him, and I won't wear his ring." Sophie reached for the bedside table where the ring sat. "You can return this for me." She placed the ring in her father's hand.

"I think the stress is getting to you, honey. You were so happy the night we celebrated your engagement." He tried to press the ring back into her hand.

"Dad, I love you, I do." She pushed the ring away. "But sometimes I wonder if you have a selective memory. Don't you remember my reaction to the engagement at all? I screamed at everyone. Told them I was dying. I ran away. Does any of that sound like the behavior of a happy bride?"

"Knock-knock." Someone walked in without knocking at all. "I brought you something I made." Gulliver walked in, and a smile stretched across Sophie's face. She immediately regretted asking the nurse for pain medication that would make her fall asleep soon.

"Gulliver, welcome." Sophie's father stood up to shake Gulliver's hand. "Good to see you again." Claude Devereux clapped him on the back and offered the strange boy his own seat beside Sophie. He loved Gulliver, and for a second, Sophie wished she'd met him a long time ago. Things might have gone differently if there was a boy that both she and her father liked. But then, her father only liked him because he'd been the one to get her to the hospital so quickly when she'd passed out at work. As far as her dad was concerned, Gulliver was a hero, and he trusted him.

"She's a little stressed out today. It's been a hard few days for my girl." Her father stood by her bed, holding her hand. "I have to thank you again for being there for her when she collapsed."

"I'm just glad I was able to help." Gulliver smiled, but there was something odd about him today. Odder than usual.

"I blame the fae." A shadow passed over her father's face. "She didn't get sick until that cursed darkness nearly destroyed our world."

"Dad, kids get leukemia." Sophie yawned, her eyes drooping. "The darkness didn't cause it." She forced a laugh, trying to make light of her father's rantings, but she could tell he was getting worked up and a classic Claude Devereaux lecture was heading their way.

"And we're right back in the hospital because of the stress of the bombing. We have to eliminate these evil creatures from our world, but my Sophie has a tender heart. These battles with the fae are too much for her."

"Did you say you made me something, Gulliver?" Sophie shook off the fog of sleep that wanted to claim her.

"I did." Gulliver smiled.

"I'll leave you two to visit for a little while. Yours is the first visit to put some color back in her face, Gulliver." Her father gave her a sad smile before he left the room.

"I saw something, and it made me think of you." Gulliver searched through the messenger bag at his feet. "I found this really cool rock at the park the other day. It's white with lots of iridescent colors, and it reminded me of those big white flowers that grow in the trees by your cafe."

"The magnolias?" Sophie laughed. "They grow everywhere in New Orleans."

"Well, they remind me of you." Gulliver pulled the stone out of his bag, but it wasn't a stone anymore.

Sophie gasped. "Gullie, you made this?" She took the beautiful magnolia blossom in her hands. The quartz was smooth and a rainbow of colors sparkled in the fluorescent lights.

"It's gorgeous." She turned the flower over in her hands. "You're very talented." She barely had the strength to lift it, so she laid it in her lap. "I'm very tired," she whispered.

"It's okay. I just wanted to bring you this. I hope you feel better soon." A frown marred his face for a moment. "You don't look so good, Sophie. I'm sorry you don't feel well."

"I'm dying, Gullie."

"That doesn't sound good." He leaned forward and touched her arm where the purple and yellow bruises sat as a stark contrast against her pale skin.

"I need to go to sleep now," she murmured.

"I'll just sit here with you for a while. Rest. It'll all be okay soon. I promise."

"Thank you. You're beautiful." She fell asleep with a smile on her face, and Gulliver's gift in her hands.

Chapter Eighteen
GULLIVER

Two days and Gulliver had heard nothing from Toby. Not since their argument. He'd searched the French Quarter from top to bottom but found no trace of Toby or the fae village. He couldn't imagine where Toby and Xavier had gone.

None of the prince's behavior had made any sense since their arrival in the human realm. Really, not since the death of Logan. Gulliver didn't expect Toby to get over the loss of his intended so quickly, but it had been more than six months since the young prince of Eldur had perished on the fire plains. And Toby's wounds were still as fresh as they must have been on that horrible day.

Toby wasn't letting himself grieve properly, and Gulliver didn't know how to help him.

Gulliver tossed and turned restlessly on the narrow bed in the hotel room. For most of his life, he'd never had a room to himself. Even now, as an adult with his own home, his sisters and friends or family were often visiting, and he was rarely alone.

Here in the human realm, without Toby or Tia to keep him sane, and with Sophie fighting for her life in the human healer ward, Gulliver felt more alone than he ever had. The weight of his responsibilities pressed in on him, and he couldn't sleep.

Tia sent him here to help the fae living among the humans, and he was failing miserably. Mostly because he only wanted to help Sophie. He couldn't stop thinking about taking her to the healing pools of Lenya.

"Maybe Toby was right." The pools might not work on a human, but he wanted to try. If the pools could save her life, it was worth her hating him for what he was. He knew she'd never look at him the same again once she saw his true form, but he couldn't bring himself to care.

If only he could open portals. Without Toby's help, Sophie would die. Likely soon. She'd said he was beautiful. Right before she fell asleep. He knew she meant the flower he'd given her was beautiful, but it still made him smile.

Tossing the light blanket aside, Gulliver rolled from the bed to look through the window again. Moonlight illuminated the courtyard outside their room. "Come on, Dad," he whispered in the night, willing his father to hear him, to show up when the sun rose. He was supposed to check on them any day now. Gulliver just hoped it wouldn't be too late for Sophie.

By the next afternoon, Gulliver was frantic. He'd walked the streets of the French Quarter and the surrounding sectors until his feet were blistered and his face was burnt to a crisp from the hot sun that rivaled the unforgiving sun of the Eldurian desert and the Vondurian borderlands where the fire plains once raged.

Sinking down onto the curb, Gulliver let his shoulders droop as he hung his head.

"You come back for that tour, young sir?" A familiar voice had him craning his neck to look behind him. The Voodoo shop.

"I don't suppose you have healing potions in your shop? Or a way to find someone in this overcrowded city?"

The woman's shadow loomed over him, shielding him from the brutal sun. "This person you want healed, is it the same person you want found?" She sat beside him.

"No." Gulliver sighed. "I want to heal my friend Sophie. But to do that, I either need a miracle or to find my friend Toby."

"He's the boy running around the Quarter with Xavier, isn't he?" she muttered into a cloth bag, digging around the contents for something.

"Yes! Have you seen them? I really need to find them."

"You stay away from Xavier. That boy has a kind heart, but he's headed for trouble." She pulled something out of her bag. "Your friend, Sophie, she is sick, yes?"

"She's going to die," Gulliver whispered.

"Maladi Bondye." The woman nodded. "A disease of the Lord."

"I don't know what that means."

"A natural disease, like cancer. It is not always something magic can heal. Take this. It will not restore her, but it will give her peace as she leaves this world." She held out her hand, smooth and dark like umber.

Gulliver took the odd-shaped pendant.

"It's filled with herbs that will ease her passing. A little bit of this world and some of the world beyond." The woman set her bag on the curb and turned toward him, kindness in her eyes.

"I don't want her to die. I need magic that will save her."

"Sometimes, even magic isn't enough. Good people die every day. This charm will show her the way through the spirit world when she passes. The spirits will recognize her and embrace her."

"Are you fae?" Gulliver took the pendant, tucking it into his pocket. It helped to know if he failed in saving Sophie that he could at least give her this magic.

"Are you?" She gave him a knowing smile. "It is not a good time to admit such things if you are. I hope your friend recovers, but if she doesn't, she will be fine. You might miss her, but the spirits will care for her. She will be happy with them."

"Thank you." Gulliver stood. "I have to go see her." He clutched the pendant in his pocket, searching the sky for traces of the moon. It often rose during the afternoons here, the perfect time for Griffin to visit when he'd have magic in both the fae and human worlds. "I just have to go home to get something first." He took off down the street, hope swelling in his chest. Today would be the day his dad checked in on him. He knew it.

He raced down Esplanade Avenue and skidded to a halt just outside the gates to Lamothe House. It was still afternoon, but the sun would fade soon. Gulliver's heart sank like a stone when he saw no signs of Griff. He crossed the street to sit on a stone bench under the gnarled Cypress trees that looked as though they had been there for as long as New Orleans had.

He sat there for over an hour, just hoping his father would feel how much he needed him. The streets emptied as locals went home to their families and tourists went out to dinner or to the smelly Bourbon Street Gullie avoided as much as possible. The tourists really seemed to like that place. They walked around with drinks in funny-looking glasses Gulliver wanted to try. Though, he didn't hold his drink very well.

Someone sat down beside him, and Gulliver thought about going to get one of those drinks they called a hurricane. He imagined a drink like that could make him forget.

"I see you've been waiting for me." A familiar hand rested on his shoulder. "What's going on, son? You look like you've got the weight of the kingdoms on your shoulders."

"Dad?" Gulliver rubbed his tired eyes. "You're really here?" He lunged for him, letting his father wrap his arms around him.

"I just stepped out of a portal right in front of you, and you didn't flinch." Griffin's arms held him tight. "Tia wanted me to check on you yesterday, but I couldn't get away until just before sunrise this morning. I almost didn't make it." If he'd waited past dawn, he wouldn't have been able to use his magic to open a portal until the moon rose again in the fae realm, which would have coincided with the sun rising here.

"I'm really glad you're here." Gulliver buried his head against Griff's shoulder, his back shaking with relief.

"Come inside and we'll talk about whatever's bothering you. Tia gave me one of her spelled books so you two can communicate. She sent you and Toby here, but I don't think she thought about what that would do to her to have you both gone at the same time. Keir is ... a very patient man." Griffin chuckled. "With a very distracted wife. He asked me to bring you home. Just short of begged, actually."

"I can't go home. Not yet."

"I told him that was not the way to help Tia. She'd just send you right back, and she'd be even more cranky from his attempt to help."

"We don't have much time, Dad. I need to go see Sophie."

"Sophie? Who's Sophie?" Griffin gave his son a long hard look. "Have you met someone?"

"She's a waitress. She's sick. Really sick." Gulliver hopped up from the bench, eager to be off. "I need you to make a portal to Lenya. Tonight."

"Wait, where is Toby?" Griffin pulled him back down on the bench. "Take it easy, Gullie. Start from the beginning and tell me everything."

With an impatient sigh, Gulliver told his father the whole story.

"And you haven't seen Toby since you argued?" Griffin finally spoke when Gulliver finished his hurried explanation.

"No, and if I can't get Sophie to the healing pools in Lenya, or if they don't work for humans, then I at least have a magic token from a voodoo priestess—at least, I think she was a priestess—to help ease her passing."

"And you like this girl? This human girl, who is the daughter of the man causing so much trouble for our fae here in the human world."

"I don't know how I feel; I just know she is a good person, and she doesn't deserve to die. She's only twenty-one. It's not fair that she has to die when we have the magic that could save her."

"And have you mentioned to this waitress, who brings you the best sweets in the land, that you're fae? That you intend to take her to our world and heal her with magic she doesn't understand?"

"No." Gulliver's shoulders slumped, and his bound tail wanted to thrash in agitation and impatience. "I don't exactly know how to tell her."

"Have you thought about what will happen when you take her to Lenya, where she will see your true features? No one I know has a tail as magnificent as yours, and your mother thinks you have the loveliest eyes of any man she's ever seen, but to humans, those things are strange. She might not react well. At least, not at first."

"I know what you're doing, Dad. And I appreciate it. I know my family loves me and the people who care about me think I'm perfectly handsome and whatever. But the truth is, I am strange. And not just because I have a tail and cat eyes. Or because I'm an orphaned street rat, who happens to be the adopted son of a prince and best friends with a queen. I'm just me, and Sophie seems to like that. If she doesn't care for my tail or eyes ... well, I don't care if she never wants to see me again if it means she gets to live."

"I think you have your answer. You like her. And you might love her enough to risk losing her. Follow your heart, not your head. If risking your heart is worth it, then we have to help this girl. But you have to decide."

"Let's go. She doesn't have much time left."

"We're leaving tonight, then?"

"I think we have to."

Chapter Nineteen
SOPHIE-ANN

You're beautiful. Had she really said that to Gullie's face? Mortified, Sophie tossed and turned, searching for a comfortable position in the horrible hospital bed. That was the bad thing about the medication. She'd slept hard all day, and now she was restless and didn't want any more drugs that would only leave her with a pounding headache and no energy. If she was going to survive a few more days or weeks, she was going to be present for the time her father wanted so desperately.

Even now, he sat beside her, chattering away about HAFS people she really didn't know. But she let him talk. It made him happy. And if she could rally enough, maybe he would even take her home soon.

Though, this time tomorrow, she would be back to asking for something to send her into oblivion. The day after treatments was always the worst.

"Gabe and his boys are working hard to get things ready for

our next big move against the fae. They've really stepped it up this time."

Sophie focused on what her dad was saying. "Another attack?" Her voice came out in hardly more than a whisper. "That's not a good idea when the dust hasn't even settled from the bombing." Her heart raced in her chest as she tried to sit up. "Please don't kill any more people, Dad." The machines beside her began to beep, and she did her best to calm down.

"Hush." He pushed her gently back against her pillows, fussing with her blankets, trying to make her more comfortable when that wasn't possible in her current state. "This time, we have the right intel on the location of one of the biggest fae villages in the entire state. The fae in the city live in scattered neighborhoods, but we found a real village out in the bayou, not too far outside the city. Nothing but fae families as far as you can see, and no humans in sight. This is going to be big, honey. Even the leader of HAFS in New York City is coming down to help us."

"But—"

"We'll talk about it more once you're feeling better. You're going to need your strength back so you can be part of this."

"You and I both know I won't be getting my strength back. Not this time." Her breath came in short gasps, and her father moved to put the oxygen cannula in place so she could breathe better. "Right now, I need you to be my dad and not the leader of HAFS."

"Just rest now." His eyes clouded with worry, and she reached for his hand.

"I need you to promise me one thing."

"Anything." He clasped her hand in his calloused fingers.

"I know we can't allow the fae to use their magic on us. What happened to Mom can never happen again. Their darkness can't be allowed to spread to our world ever again."

"We're going to stop them, baby. I promise."

"No, just listen." She panted; even the oxygen flowing in through her nose wasn't enough. "I need you to promise me that you won't hurt those families. The fae families. The innocents."

"They're not innocents," her father insisted. "They tried to bring eternal darkness to our world. Can you imagine what that would have done to our people? Our world? You don't remember, but in just a few short weeks, everything started dying. We were worried about widespread famine and long-term depression. It was anarchy. People died in the streets. People like your mother. Suicide rates were up. It was hell on Earth."

Sophie glared at him, and he quieted, letting her go on. "But the light returned. Have you ever wondered why that just happened one day? Who knows, maybe they fixed it. There are two sides to every story." Sophie sucked in a breath. "There are good and bad people. Good and bad fae. I'm sure of it. I don't want you to become a bad person, Dad. Make sure the fae you attack are the ones responsible for the darkness and the deaths like Mom's. The others have done nothing but try to live in peace. I need you to let them."

"I—"

"Leave that village alone. Look for the ones who deserve it, and remember ... even for fae ... they should be innocent until proven guilty."

"Looks like someone's having a hard time in here." The night nurse came in, all smiles as she checked Sophie's oxygen and vitals. "She's a little worked up, isn't she?" The nurse smoothed a hand over the faded blue of Sophie's hair. "I'm just going to turn your oxygen up a bit and change you over to a mask to help you catch your breath, but I need you to try to calm down."

Sophie nodded, sitting back and taking a deep breath from the oxygen mask. "Promise me." She held the plastic mask to her face, dragging in another breath.

"I-I promise." He stepped away from the bed, letting the nurse do her job.

"I need you to keep your word."

"Of course. You have my word, and I'll not break it. I just need you to get better so we can make a new plan."

"Do you want something for pain, Sophie, dear?" the nurse asked.

"No. I'm okay." Sophie winced as she shifted onto her side.

"I'll bring you some more pillows when I come back to check on you next. If you're better then, we'll switch you back to the cannula so you can be more comfortable."

"Thanks." Sophie nodded, the rush of oxygen loud in her ears. Whenever the high-flow oxygen mask came into play, it was never a good sign.

"And it sounds like maybe your dad needs a bit of a break too." She eyed Sophie's father. "It might be a good time to go home and get some rest and a good meal, Mr. Devereaux. I'll call you if anything changes."

"She's right, Dad, you need to take care of yourself. I'll be fine. I think I'll watch a movie and maybe play a game on my phone." She would likely just stare at the wall. She didn't have the mental energy for either of those activities, but it would make him feel better.

"All right. I'll call to check on you in a little while." He leaned down to kiss her cheek, and Sophie let out a sigh when he and the nurse left.

It was the thought of all those families living way out in the bayou that changed her mind. It was one thing to attack a cell of fae actively working against the humans, but it was another thing entirely when it came to families with young children. Over the years, Sophie had often wondered where her line in the sand might fall in this war against the fae. Her father had stumbled onto it tonight.

She rolled over, staring at the magnolia blossom on her bedside table. It twinkled back at her in the dim glow of the nightlight, and it made her smile to think that Gulliver—kind, sweet, strange Gulliver—had made it for her simply because the flower reminded him of her.

No. You're young. Even humans don't die this young. It's a lie.

His words had come back to her at some hazy point earlier in the day when the chemicals in her body started to work. She didn't really feel better. Not yet, but it was a familiar feeling, as if her body might rally one last time. But she knew for certain it wouldn't last long. When she'd felt like this before, she'd had months, sometimes even years of feeling better. This time it would be days. Perhaps long enough to see him again before she went home to die.

Gulliver. The nice man who said the oddest things, had the biggest sweet tooth she'd ever seen, and wouldn't hurt a fly. The man who made her smile whenever he walked into the cafe. The one who talked of healing herbs, plastic money, and feletisions. The one she just might have fallen for if she'd had a little more time.

Chapter Twenty
GULLIVER

"What about Toby?" Griffin followed Gulliver along Esplanade Avenue to the trolley stop. "We can't just leave him in the city by himself."

"Toby will be fine." Gulliver's long strides quickened as they neared the stop. The trolley would be along in a few minutes, and he didn't want to miss it.

"We'll come back for him after we help Sophie. You're more familiar with Lenya than I am. Once we find Sophie, I'll open a portal for you, but I'll stay here to look for Toby. He's a grown man, but Brea would never forgive me for leaving him here in his current state."

"He seems to be doing better in some ways." Gulliver rushed across the street to the small covered station where the streetcar waited to take them through the Quarter. "In other ways, he's still not dealing well with Logan's death." Gulliver took the two steps onto the trolley and slipped into a seat at the back of the empty car.

"Which is why we can't leave him behind." Griffin sat beside him, looking over his shoulder. "This is a strange sort of automobile, isn't it?"

"They call it a trolley or a streetcar. Either way, it will take us close to the Tulane Medical Center. It's supposed to be a very good place for healing."

"Shouldn't we let the humans treat her illness? Their potions and medicines can take much longer than ours to work, but wouldn't it be for the best?"

Gulliver shook his head. "They say they don't have anything left to give her. Just herbs to keep her comfortable until she dies."

"That seems wrong." Griffin clutched the grab bar in front of him as the trolley picked up speed.

"Canal Street!" the driver called as they neared the end of the route.

"We'll get off here." Gulliver stood as the car rolled to a stop, and they exited to the busy intersection.

"I don't think I like trollies." Griffin followed Gulliver across the street, matching his stride to Gulliver's pace.

"You get used to them. I like it better than taxis. You're less likely to abduct someone when you know where all the trollies stop."

"You're going to have to explain what accidental abductions you've made when we have more time."

"It's easier than you think." Gulliver guided them down Canal Street to Tulane Avenue and the large brick building that housed the healers.

"This is it?" Griffin stared up at the large square building. "It looks like something from the prison world before the barrier came down."

"Depressing, isn't it?" Gulliver stared up at the rows of dark windows. "Sophie has so much light in her. I can't bear to think of her dying in such a terrible place."

"How do we get in?"

"I tried to come see her last night, but they yelled at me when I walked into the building. Something about it being after visiting hours."

"We'll have to sneak in." Griffin tapped him on the shoulder. "Perhaps we can find a door back there?" He pointed to a dark alley between the medical center and another building.

They crept down the alley, where large garage doors seemed to be locked up tight. He wasn't sure how anyone could drive a car through those doors as high up as they were.

"It says this is the loading docks," Griffin whispered. "No public access. I think that means we're not supposed to be here."

"Let's try that door over there behind those big green bins." He'd seen plenty of those things in the city. It was where the humans put their garbage, and they had a lot of it.

"Locked." Griffin pushed his shoulder against the door, but it wouldn't budge. He turned and looked down the alley before he ducked back into the shadows.

"Wait!" But Gulliver didn't have time to stop him before the purple light of his magic illuminated the door and it opened.

Griffin smiled, holding the door open for him.

"You have to be careful here, Dad. HAFS is always watching for any signs of magic." Gulliver darted into the dark room.

"Are they everywhere?"

"We don't know." Gulliver closed the door behind them. "Just be more careful about using your magic while you're here. I'm serious; it's not safe."

"Correct me if I'm wrong, but aren't we here to save a girl using my magic portals?" Griffin searched the wall for a light switch.

"Just don't use your magic unless there is literally no other choice."

"Fine." Griffin found a switch, and the room flooded with bright light. It was a kitchen.

"They make food here?" Griffin seemed bewildered by that.

"Not very good food, I can tell you that much. People like Sophie have to stay here for days and days to get their healing potions, so they have to feed them. But sometimes, I wonder if it's the food making her so sick. It's really awful."

"This coming from the boy who would eat anything. It must be bad."

"We need to find a way out of here." Gulliver pushed through a swinging door and relief flooded him. "It's the dining hall. I've been here before." He waved Griffin over, and they made their way across the hall to the locked doors.

"Want me to open them?" Griffin asked.

"No. The lock is on this side." Gulliver turned the latch and pushed through the double doors, peeking into the main corridor of the medical center. It was quiet. "Let's go. We can catch the elevators down the hallway."

Outside of the dining hall, the way was clear, but the lights were dim and a thick rope closed off the area.

"What's that?" Griffin walked past a window filled with pastries and sandwiches.

"They call it the coffee cart. The food is much better there than in the dining hall, but they don't take plastic money. And they really don't like it when you order a lot and then don't have the paper money to pay for it."

"Hey, what are you doing back there? The cafeteria is closed!" A bright light flashed in Gulliver's eyes, and he couldn't see anything. Throwing his hands up to shield his eyes, he called out, "We were just looking for the elevators, sir."

"It's after hours. You shouldn't be here." The security guard marched toward them. "And you shouldn't be back there. Didn't you see that the area is closed to guests? Are you trying to steal something?"

"No, my good man," Griffin said in his most princely voice. "My son and I were here earlier today visiting a friend, and he lost his plastic money card."

"I see." The guard relaxed his stance. "I'm afraid you'll have to leave. You can come back in the morning to find your credit card."

"It's really important that I find it." Gulliver took a step back from the officer. "We'll just be a minute." Gulliver ducked behind the coffee cart, and that seemed to be the worst thing to do.

"All right, you two. Come with me." The guard grabbed Gulliver's arm and hauled him and Griffin down the hall. He was very strong for a human.

The man marched them to the front entrance and shoved them through the magic doors and onto the sidewalk. "Come back when the hospital is open, or if you have to be here, stay in the emergency room area only."

The magic doors slid shut, and Gulliver sank down onto the curb. They needed to get to Sophie tonight. Griffin's night magic wouldn't work tomorrow, and then they'd be back in the same situation tomorrow night, unable to enter the building.

"What's that he said about the emergency room?" Griffin asked.

"I think that's where they take the really sick people who need immediate attention."

"Is that it over there?" Griffin pointed to a sign they'd missed earlier. Bright red with glowing white letters, Gulliver wasn't sure how he'd missed it before.

"Looks like it's just over there." Gulliver stood, brushing off his pants and following his father down the sidewalk and around the corner.

"Oh. This looks promising," Griffin said. "You think you can pretend to be sick?"

Gulliver's brows shot up in surprise as he realized what his father was suggesting. "I do think I'm feeling a bit peaky. Plus, all those humans on TV are always sick and telling me I might be too." He coughed, hunching his shoulders as they neared the magic doors. Here, the lights were bright and the waiting room filled with people.

"You can act human, right?" Griffin whispered at the last minute.

"I've been doing it for weeks." Gulliver shuffled up to the counter, where a frazzled-looking nurse sorted through a pile of folders on her desk.

"Help me!" Gulliver crashed into the counter. "I have the mesothelioma!" He sucked in a breath, choking and gasping. "It's bad, nurse. Oh, nurse, I can't breathe. My chest ... hurts." He clutched his heart and collapsed.

"Help my son!" Griffin cried. "He needs a healer now!"

"Oh my, he's not breathing." The nurse rushed out to the waiting room with a wheelchair, and Gulliver groaned, making his body go limp as she maneuvered him into the chair.

"You his father?" she asked.

"Yes. Please help him. He's all I have left of his mother!" Griffin sprinted behind her, letting out a sob as she called for a doctor.

"We'll get him in triage." She wheeled him into a room, pulling the curtain shut behind her. "He's breathing now." She grabbed a funny-looking device and shoved the stems into her ears.

"That's cold!" Gulliver whimpered as she pressed a flat disc against his chest. "It hurts! Oh, it's like knives stabbing my lungs."

"Shhh. We'll take care of you." She helped Gulliver stand, moving him onto the bed. "Your heartrate is high. Can you take a deep breath for me, son?" She grabbed another weird-looking device and wrapped it around Gulliver's arm.

"It hu-rts ... too much ... to breathe."

She pushed a button, and the thing around Gulliver's arm swelled, gripping his arm in a painful vise.

"Ouch! That really hurts!" His eyes widened in alarm. That really did hurt. "What's she doing?" It felt like she was trying to amputate his arm. "It's my lungs, not my arm, lady."

"Relax, I just need to take your blood pressure."

"She wants to take my blood? You can't do that!" Gulliver tried to lunge from the bed, but Griffin pushed him back down.

"Relax, Gul. Let her work, and then she'll go get the doctor."

"Did he say he has mesothelioma?" she asked, her torture device cutting off Gulliver's circulation. "He's awfully young for it. Does he work construction?"

"Yes. It's my fault." Griffin ran a hand through his hair. "I've always worked construction since he was a little kid."

"I see." She frowned. "He's awfully thin. How long has he been experiencing symptoms?"

"Uh, a few weeks," Griffin said.

"Weeks? And you're just now bringing him in?"

"He's a grown man living on his own. I, uh, came to visit and found him like this."

"Good thing you brought him in. His BP and pulse are dangerously high, but he's breathing on his own. I'll send the doctor in right away, and we'll get figure out what's going on."

"Can I get a room? On the fourth floor?" Gulliver asked. That was where Sophie was.

She nodded. "You've been here before, haven't you? We'll get you settled if we decide you need to stay, and the doctors will run some tests to see what we're dealing with. I'll be right back with something that will help you get your breath under control."

"Thank you." Griffin followed her to the curtain. "I don't know what I'd do without him."

"We'll take good care of him, sir."

"Thank you!" Griffin closed the curtain behind her, and Gulliver leaped out of the bed. "What was that thing she put on my arm? I can hardly feel it." He clutched his arm against his chest.

"What the heck is mesothelioma, and how did you know what to say?"

"Saw it on TV. It's a terrible disease people get, and the man on TV says I can get a lot of money as compensation for it. I mean, if I really had it. He's on TV a lot during the day, so I imagine lots of humans have it."

"Quick thinking. You were very convincing." Griffin peeked through the curtain. "Let's hurry before she comes back with whatever that thing was she mentioned. I don't think you want that if it's like what she used to remove your blood. Are you okay?" Griffin examined his arm.

"Fine now that it's not squeezing the life out of me."

"Okay, let's go that way. Looks like there's a door we can use to get away from the nurse with the scary contraptions. What was that thing she put in her ears? Did it hurt?" Griffin led them down the quiet hall to the door.

"No, it was just really cold. Not sure what it did to my chest." Gulliver tugged his shirt and looked down at the smooth skin of his chest. "Seems fine."

"It's a room with stairs." Griffin stared at the steps that seemed to lead to nowhere.

"It should take us to the fourth floor, shouldn't it?" Gulliver rushed up the first flight and called back down to Griffin. "It says second floor up here."

Griffin took the steps two at a time to reach him, and they made their way to the door with a sign for the fourth floor. It was the cancer wing.

"Shh." Griffin peeked through the door into the long hallway. "Look familiar?"

"She's in room 467." Gulliver stepped into the hall. "The sign there says this is for rooms 440 to 470. This is it." Gulliver picked up his pace, skidding to a stop outside her door.

"She's sleeping." Griffin peered through the narrow window, carefully opening the door.

Quietly, they crossed the room. The only sound was the beeping of the machines and the rush of air from the tube in Sophie's nose.

"She looks so fragile." Griffin stepped to her bedside. "Are you sure about this?"

Gulliver nodded. "Positive." He watched her sleeping, the magnolia he'd carved for her clutched in her hand.

"She has blue hair? I didn't think humans had things like blue hair."

"Me either, but I think it's beautiful."

"Well, grab your girl and let's go."

Gulliver hiked his bag higher on his shoulder and leaned forward to remove the tube from her nose and the needle from her arm. He hoped he was doing it right but there was no time to second-guess the decision. He tried not to hurt her before lifting her into his arms.

Griffin already had the portal open, and Gulliver could see the sunny castle grounds of the one place he swore he'd never return. Vondur, though it was known simply as Lenya now.

"Good luck, Gullie. I'll come to check on you as soon as I

find Toby." Griffin reached through the portal to grasp his shoulder. "I hope your girl makes it."

"Thanks, Dad." Gulliver cradled Sophie's head against his chest and stepped into the portal. He turned around before it closed. "And be careful!" But the portal closed before Gulliver had a chance to tell him anything else he needed to know.

Chapter Twenty-One
GULLIVER

"Wha—" Sophie tried to lift her head, but it dropped back over Gulliver's arm. Her chest rose with raspy breaths that seemed to take a great deal of effort.

She was cold, her skin damp with sweat. Soft murmurs escaped her lips, but no full sentences. Her eyes remained shut as Gulliver sprinted toward the palace, where he once was held captive. The palace where a noose once slid over his head. He could still feel the rope burning into the skin of his neck.

This place wasn't the same. Vondur no longer existed, melding with Grima to become one kingdom under the rule of Queen Bronagh. And still, it held only nightmares for him.

The fire plains closing in, fleeing to the mountains above Grima.

The walls still held signs of the battle with the vatlands, black scorch marks stretching across stone and mortar. A new wooden gate now replaced the one that had held out enemy armies for many years. Unlike before, it stood open, a welcome to visitors who stopped by to see the current residents of the castle.

Gulliver wouldn't be welcome once they learned of his request. No, he wouldn't request the use of the healing pools. He'd demand it. He never asked the Lenyans for a single thing after everything he suffered at their hands. They owed him this.

"Gul ..." Sophie tried to say his name, but she couldn't seem to get it out. Her lids opened slowly like doors on rusted hinges, and her eyes were cloudy, as if she no longer saw the world.

"Shhh." He shifted her in his arms. "I'm going to save you, Sophie-Ann Devereaux. I promise. You're not dying today." The magic had to work on humans. If it didn't, what was the point? Fae, human, it didn't matter. Their power was meant to help those who needed it, to make the worlds better places.

How would any world improve by losing such a bright soul?

His legs ached as he finally reached the gate and skidded to a halt. A line of soldiers in Vondurian red greeted him. They didn't draw their weapons, but they didn't need to.

Gulliver's breath wheezed as he tried to calm his heart. "I ... need ..." He looked down at Sophie, at the way she stared at the cloudless sky motionlessly, still. Dead.

"No." The words were only for her. "Don't die on me." A tear slid down his face. "It isn't your time." He lifted his gaze to the soldiers as one of them stepped forward.

"We saw the portal open. Do you have word from Iskalt?" There was distrust in his voice, suspicion in his gaze. Gulliver was used to such treatment with his appearance.

He tightened his jaw, lifting his chin. "Bring Lady Eavha to me. I have a friend in need of a kind of help only this palace can provide. She will know where I am."

He tried to bull through them, but the fae in charge lifted a hand to use his magic, most likely to bind Gulliver to the spot. "You will wait for her here."

"No." Gulliver's defensive magic threw up a shield around both him and Sophie. "I will not."

Again, the guard tried to hold him in place with his power. There was no time for this. Anger ripped through Gulliver. Anger at Sophie's illness, at Toby for keeping him from bringing her here days ago, at these guards who wasted precious moments that could be the difference between saving her life or losing the one person who truly saw him.

A burst of defensive Myrkurian magic exploded out of him, reflecting the guard's own power. Gulliver saw the moment the fae went stiff, his rapidly blinking eyes the only part of him not frozen in place.

Sophie didn't move in his arms. Not even her chest rose with signs of life.

"This isn't happening." He charged past the rest of the guards, who only watched him in shock. The palace looked different after the repairs, but the layout was the same. He rushed through the halls, ignoring servants yelling after him, others jumping out of his way.

"Stay with me, Soph." His arms had long gone numb from carrying her, but nothing would stop him. He kicked in the door to the old sitting room and went straight for the opening to the tunnels. It was secret to most fae, but he wasn't most fae.

Sophie's toes scraped the damp wall as he hurried farther and farther into the heart of the castle. Giant caverns spread out before him, crystals sparkling in the walls, their magic now in their beauty rather than any real power.

Gulliver's heavy steps echoed in the damp space. His own breath sounded like a roaring in his ears. A bubbling sound grew louder as he neared the wide pools that held the magic of a thousand crystals crushed into the stone. They held the most powerful magic in all the kingdoms, healing even the gravest of wounds.

Yet, they did not bring a soul back to life.

Could they cure a disease?

"Gulliver, stop." Eavha ran into the cavern, her giant cat, Sheeba, loping behind her. They both skidded to a halt. "You can't do this."

"Don't come any closer, Eavha." He stared down into the frothing water. "I can't let her die."

"That's not your decision to make."

He didn't look at her, couldn't. "And whose is it? Who gets to choose those worthy enough to save? You and Declan? Do you know how hard it is for me to set foot in this castle?"

"I do."

"Then, you know how much Vondur owes me."

"Of course we do, and if that were a fae in your arms, I would help lower her into the water myself, but she's human; I can see it from here. We don't know what it would do to her. They aren't the same as us. What if it only prolongs her pain? Would you do that to her? Have you even given her a choice?"

He choked back his tears. "What if it doesn't? I can save her."

"Gul—"

"No. I care about you, Eavha, and I'm scared of Declan, so I won't insult you by calling out your fear of humans—"

"You just did."

"But I'm not scared." If Sophie survived this, she'd wake up, see his true self, and despise him. Yet, he wasn't afraid. Not this time. "We keep ourselves so separate from humans and claim they are not like us, but you do not know them. You don't know her. She deserves a chance to live."

Sheeba growled, but Eavha put a hand on her head to quiet her as Gulliver looked back over his shoulder. "Your guards can drag me away after." He lowered Sophie to the ground, gently cradling her head until it rested against the stone and let the canvas bag hanging over one shoulder thump to the ground beside her. "Throw me back in those horrid dungeons." He sat on the edge, not bothering to remove his shoes or clothes before sliding into the pool. "I'll go through it all again as long as I save her first."

The warm water enveloped him, wrapping him in a layer of magic that buzzed along his skin. All weariness faded away, any ache in his limbs was gone. His tail rose to the surface, flicking the water. His feet scrambled for a steady footing on the loose bottom, covered by fresh layers of crushed crystals.

Wrapping his hands around Sophie's ankles, he pulled her toward him. When it grew easier to move her, he looked up to find Eavha pushing her shoulders. "You're right." She met his gaze. "We have to try."

Keir's sister had always been Gulliver's favorite Lenyan, but he'd forever remember the kindness and gentleness she showed him now. Even Sheeba shoved Sophie with her nose, trying to help.

"Thank you."

Eavha smiled. "You love her, Gullie. That means I do too."

Love. Did he love her? The only love he'd ever known was for his adoptive family, for Tia. This wasn't like that, yet the thought of losing Sophie sent him plummeting into the darkness not unlike what Toby currently found himself in.

Sophie's body slipped the rest of the way into the water, and he caught her against him, looking down into her pale face. It wasn't long ago she smiled at him for the first time, and it stole the air from his lungs. He saw the signs now, thinking back on each interaction. Through all that time, she'd been suffering, just trying to get through her days, trying to survive as long as she could.

"If I'd known, I could have saved her earlier." He brushed

wet hair back from her cheeks. There were no signs of life, no movement in her chest or flushing of the skin.

Sophie was as cold as she'd been before he brought her into the warm water.

Eavha lowered herself to the edge of the rough-cut pool that was hewn right into the rock generations ago. She dangled her feet over the edge, ignoring the fact that water soaked into the bottom of her gown.

"I'm sorry, Gullie." Her face said everything he needed to know.

It should have worked by now.

He shook his head. "There's still time."

Eavha gave him a sympathetic look that on anyone else might have resembled pity. Not with her. The empathetic Lady of Vondur truly cared that he was hurting. "What was her ailment?"

"The humans called it cancer." He couldn't stop staring down at Sophie's still form as he clutched her to him. This couldn't be the end. Tears slipped down his cheeks. "She didn't even get to live, not really." Under her father's thumb, she'd never experienced the good in life. Only fear, hatred, darkness. She died not knowing who he truly was.

Eavha sighed. "There is so much we don't know about these pools. They may not know what to do with human ailments."

"I promised her." He wasn't sure Sophie had heard him, but it didn't matter. He'd said the words, told her he'd save her. His chest shook with silent sobs.

Eavha sniffled and wiped her eyes. "I wish this could have worked for you."

Keir would have guarded the pools more staunchly. Declan probably would have followed his friend's rule. Most fae he knew wouldn't take a risk to save a human, but Eavha wasn't like most. She reminded him of Tia. He thought of the book in his bag that would let him contact his best friend and tell her he needed her.

Gulliver wasn't sure what made him do it, but he pressed the voodoo charm into her hand and released Sophie, letting her sink into the pool. He closed his eyes for a brief moment, picturing her as the kind girl he'd met in a cafe in the weirdest city he'd ever seen. She grounded him when his mission left him so alone. And now, she was gone.

He hoped the voodoo priestess was right. "The spirits are guiding you now." He pulled himself onto the ledge to sit beside Eavha, letting tears run unashamed down his cheeks. "I tried."

She reached over, taking his hand. "She knew that."

His shoulders shook, and Eavha slid an arm across his back, pulling him down to rest his head on her shoulder. "What was her name?"

"Sophie-Ann." He closed his eyes.

"Tell me about her."

He drew in a breath. "Well, for starters, she hated the fae." And then, he told her everything. All of it. Leaving nothing out. When he was finished, there was nothing left inside of him. No tears, no more stories. He was a hallowed husk of a fae.

For the first time, he truly understood Toby. It was not a lesson he'd ever wanted to learn.

Chapter Twenty-Two
SOPHIE-ANN

Sophie floated through space, unable to grasp anything to slow the momentum, unable to break free of the darkness surrounding her.

Her entire body burned. Muscles contracting and lengthening too quickly, veins pulsing as her head hammered rapidly. Heat seared through each organ, every blood vessel. She wanted to scream, to tell someone, anyone, to stop the agony.

Had she died? She'd been so sure it was the end. Staring at a sky that was somehow too blue, unnaturally painted against a barren landscape she didn't recognize, she'd said her final farewells, readied herself for God.

Her body writhed as the scorching wave washed up through her abdomen, inflating her lungs and filling the cavity around her heart with a feeling she couldn't decipher.

Power. She felt powerful as she bore the agony, as her body broke and healed and burned from the inside out.

She opened her mouth to speak, and water flooded it, traveling down her windpipe and into her lungs. She coughed, and more water streamed in. Which way was up?

When she pried her eyes open, all she saw was the brilliant glittering sand that brushed her toes. It was the most magnificent sight she'd ever seen. Was she on her way to heaven?

If so, she was ready. Her time on Earth was finished, and she'd soon join her mother. Maybe she'd finally find peace.

A voice, muffled by the water, yelled something that sounded like, "Eve, look!"

Eve? A hazy part of her brain wondered if it was *the* Eve.

Water splashed around her, and large hands gripped under her arms, pulling her to the surface.

"I swear I saw her move." A man's voice. God?

"You're only seeing what you want to see," the woman said, sadness in her tone. "I'm sorry, but she's gone. We can't bring her back."

Another wave of pain hit her, slithering along her skin until her head broke the surface. She sucked air into her lungs, staring up at the man and woman who were no longer looking at her.

"We should prepare her body." The woman bowed her head. "You know it's all we have left. Do you wish to bring her back to the humans?"

"Don't you dare tell me to give up hope, Eavha. I know what I saw. She moved in that water."

Sophie's eyes were closed now. She couldn't bear the torchlight or the shining of whatever gems these walls held. There was no more strength left in her. Her entire body ached with remnants of a pain she didn't understand, but she managed to draw breath into her lungs, something she'd struggled with for days.

"Just help me get her out." The man sounded familiar, but she couldn't place his voice. It was too rough with emotion.

"Coming to Vondur was a waste of her remaining strength. Maybe human medicine would have been a better route."

"I tried to tell you that," the woman said, "but you wouldn't listen."

"Nothing good ever happens in this castle. I shouldn't have expected this time to be different." He wiped a hand across his eyes.

"Give me a break, Gulliver. It's not the same here as it used to be, and you know it."

Gulliver? Sophie wanted to reach out to him, to make him tell her what was going on. But she couldn't move her arms. They were frozen, held down by exhaustion. She couldn't remember ever feeling this drained of energy.

Gulliver held Sophie just above the water, her short hair fanned out over one arm. It felt like a living thing atop her head, writhing with power.

I'm okay, she wanted to say. *I'm right here*. But the words wouldn't come. How was she there?

Had the treatment finally helped? Was her father getting the news from the doctor that she was still alive? She'd felt herself fading from the world, felt the world fading from her.

But now, it was back in full, painful focus. *I wanted to leave*. She hated that thought but couldn't help it. *Why couldn't they let me go?* It was still just a matter of time. She was dying, and each treatment only gave her a short time, if any at all. *Let me be at peace*. "Please," she whispered.

Neither Gulliver nor the woman heard her. A tear trickled from her eye, mingling with the water warming her cheeks.

Something brushed her arm, but she didn't see what it was, only felt the comfort it tried to provide her. It was soft, like the end of a brand new paintbrush. It wrapped over her back, comforting in its embrace.

She should have been afraid that something was in the

water. A snake, maybe? Instead, calm flooded her, overpowering the pain, the fear. Her eyes opened halfway.

"Eavha." Grief laced the single word.

The woman didn't respond, but she pulled her legs from the water, ringing out the bottom of a beautiful dark purple dress with black gems sewn into the hem. She looked like she belonged in a different era, with dark curls tumbling down over her ears and across her shoulders. She wore a simple carved heart necklace that looked like it was made of the same stone as that on her dress.

This woman, this ... Eavha ... she looked like a princess straight from a storybook.

Teeth grazed Sophie's shoulder before latching onto the collar of the hospital gown and pulling. Sophie looked up into the eyes of an animal that belonged in a zoo, with barriers between it and the humans. She wanted to scream, but her throat closed up, and she couldn't even breathe.

Eavha pulled her toward the lip of the pool, and rough stone scraped her back, bare where the gown opened. She didn't have time to be embarrassed by her state of dress, by the way the sopping garment clung to her frail body. The cool floor made her want to stay in the warm water.

Her eyes met the other woman's, and Eavha's mouth fell open. She clapped both hands across it.

Gulliver pulled himself from the pool, and Sophie's gaze found him. But it wasn't him at all.

A beast stood in his place.

Her entire body seized as she finally found her voice, her scream echoing through the giant cavern she found herself trapped in.

Chapter Twenty-Three
GULLIVER

Sophie's screams tore right through Gulliver, and he screamed with her. Their voices bounced off the stone walls, and Eavha pressed her hands over her ears.

He crouched beside her, so surprised and overjoyed to see her beautiful eyes bright and alive ... and frightened. He hadn't realized through his elation that Sophie was utterly terrified, but he couldn't seem to stop screaming.

"Wait," he gasped, reaching for her hand. Sophie pulled away, scrambling back across the cavern floor as far as she could get. "What are we screaming about?" His heart plummeted at the look of horror on her face. His shouts had been from relief that she wasn't dead, and for a moment, he'd thought hers were the same and they were celebrating together.

Sophie gaped at him, her cries fading to whimpers.

"It's okay, Sophie. You're going to be fine now." His voice faded, and he fell back, unable to meet her gaze.

"Your eyes," she whispered. "You have a tail!" Sophie's voice shook with something akin to revulsion.

The tail in question snaked up over his shoulder, and Gulliver clutched it to his chest. "Well, it's a really good tail."

"Gullie," Eavha approached where he sat on the cold stone floor, "we should get her into some dry clothes. Both of you."

"Let me help you." Gulliver moved slowly to help Sophie, but she seemed to shrink into herself, hiding among the shadows of the cavern. "It's just me." He waited patiently for her to take his hand, but her eyes grew frantic as she searched for a way around him.

"Hi there, Sophie." Eavha moved to stand between Sophie and Gulliver. "My name is Eavha. You're going to be just fine, though I'm sure you have lots of questions. Can I help you up to one of our guest rooms in the palace? It's much nicer than these old caves. And I promise we'll get you home safely very soon. Gullie here is such a gentle soul. He couldn't bear to see you suffer, so he brought you to the one place that could help you. And the healing pools seem to have worked. How do you feel?"

Gulliver backed away from Sophie while Eavha did what she could to set her at ease. Eavha was a beautiful young fae woman whose only distinctly fae features were her delicately pointed ears. She was much less alarming than Gulliver was himself.

He watched as Sophie finally nodded and took Eavha's hand, pulling herself up from the dusty floor. It was worth every risk Gulliver had taken to get her here.

"I do feel ... better. I think," Sophie said in a soft whisper. Water streamed from her body as she stood, leaving her hospital gown clinging to her and nearly transparent. Gulliver averted his eyes but gasped as every drop of water fell to the floor, collecting in a puddle before it ran back into the pool in a steady stream.

Sophie was still damp, but mostly dry, and her gown now hung loosely around her.

"We are more powerful now, thanks to Tierney," Eavha explained. "The healing crystals have been replenished, and this place is far more magical and unpredictable than it has ever been."

Sophie let out a startled gasp, covering her mouth in surprise as she studied Eavha.

"Magic is just a word, dear Sophie. No need to fear it. I promise." She took Sophie's hand and led her from the caverns and through the palace walls she knew so well.

Gulliver followed, leaving a careful distance between himself and Sophie. He couldn't stand to see the fear and revulsion in her eyes when she looked at him. He'd expected this, knew it would happen, yet it still hurt to see her rejection. Her fear of his strange features.

"Here we are." Eavha led them into a guest room Gulliver had never seen before.

"We're in the west wing, Gullie. The royal residence is the only part of the palace we use now. The east wing, where you've stayed before, has been opened to the refugees of Lenya. All who have lost their homes or livelihoods to the fire plains have a place here or in the old Grima palace with our new queen. At least until we finish rebuilding. We've recovered so much new territory that was lost to the burning lands. It's been an exciting time here in Lenya." She swept around the room, opening curtains to let the light in, fluffing pillows, and checking the linens. "Isn't Lenya such a wonderful word?" She danced around in a circle. "You won't believe just how much our kingdom has changed since we've united under a single banner."

"What is a Lenya?" Sophie turned to Gulliver for answers. "I don't think I understood a single thing she just said."

Gulliver smiled, relieved to hear a bit of the old Sophie in her voice. "Lenya is a where, not a what." He took a hesitant step closer, pausing when she seemed to tremble at his presence. "I've brought you to the fae world. I'm sorry it was such a hasty decision, and that I didn't give you a choice." He ducked his head, shoving his hands in his pockets to appear less threatening. "You were dying. There wasn't enough time. Bringing you to the kingdom of Lenya was the only thing I could do to help. The healing pools ... I didn't even know if it would work on a human, but I had to try. I couldn't let you die in that cold, awful place all alone, knowing there was a chance you could live."

"And your ... friend?" She looked at Eavha.

"She's the best fae you'll ever meet." Gulliver smiled. "Though there are plenty more that are kind and generous too." He shuffled his feet, his tail flicking furiously behind him. "Not all of us are bad," he whispered to his feet as he grabbed his tail. "You're completely safe here."

"I'll have my maid bring you some tea and refreshments in a moment." Eavha flipped the covers back. "But let's get you settled in bed. The healing will make you very tired, and you'll need to sleep for quite some time. I imagine as a human, you will need even more rest before you are fully restored."

"I am very tired." Sophie yawned. "It almost seems like I'm asleep and I'm just dreaming." She took a step toward the bed.

"I'll bring you something comfortable to sleep in." Eavha moved to the armoire beside the bed and searched for a nightdress. "You can change in the bathing chamber." She opened a narrow door in the corner of the room.

"Oh. It's a bathroom." Sophie's legs trembled as she made her way across the room, closing the door behind her.

"She didn't know anything about the fae world?" Eavha whirled around, hands on hips. "Gullie, you know better than to bring a human here like this!"

"I don't care. It worked."

"Bron and Tia will have your tail for this. You know that, right?"

Gulliver shrugged. "I'll do my best to explain myself to them." He sank down onto the edge of the bed. "I had to save her."

"You should have asked for permission from the rulers of the five kingdoms. The healing pools have grown more powerful since new crystals were added. Everyone from Myrkur to Eldur and beyond would be desperate to have access to what you just took."

"It's better to ask for forgiveness than permission when a life is on the line. Even if that life is human."

Eavha sat down beside him. "Can she be trusted?"

"I don't know," he answered honestly. "But if it were Declan, what would you have done?"

Eavha snorted a laugh. "The exact same thing." She reached for him, smoothing a hand across his cheek just as Sophie opened the door of the bath chamber. Her face was pale, and she looked exhausted as she gripped the door to keep from falling.

"I don't think my legs work."

"Sophie." Gulliver darted to her side and lifted her into his arms. "You need to rest." He moved to lay her on the bed, tucking the frilly white nightdress around her before he settled the blankets over her.

She didn't say anything, but she didn't shy away from him either. He'd take that for a win.

"We will let you get some sleep." Eavha laid a hand on Gulliver's arm. "When you wake, there will be refreshments on your bedside table. If you need anything, just ring for the maid." She showed Sophie how to pull the golden silk cord hanging from the wall by the bed. "It will ring downstairs, and Ariella will come to check on you. She is discrete enough not to let the whole palace know we have a human guest."

"I'll come by to check on you later." Gulliver followed Eavha to the door, unable to tear his eyes from Sophie. She was so tired that it scared him. Maybe the pools hadn't healed her after all. What if she died while he was gone? He didn't want her to have to die alone.

"She will be fine, Gullie. It's just the cost of healing. It makes any fae more tired than they have ever been. Sophie is human, so we just need to give her time to sleep it off."

Gulliver nodded, moving to close the door behind them.

"Gullie," Sophie sighed his name.

"Yes?" He leaned back into the room. "What do you need?"

"My father is going to kill you for this."

Chapter Twenty-Four
SOPHIE-ANN

Sophie stirred under the soft, cool sheets, finer than anything she'd ever slept in. She didn't want to open her eyes and break the spell of the best sleep she'd ever had. Stretching under the covers, she relished the comfortable bed as the last vestiges of sleep left her and reality started to catch up.

"What the heck?" She sat up straight, glancing around the small but elegant room. The soft supple blanket was a pale dove gray wool with fancy embroidered flowers around the top.

"Not dead." She patted her hands down the odd nightgown she didn't remember putting on. It was the kind grandmas everywhere wore, but Sophie had never worn a nightgown in her life.

She looked around the room. A thick carpet in shades of blush and pearl covered the floor, and the large windows sported long drapes in a sparkling silver fabric tied back with ropes of pearls. It was a room fit for a princess in a fairy castle.

Sophie sucked in a breath as she looked out the window to the rolling green lawns and puffy white clouds painted across blue skies. Mountains rose in the distance. She was clearly not in New Orleans anymore.

"Gullie." She scooted to the edge of her bed, thoughts of the previous night flooding her mind. The healing pool. Eavha and her pointed ears. "Gullie has a tail." A hand came up to her mouth as she gasped. She was in a place called Lenya. In the fae realm.

And she felt great. Better than she'd felt in a decade. But she was in the fae world with no idea how to get home. Her dad would be frantic, and if he ever found out Gullie was fae and that he'd brought her to the fae world—even if it had been to heal her—he would kill him before he had a chance to explain.

She had to go. She had to find her clothes and figure out how to get home. Sophie lurched out of the bed and stumbled to a stop. A scream welled up in her throat, and she grabbed a pillow from the bed, clutching it in front of her for protection from the huge cat sitting on its haunches between Sophie and the door.

The cat stared at her with a predator's eyes, and Sophie couldn't breathe as it yawned, showing off fanged teeth and powerful jaws.

"Please don't eat me," Sophie whispered as she backed toward the bathroom, holding her pillow out like a shield. "I'm human, and we're really gross. You don't want to bother with me in particular. I'm full of powerful medications that turn my insides to goo. You won't like the taste at all."

"Sheeba, shoo." Eavha swept into the room carrying a tea tray.

Sophie gasped as she gave the huge cat a shove with her foot.

"You shouldn't be scaring our guest. It's not polite. I'm so sorry if Sheeba freaked you out." Eavha set the tray on Sophie's bedside table. "Isn't freak out such a marvelous human phrase?" She let out a giggle. "My friend Tia taught me all the best human slang she learned from her mother, Queen Brea.

Well, she's the former queen now. Tia is Queen of Iskalt these days."

Sophie sank onto the blush-colored settee behind her, her knees still trembling from her encounter with the fierce cat, who was apparently Eavha's idea of a pet.

"What's Iskalt?" Sophie asked.

"One of the five kingdoms. Up until recently, Lenyans believed there were only the two kingdoms of Grima and Vondur. We're in the old Vondur palace, by the way." Eavha poured two cups of tea from the steaming pot, adding copious amounts of honey to each. "That was before Tierney and Keir brought the fire plains down." She piled a plate high with pinwheel sandwiches and fruit. "But that's probably more information than you wanted to know." She sighed. "I tend to babble, so you'll have to ignore me." She set the plate and a cup of tea in front of Sophie.

"Did you say five kingdoms? That seems like a lot."

"It is. The fae world is far larger than we once thought, but the wonderful thing about our new discoveries is how united we all are now. Keir says the peace we've earned will do more healing than the healing pools themselves. And that's saying a lot because our healing pools have become quite powerful, as you can attest."

"Who is Keir?" Sophie asked, trying not to let her hunger get the better of her. She didn't know much about the fae world, but she knew a human couldn't eat their food or ... bad things would happen.

"My brother, the former King of Vondur and current husband to the Queen of Iskalt."

"Your brother is a king? Doesn't that make you a princess?"

"Vondur doesn't exist anymore. Neither goes Grima. We are all Lenyans now, and that means more to me than the title of princess ever did. Queen Bronagh has made me and my husband custodians of the region. I'm called a duchess now, I suppose." She waved a hand like that was of little consequence. "Eat, Sophie, you must be starving."

She was, but she refused to touch a morsel on her plate.

"I must get home as soon as possible. My father will be beside himself when he realizes I've been gone all night."

"All night?" Eavha stared blankly at her. "Sophie, you've been sleeping for three days. Now, you must eat and replenish yourself before you can think of leaving."

"I can't." She shoved the plate away from her just as her stomach gave an audible growl.

"Why not? Clearly, you are hungry, and you must be terribly thirsty too."

"It's not safe. For a human, I mean."

"However do you mean?" Eavha took a sip of her tea.

"All the stories say humans who eat fae food will ..." She trailed off, uncertain what the stories actually said. "It will end badly for them," she finished lamely.

"Oh, I've heard all about human fantasy stories from Gullie and Tia. They're positively hilarious." Eavha dissolved into a fit of giggles. "And purely fiction. I promise, on my honor, the food is just food. Very similar to what you might eat in your world, though I'm told Vondurian food is spicier than most other fae like. Though, Queen Alona quite enjoyed our fare when she came for a visit, and she is human."

"You have a human queen?" Sophie gasped.

Eavha nodded. "Alona is Queen of Eldur. She was a changeling child taken from the human realm—from a place called Ohio—when she was a babe and switched with a fae child to protect her. Both of them, actually. Alona's human parents were dreadful people. She grew up as a princess of Eldur and is now their beloved queen. But that is a fascinating tale for another time. Please eat, and do not worry that any harm will come to you while you're here in Lenya. As soon as we can return you to your people, you'll be on your way."

Sophie picked up her plate and sniffed the contents. It smelled delicious, and she loved spicy food.

"Watch out for the purple peppers; those are very hot. I forgot how much Gullie and Tia hate them, or I would have asked the cook to leave them off."

"It's okay. I like hot peppers." She nibbled on the edge of a sandwich and moaned. The sausage and peppers had a familiar flavor, but there was something exotic about it at the same time. She'd eaten two of the small pinwheels before she could think better of it.

"I'll ring for something cool to drink." Eavha pulled the cord by Sophie's bed, and a moment later, a maid popped in carrying a tray.

"I thought the young miss might like some iced berry tea." She set the tray on the table between Eavha and Sophie.

"Thank you, Ariella." Eavha nodded, and the girl bobbed back out of the room.

Eavha poured the pink drink over strange-looking chunks of ice. "We've only recently been introduced to Iskalt's wonderful ice. Everyone in the palace is obsessed with cool drinks now."

Sophie took a careful sip of the drink. It was like strawberry lemonade, and it was wonderful. She chugged the whole glass and wiped her mouth. "That was delicious."

"Isn't it?" Eavha smiled as she poured Sophie another glass. "Drink as much as you like. We have plenty for everyone, and that's not something I've been able to say here for a very long time."

Eavha seemed so happy, and there was something trustworthy about her. Sophie couldn't help but wonder if all fae were like Eavha and Gulliver and maybe her father had been dead wrong about them all along.

Gulliver. She shuddered at the memory of his tail and strange cat eyes. She couldn't seem to reconcile the odd features with the nice young man she'd known in the human realm. The one she'd thought she could maybe sort of have feelings for in a world where she wasn't dying.

But was she still dying? Or was she healed by some magic she couldn't comprehend?

"Am I truly healed?" she blurted the question she'd wanted to ask the moment she woke up feeling so much better.

"It will be difficult to know for sure, but you look like the picture of health to me." Eavha smiled and smacked her lips after a sip of the sweet drink. "Compared to the state you were in when Gullie ran through the palace screaming for help, I'd say there's a pretty good chance you're all better now. He was so distraught when he arrived, and we got you into the healing pool just in time. For a moment, we'd thought it was too late. I believe you were on death's door. At any rate, Gulliver saved your life by bringing you here. Whether that is a permanent state, I don't know."

Could it be so easy? Sophie held her breath, not wanting to believe it and then have her hopes dashed when the leukemia returned and took her life anyway. Could a person really take a bath in a fae pool and walk out completely healed from end-stage cancer?

"Gullie, don't lurk in the hallway. It's rude," Eavha called out, glancing at the shadow of two feet under the door.

He pushed the door open but still didn't enter Sophie's bedroom. His head hung low, and he refused to look at either Sophie or Eavha. His tail swished behind him like an agitated cat's.

"You're not dying anymore." He shuffled into the room.

"I'll just leave you two to catch up." Eavha slipped past Gulliver, laying a kind hand on his shoulder as she passed.

"How do you know?" Sophie asked, fussing with the linen napkin in her lap. She was suddenly nervous to be left alone with a strange man. She glanced up and met his concerned gaze. He wasn't really a stranger though, was he? She'd known him for weeks and looked forward to his visits at the cafe. But this version of him scared her. Had he only wanted to get close to her to reach her father?

"I've seen you there in New Orleans, and I've watched over you here in Lenya. You've been sleeping, but you're so much better, Sophie. I have no doubt in my mind that it will last, and you will get to live the life you should have had all along."

"I need to go home," she said firmly. "Immediately."

He nodded. "I will take you home as soon as I'm able."

"I want to go now." Her pulse pounded with fury. "Open one of your portal thingies and take me home. Now."

"I can't."

"You won't." She narrowed her eyes at him.

"No, I literally can't open a portal. Only O'Sheas have the ability to open portals—blood born O'Sheas, I mean. My father was supposed to come yesterday to check on us and take you home." Gulliver's feline eyes filled with worry. "I just left him there." His shoulders drooped.

"Is he just late?" Sophie's voice softened at the look of fear on his face.

Gulliver shook his head. "When my father makes me a promise, he keeps it. Nothing would have stopped him from coming to meet us when he said he would. Unless something terrible has happened."

She didn't think about it before she reached for his hand. Not until her skin met his and she flinched away. "What does that mean for me? Am I stuck here?" She forced a firm tone, refusing to let herself feel sorry for a man she wasn't sure she could trust.

"No. But if he doesn't show up soon, we will have to travel to Iskalt. Technically, Tia can open portals, but she's really bad at it. Her little sister is just learning how now that she's inherited her magic."

At her look of confusion, he explained, "Most fae don't get their magic until they come of age. Usually around the age of eighteen. Princess Kayleigh has had her magic for a bit now, but she's only successfully opened a portal on her own a few times. She's our best shot until the three O'Sheas currently in the human realm decide to come home."

"How long will it take to reach Iskalt?"

Gulliver sighed. "We can go by ship. It's faster, but it's still a difficult journey through the Vale of Storms. There used to be a violent maelstrom that blocked the sea path to Iskalt, but it's been healed now. We thought the vale would also calm, but it hasn't. We will have to sail around it, and that could take weeks."

"*Weeks*?" Sophie paled. "Gulliver, if my father doesn't murder you, I will."

Chapter Twenty-Five
GULLIVER

Gulliver wasn't sure what he'd hoped for. That the girl raised to hate fae would look at his extremely fae features and be so overcome with gratitude she wouldn't see him any differently? It was ridiculous.

Sophie wasn't sick anymore. Eavha didn't seem sure about that, but he knew it. In his heart, he knew Sophie had so much more to give both worlds and now she had the time to do it.

But that look in her eyes was one he'd seen too many times before. Even in most of the fae lands, they looked at Gullie with his tail and cat-like eyes and backed away. Myrkur was the only kingdom where anyone understood him. There, everyone was different.

If Sophie was truly healed, she wasn't different anymore. She could choose to be just like everyone else, to fit in and be happy. Without him.

Gulliver paced the courtyard, trying not to feel bad for himself. This palace always brought out the worst feelings in him. He couldn't stand here and not see the scaffolding that once stood at the other end of the courtyard.

Bringing a hand up, he rubbed his throat as if the fibers of the rope still scraped against his skin. His hands were smooth now, the callouses mostly healed after so long without wielding a sword, but when he looked at them, a flash of dirt-crusted, cracked palms made him stumble back.

Stone walls rose up around him, and he shook his head, trying to rid himself of the dungeon that wasn't there. But hopelessness wasn't a place. One couldn't walk away from it as easily as they could from their false imprisonment. It lived in him, spreading with every beat of his heart.

"What are you doing out here?" A familiar voice brought him back from the edge, and Gulliver turned to Declan.

"About time you showed up." Gulliver bent at the waist in a mock bow. "Your Grace." Declan hated his title, hated that it put him at a level above the common Lenyans he'd grown up beside. He wasn't born for riches and palaces, but he had been born to lead.

Declan swatted Gulliver's head and scowled. "Stop that." Through Gulliver's duties for the crowns of both Myrkur and Iskalt over the months, he'd crossed paths with Declan a few times. Despite the man's seriousness, Gulliver liked him. He'd never forget that Declan once risked his life for him or that he'd stood right beside him at the gallows.

"Anything you say, *My Lord.*"

A low growl emanated from his throat. "Don't be a fool, *Lord* Gulliver."

"But then, where would my favorite Lenyans find their entertainment?" It was so easy for Gulliver to slip back into the laughable fellow to hide what he was really thinking. Tia did the same thing, resorting to jokes, sarcasm, and humanisms to overcome dark thoughts. It drove Keir nuts when they were both together.

Declan lifted his eyes to the night sky. Thousands of stars dotted the heavens, casting Lenya in their glow. Despite the painful past here, Gulliver always loved that about Lenya. There was no other place in the fae realms with such clear nights now that the fire plains were no more. "I didn't believe Eavha when she told me you were here with a human."

"Yeah? Where have you been anyway?" Deflecting was a talent. "It's been days. I was starting to wonder if you'd fallen down that terrible staircase Keir once forced us onto and now floated down the river."

Declan finally cracked a smile. "My queen demands a lot from her vassals."

Gulliver snorted. "Bronagh would be an easy queen to serve compared to Tia. Did you know she's had me in the human realm for weeks?"

Declan winced. "My apologies. That's worse than sitting in the Vondurian dungeons."

"Thanks for the reminder that this place is terrible."

"Too soon?"

"Just a bit." Gulliver walked forward to the wall near the gate that had been closed for the night. He sat on the dusty ground and rested his back against the newly repaired stone.

Declan sighed, sitting next to him. "I've been at the queen's palace for a council meeting. Your turn. Why would Tia send you to the humans?"

"Bronagh didn't inform you? They're killing fae." He scrubbed a hand over his face. "And I didn't manage to do a thing to stop them. I failed. Completely."

They were both quiet for a long moment before Declan spoke again. "And the girl? The one I hear you ran into the palace screaming about."

"I wasn't screaming."

"Gulliver ..."

"She ..." He sighed, wondering what she'd ever be to him. He'd never regret saving her, but he'd barely been able to visit her room because of the disgust in her eyes when she looked at him. The fear. "Her father leads the humans who are killing fae."

Declan whistled. "So, you've abducted her?"

"No!" That was exactly what he'd done.

"She chose to come with you?"

"Fine, yes. My father and I broke into a human healing ward and took her through a portal right into Lenya. She was dying, Declan. Actively dying. As in, she had minutes left. Seconds. I thought I was too late, that the healing pools wouldn't work. But they did. I would abduct her all over again if it meant she got to live."

"Sounds like you care about her."

Gulliver only glared at him.

"Are you going to use her?" he asked.

"What does that mean?"

Declan leveled him with a stare that seemed to say he shouldn't have to explain it. "Her father is killing fae and instructing others to do so. He's effectively starting a human and fae war. You have his daughter. Are you going to use her against him?"

"I ..." Was he? Could he? Sophie wanted nothing to do with Gulliver, but that didn't mean he could treat her like a bargaining chip. That wasn't why he'd fallen for her, why he'd saved her. But there were a lot of lives on the line. "I don't know."

Nodding, Declan sighed. "Eavha is pregnant."

Glad for the distraction, Gulliver perked up. "Really? That's fantastic. Congratulations."

"I grew up during a never-ending war. I don't want that for my child."

His meaning was clear. A war with humans would only hurt them, hurt future generations. "I don't know what to do."

"You'll figure it out." He patted Gulliver's leg and stood. "If Tia sent you to the human realm, she trusts you to do what's best for our world."

As soon as Declan walked away, Gulliver could no longer stand this courtyard or the stars overhead. He wasn't even sure he wanted his own company.

Jumping to his feet, he headed for the one person who hated him more than he hated himself right now. He was a sucker for pain, apparently.

When he reached Sophie's door, Eavha was coming out of it, carrying a mostly full tea tray. If Gulliver's stomach wasn't twisted in knots, he'd reach out and snag one or five of those pastries. Eating always gave him comfort, but he couldn't even allow that for himself.

"What are you doing serving her yourself?" he asked, stopping in front of the duchess.

Eavha shrugged. "I don't mind. She's still so freaked out that I thought it would be better to expose her to fewer fae. Just me and my maid are allowed in there. And you, of course, though you come mostly when she's sleeping or leave after brief conversations."

"She doesn't want me in there."

"True." Eavha didn't soften her blows. "But that's only temporary. She's mad about the delay in her return home. Let her come to terms with the trip to Iskalt and how long she will have to be in the fae realm before she's forced to deal with a man she thinks betrayed her."

"But I—"

"Saved her. Yes, I know. And she does too. Don't mistake her fear for being ungrateful." She set the tea tray on the floor by the closed door. "I am not carrying that all the way to the kitchens. Come with me. I have some Gelsi berry wine hidden away."

Gulliver fell in step beside her. "Why is it hidden?"

"My husband would drink it." She smirked.

"But you're..."

She stopped, turning to him. "He told you." She crossed her arms over her chest.

"Uh, yes?"

"That's just great. I don't even get to break the news myself. Now, he definitely doesn't get the wine. And for the record, no, I'm not going to drink it. I'm saving most of it for after this baby stops using my body like its own personal healing bath. You, on the other hand, definitely need a drink. But only one. We all know how well you hold your wine."

Gulliver couldn't argue with that. They made their way to what was once Eavha's father's rooms and then Keir's. Now, all darkness was gone, and the once morose space was awash in color.

The mahogany bed had been replaced with one of lighter wood. Everywhere he looked there were flowers of varying colors from each of the kingdoms.

Eavha smiled when she caught him looking around. "I like to remind myself that we aren't alone in the fae world any longer." She dug through a wooden chest stuffed with clothing. "Got it." She pulled out a full bottle of brilliantly purple wine. It seemed to swirl with color in the bottle, the nature of Gelsi berries.

Most fae couldn't eat them because they dampened magical ability, but they had no effect on Dark Fae. Nor on Lenyans, who derived their power from crystals. It opened up an entirely new market for the delicacy.

Eavha retrieved a small glass goblet from a shelf, filled it with wine, and passed it to him. She brought the bottle to her nose and inhaled with her eyes shut. "One day," she whispered. "You and I will be back together again." Reluctantly, she pushed the cork back in and stashed it where presumably Declan wouldn't find it.

"Drink up." Eavha watched him intently while he sipped the wine.

"Why do I feel like you're trying to soften me?" Gulliver let the flavors burst on his tongue in a symphony he'd missed. There was nothing in any world like Gelsi berries.

"Because I am." She gestured to a cream settee before folding her skirt behind her legs and taking a seat herself.

Gulliver hesitated before joining her.

"We need to talk about Sophie's unique position as one of very few humans who have ever gotten a glimpse of the fae realm."

He'd known this was coming since the day at the healing pools. Wandering the palace while waiting for Sophie to wake had given him a lot of time to think, and yet, he'd come to no conclusions.

"Declan wants me to use her to prevent a war."

Eavha rolled her eyes. "Such a man thing to say." She reached out and put a hand on Gulliver's arm. "Honey, we don't use innocent women for our own gain."

"I know." He rubbed his eyes. "But what about the innocent fae in the human realm being blown to bits by HAFS?" He took a long sip from his pitifully small glass of wine.

"I'm guessing this ... HAFS is the group targeting our kind?"

"Yeppers." He nodded, smacking his lips. "And Sophie's dad is their leader."

"Oh dear." Eavha sucked in a fortifying breath. "Well, if a war can be prevented by the abduction of one girl—which I'm not convinced it can be—then there has to be another way as well. Has Sophie taken part in these attacks?"

"No, no. Nope." Gulliver was quick to shake his head. "Pretty sure she hates all the violenshe," he slurred.

"I hadn't thought so." Eavha pursed her lips, urging him to slow down on the wine. "She seems ... sweet. For a human, at least."

"She is. I couldn't stay away from her. She's so pretty and kind. And she ... she looked at me like I wash normal." He hung his head, letting the last of the wine swirl in his glass. "Tia shent me to New Orleans for a job, and I didn't do it because of Shophie. Wh-what if I'm the reashon some of those fae are dead?"

Eavha squeezed his free hand and plucked the nearly empty glass from his other. "You really can't hold your wine, can you?" She gave him a sad smile. "I have a better question for you. What if you're the reason even more fae in the human realm *won't* die? Gullie, all we can control is our future because the past has already been written. So, what really matters is what you do next."

Gulliver tilted his head, studying the former Princess of Vondur. "When did you grow up?" Eavha had always been kind, but she spoke with a calmness and maturity she hadn't had before.

"I'm a duchess now." She laughed. "That comes with real responsibility." Growing up as a princess meant little in Vondur. She hadn't been afforded any responsibilities or duties just because her father was the king. Now, she had a purpose.

"I need to let Sophie choose her own path." His shoulders drooped. He'd suffered as a prisoner and could never imagine holding anyone against their will. "If she wishes to return home, we'll travel to Iskalt so an O'Shea can open a portal for us." Right now, those he trusted to reliably open portals were in the human realm, but there were others.

"You'll have a bigger obstacle once you get there."

"Tia." He took the glass back from Eavha and drained the

rest of his wine. The liquid buzzed through him, but it didn't give him the warmth he expected. He bent forward, putting his head in his hands. "This is the first time I can't anticipate what she's going to do."

Scold him? Demand access to Sophie to save the fae in the human realm? Would she even allow Sophie to return home after witnessing the kind of healing magic humans might kill for?

"Tia will do what is best." Eavha had so much faith in her. Gulliver did too, but he also knew her.

"No. Tierney O'Shea will always do what she *thinks* is best." Those weren't always the same thing.

Chapter Twenty-Six
SOPHIE-ANN

This place was straight out of a story—the kind her father never let her read growing up. It didn't mean she hadn't. Reading fantasy novels had been Sophie's one rebellion. In their house, magic was evil, something to eradicate from the world.

Until she was older, Sophie hadn't known just how real that magic was. Her father kept the truth from her until she was ready, making up stories about what created the dark months, but how does one ever prepare for that kind of revelation? That her father wasn't just an eccentric old man, but rather the leader of a radical and violent organization who knew things about the world most turned a blind eye to?

"Where am I?" Sophie whispered to herself as she stopped, realizing just how lost she was.

Needing to clear her head, she'd tried the door to her room and was surprised to find it unlocked. So much for keeping an eye on their prisoner. There were fewer servants than she'd expected and none in this part of the castle.

The royal residence behind her, she kept walking until she didn't know how many turns she'd taken. This place was huge, but it had obviously been a long time since anyone used this wing.

Broken stone coated the floor like a layer of lost dreams. She ran her hand along the black scorch marks reaching toward a ceiling held up by only the occasional wooden beam. How did the roof remain overhead with so little support?

Something happened here. Something bad. She looked back over her shoulder to make sure no one followed her before turning into the largest room she'd seen yet. Shreds of carpeting stood out as the only color in the otherwise grim room. Sunlight streamed in through arched windows, casting the shadows aside to reveal a tarnished seat.

"A throne." Her eyes widened as she neared it. This was a throne room. Bending, she picked up a scrap of carpet that was singed at the edges and ran her fingers over it. Velvet. Closing her eyes, she pictured what this place once was, a bustling center of activity for a powerful kingdom. She saw kings and queens alike taking that throne as their own, fighting for their might.

From the looks of things, the story of Lenya wasn't a fairytale. It was a tragedy.

Taking the steps up to the throne slowly, she lowered herself onto it, wondering what it was like to have any power at all. She'd spent her life at the mercy of her illness, of her father's whims. Even at her death, he demanded she marry to cement his legacy.

She brushed rubble from the arms of the throne and leaned back, seeing the room from a new view, with velvet carpeting stretching from the door and brightly dressed courtiers elbowing each other for their sovereign's attention.

Yes, your Majesty. No, your Majesty.

Yes, Father. No, Father.

It was all the same. She'd wanted him to love her, to trust her. So, she kept her mouth shut as HAFS destroyed lives, created havoc. Even if she could tell herself they only ever hurt fae, how could she justify that now? If their kindness was any indication, they weren't the barbarous race she'd believed.

Yet, they also weren't human. Magic wasn't natural. No man should have a tail sprouting from his butt.

"Mom," she said, "I don't know if you can hear me in this world, but I don't know what to do, how to get home." She waited for the comfort of knowing her mother was there with her, but all she felt was a seeping cold. Her mother wouldn't follow her into a world full of the creatures that caused her death.

And Sophie shouldn't be here either.

"They saved my life, Mom." How could that kind of magic be sinful? She should be long dead now, free from the human world and sitting at her mother's side. But as much as she wished for that reunion, she wasn't ready. "I'm still alive." A tear tracked down her cheek, and she let it fall. She was alive and healthy for the first time in as long as she could remember.

Was it a miracle or a curse? Those she needed to hate were the very ones who gave her life back to her.

Yet, it wasn't only that. Here, so far from New Orleans, she could feel pieces of her heart stitch themselves back together. Every time her father and the group she too belonged to hurt others, it tore at her. She could still see the faces of those suspected of being fae, the ones HAFS made examples of. Could still hear the gunshots, the thud of their bodies hitting the ground.

But here, their lives didn't weigh on her. She had space to think, to search for some kind of clarity in the mess both worlds had become. The sins of her father were not her own; those faults did not belong on her shoulders.

Staying silent did.

She vowed to change if they ever allowed her to go home. No more indiscriminate killing, random bombing. Those were the acts of terrorists, and she refused to let her father's anger and grief take him further down that path than he could return from.

"I always wondered what it would be like to belong in that chair," Eavha spoke from the doorway, arms crossed over her chest.

Sophie sat up quickly. "I'm sorry, I—"

Eavha waved away her apology. "By all means, stay there for a moment. It was never my throne. Here in Vondur—what this kingdom was called before simply becoming part of Lenya—the crown was taken by force. Death. As much as I'd have liked to see the world from the height of power, I never would have been willing to do what was needed to get there."

Nausea curled in Sophie's stomach. Like so many other things, it was a throne stained in blood. "What happened in this place?" She gestured around to what once must have been a grand room.

Eavha sighed and stepped closer. "A battle. One in which we were victorious."

This was what victory looked like? "Who did you fight?"

"Not who. What. A great wave of heat threatened to turn all of Lenya into a wasteland of ash and bone." One corner of her mouth curved up. "But the five kingdoms worked together and managed to win the day with our magic. We've only managed to restore a small part of this castle, but we will keep going. It's honestly amazing this room still has a roof. Most in this part of the castle is open to the elements."

Sophie couldn't help wanting to know more, to understand this world and what it had been through. Yet, the questions couldn't break through her determination to hate it. "Are we in danger here?"

"Probably." Eavha shrugged. "The roof is still there, mostly, but the wooden beams are now ash underneath our feet."

"Yet, you still came here."

"Sophie-Ann ... Gullie told me that's your full name. Is it okay if I use it?"

Sophie nodded, shrinking back at the mention of Gulliver.

"It's a beautiful name. Anyway, Sophie-Ann, I live in a palace that is half in ruin with only a few maids, a household guard, and a host of refugees when my husband is away. We are not even a year displaced from a civil war that lasted far longer than you can fathom. We've faced famine, the fire plains, and learning of four kingdoms we didn't think existed."

"I don't understand most of what you just said."

Eavha smirked. "What I'm getting at is, Lenyans aren't scared of anything, not anymore. We've already faced the worst. So, if I wish to walk around the old part of the castle and remember what it once was, I will."

What was it like not to fear? For so long, Sophie went to bed each night wondering if she'd wake up in the morning. She worked at the cafe when she shouldn't have because being alone while her father worked was terrifying. She'd never been as scared of anything as she was of herself. "That sounds wonderful. Not living in fear."

Eavha sighed and lowered herself to sit on the step in front of the throne, right in the dust. "You do not have to fear us."

"I don't."

"And you also do not have to lie." She shook her head. "Gulliver would not have brought you here if he did not think you'd be able to understand what it is we are."

"And what is that?"

"Not human, that's for sure. But there's a reason we can pass so easily. We are a sophisticated species. We love and hate and are quick to both anger and forgiveness. Fae make mistakes, just as humans do. We are not so different."

"But Gulliver ..."

"Is not so different." This time when Eavha said it, there was more emphasis on the words, almost an anger behind them.

Sophie leaned her head back. "He tricked me. That's what fae do, isn't it? He chose me because of who my father is."

"And he failed his queen because he chose to save your life over the mission she sent him on."

They locked eyes, and Sophie couldn't look away. "A queen sent him ..."

"Not just any queen. Tierney of Iskalt. She is the most powerful magic wielder in the five kingdoms and also the most important fae in Gulliver's life. Those two ... Let's just say Tia has no more loyal friend."

Gulliver was an arm of a queen. Sophie wasn't sure if she should feel comforted or angry. He deceived her, played her because the fae were operating missions in the human realm. They didn't belong there, just as she didn't belong here in their world.

If Eavha thought she could tell tales of the great Gulliver and make her see him as something other than the beast who betrayed her, she was wrong. He was nothing more than a fae spy.

She left the woman to her thoughts in that dangerous throne room and managed to make her way back to the residence wing with the help of a maid Gulliver sent to look for her.

He was waiting outside her door when she arrived. "Not now, Gullie." She tried to push past him, but he stopped her with a hand on her arm.

"Where were you?"

Yanking herself free, she shoved open the door. "Trying to

make myself forget just where I am." With that, she shut the door in his face, hiding her tears from him.

She kicked off her boots and pulled at the laces of the silly dress they'd given her to wear. They'd even made her wear a corset—the most vile, uncomfortable creation any world had ever known. Finally getting the contraption loose, she slid the corset and dress down her legs and drew in a deep breath, her chest heaving for more oxygen.

Breathe. She had to breathe.

She grasped the bedpost to stabilize herself and clutched her waist with the other hand. The silken underthings she wore were cool against her heated skin, but it wasn't enough.

Rushing to the bathroom, she searched for anything to calm her down, to make her forget. But all she found was a basin of water left over from her morning bath.

Without thinking, she dropped to her knees and plunged her head in, letting cold water trickle down her back. Silk clung to her skin as she flipped her hair back, and her breathing returned to normal. *You're an idiot, Sophie.*

Before she had a chance to dry herself, her door burst open. "You have to talk to me." Gulliver froze, his eyes trailing the length of her in open shock and dismay. A tiny squeak escaped his lips, and she worried he was going to pass out right there on the spot.

Chapter Twenty-Seven
GULLIVER

"Your skin looks so soft." Gullie slapped a hand over his mouth to keep himself from blurting out anything even more embarrassing. He whirled around to face the door, stammering something unintelligible. "I'm sorry, Sophie! I didn't mean to barge in. Didn't mean to stare." He covered his eyes but couldn't seem to make his feet move to leave the poor girl alone.

"What are you babbling about?" Sophie sounded irritated.

"Are you decent? I need to talk to you about the journey to Iskalt."

She heaved a sigh he heard in his bones. Fae she was mad at him. "Of course I'm decent."

Gulliver slowly turned around to find her still sopping wet standing with her hands on her hips and glaring daggers at him.

"I told you I wasn't in the mood to talk to you, so make it quick. When are we leaving? And why are you facing the door again?"

Sometime in her yelling at him, he'd turned his back to her

once more. “I thought you said you were decent.” Heat crept up his neck, and he could feel his ears turning scarlet.

“I am. I just had a little dunk in the wash basin to cool off. I’m better now.”

“But you’re in your underthings, Soph.” His voice squeaked, and he rolled his eyes at himself, his tail twitching in agitation.

“I have more clothes on now than at any time you saw me in New Orleans. I wear shorts and t-shirts.”

“But you’re ... you’re all ... wet, and things are ... sticking.” He covered his flaming face with his hands. *You’re such an idiot, Gulliver.*

She gasped, but Gullie still didn’t turn around. “Can you see through everything?” He heard rustling sounds as she crossed the room to the mirror in the corner by the dressing screen. “Gulliver,” she groaned, “you can’t see anything but my belly button, you dork. You’d see more of me in a bathing suit. Now, turn around and say whatever you came to say.”

“It’s fine; I can just talk to the door.” He crossed his arms over his chest, refusing to look at any woman in such a state of undress. It wasn’t gentlemanly behavior.

“Now, wait just a minute. I am not indecent! I’m covered from neck to toes in this awful underdress thing.”

“It’s a shift, and it’s wet, and I can see your under-under things.” For the first time in his life, he really wished he had magic so he could vanish in a poof of blazing light. Not that he’d ever seen a single fae do such a thing. Tia probably could manage it if she wanted to, but she didn’t really get embarrassed.

“Okay. Whatever this sack dress is, it’s not much different than the one I had on when I came into my room. Are you seriously not going to turn around and look at me?”

“Nope.” He shook his head. “Could you just put on a robe or something? I’m trying to be a gentleman here.”

“Oh for heaven’s sake. What you’re being is ridiculous.”

Gullie couldn't tell what she was doing, but he wasn't about to turn around until he was certain his eyes would stay in his head and focused on her face and not on other parts of her.

"There is nothing immodest about a woman's body in a shift. Even if it is a little damp."

"You aren't wearing a ... a *corset*." He whispered the last word like he was ten and didn't know anything about women. Well, he was twenty-two and didn't know anything about women, but that was beside the point.

"No, and I don't plan on wearing one ever again, so get used to it. That thing was suffocating the life out of me."

He heard more rustling and the sound of fabric hitting the floor.

"You'd think fae women would just magic them in place rather than wear a torture device probably invented by a man." Her voice was muffled, and he prayed she was putting on several more layers.

Gullie flinched when she threw something wet at him and it landed on his head. He pulled the fabric away and leaped toward the door when he realized he was holding the only stitch of actual clothing she'd had on.

Her laughter followed him, and he stopped with his hand on the doorknob, his shoulders falling and his face flaming. "You're just making fun of me now, aren't you?"

"You do make it easy. You can turn around now. I'm in my robe, still fully covered from neck to toes in a non-see-through shade of purple."

"Are you sure?"

"Positive. Now, tell me whatever you came to tell me and leave. I have to pack for this *weeks*-long trip you subjected me to when you brought me here against my will."

"But I—"

She held up a hand to stop him. "Saved my life? Yes, I know, and don't think I'm not grateful for it. I just really don't like it when men and ... *fae* make decisions for me without asking what I want. I'm tired of it."

"I understand." Gulliver dropped his head, not sure how he would ever make this right or if she would always see him as a monster who took away her free will. "I'll just go." His tail dragged behind him as he opened the door.

"Wait," Sophie called after him.

He turned around, hope in his eyes. "Yes?"

"You came here to tell me something about our trip to Iskalt. Have you figured out how to fly us there or something hopefully as fast?"

"I-I don't have wings. Though, my mother and sisters do. But they're in Myrkur."

"So ...?" She seemed to be growing more irritable with him as the seconds wore on.

"Um, just, we will be leaving by ship in four days."

"I can't wait that long. I have to get home before my father does something drastic."

Gullie gulped a breath before he continued in a rush, "Well, you see ... um, the shores of Vondur are too shallow for most ships. Um, so we have to travel east to the palace of Lenya. It takes three days to reach the new palace over land."

"I assume we're going by some sort of fae version of a car, right?"

Gulliver shook his head. "Um ... not exactly. We ... um ... we tend not to move as fast as humans do. We live more simply. Unless it's an emergency, and then we use portals."

"And that means what?" She prodded him, forcing a patient tone he knew she didn't feel.

"Horses," he blurted. "We will travel on horseback. Er, just the two of us. I've, uh, made the trip many times, so we won't get lost or anything."

"Gullie! I've never ridden a horse in my life."

"Really?" His eyes widened at the look of menace on her face. "We can take a wagon if you'd be more comfortable, but it will be slower. Or if you're worried about traveling with me alone, I can ask Declan to escort us. You can ride with him if you feel safer that way."

"It's fine. I'll manage."

Gulliver took a hasty step toward the door, hoping for a quick escape before he had to tell her how much harder this trip would get when they had to go around the far northern reaches of Iskalt they'd discovered after the fall of the Vatlands. It was an insanely cold and treacherous path. "We'll leave tomorrow. So, um, just let me know if you need anything. Eavha is packing some travel clothes for you."

"Honestly, for a fae with magic, you're kind of hopeless."

"I-I'm sorry. I thought you knew. I don't actually have magic." He halted in the doorway of her room. "Dark Fae have defensive magic only. Meaning magic doesn't really work on us. It's kind of like armor, so magic just kind of bounces off me. It's also what makes me look ... normal in the human world. Other than that, I have no more magic than you do, Sophie."

"Oh. I see." Her face paled, and the tension seemed to leave her body.

Gulliver fled the room as quickly as his feet could carry him. He couldn't stand the strange look on her face a moment longer.

Feeling defeated and uncertain of what to expect when he arrived unannounced at the palace in Iskalt with a human woman in tow, Gulliver sought the privacy of his room. He was itching to leave Vondur as soon as possible. The palace brought nothing but bad memories, and he was eager to make things right for Sophie.

Reaching for his pack under the bed, he started tossing things haphazardly into his bag. He wouldn't need much on the journey. Just plenty of food and water. This side of Lenya was still hot. Nothing like it had been when the fire plains caused temperatures to rise, but the southwestern lands were similar to Eldur in temperature and in landscape, if a bit milder in comparison.

Judging by their conversation this afternoon, it was going to be a long journey with just the two of them. And there would be hell to pay when Tia found out what he'd done.

His hand landed on something he'd forgotten about at the bottom of his pack. The spelled journal his father had given him so he could communicate with Tia.

That was days and days ago. He sucked in a breath and sat on the bed, fully prepared for an earful when he opened the book and found a page of messages from Tia.

Gullie, how are things going in the human world? I'm anxiously awaiting news.

Gullie? Is everything okay?

Gulliver Muriel O'Shea, where are you? Your queen demands an update.

Gulliver snorted at that. He didn't have a middle name. That was more of a human thing Brea had brought into fashion when she named her children. It was all the rage now across the kingdoms. When they were kids, Tia had felt bad he didn't have one, so she gave him one. Back then, it was Alexander, which he quite liked, and if anyone asked him if he had a middle name, that's the one he gave. But whenever Tia was really mad at him, she three named him with whatever insulting name she could come up with in that moment.

Muriel? Really, Tia? I've been a bit busy, and though you are my best friend and a queen I admire, you are technically not my queen, as I am from Myrkur. He slammed the book closed and went back to packing his few belongings. He loved Tia, but sometimes she was infuriating with her demands.

The journal started to smoke and spark on his bed, and he leaped for it, stamping out the smoldering blanket. "For the love of magic, Tia, learn some patience!" He flipped to the last page he wrote on and waited for the words to scrawl across the page.

What is going on? Why haven't you responded, Gul. It's been too long since Griffin left. I demand an update.

Gulliver's blood boiled as he snatched up a quill and began to write.

Tierney James O'Shea, sometimes a fae can't be at your beck and call every moment of the day. I forgot about the book till just now. It's been difficult the past few days.

James? That's the best you could come up with?

Gulliver dreaded the next part. Telling her everything he'd done and how he needed her to help fix his mess.

Tia, don't get mad. I'm in our least favorite place in all the worlds, and I desperately need you ...

Chapter Twenty-Eight
TOBY

"Toby, get down!" Xavier nearly tackled him in the darkness, pulling him out of the human's way. They were everywhere.

"What do we do?" Toby panted, his eyes searching the dark for the source of all the noise and sparks of human magic he didn't understand. Fae were running from their homes in the middle of the night, trying to flee the attack.

"I don't know how they found us," Xavier whispered in his ear as they cowered behind the well house in the town square. "This village is protected. Only one of our own could have led them here."

"We have to fight back." Toby wrestled away from his embrace. "We can't let them win."

"We don't have weapons." Xavier lunged after him, but Toby had already found his target. A human boy not much younger than himself backed toward them, his odd human sword pointed in the wrong direction.

Toby charged him, landing a forceful blow against his shoulder.

"They have guns!" Xavier shrieked, though Toby didn't know what a gun was.

"There are children here!" Toby pushed his opponent to the ground with a kick to his ribs. "You can't do this."

The boy turned hate-filled eyes on him. "Die, you fae freak!" He pointed his gun-sword at Toby. "If you won't go back to your own world, I'll send you there myself."

His weapon jerked, and a blast of power erupted inside Toby. He slid to the ground in a daze.

"Toby!" Xavier screamed for him, but his vision flickered and heat shot up his arm and into his chest. He couldn't breathe, and the night went silent around him.

Toby saw a figure crash into the human with the gun that wasn't just a sword, but he saw another blurry figure standing over him. One he'd know anywhere.

He reached a hand toward the man. "Logan?"

There's so much more to Gullie's story!
Keep reading for Fae's Enemy!

Queens of the Fae book Eleven

FAE'S ENEMY

MELISSA A. CRAVEN
M. LYNN

Chapter One
GULLIVER

"Gulliver! What do you mean, *'don't get mad'*?" The disembodied voice reverberated across the courtyard in a burst of wind. Gulliver flinched, knowing exactly what was coming for him. Familiar power wrapped around his chest, like the tendrils of some unseen vine, squeezing the air from his lungs until he gasped for breath.

It released him, but not before tugging on his tail. His feet skidded across the stone as the magic gave him a final push. A scream ripped from his throat, and he stumbled. As he looked up, he caught the terror in Sophie's eyes. Eavha had just managed to convince her to join them in the courtyard for some fresh air and a simple game of liathroid.

"Heads up, Gullie!" Eavha called, not bothering to pause the game to let him recover his bearings. The ball sailed toward Gulliver, hitting him square in the stomach.

"Oof." He fumbled the ball and scrambled to catch it but was jerked backward again.

"Eavha," he yelled, exasperated with the one queen who was normally his favorite person in all the worlds. "Make her stop."

Annoyance sparked through him when Eavha only laughed. Declan shook his head with an affectionate smile for his favorite person. But Sophie-Ann... she looked horrified. This was exactly the kind of magic he hadn't wanted her to see. She still wouldn't speak to him, and this would only make it worse.

He stumbled toward the open front gates, his tail aching where it met the base of his spine. "Tierney O'Shea," he growled. "You've had your fun, isn't that enough?"

"*Don't get mad?*" Tia said again, this time her voice closer, more dangerous.

Gulliver sighed as the magic pulled him from the courtyard into the wide-open space between the castle and the mostly dead forest surrounding it with twisted and burned trees that would take generations to recover.

He stopped abruptly and would have fallen forward if not for the magic holding him up. His legs wobbled as the unseen force turned him quickly to meet the visitors.

"Don't get mad?" Tia seethed, hands on her hips. "Are you kidding me, Gulliver?"

Her parents stood on either side of her, looking amused in a subdued sort of way. Worry was etched into every line of their faces.

"Erm, nice to see you, Majesties." Gulliver bowed. Brea and Lochlan weren't the king and queen any longer, but he would always see them as such.

"Don't look at them." Tia narrowed her eyes. "They're not the Queen of Iskalt who sent you on a simple information-gathering mission and found you holed up in Lenya, of all places."

He rubbed the back of his neck. "Well, you didn't exactly find me did you? I sent you a note."

"A note." Tia lifted a hand, curling her fingers in so her

power took hold of him once more. Only, this time, it propelled him toward her to collide against her in a tight hug. She gripped him as if she'd thought she might never see him again.

"I have been so worried," she whispered, burying her face in his chest.

Gulliver held her, realizing just how much he needed his best friend. They were soulmates, connected in a way he'd never had with anyone else. When she wasn't by his side, he wasn't fully himself. As though he was missing a limb.

"Did you really have to yank me from the courtyard?"

She laughed. "Absolutely. That was the fun part."

"What if I'd been inside? Were you going to pull me through the walls?"

She leaned away and looked up at him. "I hadn't really thought about that."

Lochlan cleared his throat, sliding his arm through Brea's. "Think we could take this inside?"

Gulliver looked back at the castle, where the guards along the wall watched them with open curiosity.

"Tia!" Eavha ran toward them, lifting the bottom of her dress to keep from tripping. The two girls hugged. "You have got to teach me how to do that. Gulliver was all, 'make her stop'! You should have seen his face. It was hilarious."

Gulliver turned away from his diabolical friends as Sheba bound across the distance toward them, looking like she wasn't going to stop. A squeal escaped Gulliver moments before the giant cat reached them. She stopped at Brea's side, staring up at her in expectation.

"Oh." Brea covered her mouth in surprise. "A cat. How precious."

"That's not a cat, my love." Lochlan tried to pull her away, but she didn't budge. "It's much too big."

Brea didn't listen to him as she buried her hands in Sheba's fur. The cat let out a sound somewhere between a purr and a roar.

Lochlan started toward the castle. "Let's get out of this sun before this old ice king melts into a puddle."

Eavha and Tia linked arms and ran after him, leaving Gulliver with Brea and Sheba. Brea fell in step beside him. "Sorry for the dramatic entrance." She sighed. "The moment we stepped out of the portal, Tia took off like a rocket."

He was used to Brea saying human things he didn't understand, so he didn't ask what a rocket was. Her explanations never made much sense anyway. "I guess I should have explained more in my message."

"You don't say?" Brea took his arm as they stepped through the gates. "We have much to discuss. A lot of questions."

They had no idea.

Declan met them in the center of the courtyard.

"Where's ..." Gulliver stopped himself, needing to explain things to Tia before revealing the human girl's presence.

"In her room." Declan's dour expression told Gulliver there was more he wanted to say, but he didn't need to.

Gulliver pictured Sophie's face, the fear, as he flew backward. He'd exposed her to so little magic, but Tia was in no way cautious with her power. He should have known something like this would happen.

"Now that we have our greetings out of the way, is there someplace we can speak privately?" Lochlan clasped his hands behind his back, looking ever the king. Yet, there was something lighter in his stance ever since he'd handed the crown of Iskalt over to his daughter.

Declan nodded. "We've been using the dining hall for meetings of this sort."

"Perfect." Gulliver's stomach rumbled. "Then, we can eat while we talk."

"Some things never change." Tia rolled her eyes to Eavha.

Gulliver shrugged. "A leopard can't change its stripes."

"Spots," Brea whispered, patting him on the back. "Leopards have spots, honey, but nice try."

He wasn't even sure what a leopard was, but he'd grown up hearing Brea say it quite often about her husband.

They crowded together as they entered the quiet castle that now buzzed with activity over the arrival of their visitors.

"Ariella," Eavha called. "Ready two guest rooms."

Ariella hesitated. "Lady Eavha, we only have one more usable room. The—"

Eavha cut her off. "That's right. Our other is occupied. Fine, just the one then. My sister-by-marriage can stay with me. Declan will sleep in the guard's quarters."

"Sleepover! I've seen them in many human movies. But don't we need to find some paint for our nails?" Tia gave her mother a concerned look. "I don't want to do it wrong."

Eavha shrugged. "There might be some left over from the renovations of the east wing."

"That's not quite right, girls." Brea laughed. "I'm not sure there's a fae equivalent of nail polish, but you can do a girl's sleepover without it in a pinch."

"Oh good." Tia giggled.

"Aren't you supposed to be a queen or something?" Gulliver bumped Tia with his shoulder.

She straightened. "Just worry about yourself. You'll see how much of a queen I am soon enough."

He swallowed. That sounded ominous. Sure, he'd failed in his mission, but he had a good reason, and she'd understand as soon as he explained. Tia was well-versed in the healing pools and using them to save the man she loved. She couldn't blame him too much. Could she?

Not that he loved Sophie. The woman wouldn't even speak

to him. The thought tugged at his heart, but he tried to ignore it as a servant appeared with a tray of glasses and a flagon of wine.

"No, no. Not the Gelsiberry!" Eavha shrieked and chased them back toward the kitchens, issuing orders.

"Lord Declan?" A soldier walked toward them. "We've received a message from Queen Bronagh."

Declan nodded before turning to the others. "Please, have a seat. I will return shortly."

When he hurried off, it left Gulliver staring at the three O'Sheas. He lowered himself into a chair at the long wooden table, wishing Eavha would hurry up with that wine.

"We have many things to discuss." Lochlan sat beside him. "Tell us of your mission in the human city."

The two women took the chairs across the table from him, and Tia shot an annoyed look at her father. "Dad, I know the whole taking a backseat thing is still new for you, but I'll handle this."

He looked confused for a moment before he gave her a sheepish smile. "Apologies, my little queen." He nodded for her to continue.

Tia reached into the pocket she'd had sewn into of every one of her dresses. She got the idea from her mother's human clothes, stating that if fae were superior beings, they must put pockets in dresses.

Pulling out a folded paper Gulliver instantly recognized as a page from a human newspaper, she slapped it on the table. "Go on. Look at it."

He glanced at each fae in turn. Lochlan was tense, his jaw tight. Brea had tears shining in her eyes. Tia was defiant. It was how she acted when she didn't know what to do.

Fear struck him. For whatever that page said, whatever it would mean.

Slowly, he unfolded it, his eyes swimming over lines and

lines of text but he couldn't absorb a single word. The pictures took his attention. Two of them were side by side, blurry but recognizable.

Toby and Griff stared back, warning him that whatever he was about to read would shift the axis of his world.

"What was Griff doing in the human world long enough to cause trouble?" Lochlan asked.

"He came ..." Gulliver couldn't stop staring at his father's picture. "For me. He wanted to check on me and I, um. I needed his help with something," he finished lamely.

"He was supposed to drop in on you and Toby and come right back with a report," Tia practically growled. "He should have returned before dawn so *all* of our reliable fae with portal magic weren't *all* in the human realm ... at the *same* time." By the time she finished, her teeth were bared in a grimace and Gullie knew he really was in trouble this time.

And yet, his father had stayed. To help with Sophie. Guilt gnawed at him. His father had broken his promise to the Queen of Iskalt just to be there for his son and to make sure he was okay.

"He was supposed to go back right after he checked in with Toby." Gulliver could hardly breathe. Griff could get out of the human realm at any time during the night, but still, he was there. Because Gulliver hadn't looked out for Toby, hadn't kept him from getting involved with Xavier and his friends. And something horrible had happened.

When Brea spoke, her voice quivered. "They're calling them terrorists. I know the kinds of people humans put that label on. Why haven't they come home?" Both could open portals, and yet, neither have.

Gulliver pulled the paper closer, his eyes skimming the words. He shook his head. "This can't be right. They're saying the two men pictured are suspects of a terrorist attack on some remote village outside the city. The victims were largely families with small children." It didn't make sense. "The fae are trying to prevent more attacks, not carry them out."

"But how did they get their pictures?" Lochlan asked.

"From the crosswalks in the city," Brea said. "They can get a picture of anyone that way."

"Then how do they know they were involved in this attack?" Tia demanded, scowling her fury at Gullie.

"It's likely that someone has accused them," Brea said. "But who?"

"HAFS," Gullie said with a deep sigh, bracing himself for Tia's temper.

"Okay, why don't we back up and let Gullie tell us everything that happened before he left for Lenya." Brea had a much kinder look for him than Tia.

He explained everything about his time in New Orleans, about Toby and his new fae friends. The bombings, the attacks on fae. Tia had been right when she sent him there. It was escalating.

"If the humans capture them …" Brea covered her mouth with her hand. "My boy."

"No." Tia leaned forward, staring at her brother's image. "If they capture him, he can escape through a portal. And Griff has Iskalt magic along with his O'Shea portal magic. Neither should be in any real danger."

"But why haven't they contacted us?" Lochlan asked the question they were all too afraid to voice.

"Because." Eavha stopped at the end of the table, "they probably can't." Two servants set silver mugs of chilled cider in front of each of them. "No wine. I figured you all wanted clear heads tonight."

All eyes were on her now.

"What do you mean, they can't?" Tia said.

"With our crystals, a Lenyan can be as powerful as any Iskaltian, but there are limitations. We cannot draw on our magic when we're ..."

"When you're what?"

"There is so much about the portal magic still unknown to you. Maybe it has similar rules to ours."

Tia stood. "When you're what?" she repeated.

"Near death."

"No." She shook her head. "Absolutely not." She picked up the paper and shook it. "We have proof they survived the attack."

"Not necessarily, Tia," Brea said with a shaky breath. "Those pictures could have come from before the attack. But the good news is that the humans are looking for them. That means they haven't been caught yet. So wherever they are, if one or both of them are hurt, they're likely on their own."

Gulliver didn't want to think about losing anyone else he cared about, but he couldn't ignore the truth. "This group, Human Alliance For Survival, never just plans one attack. This attack is part of a greater objective. We don't know where Toby and Griff are, but if they're fighting HAFS, we need to figure out what's coming next to learn where they might go."

Everyone stared at him, no one speaking. Waiting. Two ex-sovereigns, one current one, and a duchess of Lenya thought he —Gulliver—would have the answer.

"Gullie." Tia reached out and grabbed his hand, her voice softer now. "You spent time in New Orleans around these people. Did you learn anything at all that might tell us of this objective of theirs?"

He hadn't. He still had no idea what HAFS really wanted, but he didn't think it was random chaos or just killing a few fae. Yet, he knew someone who might.

He closed his eyes for a moment, drawing in a deep breath.

This wasn't why he'd brought Sophie here. She wasn't a prisoner forced to give up information.

Still, Toby and Griff were on the line.

"I wasn't there long enough." The tension in the room deflated, a balloon of hope losing its air. "But there is someone here who might help us."

Chapter Two
SOPHIE-ANN

"This isn't happening." Sophie rushed into the room that now felt like her only haven in a sea of strange and foreign things. "It's not real." That power. The way Gulliver skidded across the courtyard and couldn't stop himself.

Her dad was right.

Magic had no place in any world, not if it took free will so completely. It was an abomination. Slamming the heavy door shut, she searched the room for anything she could use to barricade it. The tea table would have to do.

She gripped the edge of the heavy, black furniture that seemed to spark and come alive. A strange vibration ran the length of her arms, but she had to have imagined it. It took all her strength—a strength she hadn't had in years—to pull the table across the room to the door. She cleared off the silver tray on top of it and braced it beneath the door handle.

Backing away from the door, she put her hands on her hips

and drew in a breath. Her heart thrummed against her breastbone, the pulse pounding in her ears.

That woman out there terrified her. She'd used her power so casually, as if there was nothing wrong with forcing it on Gulliver. Was that what they all did? She could still hear that voice echoing against the stones. *Don't get mad?* She didn't understand anything that was said, but it was clear Gulliver knew who she was and that he had angered the powerful fae woman.

Sophie fumbled back farther into her room and managed to sit on the edge of the bed before her legs collapsed beneath her. She wanted to scream, or throw up, or run away into the wilderness of this awful world.

But, no. That wasn't what she wanted at all. "I want to go home." She flopped onto her back, staring at the pearl gray canopy above her head. There was luxury here of a kind she wasn't used to, but she'd give it all away to curl up in her own bed.

Thoughts of home calmed her mind enough for her to truly consider her situation. She was a prisoner in the fae world, the same fae who turned most of the human world dark for months. If they could do that, could take her mother from her, what else were they capable of?

If only her father could have seen her today playing a strange game with those he despised. He'd have been ashamed of her. But would he have also been grateful they saved her life? There was the problem. She couldn't remember the last time she felt this good, and it was because they saved her with their magic.

Did that erase everything else they'd done? The danger they posed to her entire world? Or was the fact that Gulliver had to force his way into the healing pools just another sign of their corruption? That they had healing pools capable of bringing her back from the brink of death, yet they didn't allow free use of such magic when untold lives—human or fae—could be saved from illnesses like hers.

A soft knock sounded on the door, and she sat so fast her head swam. Clamping her lips shut, she didn't say a word.

They knocked again. And waited.

Sophie's gaze darted around the room, searching for anything she could use as a weapon. Her eyes fell on the fireplace and the tools sitting next to it. She climbed off the bed and tiptoed across the room, wrapping her fingers around the cool iron poker.

Her father said fae couldn't touch iron. It burned them like the demons he believed them to be.

"I know you're in there," an irritated voice said as the woman jiggled the doorknob. "You do realize I can open this door no matter what you've done to it, right? I'd rather you not have to see that, but I am coming in. It's your choice how."

Sophie couldn't find the words to respond, so she readied herself, planting her feet as far apart as the obnoxious dress she'd been given would let her. She lifted the poker, prepared to attack.

A sigh came through the door. "Guess we're doing this the hard way." The tray slipped from underneath the knob and shot across the room. The table moved, seemingly of its own accord, scraping across the floor until the door was clear.

When it finally opened, a small woman stood there, arms crossed and eyebrows raised. "Well, I can see why Gullie likes you." She stepped into the room. "Give me the poker. I'm really not in the mood to fight with a human."

Sophie stepped back, shaking her head. "Stay away from me."

The woman rubbed her eyes. "I am way too tired for this. Do you know what I've been through lately because of your father?"

"No more than you deserve."

"Come now, I know you don't believe that. Gullie wouldn't be so ... attached if you did."

Sophie narrowed her eyes. "He can keep his attachment to himself." She wasn't sure if she meant it. The Gulliver she met at the Vieux Carré Cafe was still lodged deep in her heart. He'd cared for her, and she'd thought he was the kindest man she'd ever met.

The woman reached out, and the poker slid from Sophie's fingers, dropping to the floor with a loud clang. "I might have let you keep that so you'd at least have the illusion of protecting yourself, but then you had to go and insult Gulliver. You'll learn quickly that's the best way to get on my bad side."

"Do you have a good side? You're fae." The words sounded too much like her father's, and she wasn't sure she liked it.

The woman's shoulders dropped. "This is going to be harder than I thought. Look, I'm trying really hard not to go all angry, scary, magical queen on you right now."

She sounded so human. "Y-you're a queen?"

A smile curved her lips. "Queen Tierney of Iskalt, at your service. You can call me Tia because, honestly, my parents were daft naming me Tierney after the grandmother I never met. It's such a stuffy old name, and I am fun."

She said it with a growl in her voice, and Sophie shrank away. "You sound fun."

A surprised laugh popped out of Tia. "I think I'm going to like you once you stop acting so freaking terrified of me. I'm really not so scary. Sure, I'm more powerful than just about any other fae, but I mostly use my magic to play pranks on Gullie and my siblings. Sometimes, I break out of dungeons or destroy ancient magical barriers, but only when I'm really looking for a good time."

This woman was insane. Sophie knew it without a doubt. From the casual way she spoke of magic to the feats she claimed.

"I can tell you don't believe me. Was it the pranks? Do you think queens don't get to have some fun?" She shook her head. "Look, what you believe or don't isn't my problem. I have bigger friends to fry."

"Fish," Sophie whispered, not sure why she felt the need to correct her.

Tia winked. "Oh, I know. I prefer my way, mostly when I'm talking to Gulliver after he has brought a human into the fae realm to use some of our most protected magic. You're lucky I wasn't here when he arrived. I'd have let you die."

"Thanks?"

"Don't take it personally. Humans really aren't my problem. Not unless they're hunting down my brother and my uncle for crimes I know they couldn't have committed."

Sophie didn't know what she was talking about.

Tia continued. "Look, I don't want us to be enemies, but I've never really cared how many of those I make. Just ask my husband. He was my enemy once upon a time, and then he realized I was always right. But you owe me."

"How do you figure that?" Sophie was waiting for the queen to use her magic to get information, was prepared for the pain to come. Yet, it didn't.

"My uncle Griff brought you here. He saved your life."

Sophie shook her head. "Gulliver—"

"Can't open portals. His father helped him, and now, that father is in danger because of some idea that he can save my harebrained brother. They've attached themselves to a group of fae in the human realm, and the newspaper claims they are terrorists."

Guilt gnawed at Sophie. If it was true that this man saved her, did she have an obligation to him?

Tia pointed to the settee. "Sit. We have much to discuss and only so much time before Gulliver runs into this room to make sure I'm not roasting you over the fire."

"You would do that?" she breathed.

A smile parted the fae queen's lips. "Man, you humans. You really do believe we're awful. Well, we're not the ones currently attacking our own people to seek out those different from us. I suggest you sit and tell me everything you know, or I might have to revise the whole roasting over the fire bit."

This time, Sophie knew she was joking. It seemed the woman did that a lot but didn't want others to know when something was a joke. Sophie did as told, lowering herself to the settee in front of the cold embers, thankful there was no fire at the moment. It meant there'd be no roasting.

Tia didn't sit, instead she paced in front of the settee. "Your father is the leader of this anti-fae group, is he not?"

Sophie nodded. "Well ... one of them, at least. But Just in New Orleans."

"The attacks are escalating. We've tracked his activities for a while. It's why I sent Gulliver to New Orleans. He was meant to gather intel from local fae." She rubbed the back of her neck and stopped walking. "I should have acted earlier, should have sent more than my friend and my brother into the human city, but we do not want a war with the humans."

"Is that why you turned our entire world dark?" Sophie looked up at her, defiance burning in her eyes. "That wasn't war?"

Tia's brow furrowed. "That was over ten years ago, and we didn't—"

"Ten years or not, some of us never got to move on." Like her mother. Like her family.

"Is that what this is about? An accident that we did everything we could to fix?"

Sophie didn't believe for one second it was an accident. How does one accidentally block the sun from shining?

Tia dropped to the settee beside her. "We were at war, human. Yes, an evil fae king ripped open the world and let darkness seep into yours, but we defeated him. My brother, who your people currently call a terrorist, helped me return order and good to both our worlds. And now, he bears the blame for acts your father commits. How is that justice?"

"Justice?" Sophie jumped to her feet. "Do not speak to me of justice." If that truly existed, her mother would still be alive.

Tia was quiet for a long moment. "We've lost those we care about too."

It wasn't just someone she cared about; it was her mother. "It's not the same thing."

"Of course it is. You think we're so different, but you're wrong. My mother grew up in the human realm, and I've spent a lot of time there. Our main differences are only perception. As the existence of fae and magic comes into the open, it's natural for you to fear us. But we have families too. We laugh and love and play with our children. There is good and bad in both our worlds, but all we can do is fight so that the good wins out in the end. I wish that meant we could prevent evil, but that's impossible."

Sophie turned away, not wanting Tia to see the tears burning in her eyes. Most of her life, she'd been so angry because she thought her mother's death had been preventable. That the very existence of the fae caused that tragedy.

But when Tia continued, she heard every word. "Last year, I stood on the gallows of this very castle with Gulliver at my side and a noose around my neck."

Slowly rotating back around, Sophie met her gaze, her heart plummeting at the thought of Gulliver facing his own demise. He must have been so scared.

Tia nodded. "It was bad. My husband saved us, but I will never forget how it felt to stand in the face of evil and lose. Weeks later, my brother lost the love of his life as we fought to save those very fae who'd tried to kill me so many times."

"How did you do it? How did you forgive them?" Sophie blurted, half wishing she could call the questions back.

She drew in a deep breath. "I realized there was nothing to forgive. Most of the fae in Lenya had nothing to do with my almost execution. They just wanted to live their lives and hope to avoid the noose themselves. The man who'd sentenced me was already dead, and that was good enough for me. I couldn't punish an entire kingdom just because something bad happened to me."

For so long, Sophie only focused on herself. Such was the nature of a disease like hers. Every day, every moment, her inner focus was on how she was feeling. Could she take her shift at the cafe? Did she feel capable of getting out of bed? It could make a person imagine they are the only suffering one.

But Tia suffered too. She saw it in the queen's eyes, heard it in her voice.

Even with that bit of understanding, the anger didn't subside. She once again pictured Gulliver as the magic pulled him through the gates. No matter the intentions of those wielding such power, it was too dangerous to be allowed to exist.

The fae might be similar to humans in some ways, but if they chose, they could destroy her world. Her father was wrong about a lot of things, but at least he knew the only way to survive was to strike first, to never back down.

If they did, all was lost.

Chapter Three
TOBY

"Watch it, Xavier." Toby winced as his half-fae friend removed the bandage from his shoulder.

"Then, sit still and it might not hurt so much." Xavier examined the open wound on Toby's shoulder. During the last skirmish with the humans, Toby was shot, and he was still recovering. The bullet had hit him straight on but passed clean through muscle and tissue just below the joint. He was lucky, but the injury let him with a wound that had bled a lot. He'd thought he was dying at the time. He'd even thought Logan had come for him, but the person he saw just before he passed out was his uncle. It seemed Griffin had arrived not long after the fighting began in the small village.

Xavier dabbed a potion over Toby's injury, and the sting set his whole arm on fire.

"I'm sorry, all we have to clean injuries is alcohol." He frowned at the state of the wound. "It will only sting for a minute, and then it'll subside."

"Hot water works too," Toby muttered.

Xavier chuckled. "Not enough to kill germs." He rummaged around his potions kit and smoothed a layer of salve over the stitches the local healer had given him. It didn't seem to work as well as fae potions did. Toby had a throbbing headache and his whole arm ached from shoulder to wrist.

"What are germs, and why do they need killing?"

"They're what are making this injury swell up and throb." Xavier looked worried about the wound, but Toby felt fine except for the terrible headache that plagued him.

"That looks awful." Griffin peered over Xavier's shoulder. "When I take you home, you're going straight to the palace healers." Griffin tapped his foot impatiently against the rough wooden floor of the barn where they were currently hiding out. With their faces splattered all over the news and in the human papers, Griffin and Toby were stuck, and the village elders wouldn't let them use their portal magic within the town limits. It was too dangerous to use magic when HAFS members were scattered across the city and surrounding areas in droves, just looking for anything that resembled magic.

"I've told you, Uncle Griff, I'm not going back." Toby sucked in a breath as Xavier re-wrapped the bandages tightly around his shoulder. "I know you've come to check up on me, but you should go home and give my sister an update. "Ouch! Take it easy Xavier." He winced

"Sorry." Xavier eased up on the pressure against the wound. "You have to promise me you'll keep ice on this. It will help with the swelling."

"That's such a weird thing. It can't possibly be true. I come from a land of ice, and I can promise you it's not good for much."

"Just do it, Toby." Xavier stood, forcing Toby to lie back against the cot.

He was sick of resting. Resting meant there was far too much time to think about things he didn't want to think about. He preferred action. Fighting the humans gave him a purpose, and he wanted to protect the fae living in a world that would never accept them. He knew something about being different from everyone around him. Luckily for him, his people had never hated him for his lack of magic.

"Fine. I'll ice it, but I'm not staying cooped up in this smelly old barn for another minute." He tried to sit, but Griffin pushed him back down.

"Your mother would have my head if I let you out of that bed before you're completely healed."

"I'm fine, Griff. Just a headache is all." Toby compromised by sitting on the edge of the cot. He and Griffin were the only ones staying in the barn at the moment, but there were several other cots laid out in rows across the hayloft. The fae community was a small one made up of a few farms and a central town square. The barn stood near the square and served as a meeting hall and winter storage when it wasn't being used as a hospital.

"I'll come back to check on you later," Xavier said. "If the swelling doesn't go down by then, I'll send for the healer again. You might need a shot of penicillin."

"I've been shot once already. I don't want to go through that again any time soon."

Xavier chuckled, shaking his head, probably at something Toby said that sounded funny to him. He did that a lot, but Xavier seemed to enjoy it. "Get some rest." Xavier scaled the ladder to the lower part of the barn.

"He's right, you know." Griffin sat on the cot opposite Toby's. "You need to rest. I don't think you've slept much since we got here."

"I don't sleep well most nights." Toby watched through the huge hayloft window as Xavier made his way down the well-worn path to the town square. With a sigh he rubbed a weary hand across his face. He hadn't slept well since Logan died. When he did sleep, he woke from horrible dreams where he relived the moment of his death over and over. Staying awake or drunk was easier than facing his dreams.

"I could open a portal right now, and we would be gone before anyone even knew what happened."

"And what if someone saw us?" He shook his head stubbornly. "It's too risky when these people don't know who they can trust. There could be HAFS members right here among them, and these fae wouldn't know since half of them don't have strong fae features. It's hard fighting against something you can't really see."

"I am very familiar with such things." Griffin's voice dropped into a sympathetic tone. The kind of tone fae had adopted around him after he'd lost Logan. It made him so angry to hear the pity and sorrow others would never understand.

"I need to stay and fight, Uncle Griff." Toby stood and crossed the loft to the big window overlooking the small village on the outskirts of New Orleans. The countryside was beautiful here. It reminded him of Fargelsi along the marshlands, but even more beautiful and less scary than what the Southern Vatlands used to be.

"Is it this Xavier fellow?" Griffin asked carefully. "Is he someone ... special to you?"

"No." Toby's voice came out in an angry rush. "It's not about that."

"Then, tell me what it is about. Every time I mention going home, you get defensive and refuse to leave."

"I can't leave when there are fae who need help. These people live with very little magic. Most of them are half-human and half-fae like Xavier. Their magic is weak if they have it at all. The ones they believe are powerful pale in comparison to even the weakest of fae in the five kingdoms."

"I see." Griffin looked down at his hands. "They are more like you."

"Yes. And I won't leave them when I know something about fighting against a formidable foe without the benefit of magic."

"Prince Tobias, the Ogre Killer," Griffin said softly. "It's ... admirable, and I can understand your reasons for wanting to stay, but our faces are everywhere. It isn't safe."

"I don't care about that. I can protect myself."

"I know you can. You've been trained to fight. You understand strategy and warfare, but no matter what you feel, this isn't your fight. You've learned the hard way that humans have weapons we do not understand."

"I know now." Toby ran a hand over his fresh bandage. "And I will be more careful, but I won't leave, Uncle Griff. But I think you should find a quiet place, late at night, and slip back home to tell Tia what's happening here."

"Your sister will just come here looking for you."

"Don't let her." Toby smirked. "You control portals, and we all know she can't."

"And you know very well that would be like trying to hold the waves back from the shore. If she thinks you're in danger, she'll try portaling here herself if she has to."

Toby looked up into the familiar eyes of his birth father, begging him to understand. "When you lived in Gelsi, back when Queen Reagan was at her most powerful, you lived alone in your cottage away from palace life."

Griffin nodded. "It was easier for me there."

"Because you were an Iskaltian prince who couldn't go home to Iskalt?"

"Yes. And no." He hung his head. "I look back on that time now, and I believe I preferred living at the cottage so I didn't have to see the Fargelsian people suffer under her rule. I loved her. She was my mother, and for a long time, I refused to see her as she was."

"You felt for the people of Gelsi?"

"I did. I was ashamed of my inability to help them." Griffin studied Toby's face. "You feel for these fae here in the human world?"

"I do." Toby nodded, dragging in a deep breath. "And it's been a very long time since I've felt anything."

"Uncle Griff, wake up." Toby shook his uncle, just short of rolling him off the cot he'd slept on for the three nights they'd spent in the fae village. "It's time for you to leave."

"Leave?" Griffin groaned, his bones creaking and popping as he stretched. "Where am I going?" He sat on the edge of the cot, rubbing the sleep from his eyes.

"I need you to go home," Toby said simply. "There's been an attack on another fae village farther to the south of New Orleans. This isn't going to stop." He studied his uncle's eyes. "We've seen this all before, Griff. We know what it leads to, and we can't let that happen here."

Griffin nodded. "It will be far worse here with the humans and their killing machines." He reached for his pack. "Are you sure I can't talk you into coming with me?"

"No. I need you to tell Tia everything that's happening here. I'm not so certain the fae in the human world can protect themselves from HAFS much longer." He moved to the window to peer out into the darkness where fae were gathering to discuss the latest news.

"I brought you one of her spelled journals; you can tell her yourself." Griffin moved to stuff his feet into his boots.

"I won't use it." Toby shoved his few belongings into a pack.

"Once I open that book, Tia won't shut up, and I can't have her tie my hands while I'm trying to help these people save their little corner of this world. I need you to be the messenger."

"And what am I to tell your sister, the queen, when she asks why you refused the journal?"

"I don't care. Make something up." He shrugged. "Better yet, tell her I'm trying to do what she sent me here to do."

Griffin quickly gathered the last of his things. "Where am I going to open a portal where no one will see me?"

"Xavier will be here in a moment to take you deep into the bayou where it should be safe and no one will see the light. You'll portal home just before dawn."

"Very well. What do you propose your sister do to aid you in this fight against HAFS?"

"To start, we need more trained soldiers. Not an army, but advisors to help the fae here protect the innocents. These minor attacks are just the beginning. This unrest is about to burst wide open, and the fae are going to need representatives to act in their best interests."

"You act as if a war is brewing."

Toby lifted his pack over his shoulder. "That's exactly what I'm saying, Griff. War is coming to the human realm, and we need to be ready for it."

Chapter Four
GULLIVER

"Tell me again how the humans got their pictures in the first place?" Tia paced across the large sitting room in the royal residence where Eavha and Declan now lived. "It looks like they're being followed." She snatched the newspaper from Gullie's hands as he stalked past her in the opposite direction. "Just look at them!" She threw her arms up in the air. "They look like ... like they're up to something ... like ..."

"Terrorists? No." Gulliver ran a hand through his hair as he hit the end of the sitting room and turned around, pacing back across the plush navy blue carpet. It glittered with tiny specks of crystals, making the floor look like the midnight sky. Eavha had done a lot of redecorating since he'd last visited the Vondurian palace. "They look like two fae trying to blend in with the humans around them and neither one of them is very good at it. They're just crossing the street, probably trying to figure out how the trolly cars work, but in the paper, along with the article about how fae are attacking humans, they look guilty."

"But how did a street corner manage to get a picture of them?"

"It's from something called a traffic camera, Tia." Gulliver's tail swished behind him as he passed her again. "It works on its own, but I don't really know how. It does seem like they're being followed, though. Maybe there's more to it than a traffic camera?"

"Like what, Gullie?" she snapped, magic crackling at her fingertips, making Sophie flinch from her seat on one of the many settees scattered across the room. "What is happening to my fae in the human world?"

"Keep your hair on already. We already knew people of HAFS were attacking the fae communities, and they don't care if humans get hurt too. They're getting bold now, trying to blame their terrorism on the fae. That's really all I can tell you. Griff and Toby were just in the wrong place at the wrong time. Easy scapegoats to pin the attacks on."

"These people sound like lunatics."

Gulliver winced, averting his eyes from Sophie's. "None of that matters. We just need to get in there, find those two idiots, and bring them home."

"But where are they?" Tia marched back across the room, biting her fingernails—a nervous habit from her childhood she'd never quite kicked.

"The paper says they're wanted, which means they haven't been arrested yet." Gulliver had watched enough local news on the feletision box that was stuck on the news channel during their stay at the Lamothe House Inn. There were always criminals wanted for some crime or another in the city.

"Which means they're hiding somewhere, likely injured or unable to use their portal magic, and we have to find them before the human authorities do." Tia balled her hands into fists at her sides. "I don't want to even think about the nightmare of them getting arrested and then disappearing from their jail cells through magic portals the humans won't understand. We cannot afford to cause any more magical commotion or we really are going to have a confrontation with the humans."

"Exactly." Gulliver whirled around, his tail nearly knocking over a priceless Vondurian vase perched on a marble pedestal. He leaped to catch it and set it back carefully before he continued his movements. "They're probably hiding out with Xavier somewhere in the city."

"Who is this Xavier, and can we trust him?"

"He's a friend of Sophie's. That's why I asked her to meet with us." He turned to Sophie where she sat wide eyed and silent on the settee. "Where would Xavier hide any friends who were trying to avoid your father?"

"I don't know. He wouldn't tell me." She held a fluffy, cream-colored pillow in her lap like a shield that would protect her from Tia's magic.

"Would you know how to find this friend of yours?" Tia demanded, striding across the room toward the girl. "Could you get a message to him?"

Sophie let out a startled squeak as Tia approached her.

"Tia, take it down a notch." Gulliver put himself between the two women. "She's not your subject, and she's scared."

"I'm not scared." Sophie lifted her chin in defiance. "I'm furious I've been brought here against my will."

"You honestly would have rather died than let Gulliver save your life in the healing pools?" Tia turned on Gulliver. "Which I have not forgotten about, by the way. We're going to have to talk about your punishment when all this is over. King Hector is furious with you, and Bron is itching to get her hands on you. You broke about a dozen new laws when you took it upon yourself to heal this girl. You might be my most favorite person in all the worlds, but even I can't save you this time."

"Focus, Tia. We can talk about that later. Right now, we need to save my dad and your brother."

"Griff was my uncle before he was your dad." Tia crossed her arms over her chest.

"You people are so strange," Sophie muttered, glancing between the two old friends.

Gulliver's tail twitched furiously as he pointed at her. "You didn't even know he existed when Dad found me in the slums of the Myrkur palace."

"I knew him from my dreams." She stood with her hands on her hips. "Besides, Uncle Griff likes me better than you." She returned to her pacing. "Sophie, what about getting that message to your friend in the city? Is it possible?"

"Maybe. I don't really know." Sophie shrank back from Tia's intensity.

"We need to find out what's happened to our family, Sophie," Gulliver said, approaching her like he would a startled deer. "This is my dad and Tia's brother we're talking about. I know you're overwhelmed with everything that's happened these last few days." He sank down onto the chair closest to her without invading her space. "But neither Griff nor Toby would ever hurt anyone. I promise you, they are good fae. We have to get them out of there before they suffer the punishment for someone else's crimes." He left it unsaid that some of those crimes were committed by her own father.

Sophie nodded. "If you let me go home, I'll do whatever I can to find Xavier, and then he can help you find your family if he wants to. I want nothing more to do with any of this." She sniffed back her tears and put on a brave face. "I am grateful for whatever you've done to heal me, but I-I can't be involved with this ... unrest between the fae and the humans."

"Well, from what I hear, you and your family are already

involved." Tia glared at Sophie, looking every inch the scary ice queen.

Sophie shook her head. "My father isn't a bad man."

"So, he's the good kind of man who kills innocent fae children and humans who happen to get in the way?"

"Tia, that's enough." Lochlan strode into the room with Brea right behind him. "We could hear you two bickering all the way down the hall. You'll wake the whole palace with all your shouting."

"Sorry, Dad." Tia waved a hand at him.

"Well, I had hoped you two would come to an agreement for once in your lives, but as much as I don't care to admit it, my brother can take care of himself."

"And so can Toby," Brea added. "They will do whatever it takes to stay hidden until the dust settles. If they get into too much trouble, they can portal home whenever they want. That they haven't just tells us they are still trying to help the fae who might not be as capable."

"What are you saying, Mom? That we should just let them fend for themselves?" Tia demanded.

"That's exactly what she is saying," Lochlan said.

"But what if Eavha was right and they can't portal home because they're hurt, or dying?"

"We can't think like that, sweetheart." Brea crossed the room to pull her daughter into her embrace. "There is a lot more at stake here than Griff and Toby ending up on the FBI's Most Wanted list."

"What's the FBI?" Tia muttered into her mother's shoulder.

"Nothing to worry about right now. We need to focus our efforts on ending this unrest between the fae and this HAFS group before it gets out of hand."

"It's already out of hand," Sophie said, seeming surprised that she'd spoken her thoughts out loud.

Brea moved to sit opposite Sophie. "I grew up in the human realm, Sophie. I know firsthand how scary it is to wake up one day and find yourself in a world of magic you never knew existed. And having a bunch of scary fae demanding your cooperation. I am so sorry you've ended up here in the middle of all this, but I promise we will get you home just as soon as we can."

"But you're fae." Sophie stared at the former queen's pointed ears.

"I didn't know that until I was almost eighteen. At heart, I'm a human girl who grew up on a farm in Ohio. And I care about all the people—fae and human—that could die so needlessly, simply because they do not understand each other. We need to know what the HAFS group is planning so we can try to end the violence. If you could help us find my son and his uncle, I would be forever grateful."

"You don't understand." Sophie sucked in a shaky breath. "The fae killed my mother. My father will never trust anyone who has magic. Even if they did heal me. He'll see it as some form of manipulation to get close to him and HAFS." Her whole body trembled, and Gulliver wanted to comfort her. "I won't betray him. I-I'm sorry. I can't help you." She shot up from her seat, still clutching the pillow to her chest. "Especially not when you continue to keep me here against my will. All I've heard since I woke are promises that I will get to go home soon. So far, that seems to be the very last thing any of you intend to do. Yet, you expect me to betray my people to help you."

"We healed you!" Tia's eyes flashed with magic. "The least you could do is help us save our family."

"With all due respect, your Majesty," Sophie spat. "You didn't heal me. Gulliver did. And he used the healing pools of this kingdom to do it. Correct me if I am wrong, but you are not the sovereign here. I don't owe you anything." She dropped the pillow to the floor, clutching the skirt of her gown in her fists. Her chest heaved with fury.

Secretly, Gulliver was proud to see the sweet, mild-tempered girl stand up for herself.

"So, how's everyone's week going?" A familiar teasing voice broke the tension in the room.

"Dad!" Gulliver whirled around to gape at his father leaning against the entrance to the sitting room. "You're okay?" He darted across the room and flung his arms around his father. "Are you hurt? You look awful." He studied the bruises on his face and the cracked knuckles of his hands. The dark circles under his eyes.

"Griffin, you look like you've been in a fight." Brea ushered him to a nearby seat.

"A fight with a human bomb sending a poor defenseless fae village into unnecessary chaos." He sank into the chair, looking more exhausted than Gulliver had ever seen him. "The unrest there is growing by the day."

"Where is Toby?" Tia asked as she and Lochlan crowded around him.

All the color drained from Griffin's face as he turned toward Brea. "He's okay, but he's been shot."

"Shot!" Brea clapped a hand over her mouth.

"He's fine. Or he will be with a little more rest. It hit him in the shoulder, but the human-fae healer said it was a clean shot. Toby's in a lot of pain from the swelling, but he has people caring for him."

"It's infected? Has he seen a doctor? No, of course he hasn't because you and my son are wanted terrorists." She punched his arm and appeared on the cusp of a tirade Gulliver usually only saw from Tia. A talent she got from her mother.

"Brea, that son of yours got himself into trouble without my help." Griffin threw up his hands to block any further punches.

"He's working with the fae to fight HAFS and stop the hate crimes. He's determined to end the struggle between fae and humans. You'd be proud of him."

"How did you know we were in Lenya?" Brea's anger wilted for a moment.

"I didn't. I came to check on my son first." He glanced apologetically at Gulliver.

"You intended to wait two more days before you brought this news to me?" Brea's eyes flashed gold with the intensity of her Eldurian magic.

"No, that's not what I intended at all." Griffin held a hand out to stall her yelling. "I was going to send you a message."

"Wait, you gave Toby the spelled journal, didn't you, Uncle Griff?" Tia said, excitement making her eyes seem larger than normal. "I forgot all about it. I have mine in my rooms. We can write to him and make a plan!" She turned to leave.

"He wouldn't take it." Griffin reached for his bag. "I was going to use it to send you a message about Toby once I had a chance to check in on Gullie and his friend." He turned to Sophie, where she still stood frozen with uncertainty. "I am glad to see you are still with us, Sophie." He gave her a polite nod. "And I must say you look much healthier than the last time I saw you."

"Th-thank you," she muttered, some of the tension wilting from her shoulders.

"Now that we're all here and we know Toby is safe for the moment," Lochlan interjected, "I think it's time we all return to Iskalt and discuss our next steps with our peers across the five kingdoms. It's the most central location, and Neeve and Myles are already there with King Hector. The council of royals will need a say in whatever is to happen next. In the meantime, perhaps we can get a message to Sophie's friend Xavier if she is willing." He turned toward Sophie. "No one will force you to do anything you don't want to do, but we would appreciate it if you could help us find our son. Either way, I will take you home myself as soon as we've explained your situation to the other rulers of this land. They will need to know of your healing at the very least. You have my word."

Sophie stared at the formidable Lochlan O'Shea for a long moment before she gave one solitary nod.

Chapter Five
SOPHIE-ANN

Nothing here made any sense. One moment, the man they called Griffin was a wanted terrorist in the human realm, and the next, he stood before his family in Lenya, speaking to her as if they'd met.

What kind of person showed up in the middle of the night like it was no big deal? Sophie yawned, trying to shake off her need for sleep. Things were happening and she needed to pay attention. She just wondered if these fae ever slept.

Over the years, one of the greatest mysteries HAFS tried to uncover was how exactly the fae got to their world. Now, she was so close to learning their deepest secret. If only she could get a message to her father and explain everything she'd learned. Maybe it would help him bring an end to this decade-long struggle.

Sophie shrank in on herself under the curious gaze of the handsome newcomer. He spoke as if they were old friends. Surely she'd remember such an encounter?

Gulliver walked across the room with a purpose, and she turned so she didn't have to look at him, didn't have to meet his startling eyes with Tia's words still rattling in her mind. Forgiveness had never been a Deveraux strength, and she wasn't there yet. If she ever would be.

Steps echoed off the high ceilings of the hall as Gulliver joined his father. "I sent Mom a message with Loch." He sighed. "She's going to be so angry with you."

Griffin's lips split into a smile. "You mean she'll be vexed I didn't invite her along."

"Probably both. The message won't reach her before Hector tells her of the summons to the Iskalt palace, but at least this way, we can say we sent it."

"Good man." Griffin draped an arm over his son's shoulders. It looked so natural, so ... human. Sophie stole glances their way as the two of them continued to chat like the world wasn't on the brink of disaster.

Tia clapped her hands. "Okay, my parents have left for Iskalt and to gather the other royals for an emergency meeting. Eavha will stay here and keep Lenya running in the queen's absence. Now, the four of us need to go. Dawn will be upon us soon."

What did dawn have to do with anything? There was so much Sophie didn't know, and she was torn between wanting to absorb everything for some later advantage and just wanting to find her bed for whatever remained of the night.

"Uncle." Queen Tierney nodded to Griffin. "If you will."

They brought no supplies for a long journey, had packed few belongings, and yet, no one appeared to notice.

Eavha stood in the doorway, a sad smile on her face. "Be careful, Tia."

Tia didn't respond because at that moment the atmosphere grew thick, distorting the view of the opposite end of the room.

Sophie scrambled back as the power trailed down her arms. That was when she saw his eyes.

Griffin's normally green eyes shone violet as he concentrated on the air before him that began to swirl and take on the same hue. It was light at first, mesmerizing. For a moment, Sophie forgot to be scared. For a moment, she wanted a closer look.

That moment snapped as his magic expanded and a blast of wind blew the hair away from her face.

"Go!" Griffin yelled.

Without hesitation, Tia disappeared into the violet tunnel. A scream lodged in Sophie's throat, but it didn't make it past her lips. She couldn't move, not until she felt Gulliver's hand in hers.

He tugged her close, wrapping an arm tightly around her. "There's no time to be human right now." He yanked her hard, and together they fell. The drop seemed to go on forever. There was nothing to hold on to except Gulliver. No point to focus on in the horizon. Every part of her body propelled her forward at a nauseating pace, and when she resisted the pull of magic, pain seared through her like her limbs might rip from her body. But Gulliver's embrace kept her from spinning out of control.

She cried out, but there was no sound. This was it, the end. Was this how her mother died? Was this what it felt like to be killed by fae magic?

Color receded from her vision until all she saw was bright green grass barreling toward her at the speed of a New Orleans tram. At the last moment, Gulliver twisted himself toward the ground, and they hit hard, the impact rattling every bone in her body.

The only sound that escaped her was a long groan. She lay sprawled across Gulliver's chest, unable to move.

Someone coughed. "Not one of your best landings, Dad." Gulliver rolled Sophie onto her side, giving her some distance between them. With another groan, he spit out a mouthful of grass.

Sophie flopped onto her back and grass prickled her skin, the ground beneath her softer than she'd expected. Gulping in a breath, she studied the sky overhead, unable to wrap her mind around what just happened.

Griff picked himself up off the ground as if he hadn't just collided with it, brushing off his pants. "It would have been easier if someone wasn't fighting the portal the entire way." He started walking away. "I need some human food."

Human food? Sophie lifted her head, taking in her surroundings. They'd landed on the lawn in front of a small farmhouse that looked like it had seen better days. A rickety porch held no furniture, only a welcome mat that said, 'leave your packages at the door, we're probably not wearing pants'.

Across the yard, the barn didn't look fit to house a pig, let alone a horse.

Tia sat up. "Well, it's a good thing my mom had the lawn reseeded."

Gulliver cracked a smile, turning it on Sophie. "We land here a lot. The ground used to be a lot harder if you can imagine that."

"Mom loves doing projects in the human realm now that she's not ruling a kingdom anymore." Tia rolled her eyes. "You can take the fae out of the human world, but you can't, well, you know ..."

How many fae grew up here without even knowing their true origins? If one with royal blood remained hidden for so long, how did HAFS stand a chance of rooting out all the others?

Before standing, Sophie took a moment to breathe in the fresh air, the air of her world. She was home. It might not be New Orleans, but wherever this farmstead was located, it was a lot closer to her beloved city than any part of the fae world.

"Ohio," Gulliver said as they walked toward the house. "That's where we are."

Tia held the door open for them. "And no, you can't run from us here. So don't get any ideas."

"Tia," Gulliver growled her name. "Enough with the threats. She's not a prisoner."

"No, but she's not quite free to go just yet." Tia gave Sophie a long stare before she entered the house.

In the kitchen, Griffin dug through cabinets, curses falling from his lips. He looked worse than he had when he first arrived at the palace in Lenya. The circles under his eyes were darker and he looked haggard.

"Something wrong, Griff?" Tia asked.

He muttered something unintelligible and kept searching. "It has to be here somewhere. I know there was at least one box left."

"A box of what?" Alarm entered Gulliver's voice. "Dad, tell me ... is it ..."

Sophie wasn't sure if she should be worried, or why the two men looked so scared. She gripped the counter, still trying to recover from that dizzying magic she had so many questions about.

"It's gone." Griffin slammed a cabinet. "I'm going to have some words for your mother, Tia."

Tears welled in Gulliver's eyes, and he blinked them away. Sophie took in the angry Griff, the upset Gulliver, and the smirking Tia, confusion clouding her mind.

"What are we going to do?" Gulliver plopped himself down on a stool at the counter and buried his head in his hands.

"It'll be okay, son." Griff put a hand on his shoulder. "I promise we'll get through this."

Sophie couldn't handle this anymore. "Does someone want to tell me what you have to get through?"

Gulliver sniffed. "Dad ... we had ..." He shook his head, falling into silence.

"I had an entire box." Griffin looked like he wanted to rip someone's head off, and Sophie just didn't want that to be her.

"A box of what, Uncle Griff?" Tia hopped up to sit on the counter, her lips twitching.

"They were shaped like tiny square ... What do you call them?"

"Sponges, Dad." Gulliver wiped his eyes. "Adorable sponges."

"What was shaped like sponges?" It seemed as though Tia was just taunting them now.

"I don't remember what you call them."

Gulliver reached out and squeezed his father's hand. "Fruit. Sponges shaped like fruit."

They couldn't possibly ... "Are you guys talking about SpongeBob SquarePants fruit snacks?" No, that was a ridiculous thought. They couldn't possibly—

"Yes." Griffin snapped and pointed at her. "They're the best food humans have to offer."

He'd obviously never had prime rib. Or cheesecake.

Griffin wasn't done. "Last time I was here, I hid a full box in the cabinet, but it's gone. If someone is going to challenge me, it should be with a sword and shield."

Sophie shook her head, throwing her hands up as she turned. "You fae are insane." She had to get away from them. Getting back home was paramount, but for now, she just needed some space to gather her thoughts and then she would plan her escape. Pushing through the swinging screen door, she sat on the top step, tucking the fabric of her too-long gown around her legs. The sun had started to sink on the horizon, and she tried to remember the last time she watched the sun set in her home world.

Many evenings, she'd already fallen asleep by this point, worn out by both work and treatments. She couldn't fathom a time before the illness controlled her life, dictating the wonders she got to take in.

"I'm here, Dad," she whispered, knowing the words would never reach him. She wanted him to know she was alive, that he hadn't lost her like he'd lost her mother. At least, not yet.

The door opened behind her, but she didn't turn to see who it was. The silence told her it wasn't Gulliver. Probably not Tia either.

"My son has this need ..." Griffin sat down on the step beside her, a half-eaten sandwich in his hand. "To save people. I've known him since he was two years old, and even then, he knew when someone in our village needed the kind of love he possessed. That's all he's ever wanted to do. Spread love, care for fae and humans alike. He has a big heart. Yet, he's found himself in the middle of too many wars, fighting too many battles that have all taken little pieces of his heart." He turned green eyes on hers, his no longer swirling violet with his unpredictable magic.

"Why are you telling me this?"

Taking a leisurely bite of his sandwich, he shrugged. "I know your mother died during the months of darkness, possibly by our magic, and that has to affect the way you feel about all of us."

"Possibly?" she scoffed. "A fae killed her after you turned the world dark."

His sigh echoed beside her. "Did you know one of the origins of that darkness was here in Grafton?"

She nodded. "It was the first town to go dark." She knew everything there was to learn about that time. When she didn't respond further, he continued.

"Tia's grandfather has a theory about that. Grafton, this house, is where we normally portal—at least for our generation—those few of us who have the power. He thinks we've created a thinning of the veil between worlds at each location we've entered through our magic. The more frequently we pass through the veil in one place, the weaker the veil becomes. My brother and I both used to travel here frequently when Brea was growing up. Loch more often than me. He came to watch over her. I came to spy on her. Though, that's a story for another time."

So, it was true. They were tearing her world apart.

"Why should I care about any of this?" Sophie rested her arms on her knees and leaned forward.

"Because none of it was intentional. We did not declare war on the humans, nor was your mother's death Gulliver's fault. Hate the rest of us, if you must. But Gullie is someone you can trust with your life. He's already saved it once." He stuffed the last bite of his sandwich in his mouth and some color seemed to return to his face.

Before she could respond, the door crashed open. "Found Brea's stash of chocolate." Gulliver threw his father a wrapped Milky Way. "Ready to head out?"

"Head out?" Sophie jumped to her feet. They couldn't leave yet. She was counting on having time on her side here. "Where?"

"Iskalt." Tia pushed past them to reach the lawn. "It's why we traveled at dawn. We wanted to hit dusk here. Griffin's had some time to recover, and I've sent a message to Xavier through Mrs. Merrick, so now we can go."

"Wait who's Mrs. Merrick?" Sophie demanded.

"A friend." Tia crossed the lawn to the grassy area where they just landed.

Griffin locked the house. "All portals have to go through the human realm," he explained. "Well, all except—"

"Griff." Tia cut him off. "She is still our enemy until she decides otherwise. Watch what you tell her."

He offered her a salute, something so distinctly human it almost made Sophie laugh. Almost, because it was followed up by the air rifting once more to open that violet tunnel. The one Sophie was never setting foot in again.

She backed up. "Not happening."

"Don't be stupid." Tia grabbed her arm. "You knew you had to come back to Iskalt with us."

"But I didn't ..." She shook her head as her breath came faster and faster until it was completely out of control. "I can't." The falling. Magic coursing through her. It wasn't meant for humans, that much was clear. No one else seemed fazed at all. Didn't they see?

Gulliver pushed Tia out of the way. "It'll only last a second," he whispered. "You don't really have a choice here, Soph."

Wrong thing to say. She took off, her legs pumping as fast as she could force them.

If only she could find help, get to a human-owned house. Then, she could go home. Her lungs burned as she reached the end of the expansive lawn and circled around the back of the barn. Casting a quick glance behind her, she saw all three fae moving in.

"Tia," Gullie yelled, "don't you dare." Her eyes flicked to Tia, who'd raised a hand. "No magic."

Sophie took the momentary distraction as a chance to climb the neighbor's wooden fence, cursing whoever's idea it had been to put her in a dress. She'd almost made it over when strong hands grabbed her around the waist and yanked her back.

Kicking out, she connected with Gulliver's stomach, but he didn't release her. "Stop. Fighting. Me." He pulled her to the ground, rolling her onto her back and pinning her with his body. "I'm sorry, Sophie."

"No you aren't," she bit out.

"You have no idea what I just saved you from." He pulled

away from her, yet he still didn't let her move. "Tia wouldn't have been this gentle."

"You call this gentle?" She writhed under him, trying to break his grip on her arms.

His eyes held a sadness as he shook his head. "I'm really sorry."

"For what, Gullie? Abducting me? Taking me to your world and holding me captive? Pinning me to the ground against my will."

"For that." He heaved a sigh as his brows drew together. "And for this." In one swift movement, he hauled her over his shoulder.

No amount of screaming or hammering on his back loosened his grip on her. He wasn't a muscular man, with his lean build, but he was stronger than he looked.

They reached Griffin and Tia, but before she could attempt another escape, Gulliver stepped through the portal, and her world disappeared.

Chapter Six
GULLIVER

How could Gulliver just return to Iskalt? To the rooms Tia always insisted were his, as if he were the same fae who left?

Truth: he couldn't.

Surrounded by all the opulence Iskalt provided, and all the comfort Tia demanded, he couldn't help thinking about the fae in the human world who led hidden lives. Lives that were now threatened.

This evening, Griffin left once again, not even a full day after his arrival. He went to retrieve Bron, droped her in Iskalt, and then went back to the human realm as soon as he could to check on Toby.

Now, the only fae who had any useful advice for Gulliver was gone. Useful, because Tia would try. She'd tell him what to do about Sophie, how to interact with the woman he couldn't stop thinking about. But something told him Tia's rather blunt methods would cause more harm than good.

He could still hear the fear in Sophie's screams when he forced her through the portal. Gulliver never imagined he would ever take away a person's consent where magic was concerned. Growing up with no offensive power, he knew what it was like to feel weak in the face of so much might. And yet, he'd done that to her. Multiple times now. Taken away her choices.

He could only imagine how much she hated him for it.

Two hearths blazed in Gulliver's room, but it didn't stop the damp chill of the Iskalt palace from entering his bones. Maybe that was guilt, or maybe he was just looking for ways to punish himself.

Sitting on the four-poster feather bed, Gulliver stared at the dark blue wall opposite him. Capped with golden crown molding and dusted with the shimmer of thousands of tiny fire opals, the surface of the wall sparkled like a silver haze. Sophie was asleep on the other side of that wall, in the room where his sisters normally slept when they visited.

The wall was thin enough to hear those on the other side. He'd learned that over the years of them giggling late into the night while he tried to sleep. If he spoke right now, Sophie would have no choice but to listen to the words.

There was that word again. Choice.

He scratched his face with the tip of his tail and sighed. So much for getting some rest. Over the next few days, the royal council would arrive to meet with Tia. The last time they came together, Tia decided to send him into the human realm.

It had led them here.

None of the other rulers would be pleased Tia decided to go behind their backs for a mission they had declined to authorize. Their aim had been to remain at a distance while they watched the humans and determined if an intervention was needed. Tia had been a little more hands on than they had agreed.

Sliding from his bed, Gulliver paced the length of the room.

How was he supposed to stay here and sleep when everything threatened to crash down around him? Sophie had barely left her rooms since their arrival, and he was pretty sure she would never speak to him again.

A knock at his door had him turning. It was too late for a messenger or any of the maids. There was only one person who'd wake him in the middle of the night, but when he opened the door, it wasn't Tia standing before him.

Gulliver immediately bowed, as had become his mocking habit. "Your Majesty."

Keir slapped him upside the head with the leather-bound book he carried. "Are you ever going to stop that?"

"Not on your life."

Keir sighed. "Well, are you going to let me in, or do you wish to wake the entire wing by talking in the hall?"

Gulliver held the door open wide and swept his hand out. "Please enter my humble abode, oh great Keir, ruler of nowhere, husband to a stubborn queen, annoying—"

Keir shoved the book at his chest, shutting him up. "I didn't want to wake Tia when she'd finally gotten to sleep."

"But you have no problem waking me?"

"Not really, no."

"Such a grumpy king." Gulliver rubbed his chest where the book had hit and glanced down at the leather cover, his eyes widening. "Is there a message?" This wasn't just any book. It was the journal that let the holder communicate with its twin, no matter the location.

"Do you think I came here just for the pleasure of your company?"

"In fact, most find me a joy."

"I'll just ask the human girl what she thinks of you, shall I?" Keir grunted. "Now, stop being ... you. This is serious."

Everything was serious these days. That was why Gulliver

tried to make jokes, to keep everyone smiling. It was something he learned from his father. Strength came from the knowledge that one could win whatever fight they found themselves in if one could remain positive.

"Have a seat." Gulliver waved to a blue settee in front of the hearth. "I think we need a drink for this." Whatever information his father sent, it had to be important if he did it so soon after his arrival.

"Do you really think—"

"Keir." Gulliver's jaw tightened. "I'm sleeping in a room next to a girl I care about who hates everything about me. There may be a coming war between humans and fae. Foreign royals will soon learn everything Tia instructed me to do behind their back. And right here," he lifted the book, "is a piece of information that can only be bad. Let's stop with the keeping-Gulliver-sober talk for now."

Keir was quiet for a moment, and Gulliver expected an argument. He didn't have a problem with using too much alcohol, only the fact he was a terrible drunk.

"You're right." Keir shifted. "Have any Gelsi berry wine?"

"Only if you don't tell your wife I've been bringing it from Lenya every trip I make. My sister always keeps it around." It wasn't allowed in the Iskalt palace because of the dampening effect Gelsi berries had on the magic of the three kingdoms. Lucky for both Gulliver and Keir, neither of them had that kind of power.

Gulliver pulled out a bottle of the crimson gold Eavha sent him months ago. He poured two glasses and carried one to Keir. The king took it, sighing as he tilted the cup against his lips.

Taking a small sip, Gulliver set his on the low table in front of the hearth and sat in his favorite chair opposite Keir, staring at the book on the table between them.

"You're worried about him," Keir said. It wasn't a question.

"You're not? Is that not the true reason you brought this to me instead of waking Tia?" How many times had she said to both of them that sleep was for those without crowns on their heads?

Keir took a long drink, closing his eyes for that first glorious moment of pure bliss.

But Gulliver saw the battle waging inside the king. If Keir saw there was a message from Griff, he could have read it and reported to Tia, but for whatever reason, he'd known the message was for Gullie, and that probably wasn't good.

"My dad said Toby was okay last time they talked. He was in pain but not in danger." Gulliver couldn't think of Toby without feeling like he'd failed him and Tia both. She'd wanted someone to look after her grieving brother, and all Gulliver did was get distracted with a human woman while Toby involved himself in the very fight they were supposed to prevent.

"But we don't know anything about human bullets." Keir set his cup on the table and leaned forward, head in his hands. "What kind of damage do they do? His shoulder was injured. I've seen enough of those kinds of injuries to know what it means. There are no healing pools in Orleans."

"New."

"What?"

"It's New Orleans."

Keir lifted his head. "Do you think he'd be safer in Old Orleans?"

Gulliver shrugged. "New Orleans seemed pretty old to me, but if Old Orleans is older than the newer Orleans, then I guess it would have to be ancient."

"What am I going to tell my wife if we learn something has happened to her brother in New or Old Orleans?" He gestured at the book on the table between them. Both afraid to look at what news it might bring.

There was a time when Tia and Toby were almost the same fae. They did everything together. He was her anchor, her conduit. Without much magic of his own, he instead strengthened hers. A world with one and not the other was unfathomable. Tia's magic didn't work with the fire plains between them, and that had been the scariest time of her life. "Both Tia and Toby have beaten bigger odds than these."

Gulliver flipped open the notebook on the table. It was full of blank pages, but only the first page was ever used because the messages were erased once they were read. His eyes focused on his father's familiar script, barely legible, and a smile tugged at his lips.

"Can you even read that?" Keir leaned closer, trying to decipher the rough lines.

Following the words with his finger, Gulliver started reading. "Tia, your brother is fine." Both men let out long breaths. "Stubborn but alive. We have bigger problems. Every news show in the human realm has been running a story nonstop about Claude Devereaux and his missing daughter."

Gulliver let out a groan, resting his head in his hands.

"What's a news show?" Keir asked.

"I'm sure Tia has shown you a human feletision. If you hit the right buttons enough times on the black boxes, you can find shows where someone sits at a desk and tells of things happening across their world."

"That can't be real. It takes days for messages to travel."

Gulliver shook his head. As much as Tia tried to explain many of the human technologies to the Lenyan, he still failed to comprehend their technology. "Can you just believe me when I say it's important? That those news programs can reach most humans instantly?"

Keir's brows drew together, but he nodded. "Is there more?"

Gulliver searched for his place among the scribbles most

wouldn't have been able to read. "The fae here are losing hope as the news claims Sophie was abducted by fae."

When Gulliver was in New Orleans, only a certain group believed in the existence of the fae. The rest thought the darkness of years ago was a phenomenon of the weather, and that HAFS members were a little loony in their beliefs. HAFS was only kept in check by other humans' limited minds. But now ...

Gulliver looked up at Keir, his father's final words echoing in his mind.

"What?"

"The humans know. Everything."

Chapter Seven
TOBY

Toby's shoulder throbbed as he flipped through the stations on the television in the tiny living room of the little house he now shared with three other fae. After the last incident with HAFS, most of the fae villagers had picked up the pieces of their lives and gone on about their business as if nothing had happened. Toby was supposed to be recovering, but he wasn't very good at resting.

Scratching at the bandages covering his wound, Toby flung the remote onto the table beside the old couch. There was nothing on, and he was slowly losing his mind.

"Sophie-Ann Devereaux is not dead." A familiar voice blasted from the television. "My daughter was abducted by the fae."

Toby leaned forward, studying the half-crazed Claude Devereaux on the screen. Bleary-eyed, with rough stubble and shadows under his eyes, the man looked as though he hadn't slept in days.

"Mr. Devereaux," the talk show host halted with a dramatic pause, "tell us how the fae lured your daughter right from her hospital bed." The woman stared into the camera, her thick eye makeup made her seem more inhuman than the humans deemed the fae.

"My Sophie-Ann was so sick." Claude choked back a sob. "She's suffered from Leukemia since she was just a little girl, diagnosed right around the time when the world went dark." He glared at the camera, as if to say the diagnosis at that time wasn't just a coincidence.

Xavier came in, letting the back door bang shut behind him. "That crazy son of a chicken thinks Sophie got sick because of the fae." He rummaged through the refrigerator for the last of the beer, cracking open the can with a hiss. "Turn it up; let's hear what he has to say." He crossed into the living room and dropped down onto the sofa beside Toby, propping his feet up on the table scuffed from his boots.

"We were so lucky to get her into the clinical trial, and the new treatment was working. She was feeling better, and it was only a matter of time before she got to come home. We were hoping for another remission."

"Not likely." Xavier scoffed. "Poor Sophie was dying, and he was only prolonging her suffering."

"Did you know she was missing?" Toby glanced at Xavier's profile in the fading light of the sunset outside the window.

"We heard about it just this morning. She disappeared from her hospital room a few days ago. So Claude Devereaux would have everyone believe."

"You don't believe him?" Toby asked.

He shook his head, a sad look on his face. "She was really sick, Toby. I think she died, and he's trying to blame it on us."

"How could a father do that?" Toby couldn't imagine his

own father using the death of one of his children for ... political gain. It didn't make any sense.

"Let's see what story he's come up with." Xavier nodded toward the television.

"My girl was so happy." Claude's eyes filled with tears. "She was about to get married. She was so excited for the wedding to her childhood sweetheart."

"Ha!" Xavier snorted. "Soph couldn't stand that idiot brother of mine and their sham of an engagement."

"I forgot Gabe was your half-brother." Xavier and Gabe's mother was human, but Xavier's father was one of the few full fae in the human realm, and Gabe's father was about as human as they came. Gabe was the oldest of the two, and Toby suspected their mother had married Xavier's fae father once Gabe's father died in the darkness. That had to be a big part of why the two hated each other so much. It couldn't just be about Xavier's magic. Not that he had much to speak of.

"When did you last see your daughter, Mr. Devereaux?" the host asked in a hushed tone.

"The night she was taken. I left her sleeping peacefully. The nurse told me it was a good time to go home for a shower and some rest." He fidgeted in his seat, staring off into the audience with unseeing eyes. "I barely left her side the whole time she was in the hospital. But that nurse ... the male nurse she'd befriended —the one giving her the treatment. I swear, he was fae, and he was trying to get me to leave my daughter so they could take her."

"And why would they want her?"

"They know I'd do anything for my Sophie-Ann." Claude swiped a hand across his eyes. "They knew it would cripple me ... to lose my girl when she was so sick. To deprive her of the medicine that was keeping her alive."

"I'm so sorry for the pain you're dealing with, Claude." The host laid a comforting hand on his shoulder. "I hate to play devil's advocate, but there are rumors. Rumors that say your Sophie-Ann died in the hospital and this accusation of a fae abduction is your attempt to make headlines. To push your agenda."

"That's a lie! Sophie-Ann Devereaux is not dead. And I can prove it."

"How?" The host's eyes sparkled with excitement. "How can you prove such a thing?"

"We have a witness who saw it all happen."

"What did this witness see?"

"A boy. A fae boy ... one I stupidly trusted. He was the one with her when she collapsed, and he got her the help she needed. I let him visit her as much as he wanted." Claude shook his head. "That's the problem with the fae among us. You can't tell what they are until it's too late."

"And this boy just led your deathly sick daughter from the hospital without anyone stopping them?" The host gazed across her audience, an incredulous look on her face and a tone of disbelief in her voice.

"No." Claude shook his head. "This boy had help. An older fae man was with him this time—the one in all the papers. I'd never seen them together before. I even had my people watching over this kid, thinking he needed protection from all the fae out there." He snorted in disgust.

"This man opened some kind of ... magical doorway. Our witness saw it with their own eyes. A seam of violet light split the air, and the boy took my girl from her bed, stepped into that light, and just ... vanished."

"Vanished?" the woman whispered. "Where do you think they went, Mr. Devereaux?"

"That fae boy took my daughter to their world. Our witness heard them talking about a place called Lenya."

"For what purpose?"

Claude Devereaux sat up straight, pulling his shoulders back as he stared at the camera. "To start a war."

Toby shot out of his seat. "I'm going to kill him."

"Easier said than done." Xavier leaned forward, setting his empty beer can on the table. "We've been trying to get close enough to Claude Devereaux to kill him for years. He's surrounded by HAFS people day and night."

"I'm not talking about this idiot." Toby gestured at the screen. "When I see Gulliver O'Shea again, I'm going to strangle him with that blasted tail of his."

"Gulliver? What's he got to do with this?"

"Who do you think took Sophie to Lenya?" Toby's head throbbed harder as he paced the length of the tiny room. "I'm going to kill him. No ... I'll never get a chance to. *Tia's* going to kill him."

"What's a Lenya?"

"It's one of the five kingdoms," Toby said absently.

"I always thought there were only three, and then Gulliver said there was a place called Myrkur, where he's from, so that makes four."

"We just found out about Lenya. Long story." A jolt of sorrow hit him so hard that he faltered in his steps. Toby could never think about Lenya without seeing the expression on Logan's face the moment he died on the fire plains.

Toby closed his eyes, pushing thoughts of the man he should have spent the rest of his life with to the back of his mind.

"I didn't think Gulliver had magic. I know he's an O'Shea by adoption, but how did he open a portal?" Xavier asked.

"He didn't. Uncle Griff did. And he didn't tell me. Why would he not tell me?" Toby raked a hand through his hair in frustration. "Ow!" The bandage covering his shoulder pulled away from the skin, tugging on the stitches the half-fae healer had used to sew his arm back together.

"Watch out, you're going to rip your stitches." Xavier moved to his side, forcing him to sit back on the couch and take it easy.

A wave of dizziness washed over Toby, and he sank down onto the cushions. "He's just made everything so much worse." He reached up with his uninjured hand to scratch the itchy wound beneath his t-shirt, and Xavier slapped his hand away.

"Stop that, you'll get your germs all over it." He tugged Toby's sleeve down and studied the wound with a frown. "Stay right there; we're cleaning this again." He went to the kitchen to retrieve his healing kit.

"Just slap a fresh bandage on it. We've got bigger things to deal with." Like murdering a certain dark fae for taking a human to the healing pools in Lenya. He was almost certain that was what Gulliver meant to do with the sick Sophie. If she was truly on death's door as Xavier claimed, then Toby knew Gulliver was desperate enough to try anything to save her life. Even taking a human to the healing pools the leaders of the five kingdoms had recently ruled to be used only in the gravest of situations, and only with the consent of all five kingdoms.

Gulliver's heart was in the right place, but Toby feared Claude Devereaux was right. He'd just started a war. One that could destroy everything.

"Sit still. This wound isn't faring well, and if you don't want to end up in the hospital yourself, you're going to let me clean it as often as it needs cleaning. Now take your shirt off."

Toby winced at the bowl of hot water Xavier set on the side table. "Fine. Just be quick about it." He tugged the shirt over his head with one arm.

"Healer Maddox sent over a new poultice for you. He doesn't have much magic, but his potions always work." Xavier leaned over him, pressing a steaming hot cloth over the still swollen wound.

"Ouch. That's really hot." Toby pulled away.

"Don't be a baby. The heat will help with the swelling."

"What's that horrible smell?" Toby's nose wrinkled at the awful scent of rotted eggs and other dead things.

"The poultice." Xavier poured rubbing alcohol over his hands and dribbled some onto a clean paper towel. "Hold still. This is the part that hurts." He removed the warm cloth and dabbed at Toby's stitches.

"Watch it, that stings!" Toby pulled away again, but Xavier wouldn't let him.

"It's supposed to. That means it's working."

"By eating off my skin?" Toby winced.

Xavier chuckled. "The big and mighty prince of fae is scared of a little alcohol."

"Well, where I come from, we drink the alcohol, not bathe in it," Toby growled. "And I'm not the prince of fae. I'm just a magicless fae prince. There's a difference."

"Well, we don't have fae princes here. Here we're all just fae." He gently swabbed the wound until he was satisfied it was clean enough.

"I think that's why I like it here," Toby muttered. "Here, it doesn't matter what you can and can't do with magic."

"Huh." Xavier studied Toby's shoulder for a moment before he took up the jar of foul-smelling stuff.

"What's that mean?"

"What?"

"Your 'huh'. You say it like you've got something more to say."

"It's just ... it hasn't escaped me that your sister queen—the one with all the magic—sent two fae with very little magic between them to investigate what's happening to the fae here."

"What of it?" Toby shrugged. "We blend in better. That's all."

"Huh." Xavier bit his bottom lip as he dabbed the muddy poultice over Toby's stitches.

"Now, what?"

"I guess it seems like she probably had more of a reason for sending you two than just your ability to blend in. From what you've told me, any fae can come here and humans will only see them as human as long as they use their glamour. Even Dark Fae like Gullie can look like humans here. So, maybe your queen thinks the fae with the least magic are just as capable as those with all the magic you lack."

"Tia would never judge anyone as less for not having magic." Toby lifted his chin.

"That's ... interesting. Not at all what I would have expected from such a powerful queen."

"Ugh, that can't possibly be good for the germs you keep talking about." Toby plugged his nose to avoid the awful reek coming from his arm. "Am I going to have to walk around smelling like an outhouse?"

"Afraid so. At least until the swelling goes down." Xavier wrapped a clean bandage around Toby's shoulder. "But this is powerful stuff. At least on this side of the veil between worlds. I'm sure your fae healers back home could have you fixed up in no time."

"Not necessarily. There are some magical things that can aid healing, but for the most part, this isn't all that much different than it is at home."

"They just don't smell as bad?" A smile tugged at the corners of Xavier's perfect mouth.

"Yeah, but the smelly ones are usually the ones you have to drink." Toby gave him a hesitant smile.

"All right." Xavier hopped to his feet to clean up the old

bandages. "We've got to get to a meeting later tonight." He moved into the kitchen to wash his hands and toss the rubbish into the trash bin.

"What for?" Toby followed him, sitting on one of the bar stools at the two-seater counter that made up the bulk of the kitchen.

"HAFS is about to make a big move. Maybe their biggest yet in light of Sophie's abduction."

"She wasn't abducted. At least, not maliciously."

"What was Gullie thinking by taking her to the fae realm?" Xavier shook his head.

"Some of that healing magic we don't have that much of." Toby let out a weary sigh. "I'll tell you all about it later. What's HAFS planning?"

Xavier retrieved a bottle of spirits he kept in the freezer and poured them each a drink. "We have fae villages all over the world. We mostly live in small groups in rural areas so we don't call that much attention to ourselves."

Toby gave a mirthless laugh at that. "When we first came here, we thought it was just the one community in New Orleans."

"Well, just like us, HAFS has groups all over the world, and just like us, they are banding together to go after the largest fae settlement in the world."

"Where is that?"

"A place called Los Angeles. It's a huge city about two thousand miles from here."

"And this city is all fae?" Toby asked. He didn't know how far two thousand miles was, but he could imagine it wasn't close.

"No, not entirely, but there are thousands of fae living among the humans there. It's sort of a strange place even for humans. The people there are more accepting of those different from themselves."

"And HAFS is going to attack?"

"Not just attack." Xavier sighed, knocking back the contents of the small glass he'd poured for each of them. Toby quickly followed suit, imagining he needed the fortification for what Xavier was about to reveal. "According to our intel there in L.A., the head of all of HAFS is calling in every member from across the country to assist in the raid on the city. We suspect they're going to try to blow the entire city off the map, and we've got to figure out a way to mobilize there quickly enough to do something about it."

Toby reached for the bottle and poured them another drink. "I might have a way we can do that." He let out a worried sigh before he tipped the clear contents of the small glass into his mouth with a wince. "But there's someone I need to talk to first."

Chapter Eight
SOPHIE-ANN

This infernal castle was freezing. Sophie huddled under her blankets in the oh-so-comfortable feather bed in her huge room in a fantasy fae palace in the coldest lands she'd ever visited. Not that she'd ever traveled anywhere remotely interesting.

She'd never admit it to a living soul, but Iskalt was gorgeous. A land of ice and snow surrounded by majestic mountains, blue skies, and cute villages, Iskalt was a veritable winter wonderland. Sophie would give just about anything to explore more of the idyllic countryside she could see from her balcony window, but she wasn't here on vacation. She was here against her will, and she would never forgive Gulliver for dragging her through another portal.

She didn't understand why they'd taken her to the human realm for a brief stay at the Ohio farmhouse before they traveled by portal to this snowy realm. If she could have gotten away from these fracking fae people there, she could have made her way back to New Orleans.

She rolled onto her side, gazing at the cheery fire cracking in her fireplace. It was magic. Had to be. She'd watched the fire for hours, and it never died down. Never needed more wood. The room itself was warm, and her bed was toasty with soft fur blankets piled on top of her, but the chill she felt came from the inside.

Ever since she woke from the healing pools, Sophie was restless, and a constant chill had settled deep in her bones, as if the magic that had healed her lingered within.

She shoved the blankets aside and grabbed the dressing robe they'd given her to wear over her clothes. She couldn't stay in bed for another minute. Her mind and traitorous body couldn't seem to forget the sensation of so much power rushing through her. Just the thought of it now left her frightened. Frightened of her innermost private thoughts—the ones that admitted to enjoying the touch of magic. The thoughts that yearned to feel it again.

"Enough." Sophie stuffed her feet into slippers warming by the fire. Tossing the robe over her shoulders, she decided to go exploring. Surely there were enough interesting things to see in this castle to keep her occupied until she grew tired enough to sleep.

She wandered along the wide hallway, her slippered feet whispering against the cold stone floors. She studied the old tapestries covering the walls, keeping the chill at bay. Each was a sweeping canvas of history painted in needlepoint, depicting battles of long-forgotten wars. Newer tapestries illustrated times of peace and unity among the kingdoms. Sophie stopped to study a landscape of a valley, half shrouded in darkness and half bathed in brilliant sunlight. Both sides of the valley were beautiful in their own way. Even the darkness seemed friendly and inviting, with its shades of violet and a purple so dark it was almost black. Dark red flowers bloomed in the moonlight right alongside bright white blossoms bobbing in the breeze under the shining sun. On the hill overlooking the valley stood three children of about the same age. A girl with wild strawberry blond hair and a little boy that looked a lot like her. Sophie wondered if this was the queen with her twin brother.

Standing between them was a skinny boy, slightly taller than the twins with knobby knees and dark hair that stood up on end. His tail seemed so natural in this setting; the leaf-shaped tip laid on the girl's shoulder like a human would drape an arm around a friend.

Sophie reached to touch the tapestry, knowing without a doubt if the three children could turn around to face her, one would have the most remarkable cat-like eyes. "Gullie," she whispered, still trying to resolve the image she had of him and his human features with the odd fae features of the man she'd grown to like despite her better judgment. It was thanks to him that she was still here. Still breathing. He was the reason she felt stronger now than she ever had before.

But magic had healed her, and Sophie Devereaux did not trust magic nor the creatures that wielded it.

Leaving her conflicting thoughts behind with the tapestry, Sophie explored the rest of the hall and followed a winding stone stairway up to a tower with circular rooms. Each level revealed a different room. The first was a cheerful warm sitting room that had the look of a well-loved corner of the castle. The second level revealed a room of windows. A solarium with the most spectacular views of the lake and the silvery expanse of snow fields in the moonlight. Sophie stayed there for the longest time, just enjoying the view.

Heavy footsteps echoed overhead, followed by the sound of a slamming door. Intrigued by the silence that followed, Sophie made her way up to the third level of the tower to find a wide-open room with doorways leading to other parts of the castle. The walls here were covered in an array of swords and shields. Even an ancient set of armor stood under a tartan banner of aged dark blue and pale green plaid.

A crash of steel caught her attention, and she went looking for the culprit. Something told her she should go back to her room, but she needed to know who else was up on this restless night. Sophie tiptoed to a door left cracked open.

Cold air rushed in her face as she peeked through the gap. It was a courtyard, high above the rest of the castle, like a bridge between turret towers.

A lone figure raced across the bridge amid the quiet snowfall, his sword glinting in the moonlight and his tail lashing out behind him.

Gulliver. Even among the fae, he was unusual. During her time here in Iskalt, she'd met all manner of creatures. Some with wings and others with horns like beasts of the land. She'd even caught sight of an enormous creature she was almost certain was an ogre. Her father would call them vile devils, but they'd all been nothing but kind to Sophie since her arrival. She'd yet to meet a single fae who wasn't kind. Yet, they had magic that could destroy the human world.

Gulliver moved gracefully, fluid and sure as he practiced with his sword, like a warrior who'd trained all his life with a blade in his hand. Gone was the awkward geek who ate baskets of beignets and said the most ridiculous things.

Tonight, he seemed as though he fought demons of his own, his sword arcing through the air to strike imagined enemies, slaying the shadows of doubt and frustration that plagued his mind.

A gust of wind swept across the courtyard, and Sophie

yelped at the bite of snow and ice that billowed in her face through the crack in the door.

Clapping a hand over her mouth, she took a step back, but he'd already seen her.

"Sophie?" Gulliver dropped his sword at his side.

Sophie didn't stick around for him to ask her what she was doing out of bed. Like a coward, she turned and ran through the nearest door and down a flight of stairs, leaving the tower and its beautiful circular rooms behind.

Sophie darted into a room at the end of the short hallway and closed it behind her, leaning against it. She sucked in a deep breath, urging her heart to slow its pounding in her chest.

"Sophie?" Gulliver's voice reached her ears. Stifling a groan, she moved across the large room, realizing it was a library filled with rows and rows of books, the domed ceiling letting in the moonlight as she gazed around, breathless. It was the most beautiful room she'd ever seen.

"Sophie?" Gulliver stepped into the room, studying Sophie's face. She'd forgotten to hide. Through all the years of her illness, books were her sole companion. She escaped the daily grind of getting out of bed, faking her way through the motions of life until she couldn't take it anymore, and escaped it all through the pages of a book. "Are you all right?"

Sophie nodded. "It's so beautiful." She turned in a circle, taking it all in. The cold fireplace at the center of the room was surrounded by well-worn leather chairs. Soft rugs covered the floors and lamplight illuminated each aisle of books, coming to life as she moved closer.

"This is Tia's favorite room in the castle." Gulliver followed. "I've never been much of a reader, but when we were kids, we came here on the coldest days. She and Toby would read all the human tales while I carved some of the characters they described." Gulliver crossed the room to the fireplace, and flames erupted at his movement. "Here, check this out." He lifted a small figurine from the mantle.

"Is that ... a hippogriff?" Sophie almost laughed until she realized they might actually have such terrifying creatures in Iskalt.

"Buckbeak from *Harry Potter*." Gulliver smiled, placing the heavy figure in her hand. "Brea and Tia loved reading those books over and over. Tia gets a kick out of the humans' imagination for magic. I even carved her a wand she carried around for nearly a year when she was twelve."

"I imagine lots of people have wands here," Sophie blurted.

"No." Gulliver shook his head. "Real magic doesn't work that way. It takes a lot more than wand waving and memorizing spells to create magic."

"Magic scares me." Sophie didn't know why she said it. But with Gulliver, she always found herself being honest with her feelings.

"It used to scare me too." Gulliver placed the figurine back on the mantle. "I grew up without magic, just like you. When I first saw real magic—the kind used in warfare—it terrified me."

"Magical warfare?" Sophie shivered at the thought of such power turned against her people.

"Thankfully we are at peace now. For the first time in generations, all five kingdoms are not only at peace with one another, but we are all genuinely friends, eager for a long and happy future without war."

Sophie moved to look at all the delicate carvings adorning the mantle, so much like the magnolia carving Gullie had made for her. She saw lots of familiar characters from *Harry Potter* and *Game of Thrones*. She even saw a hobbit and five golden rings perched on a wooden stand. Such familiar sights made her smile. It made Gulliver seem that much more ... human. Despite his tail and eyes that marked him as fae.

"This library is amazing." She picked up a book from a side table, where someone had recently discarded it. "*Dune*?" She laughed. "I just read this a few weeks ago." She set it back down.

"King Lochlan ... well, former King Lochlan loves human fantasy and science fiction," Gulliver said. "Most of the human books here are ones he's collected over the years."

Sophie wandered over to a row of leather-bound books on a nearby shelf. She studied the titles. "Human tales?" She lifted her gaze to Gulliver.

"There are hundreds of them. Stories much like your fairy tales."

"Oh. I see." She smiled, turning in a circle to take in the glorious library she could get lost in. "It's just like in *Beauty and the Beast*."

"The beast?" Gulliver's voice took on a hard edge. "I suppose that makes me the beast."

She looked up in surprise, horrified by what she'd said. Of course, he wouldn't get the reference to the library. "No, that's not—"

"It's fine. I'm used to it." Gulliver turned, his tail dragging lifelessly behind him. "I'll just leave you to explore. Though, you should probably think about getting some sleep soon." He stood at the doorway, his back to her. "Just take the hall to the left and you'll find the main stairs. Go up one floor and your room is down the hall to the right. In case you weren't sure how to get back."

With that he left, shutting the door behind him.

Sophie started to follow. She got as far as the door before she stopped. She didn't know what to say to him. She hadn't meant to call him a beast, and she felt awful about it. She didn't see him that way at all. His features were alarming at first, but she was getting used to seeing his true form. His tail suited him, and to her, he was just Gulliver. The kindest man she'd ever met. He'd never mistreated her. Nor had any of his fae friends.

Gulliver O'Shea had saved her life, and she was certain he was in a lot of trouble for taking such a huge risk, bringing a human to his world. And she knew he'd do it all over again just to give her a chance at the life he claimed should have been hers all along.

"Sophie-Ann Devereaux, maybe it's high time you actually learn something about these people before you go judging them all by your father's opinions." Sophie turned back to the library and began searching for answers.

Chapter Nine
GULLIVER

It had been a long time since Gulliver felt self-conscious about the way he looked. Sure, he got stares wherever he went outside Myrkur, but those closest to him never made him feel different. Tia and Toby had been his best and only friends for so much of his life. To them, he was just Gullie.

And yet, that word. He'd heard it before. Beast.

Maybe that was truly what he was. A creature not meant for civilized life. It was how Sophie would always see him. No matter how much he cared about her, she could never truly care for him.

He rolled over in bed, squeezing his eyes shut. "Sleep, Gulliver," he muttered. "You idiot."

But sleep refused to come. That blissful darkness only got louder and louder, a void shouting in his mind.

Beast.

He flopped onto his back, shifting when his tail got stuck. Running a hand down the length of it, he tried to remember the boy who'd never questioned his identity. The one who knew this tail was as much a part of what made him Gulliver as anything else.

"I'm sorry," he whispered, his fingers drifting over the tiny hairs. "You know I don't hate you. Sometimes, I just wish everyone else could love you as much as I do."

Snickering came from the door Gulliver hadn't heard open, a familiar sound.

"Were you just talking to your tail?" Tia's laughter cut through the dark.

"No." Gulliver sat up. "Do you always creep around in the dark like a creep?"

He could practically hear her grin. "Nice use of the human word, but you didn't need to use it twice in the same sentence."

"At least I got it right this time."

"Yeah, but it was pretty funny when you called your mom a creep just for hugging you."

"Don't remind me." He groaned. His mom sometimes didn't have the greatest sense of humor. She took everything so literally, and Brea had already explained to the entire family what a creep was. That didn't go over so well.

Tia walked farther into the room, stopping at the hearth. "*Dóiteán.*" Flames spread in the cold ashes, casting the marble in an orange glow.

"Is there something you want?" A chill raced through Gulliver, and he pulled the covers up to his bare chest. "I was sleeping, you know."

"Like I'm going to believe that."

"It's the middle of the night. Why wouldn't I be sleeping?" Between Keir last night and now Tia tonight, he'd never get any rest.

She crawled onto the bed, pulling back the covers so she could burrow underneath at his side.

"Help yourself." He rolled his eyes.

"Thanks. I will." She leaned back against the feather pillows. "Now, to answer your question ... you're staying next door to a woman you lurve."

"I what?"

"Lurve."

"Stop that."

"Stop what?"

Did she always have to be obnoxious? "Stop saying that. I don't love her."

"I didn't say you did. I believe I said *lurve*."

"Well, I don't."

"You don't what?" She turned onto her side to look at him.

He sighed. "Lurve her."

"Don't be ridiculous, Gulliver freakydeaky O'Shea. Lurve isn't a word."

He was going to strangle her. "You know I don't have a middle name."

"Of course you do; I gave you one when you were twelve."

"That one doesn't count."

"Yes, it does, Gulliver Alexander O'Shea."

"That's better." Gullie grinned into the darkness.

"Ugh, you just wanted me to say it."

"Of course."

A knock at the door drew their attention, but Gulliver already knew who it would be. Where one annoying royal went ... "Come in, Keir."

Keir entered more cautiously, at least pretending he didn't want to invade Gulliver's space a second night in a row. In reality, he'd become way too much like Tia in the last year. "I thought my wife might be here."

"Guys," Gulliver whined, "it's the middle of the night."

"Right." Tia nodded, as if she completely understood. "Keir

is probably tired too." She lifted the edge of the blankets and scooted closer to Gulliver.

Keir kicked off his shoes and slid in next to his wife.

Gulliver rubbed his eyes. "And just why are the queen and king in my bed?"

"You make it sound so wrong." Tia pouted.

"It is wrong. Please go."

"Maybe we should leave him alone," Keir whispered.

Tia ignored him. "Can't I just want to talk to my best friend?"

"No. Not in the middle of the night. And not in my bed."

"Don't be mean." She reached over and pinched him.

Gulliver yelped. "Keir, tell her to stop."

The king rubbed his eyes. "Have you ever once known her to listen to me?"

"He has a point." She jabbed a thumb Keir's way.

Gulliver sank down lower in his bed. Just a few minutes ago, he'd been unable to sleep, and now, all he wanted to do was close his eyes and make the world disappear, make obnoxious royals disappear.

Wanting the attention off him and his dark thoughts, Gulliver turned onto his side to face Tia. "Have you thought about what we're going to do?"

She'd had meetings with representatives from each of the other kingdoms in the last day. He'd wanted to join her, but she didn't let him, saying he was too close to what was going on in the human world. That scared him. It told him whatever plan she'd started crafting, it wouldn't be good for the humans.

Tia and Keir shared a look he didn't trust. "We're here to talk about you, Gul."

"What aren't you saying?" He could see it on her face. Guilt.

"We've been developing a new plan, but I'm not ready to share it yet. Can you just trust me?"

"Tia, I trust you more than I trust myself sometimes. But this is an entire world of humans we're talking about. You can't go all O'Shea on this."

"What's that supposed to mean?"

Keir was the one who answered. "Your entire family has a bit of an impulse problem, love."

"We absolutely do not."

Gulliver and Keir shared a disbelieving look. Lochlan, Griff ... not to mention their mother, the woman who once stole the most powerful book in the world. The only O'Shea Gulliver once considered calm and logical was Toby, but that was out the window now.

"Whatever you say." Gulliver stared at the dark ceiling. "We done here? Some of us would like to get some sleep ... without all of the Iskalt palace in his bed."

Keir started to leave, but Tia clutched his arm, forcing him to stay. "No. Something is wrong."

"What?" He sat up so quickly his head swam. "Is Sophie okay?"

"I'm going to ignore that she was the first one you thought of, despite the fact you apparently don't lurve her. No, you fool." She slapped the side of his head. "Something is wrong with you."

He shoved her hand away when she tried to hit him again. "Thanks for that, but I'm fine."

"You are not. Keir told me you were training tonight. You only do that when whatever is on your mind is worse than the exercise."

"You make me sound like a lazy oaf."

She sighed. "You would just rather play in the snow or pick winter berries than work up a sweat."

Okay, maybe she had a point.

"I have a lot on my mind." And the worst of it was from after he worked with the sword.

She tapped her lips. "Does that explain why you were talking to your tail?"

Keir laughed. "He was what now?"

"Literally talking to it. Like it was a sentient thing."

Gulliver ran a hand down the length of it. "She doesn't mean it, little Gulliver."

"Please don't tell me that's really its name." Keir choked on a laugh.

"Wouldn't you like to know?" It wasn't, but he owed them no answers. If he wanted to talk to his tail, he could.

"I would like to know." Keir looked so confused it was almost comical. "That's why I asked."

"Babe." Tia laid a gentle hand on his chest. "It's a human saying that basically means you're out of luck because he isn't going to tell you."

"Then, why didn't he just say that?" He shook his head. "I will never understand you two and your human phrases."

"Good." She smirked. "Best friends have to have their secret language that husbands can't decipher."

"Uh, Tia." Gulliver couldn't stop his smile. "It's not exactly secret if an entire world of humans understands."

"Stop with the logic, Gulliver," Keir said. "Tia doesn't like it."

She pinched him, but he notably didn't yelp as Gulliver had. Freaking Lenyans and their toughness.

Gulliver drew in a deep breath, thankful that for a few moments, Tia had distracted him from the word circulating in his mind.

Beast.

Beast.

Beast.

He was a beast, according to Sophie.

They all went silent, even Tia, their breath the only sound

between them. As much as Gulliver protested it, he liked having the pair with him. Yes, even in his bed. Tia was his best friend, his other half. They were meant to be together forever, in a purely platonic way. And Keir ... as grumpy as he could be, Gulliver trusted him. Somehow, after everything that happened all that time ago in Lenya, Keir and he had become ... friends?

After a while, a soft snore broke the silence and then a giggle.

"Is he ...?" Gulliver didn't need to finish the question. Keir was asleep. In Gulliver's bed.

Tia nodded, slapping a hand over her mouth.

Keir snorted, making them both jump, and then snored again. Another sound soon joined in, like rushing air.

"Oh no." Tia scooted away from her husband, pressing into Gulliver, her entire body shaking with laughter.

"What?" Then, he smelled it. "He's dying." He scrambled from the bed, falling to the soft carpet spread underneath. The smell followed him.

Tia tumbled out next to him. "Rotting from the inside out."

"That's horrid."

The two of them crawled off the carpet and across the stone until they reached the wall next to the hearth. They leaned against the cool marble, gasping for breath.

"That was awful." Tia bent over, laughing.

"You're the one who married the man."

"Because I lurve him."

He stared at her. "What's it like to be loved back?"

That sobered her, and she sat up straighter. "It's ... confusing."

"That was not what I was expecting."

"My whole life, I've heard all these things about myself. I was wild, uncontrollable, reckless. Gullie, I saved an entire kingdom, and still, everyone was always just waiting for me to mess up. And when I did, it proved them right."

"No, you—"

"I'm answering your question. From the moment I met Keir, he saw me as a formidable foe. When he finally stopped hating me, he didn't lose that respect. In his eyes, I'm capable. He believes in me as I never believed in myself. Like when all the fae in the human realm need my help and I can't figure out how. I'm not sure why he still has faith other than the fact that he loves me. That's why it's confusing."

"It sounds wonderful."

"Oh, it is." Her smile dropped. "Gul, I know something is wrong."

He opened his mouth to speak, but she cut him off.

"Sometimes, I feel like I know you more than I know myself. I can tell when that dark cloud you get is growing. It's not just your normal self-consciousness. What happened? If you tell me again that it's nothing, that you're fine, I'm going to light your entire room on fire."

"In your own castle?"

"Yes. Because I care more about you than I do about a stupid castle. Speak."

A sigh rattled from his lungs. "I'm a beast."

She laughed suddenly and loud before clapping a hand over her mouth. "I'm sorry. I just was not expecting that. What do you mean?"

He told her about Sophie finding him, about the library, and how he assumed they were finally getting along. "Then, she called me a beast."

Tia looped her arm through his, shifting so they were leaning against each other, holding each other up. "What exactly did she say?"

"She said she was a beauty, and I was a beast."

Tia fell quiet, and it took Gulliver a moment to realize she was grinning. "Gul."

"What?" He was starting to lose patience with her.

"Oh, Gullie, Gullie, Gullie." She shook her head. "You, my dear friend, need to read more human tales."

"What are you talking about?"

"It's a story. *Beauty and the Beast.* A young woman falls in love with a man who has been cursed to live in the body of a beast. In his castle he had a fabulous library and she loved to read."

"Oh." Gulliver frowned. "I'm not sure that makes it any better. I'm not cursed and that wasn't my library. This is just me."

"Of course it's you. And what you are is magnificent. If she calls you a beast again, I'm going to ... cut her hair with my magic or something."

"Vicious." He bumped her shoulder.

"Shut up. I don't want to actually hurt the human, but girls love their hair. Anyway, there's something you don't understand about *Beauty and the Beast.*"

A loud and sudden snore came from the bed, and they both looked Keir's way. That had to have woken him up, but he continued to sleep.

"What don't I understand?" Gulliver drew Tia's attention back to him.

She rested her head on his shoulder. "That story has a happy ending."

Chapter Ten
TOBY

This was a bad idea.

Or the best idea he'd ever had.

Toby wasn't quite sure which, but he knew his family was going to be furious either way.

"I still don't understand what we're waiting for." Xavier paced the length of the room. He reminded Toby of Tia with his inability to sit still, his need to be constantly in motion, to know what was happening at all times.

"Then, why are you nervous?" A smile tugged at Toby's lips. He wouldn't admit it, but he found Xavier kind of adorable.

"Because ..." Xavier stopped and blew out a breath. "I have a feeling whatever you've done is going to change everything."

"That's because it is." Toby stood, his lips stretching into a full-blown grin. "I went to see my grandfather."

"Your ..." Xavier rubbed the back of his neck. "I'm confused. How is an old man supposed to help us save an entire city full of fae?"

"Don't let him hear you call him old. Besides, my grandfather ... he's not like others."

"Wait, you're a prince. He's ..." Xavier's eyes widened.

"No. He's my mother's father, so he's not of Iskalt. But he was once the King of Fargelsi." Toby shrugged. "Until his sister locked him away for about eighteen years in a magical dungeon. My mom broke him out, but he didn't want his kingdom back. His illegitimate daughter is now the queen there. She rules with her human husband."

Xavier's eyes went so big they looked like they'd fall right out of his head. "There's a human sitting on a fae throne?"

"Two, actually. My aunt Alona, the Queen of Eldur, is human. But that's not important. What is important is that we need to go."

"Where?"

Toby wasn't sure how to explain Aghadoon to someone who'd only ever seen the much-weakened magic of the half-fae living in the human realm. "My grandfather is going to meet us." It was better if the fae here just saw it. Plus, part of him wanted to see the looks on their faces when a village seemed to just drop out of the sky.

Maybe he was more like his sister than he cared to admit.

That thought sobered him. He'd never let her know this, but he missed her. He hated that she was probably angry with him for staying, angry that he'd involved himself in a war between the humans and the fae. At first, he'd hoped HAFS was just a fringe group that could be beaten easily without risking a war.

Now, he knew the truth. They had to fight for this world.

Xavier was looking at him expectantly, head cocked to the side. He opened his mouth to say something, but a flash of violet light cut him off, and he jumped back, flattening himself against the wall of the makeshift bedroom.

Toby sighed. Here it comes.

Griffin stepped through the portal in a wave of anger, advancing on Toby. So, that answered that question. He knew. Of course Grandfather would get a message to him. Toby had been a fool to think he'd keep it to himself.

"What did you do?" Griff roared.

Toby refused to cower in the face of his uncle. It was rare that Griffin showed his anger over the last few years. He was usually the one calming Father, making sure he didn't go completely to the dark side. Tia would be proud of that human reference.

"What are you smiling about, boy?" Griff's old tactic was still in play. The few times he did get mad, he made those around him feel like children. Namely, his son.

But Toby wasn't Gulliver. He wasn't even the Toby everyone back home knew. That fae died when Logan did. Now, he was a fae with nothing left to lose, one who didn't back down any longer.

"I'm smiling because it's done, uncle. You can't stop it now."

"Like magic, I can't!"

"I'd like to see you try to change Grandfather's mind when it's made up." Not only that, but his grandfather would never obey Griffin. He'd never fully trusted him again after Griffin worked for Regan during the years he was imprisoned. He'd forgiven him, but he'd never forgotten.

Griffin cursed. "Aghadoon is no longer meant to exist in the human realm. It's too dangerous."

"Why?" Toby stepped toward him. "Because it could reveal our existence to the humans? Guess what. They know about us. We're no longer a secret. Our world is no longer a secret. And this is what happens when they see us. They come for us, hunting us down in the very streets we've lived on our whole lives."

"You lived in Iskalt most of your life."

"Yes, but Xavier hasn't. Every other fae or half-fae who is part of this movement hasn't. They've never set foot in Iskalt. This is their world as much as the humans. Yet, they're also our fae. We owe it to them to make sure they can live their lives peacefully in the place of their choosing."

Griffin's anger faded away, and his shoulders dropped. "You still think that's possible? The humans will never stop."

"I don't know what's possible, only that we have to try. Aghadoon is our best shot to reach Lost Angelica in time. I've never been there so I can't open a portal."

"Los Angeles," Xavier cut in.

"Yeah, that."

Griffin sighed. "Where is he meeting you?"

The triumph didn't feel good this time. He was glad his uncle supported him, but he wished they hadn't needed to resort to Aghadoon in the first place. "There's a park near here. It's used for some human game."

"Soccer fields," Xavier explained. "Toby said his grandfather needed a wide-open space, though I'm still not sure why."

Griffin leveled Toby with a look. "You didn't tell him?"

Toby gave him a sheepish smile. "Please let me have my fun."

"You are my kid, aren't you?"

It was a fact rarely spoken of, but Tia had always been the risk taker like Griff. Toby was the opposite. Except lately.

"Wait." Xavier looked between them, confusion creasing his brow.

Toby grabbed his arm and started pulling him toward the door. "Long story. Maybe I'll tell you someday." If they made it through this, he wanted to tell Xavier everything. It hurt to admit that, made his heart ache for the one man who'd known him completely.

But Logan was gone. He wasn't coming back. And Toby had

a long life ahead of him. He didn't want to spend the rest of it in pain, living in the past.

When they got to the soccer fields, it was raining, soaking the ground and turning parts of it into mud. Toby's boots stuck, and he had to pull them free with each step.

He'd never seen as much rain as he had since being in the human realm. In Iskalt, they got lots of snow. Eldur was mostly heat. They'd have basked in this kind of weather. Fargelsi got rain, but not nearly this much.

"There's nothing here." Xavier crossed his arms on his chest and peered across the fields. "Where's your grandfather?"

Griffin blew drops of water off his lips. "Just wait, kid." He shook his head. "I can't believe Toby didn't prepare you for this."

Toby looked at the people behind them, the leadership of their group of rebels. They'd insisted on coming to any sort of meeting, and Toby had no way of stopping them. There must have been twenty half-fae and human allies waiting for something they didn't understand.

"What time is it?" Toby asked.

Xavier pulled out his phone. "One."

"He's late." Grandfather was supposed to arrive ten minutes ago. Had something happened? Did Tia stop him? Or one of the other royals? Brandon O'Rourke was beyond the rule of any kingdom. He made his own decisions and was never late. He listened to the council of kings and queens, but he did not always obey them.

That was why he'd agreed to come here.

It began with a glint of light at the furthest edge of the field, where the open space gave way to beautiful oak trees that stretched toward the sky. The trees started to bend, as if shrinking away from an oncoming storm that would crush them where they stood.

A curse floated on the air—Xavier's only word as two pillars appeared as if from nothing. The rest of the village stayed hidden, but Toby knew it was there. Calm settled in him. Aghadoon was a piece of home. He hadn't visited the village much in the years since he spent way too long there during the battle of Myrkur.

A young man who looked to be in his thirties strolled through the pillars. Toby cast a glance toward Xavier, taking in the shock on his face, the way he looked frozen to the spot.

Totally worth the secrecy.

Griffin rolled his eyes at Toby's glee and walked forward to meet Brandon. The two men shook hands before Brandon turned to Toby, his face softening. "You have a lot of fae worried, young man." He pulled Toby into a hug. "It's good to see you whole."

Toby didn't say he'd never be whole, like he would have not long ago. Because he wasn't sure it was true anymore. "I'm sorry for worrying you."

His grandfather pulled back. "We love you. You know that, right?"

"I do. And I know the fae you're mostly meaning are Tia and Mom."

One corner of his mouth lifted. "Well, you are their favorite fae in all the worlds."

"And if I didn't also know Griffin was keeping them updated on every breath I took, I'd make the trip home to check in."

Griffin shifted. "I'm not ... okay, fine. I have the book. Your mother and Tia just worry."

Brandon shared a smile with Toby. "Your mother and sister will survive. It's all Tia can do not to march her entire army here to help you. That's why she wanted me to come."

That surprised him. Tia was on board with this? No wonder Grandfather was so easy to convince.

"Before we continue ..." His grandfather met Toby's gaze.

"We must be clear on something. I am here to help protect those like us in this realm. Aghadoon will not be used to hurt humans."

Toby nodded. "If we could do any of this without hurting the humans, you know we would. I promise, we only need a ride. But ..." Grandfather wasn't going to like this. "They need to be able to see it. You know the secrets of Aghadoon better than anyone, can you make that happen?"

He sighed. "Are you certain it has to come to that?"

"The humans know everything now, Grandfather. It's time to make a statement."

With a nod, Brandon closed his eyes and muttered a series of Fargelsian words. Without magic, Toby had never learned the language of his Fargelsian heritage. Not like his mother or Tia. Still, he understood what his grandfather was doing. They weren't words to cast a spell. Instead, they lifted one.

The streets of Aghadoon appeared before them, stretching into the trees that now seemed to have moved.

Those surrounding them talked loudly in confusion.

Brandon lifted his voice. "We will explain everything. For now, you may enter Aghadoon. We will meet in the library at the center of the village." He turned to lead them through the pillars with Griffin at his side.

Xavier didn't move, and Toby stayed with him.

"How is any of this possible?" Xavier shook his head.

"You'd be amazed what's truly possible."

Xavier turned to look at him. "I used to think I knew myself, my heritage, but the fae communities in this world just barely scrape the surface. It's a little terrifying."

"Not for you." Toby hesitated for a moment before boldness struck him and he slid his hand into Xavier's, squeezing. "You never need to fear me or what those I know can do. The ones who should be scared are the humans trying to extinguish us in this world."

"Us?" Xavier gently pulled his hand free. "But you're not one of us, Toby. You come from another world, one we can't even imagine. My father was full-fae, but he was born of this world. His power was strong—for one of us. My mother is human. I have magic but it pales in comparison to this." His gaze lingered on the village. "The humans attacking us are the ones I've lived alongside my entire life."

"No matter the world I call home, I'm here now. I've been to war before. Wars I didn't choose, where too much was placed on my young shoulders. I've been kidnapped by evil kings, forced to help my sister wield untold amounts of power. But this time, I choose to be here. Don't fear me." He lowered his voice. "I don't have the abilities of most of my family, but even if I did, I would never hurt this world. I'd never hurt you. Please believe me."

"I do, Toby." He sighed. "And I know we can't win this without you and the ..." he gestured at the village, "things available to you. I'm just scared that at the end of all this, when you go home, we'll lose anything we've gained."

Toby didn't say it, but he didn't plan to leave until he was sure the fae here would be okay.

They joined the others in the library, where Brandon explained Aghadoon, leaving out the more important facts like what that library held and how the village could travel from place to place as needed. They laid out a plan, and by the time they walked outside, the rain had stopped.

A thumping sounded in the distance, coming from the sky. And then, chatter outside the pillars grew louder by the moment.

"Oh no." Xavier ran down the cobblestone street toward the pillars. He stopped at the entrance and Toby skidded to a halt beside him.

"Who is that?" Toby asked. Large vehicles were parked in the nearby gravel lot. A giant metal bird flew overhead, and Toby ducked with a curse. But it was higher up than he'd thought.

People rushed across the field, carrying all sorts of technology Toby didn't recognize.

These weren't half-fae. They weren't the humans who had risked everything to help them. There was too much eagerness in the air, too much hunger.

"News crews." Xavier peered up at the metal bird with its spinning blades. "This isn't good, Toby. We aren't ready for this."

When he'd asked his grandfather to make the village visible, he hadn't considered the humans would react so quickly.

Xavier was right. They weren't ready for this. "Everyone inside the village. Now!" Toby started running for the village square. "We're leaving for L.A. sooner than we thought!"

Chapter Eleven
SOPHIE-ANN

The stuff the fae read about humans was ridiculous. Also, not entirely untrue. Sophie lay on her stomach, chin propped on one hand as she engrossed herself in yet another human tale. This one bore a striking resemblance to roman gladiator history. Though, all from a fae perspective, of course.

The story was told with a bit of a sneer; Sophie could practically hear the disparaging tone in the way the words were written. Humans killing each other for the entertainment of humans.

"What are you reading?" Tia edged into the room, her strawberry blond hair appearing golden in the sunlight streaming through the arched windows. She could be a queen straight out of a fairy tale, with all her determination and strength.

"Oh." Sophie's face heated. She didn't want to trust any of the fae. Didn't want to believe they could be different than her father had always told her. Evil. But then, she spent the last two days reading all about how the fae saw humans. Blood-thirsty, cruel. They thought humans were the aggressors. "Just something I found in the library."

Tia's face lit up, as if someone held a glow stick underneath her skin. "You found the library?" She hopped onto the bed, having no care that it wrinkled her elegant ruby dress. "It's my favorite place in the palace. We all used to spend the coldest days there, reading all the books my dad didn't want me reading."

"Um, like ... the spicy stuff?" Sophie flushed. Somehow, she couldn't see the feisty queen diving into a romance book.

"Spicy?" Tia tilted her head like she didn't understand the question. "No, but Dad always wanted me reading all the boring books on politics and governing. You know, the stuff he thought I needed to know to be queen." She laughed. "I used to get the biggest book on Iskaltian history I could find and use it as a shield to hide that I was really reading the graphic novels and comic books Uncle Griff used to bring us."

"Your father is ..." Sophie wasn't quite sure how to describe the intimidating Lochlan O'Shea.

"Intense? Definitely. Frustrating? Absolutely. But I'll tell you a secret." She leaned in closer. "He's really a big teddy bear."

Tia loved her father. There was affection in her voice, and one corner of her mouth lifted into a small smile. Whatever Lochlan might be, his daughter idolized him.

They're nothing more than barbarians, Sophie. Her own father's voice echoed in her mind.

But were they? The fae she'd met had connections with other fae not unlike the humans formed. They cared for each other, for their kingdoms and their world. There might not be electricity and little technology, but it wasn't because they couldn't develop it.

There was no need. Magic was their technology.

Tia slid the book out from in front of Sophie. "Oh, this one."

Her face darkened. "My Uncle Myles used to tell me all sorts of stories he called human history. There was a time I thought we were so above humans because that kind of thing didn't happen here."

Sophie sensed Tia wasn't done and remained quiet.

"And then, I went to Myrkur." She closed her eyes. "It was a prison realm at the time. Fae fighting fae just to survive. It was horrible." She shivered.

Without thinking, Sophie put a hand on the queen's arm. "I don't think evil has a preference between the worlds."

Tia gave her a tight smile. "You wouldn't have said that when you first crossed the portal."

Wouldn't she? Sophie wanted to believe she hadn't painted an entire species with the same bigoted brush her father had, but maybe that didn't matter. What did was that she hadn't tried to stop him. She'd never told him how wrong it was.

The fae couldn't be trusted. They had magic, and magic was unpredictable. She still believed there was no place for them in her world. But it didn't mean they were evil. She pulled her hand back and used it to push herself up so she was seated next to Tia.

"Why are you here?" Sophie asked.

Tia sighed. "Because I love Gulliver."

Sophie blushed furiously. "I don't need to know that, your Majesty. I ... we never ..." Then, she burst out, "But you're married!"

Tia stared at her for a long moment before doubling over in laughter. "Sometimes, I forget how gloriously obtuse humans can be." She clutched her stomach. "Me? In love with *Gulliver*? Are you mad, human?" She wiped tears from her eyes.

Fury wound through Sophie. What was so funny about it? Was Tia embarrassed by her friend? How dare she laugh about that? "You ..." She couldn't get the words out past her anger.

Tia sobered when she caught sight of Sophie's face. "Oh ... oh no. Sophie, you have to understand. Gulliver is the best man I have ever known. That includes my husband, and Keir is very well aware of this fact. He even agrees. Our friend is kind and brave. Few give him the chance to show who he truly is without prior judgment, and it breaks my heart. But as wonderful as Gullie is, he is part of me. As close as my own brother. Family. That is why I laughed. You'd get the same reaction out of him, you know."

The rage abated, but tendrils of it sat unsettled in her stomach. She wanted nothing to do with Gulliver, yet the thought of another disparaging him, writing him off ... it hurt.

Tia, collecting herself, drew in a breath. "Anyway, as you humans say. I love Gulliver. That's why I'm here. You have to understand something about him. He has spent most of his life looking for the few fae who'd accept him. Sometimes, I fear he doesn't even accept himself. And you ... you're not helping."

"What do you mean?"

"You want to show us that you aren't your father?"

Sophie nodded.

Tia fixed her with a stern look. "Then, start with Gulliver. Trust him. I promise you won't regret it."

Whether she'd regret it or not, Sophie wanted to do as Tia asked. More than anything. She just wasn't sure if she could.

A knock sounded on the door.

"Enter," Tia called.

A young man in castle livery pushed into the room and bowed. "Your Majesty, I've been sent to warn you that your uncle has returned."

"Warn?" Sophie asked.

Tia's lips twitched. "Probably my husband's exact words. Griff tends to cause trouble."

"I thought he helped you?"

"Oh, he does. But I prefer it when he causes trouble for other fae." Tia jumped to her feet with surprising agility in the puffy dress. There was a grace to her, that of an athlete. From a few of the stories Sophie had read about the famed, Tia when she was just a beloved young princess, she knew it was the movements of a warrior.

Tia didn't ask Sophie to stay back, so, out of curiosity, she followed the queen. They found King Keir in the throne room with Gulliver, Griffin, and Brea. All four of them had their voices raised in argument.

No one noticed the arrival of the two women.

Griffin carried a bag that looked very much like an oversized purse on one shoulder. His lips pressed together as his eyes found Tia. "About time, little queen."

Tia grimaced at the title. "And what is your place in this kingdom? Oh, right. You don't have one, uncle."

Griff flashed her a smile. "If that's the case, I'll just return home to my wife. She's the only one I actually enjoy arguing with besides your mother."

"What have you done?" Tia sighed.

Sophie leaned against the wall, hoping no one else noticed her watching them. She eyed Gulliver, the way he seemed to hang on every word his father said. It was just like Tia's love for Lochlan. Sophie couldn't help wondering if that could have been her relationship with her own father had he never joined HAFS.

It was an old organization, one that had its hands in so many things over the years. But it wasn't until her father took over the New Orleans sector that it changed so many lives in her city.

She feared her father, feared for him. And yes, she loved him. But respect? Had there ever been that between them? The kind of trust she saw here just didn't exist in her life.

Griffin pushed a hand through his wily red hair. "It wasn't me this time."

"Is Toby okay?" Brea asked.

"He's fine, Brea."

"But is he safe?" she demanded.

"For now." Griffin nodded.

"I'm starting to think there isn't a safe place anywhere for us in the human realm. You have to convince him to come home."

There was something Griffin didn't want to tell the queen's mother. Sophie could see it in the way he wouldn't look at her.

"Uncle Griff." Tia gripped his arm. "Just tell her."

"He's in Aghadoon ... just outside a human city."

A round of curses issued from Keir and Brea. Sophie watched Brea's face morph from fear to anger and back to fear. But Sophie didn't understand what this Aghadoon was or why it mattered.

"I'm going to murder my father." Brea paced the length of the room. "How could he involve that village in human affairs?" She whirled around to face her daughter. "Did you know about this?"

Tia nodded. Moving to stand beside her husband. "I gave the order." She tilted her chin up, a powerful queen standing up to the woman who raised her.

"But it's not just human affairs, is it, Brea?" Griffin turned toward her, a softness in his eyes he didn't hold for anyone else in the room. "They're killing fae. Our fae."

"They've been killing fae in the human realm for longer than we know." Tia's shoulders dropped. "It's time we put an end to it, but we cannot start a war."

Brea ran a hand through her dark hair, a deep sigh seemed to deflate her like a balloon as she locked her gaze with Sophie's. "I don't think you fracking fae will ever understand how truly terrifying magic is to humans."

Some of the tension left Sophie's shoulders. Maybe the

former queen really did understand what it was like for her to wake up in this world of magic and fantasy come to life.

"I just hope my father has enough sense to keep that village hidden."

"There's a city in the human realm," Griffin said. "I think it's called Lost Angels."

Brea stopped moving. "You mean Los Angeles? I wanted to go there as a kid, but my human parents weren't exactly the family vacation type."

"Yes." Griffin waved away her correction. "It's full of those with fae blood. There are more of them than we could possibly imagine. Thousands just in that one city."

"Thousands?" Confused murmurs erupted around the room. Keir and Tia shared a look of alarm.

"Yes, and I'm afraid we're only at the beginning of what's to come." He dug into the bag on his shoulder and pulled out a folded newspaper, handing it to Tia. "They've done it."

"Done what?" Brea took the paper, opening it so she and Tia could read.

"Oh my," Tia whispered, covering her mouth.

"What?" Gulliver looked confused and slightly scared.

His father met his gaze. "Apparently, we've been outed to their whole world. We aren't just a HAFS conspiracy theory anymore. Human news shows, these odd papers, their governments ... the people now know about us. And they believe it."

Silence followed his words. Sophie could hardly breathe. She'd never imagined her father would do it. Revealing this secret to the wider public meant taking the battle to the next level. He was really going to war.

"So," Keir started, "this piece of paper told you that?"

Brea shook her head. "It tells us that Sophie-Ann Devereaux has been abducted by the fae." She held up the page to show a giant image of Sophie, looking as sick as she ever had.

"I ..." Sophie's eyes widened as she caught the headlines of the *Washington Post*. Her picture took up most of the front page above the fold. Her hand went to her mouth in shock.

HAFS leader's daughter abducted from her death bed by the fae living among us.
An exclusive interview with Claude Devereaux.

"No." She shook her head. But the paper wasn't wrong. The fae abducted her, but it was to save her life. "I'm sorry." It was all she could think to say after her father destroyed any freedom these people had in her world.

Tia snatched the paper, her eyes widening. "We should create one of these news pamphlets. I've seen these many times. The humans get great benefit from it. Our scribes could get to work on it. This is so cool."

"Tia," Gulliver snapped, not taking his eyes from Sophie. "Focus."

"Right, sorry."

Gulliver walked toward Sophie, and she searched for an escape, a place where she could disappear. Surely a magical palace could offer her that.

Her father had always worked so hard to keep her illness a private thing between them. She'd never wanted other people to know and he'd done what he could to protect her from prying eyes. Now, an image of her with a breathing tube and feeding tube was out there for everyone to see. And he was giving interviews with the famous news outlets? It didn't make sense.

Unless ... he wasn't calling the shots anymore.

The story was in the *Washington Post*, which could only mean one thing. This wasn't coming from the New Orleans sector of HAFS bombing single buildings to drive out the fae. They'd connected with the other chapters of HAFS. As far as she knew, they had large groups in all the major cities across the country, probably other countries as well.

If they all came together, and they had the backing of the mainstream news, the fae stood no chance. Not alone.

"Sophie." Gulliver's voice was so soft, so understanding. Yet, she couldn't look at him without seeing the devastation coming for those like him in her world.

"I'm not feeling so well." Sophie ducked around him, running for the exit. She didn't draw a breath until she reached the empty hallway outside. A door opened, and she sprinted past it, not wanting whatever servant it was to witness the tears streaming down her face.

She slammed the door behind her after entering her room and flopped down on the bed.

"Mom," she whispered through her tears, "I don't know what to do."

Her mom was dead because of the fae, because of their connection to the human world. Yet, she knew her mom would never blame them. She'd always seen the good in everything, everyone.

When had Sophie forgotten that? For so long, she'd let her father's anger and fear poison her.

"Tell me how to help, Mom." Help her father. Help create peace. She didn't want to lose anyone to a war that made no sense.

She buried her face in a pillow, and it grew damp beneath her cheek. But her tears didn't wash away the doubt nor loosen the knot pulling tighter within her.

Chapter Twelve
GULLIVER

"What are you still doing here?" Tia turned on Gulliver like a dragon from one of the human tales who suddenly found a knight trying to steal their gold. Her eyes blazed with the heat of her magic.

Gulliver's brow creased. "Uh ... standing."

Thankfully, Griff came to his defense. "Leave Gulliver alone, Tia." He draped an arm across his son's shoulders. "He's not the reason you're upset right now."

She stomped toward them. "Are you serious?"

"Tia." Keir reached for her, but she swerved out of his reach. "Don't take your frustration out on us. We're on your side. Let's figure out how to help the fae in the human realm without starting a war."

Tia rubbed her eyes. "I'm surrounded by idiots," she murmured.

Brea stepped up to her side, leaning over to whisper.

Though, it was loud enough for them all to hear. "They're men. They don't even know what they don't know."

Gulliver looked from one woman to the next, trying to figure out what they could possibly mean. In his opinion, Tia's dad was one of the smartest men in Iskalt. He'd been the one to realize Tia was meant to be queen.

The two women continued to chat in low voices before Keir let out a sound that was half-growl and half-sigh. "Would you care to inform us of our deficiencies?"

Tia's jaw tensed, and her eyes landed on Gulliver. "That girl, the human you so carelessly brought into this mess, is now both the problem and the solution."

"How?" He didn't see how Sophie could do anything about the current issues.

Tia pressed her lips together, studying him before continuing. "First, I must point out that she didn't choose this. You chose it for her."

"She was going to die."

"Yes, I know. But that doesn't change the fact that you and Griff made her a pawn in her father's schemes. He is using her supposed abduction—"

"Not supposed," Griffin interrupted. "We actually did abduct her."

"Quiet. Anyone who is not a queen does not have the right to speak at present." She clasped her hands behind her back, the friendly, goofy Tia falling away. In her place was every bit of the ice queen she'd shown herself to be. "Don't you see? Sophie is further proof we exist. When she goes home and she's seen by the humans, healthy and alive, they will know without a doubt that this drivel is, in fact, not drivel at all." She took the paper and shook it. "We can't undo this unless we keep her here against her will and I'm not prepared to do that. She has to go home to her people. And when she does this will all escalate. Yet, Sophie is also our only connection to the human fighters."

"I don't—"

Tia shut him up with a look. "When I asked what you were still doing here, it's because I expect you to fix your mess. I'm starting to like that woman, and I'm not unhappy that she is alive, but it has created a not-so-small problem for us, and you must do everything in your power to make sure she is on our side."

"Tia ..." Gullie paused. "Am I allowed to speak?"

She nodded.

"Don't think for one second I'm unaware of what I've done, of the risk I have added to our lives. But Sophie ... she's not just a player in your games. You're right that I took her choice away before. I won't do it again. I won't use her. I know you worry for Toby, and I do too. I would lay down my life for him in a heartbeat. You know that. Yet, I will not ask her to do the same. I'm sorry." He turned, hoping she'd call him back, and at the same time hoping she wouldn't.

There had never been anyone in his life he trusted more than Tia, except maybe Griff. They were his people. But this wasn't about trust. At least, not between them. He needed someone else to trust him now.

His feet knew where to take him before his mind caught up, and he found himself standing outside Sophie's door. A maid scurried past, dipping into a curtsy at the sight of him, but he focused on the door, wondering if she'd finally speak to him.

Lifting a hand, he knocked softly against the image of the carved wolf. And waited. There was no answer, and he almost knocked again but thought better of it. If she didn't want to speak with him, he wouldn't force her.

But he hoped she would listen.

His own door was only feet away, and when he entered the

room, he walked straight to the far wall, the one he shared with Sophie. The same wall he yelled through to his sisters when they stayed and he needed them to go to sleep or just be quiet and let him sleep.

Inevitably, that alerted them to the fact he was awake, and they'd show up to crawl in bed with him moments later. Their wings constantly got in the way, and they hogged all the covers, but after living his earliest years with little family, he'd never have given it up.

Did Sophie have anyone like that? While he'd observed her in New Orleans, he hadn't seen anyone who appeared to care about her. Sure, she had her father, but did he ever hug her? Did he tell her he was proud of her for fighting so hard to defeat her illness?

Would he have broken someone out of a human healer's ward and taken them through a portal to keep them alive, just because she asked?

The truth was, no matter the hardship in his early life, Gulliver was lucky to have Griffin, Riona, and his sisters.

He just needed Sophie to know she wasn't alone.

Pressing his back to the wall, he slid down until his butt hit the stone floor. A chill raced through him, and he wished he was closer to the hearth, or at least the rug that surrounded the bed.

He pushed his discomfort aside and leaned his head against the wall, gathering every ounce of courage and compassion he possessed. "Sophie-Ann?" His voice was soft, but he knew this room enough to know it reached the person on the other side of that wall.

Still, she didn't respond.

He drew in a deep breath, closing his eyes and focusing on the beating of his heart.

"I was twelve years old the first time I thought I was going to die." He wasn't sure why this story came to mind or what any of it meant in regard to their current problems. "I got trapped in a fortress in Myrkur that was owned by a favorite lord of the king's. This lord liked to keep us in line by withholding food, forcing us into destitution. I lost my parents when I was too young to remember them, but Griffin had looked out for me since the day he set foot in the prison realm. That was what Myrkur used to be. A desolate place of perpetual darkness and never enough resources to go around."

He could see it now. Kavek's giant walls, the river that ran right under them, and the village protecting them from the desperate. But Gulliver never thought about the risks, not then. "I'd thought myself brave, but that's the thing about desperate fae. We will do anything, risk anything, for some kind of hope. I'd never had much of that in my life, not until that night when Griffin showed me the one thing I needed to know."

He paused, taking a breath as images flashed through his mind.

"What was that?" Sophie's voice was low and sweet, curious.

Warmth spread through Gulliver, a kind of precious victory. Not the type one gained in a game, but the kind that was earned and protected. "What was what?"

"The thing you needed to know?"

He touched the wall, imagining she did the same. "He was the first to show me I wasn't alone. That as long as he was there, I'd never be alone again." He pictured her sitting nearby, her pose mirroring his, her heart pounding just as heavily in her chest. "Sophie," he whispered before realizing she probably hadn't heard that. "I didn't bring you here because of who your father is."

When she didn't respond, he continued. "I didn't even know you were my mission's daughter when we met in that cafe."

"Your mission." She sighed.

That hadn't been the right thing to say. "I liked you. A lot.

When I learned you were dying, I wanted to help you. Not so we'd have access to Claude Devereaux's daughter, not even so you'd stay in my life. It was that same hope Griff once gave me ... I wanted you to have it too. I just thought ... you deserved a chance. You deserved to see both worlds for the magical places they are. Whether or not I got to be there when you did, I just needed to know you would have that chance."

Gullie leaned forward against his knees, clasping his hands together as he tried to get the rest out. "But I'm sorry." His voice wavered. "Tia is right. I took the choice away from you. Now, you're in this. All over the human news, in their minds. I know all of this is beyond anything you'd have wanted, but as sorry as I am for the way it happened, I wouldn't take any of it back, not if that meant losing you."

"Gullie." One word. That was all he got.

"I can keep going. You don't need to respond, to accept my apology or forgive me. I know that you will most likely hate me for the rest of your hopefully long life. It's something I will live with. But you need to know, Sophie, that I liked you. Not for my mission. Not because you were sick and needed help. I liked you with your clumsy hands dropping plates of beignets, that tentative smile you have when you think no one is looking and you aren't sure if life deserves a smile. I liked your kindness, and your pretty blue hair. And I liked how you saw me. Even if none of it was real because my fae features were hidden, I enjoyed how you looked at me like I was good and right. Not an abomination."

His tail curled up his spine, the tip thumping in agitation. It didn't like the feeling of being an abomination either.

"In your eyes, I was just like everyone else."

He fell into silence, wishing he could take every word back and knowing he'd done all he could to make Sophie see what she could be. A force for peace. Even if he hadn't said it outright, hadn't asked for it, it was in those words. There was a way for fae and humans to understand each other.

"Sophie." He brushed the wall with his tail. "Please. Say something." Anything.

The quiet stretched for so long that his back ached from sitting on the floor. He didn't know how much time had passed by the time he finally decided to stand and prepare for bed. Nearby, the moon rose outside his window, casting the dark shadows away. In Iskalt, this was when their magic rose, when the power was at its strongest.

For Gullie, life without active power meant having one more thing that placed him on the outside in Iskalt.

He'd given up on hearing from Sophie again and had just removed his shirt when her voice reached him.

"Gullie," she said.

He reached the wall in two long strides and set a palm to it, waiting.

"You were never like everyone else."

And for once, he believed that wasn't such a bad thing after all.

Chapter Thirteen
SOPHIE-ANN

Sophie curled up on a window seat in a remote corner of the library she couldn't get enough of. Bright sunlight illuminated the stained-glass window depicting some long-forgotten queen of Iskalt. It was a strangely warm place, as if some magical force had created the optimal reading nook with the most comfortable cushions and perfect lighting.

The human tale book sat propped against her knees as she studied the fantastical drawings of what fae thought human cities looked like. She'd laughed out loud so many times her sides ached. Instead of steel skyscrapers, the fae illustrator had drawn enormously tall, slender, tent-like structures with stairs wrapping around the outside. It reminded Sophie of a kid's book. Instead of cars, there were carts sitting on streets with nothing to pull them, and men and women walked along sidewalks in the most ridiculous outfits Sophie had ever seen. People wore jeans with long skirts and shirts with ties or plumed hats with hooded sweaters and what looked to be bloomers. Some wore modern sneakers and others wore fashionable shoes from centuries ago.

She'd looked for a copyright page, but there wasn't one. Only a single title page with the year it was crafted. The book was only thirty years old. Sophie didn't know why, but that just made it even funnier.

This book wasn't like the others she'd read. It wasn't a work of fiction so much as an encyclopedia of everything the fae knew about humans, which was next to nothing. As she read about how human technology was their special kind of magic and speculations on how computers worked, she realized there was something innocent and child-like about the fae imagination.

She gazed out the stained-glass window at the snow fields, distorted by the colored glass. It was kind of like the way the fae and humans looked at each other through the invisible barriers that separated them. They were so vastly different in so many ways that it was difficult for one person to understand the other. Yet, in all the ways that truly mattered, weren't they the same?

Sophie snapped the book closed and sat up. She didn't know Tia very well, but the young woman was Queen of Iskalt and well respected among the other nobles from what Sophie had gathered. The queen was cheerful and friendly, with a very strange sense of humor. But there were a few things Sophie knew for certain about Queen Tierney. She loved her family and her people, and she only wanted what was best for them. She also respected humans and their differences. She was loyal, and she wanted to avoid an outright war with the humans.

None of those things were evil qualities, though Sophie had no qualms that the powerful woman was a force to be reckoned with when pushed too far. The idea of Tia's magic scared the wits out of Sophie.

"But can I trust her?" She chewed on her bottom lip. Matters at home were escalating quickly if the news media was talking about fae in any serious tones. That she had somehow become the face of HAFS across the United States was alarming. The outlandish claims her father had made about her ... abduction couldn't continue.

She had to get home. As soon as possible. Before things escalated beyond the point of no return.

Tossing the book aside, Sophie went in search of the queen.

"Now, there's a sentence I never imagined would cross my mind." She pulled the heavy woolen wrap around her shoulders in the drafty halls. She was quickly learning her way around the palace, and the fae were all too eager to point her in the right direction.

Sophie found Tia in a spacious courtyard just outside a study that looked as though a paper factory had exploded across the gilt-edged desk. The queen stood at the center of the circular courtyard, beautiful gray and white plumed birds surrounding her as she fed them bits of bread from her hand.

"They're cute." Sophie approached slowly. The fat little birds waddled like penguins around the queen, searching for discarded crumbs they might have missed.

"They're like greedy little chickens." Tia wiped her hand on her pearl-gray dress.

"They seem to adore you."

"Don't you have snowbirds where you come from?" Tia asked.

"Not like these little guys. They look like a cross between a pigeon and a penguin."

Tierney laughed. "I think you're right." She shooed the fluffy birds away, moving to sit on a wrought-iron bench and patting the seat beside her.

Sophie joined her, tucking the wide skirts of her dress around her legs before she sat.

"If only we could wear jeans and hoodies." Tia gave a longing sigh.

"Your dresses are so pretty, though."

"Pretty, yes. Comfortable, not in the slightest, but my fae expect their queen to look like a queen, though my mother did set a precedent for casual Friday." Tia laughed again. "Humans definitely have superior comfortable clothing."

"I can't disagree with you there."

The snowbirds had waddled their way back toward the bench, and Tia pulled out a handful of breadcrumbs, flinging them on the snow-covered courtyard. "We need a plan, don't we?"

"We?" Sophie looked up at her in surprise.

"Yes, we. I'm responsible for my fae. Since I was the one who sent Gullie and Toby on a reconnaissance mission to find out what was happening in your world, it's kind of my responsibility to fix it. And your face is all over the human news, so you're as big a part of this as I am."

"You need to send me home," Sophie blurted. "As soon as possible."

Tia nodded. "And what will you do when you get there?"

"My father and his people need to see I'm alive and that I've been healed and returned to them whole."

"And then what?" Tia asked. "Won't that just add fuel to the fire?"

"Well, maybe ... but maybe the violence will stop once they see the fae are not our enemy."

"Is that all it will take?" The queen gave her a skeptical look.

"I need to speak to my father." Sophie sighed. "He will listen to reason. He isn't the only man in charge of HAFS, but his voice holds weight. I will show him I was not abducted against my will, even though that is exactly what Gullie did."

"His heart was in the right place." Tia's mouth curved into a smile.

"I would like to have seen how he and his father managed to get into the hospital without causing a scene."

"Oh, I'm certain they caused trouble somewhere along the way." Tia laughed, and Sophie couldn't get the vision of Gulliver and Griffin attempting to break her out of the ICU out of her mind.

But her smile quickly faded. "HAFS isn't only killing fae. They're killing humans too in their attempt to flush out those with magic. I don't disagree with their mission. Magic has no place in my world, but I can't condone that kind of violence against any people."

"Can you tell me why humans fear us so much?" Tia asked softly. "The ones who believe we exist."

"Like your mother said, magic ... is a terrifying thought for most of us." Sophie fumbled with the soft edges of her wrap, unable to meet Tia's steady gaze. "That an entire race of magical beings walks among us with the power to destroy us at their fingertips isn't something most humans can just accept and move on with their lives."

"To my knowledge, our magic has never been turned against humans in any significant manner. There must be a way we can coexist peacefully."

Sophie's jaw dropped, and her hands curled into fists. "No significant way?" Her words came out in a harsh rasp as anger coiled in her belly. "What about the months of darkness we experienced? Magic was behind that disaster."

Tia blinked at her in confusion. "I'm sure it must have been alarming, but a little darkness never hurt anyone."

"Our world went dark overnight, Tia." She clutched her fists to her side. "We just woke up one morning, and the sun didn't shine. It was there in the sky like always, we could see it, but the darkness of your world choked out the light and chased away the warmth." Angry tears burned Sophie's eyes, and she struggled to keep her composure. "Of course it was terrifying. We had no idea what was happening. Do you even know how close we came to losing everything? Our society was crumbling before our eyes, crime rates soared, and people thought it was the end of the world. That our sun was dying. Our farms were failing because there wasn't enough sunlight for them to grow. People quit their jobs to be with their families, and stores closed. The supply chain broke down, and there wasn't enough food or essentials no matter how much money you had. It was anarchy. Families were starving, and people were dying, Tia. My mother died because of fae magic."

"I see." Tia's hands lay clasped in her lap. "I suppose I never thought about what that must have been like for the human world. I was very young then. But it was mine and my mother's magic that ended the darkness in your world. I guess we were so focused on fixing it and ending the battle against the Dark Fae king that when all was righted and King Egan was defeated ... we went back to our lives."

"In many ways, humans are still trying to get their lives back," Sophie said. "So many humans are struggling to find jobs now. We are still hurting, Tia. From an event that had nothing to do with us. My mother died during the worst time of my life, and I still don't understand why any of it happened."

Tia turned toward her, catching her gaze in that queenly way she had. "I won't lie to you, Sophie. The fae have a dark history of wars and death. My ancestors have done some really terrible things I am too ashamed to tell you about. During the darkness that invaded your world, we were at war with a very bad man who sought the kind of power no individual should ever have. But we stopped him.

"And now, the five kingdoms have reached a place where we

are done looking back on past wrongs. We are finally at peace and striving to do better as we move forward. I want the same things for your people."

"How can we fix this?" Sophie wanted to trust that Tia would make things better for everyone. She just couldn't see how that was possible now.

"I'm so glad you said 'we'." Tia smiled. "We're going to start by sending you home." She gripped Sophie's hand in hers. "But if I do, can I trust you? I don't expect you to choose my side over the humans. I expect you to choose the path to peace between our worlds. Can I count on you for that?"

Sophie nodded. "I will do everything I can to facilitate peace, but in my world, I'm not a queen. I'm just a sick girl without much to offer. I can't force them to listen."

"You have more to offer than you think." Tia laughed. "Just ask Gulliver." She elbowed Sophie playfully.

"What's the plan for when I return?" Sophie ignored the flush that bloomed across her cheeks.

"We could take the time to agonize over a plan and put it into motion, but in my experience, plans never work out the way you expect, and more often than not, they go flying right out the window almost immediately." She stood, grabbed Sophie's hand, and pulled her up.

"Then, what's the alternative?"

"Winging it." Tia shrugged. "We're going to make it up as we go, hoping we don't die before we can return your world to the way it was before we messed it up. Come inside my study. I have a magical object I want you to get acquainted with. It's not scary, I promise, but it will give us a way to stay in touch after you've returned to the humans. We don't have cell phones in the five kingdoms, but we have other ways of staying in touch. Think of my little spelled journals as our way of texting each other. Same technology, different execution."

Chapter Fourteen
GULLIVER

Gulliver thundered down the stairs and across the hall, peeking into rooms and searching every hiding spot he'd ever found his father in. The man was better at avoidance than confrontation, and spending so much time in this palace where both Tia and Brea lived meant a lot of the latter.

But there was only one reason he ever hid from his son.

There was something he couldn't tell him.

Over the years, as Griffin relaxed into a calm life of peace, he lost certain skills he'd needed in previous fights. Like the ability to keep a secret from his children. His face was an open book, the magic in his eyes blazing whenever he was trying to hold something back.

So, he hid.

"Dad!" Gulliver called.

A servant carrying two giant candlesticks he was probably taking to be polished nodded toward the library. Why did everyone choose the same place in this enormous castle to hide?

"I know you're in there." Gulliver tried the handle, but he couldn't push the door open. Something was blocking it. "Come on, Dad."

"Go away." His muffled voice came back through the solid wood.

"Absolutely not. Whatever you're keeping from me, you might as well come out and say it. You know it's only a matter of time."

"You won't be able to get in here. I sealed the door with my magic."

Not for the first time, Gulliver experienced the frustration of having no active power. "Well, then, it really is only a matter of time." Griffin's magic would only last until dawn, which was no more than an hour away. With a shrug, Gulliver sat against the wall, making himself comfortable.

The palace never slept. At night, while Iskaltian magic was alive, fae bustled around, using their power in small ways and large. To clean, to cook, to duel. It was a sight to see, but also incredibly annoying for those without Iskaltian blood who preferred to sleep when the moon was high in the sky.

He'd woken up in the middle of the night with the sense that something was wrong. When he checked his father's rooms, they were empty.

"Gulliver," Griffin yelled, "if you don't leave right now, I'm telling your mother."

Gulliver snorted. "Riona is more likely to punish you than me." She'd recognize immediately what he was doing. Griffin wasn't exactly a reader, not like his brother. The library was only a means to an end for him.

"True," Griffin grunted. "Can you just please walk away right now? I'm begging you."

"Begging? Well, now, I really need to know."

A sigh echoed in the hall, and Gulliver looked up to find the door open and his father standing there in a rumpled burgundy linen shirt and brown pants. He wore no shoes, and that right there was the explanation. There was only one person who'd risk Griffin's wrath waking him from bed and not even giving him time to dress.

Gulliver stood to face him. "What has Tia done now?"

"What?" He started walking, looking away to hide the lies revealed so plainly across his face. "Nothing. You should go back to bed, son. There is nothing that concerns you tonight."

Griffin's words might have told Gulliver to leave, but his steps turned in the direction of the throne room. He was leading him there.

"Why are you lying to me?"

"I'm not." He blinked rapidly, clenching his fists at his sides.

Gulliver rubbed his brow. "How in the magic did you ever fool Egan? Or Reagan? You've duped two evil rulers, and now you can't tell a single lie to your son."

Griffin's step faltered. "This isn't the same thing."

"Why not?" He'd seen Griffin fool the most conniving minds, but not in recent years.

"There is a difference between lying to those who mean nothing to a fae and those one cares about." He veered into the throne room, cutting off further conversation.

But he didn't need to say anything else. He'd brought Gulliver right to the answer.

Sophie.

She stood with Tia and Lochlan, the three of them speaking in low voices.

"No." Gulliver's presence stopped them. "This isn't happening."

"Gul." Tia frowned. "I'm not sure what Griff told you, but—"

"Nothing. He told me nothing because you obviously made him keep a secret. From me. Since when do we do that, Tia?"

"Since you wouldn't agree to this."

"You're right. I wouldn't. I don't." His eyes slid to Sophie's. "You're going back. To him." To her father, the man who wanted to exterminate the fae. "I should have known. You'll never see us as anything other than evil."

"I—"

He cut her off. "Have you been hoping for this the entire time? To return home and join the war against us? I'm sorry we're not precious humans, Sophie-Ann, but it doesn't make us worth any less than you."

"That's enough." Tia's glare cut into him. "Gulliver O'Shea, this isn't like you."

"How are you so sure what I'm like anymore?" He hadn't meant to say the words, but he couldn't call them back now.

He expected Tia to respond with her usual vigor. Instead, it was Sophie who stepped toward him. Her eyes never left his, the soft gaze melting the anger inside him.

"I can still see him." She lifted a hand, placing the lightest touch against his cheek. "That guy I met who ate too many beignets." One corner of her mouth lifted. "I'm sorry too, Gullie. I should have said it last night while you poured out your heart through that wall. I'm sorry I spent so much of my life hating those like you. You're a good man." She pulled her hand away. "For a fae."

When she stepped back and turned to Lochlan, all Gullie could do was watch as his uncle opened a portal and blue light flashed through the room. Sophie looked back over her shoulder, giving him a sad smile before stepping through. It was only then Gulliver saw the familiar journal in her hands. She wasn't going back to her father for herself. It was for them.

"No." Gullie recovered enough to run after her, to try to

jump into the portal after Lochlan. His feet hit the ground, but when he looked around, the throne room still surrounded him and the portal was gone.

Sophie was gone.

He touched his cheek, still feeling the ghost of her fingers, still not sure what had happened, what was going to happen.

A hand landed on his shoulder. "See, Gul, she doesn't hate you after all."

He ripped himself away from Tia. "You don't get to say that to me."

"Be reasonable. We all knew this was going to happen one way or another."

No, he refused to believe that. They had other options to help the fae in the human realm. There had to be ways that didn't put someone he ... cared about in jeopardy. "You talked all about choice, how I took hers away by bringing her here. What about you, your Majesty?" He spit out the title. "You don't think you did exactly the same thing, sending her back into a budding war?"

"No, I don't. There's a difference. I am the queen. It is my job to protect the fae, to make the sacrifices necessary for my kingdom."

"So, she's a sacrifice then? I'm so glad we cleared that up. It's fine for the human I love to become a sacrifice, but your brother joins the war and you do everything in your power to try to get him to come home."

Tia's indignation faded away in an instant, and her shoulders dropped. "Oh, Gullie."

"What?" He didn't like the way she was looking at him. With pity.

"I'd had my suspicions, as you know. But there were doubts too. You really love her, don't you?"

"No. I didn't say that."

Griffin cleared his throat. "Uh, you did, actually."

"No one asked you," Tia and Gulliver said simultaneously. That broke the tension, and they shared a smile.

"Go jump in the frozen lake or something," Tia told Griff, not looking at him.

Gulliver lifted one brow. "Or he could hang out on the balcony in the snow."

"Go to Fargelsi and listen to Myles talk about human movies."

"I get it!" Griffin headed to the door. "I'm leaving so you two can be mean without me."

When he was gone, the silence lasted a few moments before both Gullie and Tia laughed. Their laughter died away, and Tia sighed.

"It was her choice."

Gulliver wanted to say that was a lie, but he felt in his gut it was true. "Is she ..."

"On our side? Not likely."

"And yet, you sent her back to her father?" He would probably never understand Tia.

"She's not not on our side."

"You make no sense."

Tia walked toward her throne and collapsed into it. She patted the lower throne next to her and Gulliver sat. "She's on the side for peace."

Tia picked at the edge of the golden armrest, her gaze focused on her fingers. "She's for peace, but Sophie doesn't fully trust us. Like most humans, she sees our power as a threat to her world."

"She's not wrong."

Tia sighed. "No, she's not. But I think she sees us differently now. We aren't the barbaric creatures she'd been told we were, animals who wanted to destroy everything she loved. She thinks her return can bring peace."

"And what do you think?" Gulliver looked at her, waiting for the answer he knew was coming. He'd always been an optimist, thinking with his heart. Tia was the opposite. She expected the worst and was usually right.

"I think we're past the point where peace is possible." She rubbed her eyes, exhaustion evident on her face. "They hate us, Gul. Sophie may have started to change her mind, but the entire human world now knows we exist, that we can come take what they have at any moment."

She was right. If the fae invaded the human world, the humans would stand no chance. The darkness almost destroyed their civilization. What would a sudden onslaught of magic do?

"That's why you haven't wanted to get more involved." It made more sense now. "The half-fae living there have little, if any, power. But if an army from Iskalt suddenly appears, there's no coming back from that."

She nodded. "The humans deserve their world just as much as we deserve ours. I don't want to take it, but if I aided in this war, I'd almost have to. Just to keep our fae safe."

"So, we just sit here and watch those with our blood die?"

She fixed him with a stern look. "I didn't say that, did I?"

"Kind of."

"Gul, Sophie will try to turn her father's opinion, to make him see war isn't the answer. And that's great, but I have little faith it will work in any significant way."

Gulliver turned on the throne to face her. "You're sending me back in, aren't you?"

She gave him a tiny smile. "There's a reason you're you and I'm me, a reason we're us. You know exactly what I'd do at all times. I need that. Toby is impulsive now, apparently. Brandon is righteous. Griffin is reckless. I need an agent there to keep a cool head, to make sure Toby stays safe and that no one does anything irrevocably stupid."

Tia reached for his hand. "There is no one I trust more than you. If I can't be there myself, it makes me feel better if you are. Please, Gullie, protect our fae. And for the love of magic, keep them from destroying the humans altogether."

Gulliver would never say no to Tia, and this time was no exception. He stood, giving her a nod. A mission like this beat sitting around the palace waiting for news.

"I'll find my father and we'll prepare to leave tomorrow night." He started to leave, but Tia called him back.

"Gul?"

He looked over his shoulder. "Is there something else?"

"Sophie ... she may not want to, but I think she cares about you too."

A smile curved his lips, and his cheeks heated. "Did you see her touch my cheek?" Like he hadn't repulsed her, like she saw him. Nothing had ever felt more real.

Tia laughed. "You're such a nerd."

That was a human word he didn't quite understand, but from the way Tia smiled, he assumed it was a term of endearment, another way to tell him she loved him. "You're a nerd too, Tia."

Chapter Fifteen
TOBY

After a brief stopover in the middle of nowhere to regroup from the onslaught of the human media, Toby and Brandon moved Aghadoon to their newest location. Los Angeles.

Not wanting to cause too much of a stir this time, they'd looked for a more private area. And at first, the small park in L.A. seemed like the perfect location. It was a small green meadow in the foothills, where humans came to walk their dogs and get some exercise and fresh air away from their smoggy city. Some of the people seemed obsessed with having their picture taken in front of a weird sign higher up in the hills.

But that was the first day. Toby hardly recognized Lake Hollywood Park now. Like the first location where his grandfather had settled the tiny village of Aghadoon, the park soon swarmed with news crews and dozens of those metal birds hovered above as more and more humans came to get a glimpse of the fae village that had dropped out of the sky. But they were prepared for it this time.

They weren't a secret anymore, but Toby was one of the few who were okay with it. That was his intention all along when he'd asked his grandfather to make the village visible. It was time for the humans to get used to them being here. The fae would no longer hide in plain sight.

After weeks of living among the very human-like fae of this world, Toby knew better than anyone that this world was their home. He couldn't imagine forcing those like Xavier to move into the fae world and expect them to adapt. He intended to help them fight for the right to stay.

"Such a fuss over one little village." His grandfather stood beside him at the entrance to Aghadoon, watching the scene play out in front of them.

The local fae had flocked to the village the moment their arrival hit the news outlets. Toby had never imagined just how many fae there were in this country. "Well, a magical flying village is a rather strange thing even for us, Grandfather. I think you've just gotten used to the idea of Aghadoon over the years. For the humans and fae of this world, this kind of magic is astounding."

Toby watched the swarm of humans and their special guard force keeping the crowd at bay. No one walked their dogs in the park now. The grassy meadow was empty beyond the borders of Aghadoon, and a wide-open space stood between the human peacekeepers and their fae counterparts. The local fae communities had been quick to form a security force around the park to keep the humans out.

"I thought Aghadoon would be big enough to serve as a haven for the fae in this region." Toby shook his head at the sheer number of fae that had joined them inside the village and those outside protecting it. "I had no idea of their numbers, but clearly Aghadoon is only a start to what we actually need."

"Clearly, that is the least of our worries." Toby's grandfather pointed to the line of humans hidden behind their protectors. They carried signs and chanted.

Say no to fae!

Go back to your own world! This one's ours!

Fight today for a magic-less tomorrow!

Keep your eternal night to yourselves!

End the magic before it ends us!

We will not be victims of magic!

Others were more clearly from HAFS. Their signs and chants amounted to a single message.

Bring Sophie home.

And on and on it went. The hatred they spewed for an entire group of people they didn't even know broke a piece of Toby's heart. But others seemed to be in favor of the fae. They came with smiles and signs welcoming them to L.A. They took pictures of the village and tried to break past the human security forces.

"We have other matters to attend to, Toby." Brandon laid a hand on his grandson's shoulder. Together they turned, leaving the chaos behind. They walked up the ancient path to the library near the center of the village. Others followed, but only select fae were admitted in.

Inside, the library swarmed with activity. Xavier argued with several local leaders of the Los Angeles settlements.

"Your arrival in this manner has blown the lid off the secrecy we have all worked so hard to maintain for centuries." A formidable-looking woman slammed her fist against the worn wooden table at the center of the room. "It was not your choice to make, young man." She stood with her hands on ample hips, glaring at Xavier like she secretly wanted to tear him limb from limb and be done with him.

"It wasn't his choice, ma'am." Toby stepped forward.

She turned on him, eyes smoldering with anger. "And just who are you?"

"Tobias O'Shea, Prince of Iskalt." He gave her a regal nod, standing beside his grandfather with his hands clasped behind his back.

"Prince?" She gaped at him.

"Yes, madame. My sister, the Queen of Iskalt, is concerned over the death of fae in this land. It is our intention to help those who need it."

"You want to help?" She seemed to have gathered her wits about her, and her anger returned. "Perhaps you should return to your world and leave the humans to us. You've caused more damage than you can possibly understand."

"Oh, I understand, Ms. ...?" He trailed off.

"Meara ... er, your Highness. Leader of the Hollywood Hills fae." There were several other leaders among the small group gathered around the table, and they were all mad.

Toby had some work to do to win them over. "I understand perfectly well what we've done, and it's about time someone brought the fae out of the shadows and into the light of day." Toby moved to stand beside Xavier at the head of the table. "This world belongs to you all as much as the humans. You've been here for generations—so long none of you would know what to do with yourselves in the five kingdoms."

Toby pointed toward the park. "They would have you leave. Send you back to a place as foreign to you as the moon is to them. It's not fair. You're here. You have some level of magic the humans don't. So what?"

"So what?" A deadly soft voice rose above the noise from

outside. Toby turned toward the door where a woman had just entered.

"Orla?" Xavier moved toward her. "I'm so glad you could make it. Please come join us."

"For what?" She moved like a warrior, her eyes not missing a single detail of her surroundings. She had magic. Much more than most of the fae Toby had met in the human world. This woman had very little human in her heritage.

"We need to come up with a plan." Toby gestured for everyone to sit.

"Obviously." Orla took the seat at the opposite end of the table from Toby. The one nearest the exit.

"Toby, this is Orla," Xavier announced. "She is the leader of all the fae settlements in the Los Angeles area."

"Excellent." Toby nodded, playing the part of the royal delegate to perfection. "The fae of this world need a haven. A home where they can live openly and peacefully, without fear and without the need to hide their identities."

"You ask for too much, young prince," Meara said. "You are not of this world. You cannot understand what the humans will do to those with magic. You come from a place where magic is an effortless thing. Here, we struggle to maintain what little magic we have. We are not as strong as you are. We cannot protect ourselves from human weapons."

"First and foremost, you should all know that I have no real magic to speak of. Most of you here at this table could out magic me on your worst day. With that in mind, I still believe we can protect our fae in this realm and live peacefully among humans."

"And how do you propose we do that?" Orla leaned back in her seat. Pulling one knee up to her chest, she rested her forearm on her knee. The tips of her pointed ears protruded through her dark hair that hung like a curtain down her back. Her pale golden eyes shot right through Toby.

"For the moment, Aghadoon will serve as a haven for any fae in fear for their lives. But we need to think bigger. There are more fae in this city than there are in the largest cities of the five kingdoms. They need a sanctuary." Toby locked his gaze with Orla's. "And I need your help to protect them."

Orla studied him for a moment before she nodded. "You've pulled us into the fire already, Prince. You'll either save us or get us all killed." She let out a sigh as she gazed at her fellow leaders. "Just promise me one thing."

"If it's within my power to grant."

"If this goes poorly, will you help those who wish to leave this world?"

"Return to the fae world?" Toby asked, and she nodded. "That is the one thing I can guarantee. I will take them home to our world myself."

"Might I also ask a favor, your Highness?" Meara asked.

"You may ask," Toby said in a tone that indicated he might not grant her request.

"None of us knows one kingdom from five. Can someone here help ... educate us on the places of refuge we might seek in your world? Should it come to that."

Toby glanced at his grandfather in silent communication before Brandon gave a slight nod. "Yes," Toby promised. "My grandfather, Prince Brandon, is the authority of Aghadoon. He will see to it that all the pertinent information on the five kingdoms is available to anyone who wishes to learn about their heritage."

"For those with magic, I should be able to help them learn which of the five kingdoms they originally hailed from," Brandon offered. "That might help them make their decision on where to go if they feel they must leave their home here in Los Angeles."

"And should they wish to seek refuge in our world, I will take them where they would like to go," Toby added. "But they must report directly to the king or queen of the land they seek refuge in. I can assure you, each of the rulers of our world is every bit as approachable as myself."

"All right." Orla stood. "What's our next move?"

"We go out there." Toby pointed to the park, where the news crews had gathered. "We go as a united front to speak with your media people. The ones with the vans and the sticks they shove in people's faces."

"The reporters?" Meara chuckled. "You want to go talk to the media?"

"I have something to say that they need to hear."

"This should be good." Orla shook her head and was the first through the door.

"What are you doing?" Xavier walked beside Toby through the streets of Aghadoon.

Toby slowed his pace, letting the others pull ahead of them. Reaching for Xavier's hand, Toby laced his fingers through his. "I need you to trust me."

Xavier met his gaze for a moment and then squeezed his hand before releasing it. "I trust you."

They began walking again in silence. "There's just one thing."

"What?" Xavier's eyes widened at the sight of all the cameras and people swarming the perimeter of the park.

"What's it called here when a person or government designates a region as a sanctuary?"

"We have Sanctuary Cities all across America, but I'm not sure that's what you're getting at. Maybe a City State? Why?"

"Not sure yet." He stepped through the pillars marking the exit from Aghadoon.

"You don't have a plan, do you?" Xavier's voice came out a bit higher than normal.

"As my mother would say, I'm winging it." Toby crossed the grassy expanse.

"Greetings, humans." Toby waved at a group of news people as they approached the line of human protectors. "I have an announcement I'd like you to put on your televisions."

"He's going to get us all killed," Orla muttered under her breath as camera crews broke through the line of security and mobbed their group.

"Who are you?" Someone stuck one of their strange speaking sticks in Toby's face.

"My name is Tobias O'Shea, prince of a land called Iskalt."

"What do you want from us?"

"From humans?" Toby blinked at them. "For my people to be left alone. I wish for humans and fae to coexist peacefully, so I may return to my kingdom with the good news."

"Do you plan to kill all the humans?"

"What? Don't be ridiculous."

"What my friend here is trying to say," Xavier stepped up beside Toby, "is that the fae have been living among you for generations, and we've never intentionally harmed anyone."

"What about the long night?"

"That was a long time ago," Toby said. "It was an accident that my sister and I worked tirelessly to fix. I can assure you that nothing like that will ever happen again." Another reporter tried to interject, but Toby cut him off. "I came here to announce that there will be changes in our future. Necessary changes to ensure the safety of my people. As a Prince of Iskalt, I claim the city of Los Angeles and its surrounding areas as a City State for the fae living in this world." Xavier turned him toward the nearest camera, urging him to continue as silence fell across the park. The only sound was the clicking of their black, flashing boxes.

"Wherever you are in this world, all fae are welcome in this city. Los Angeles will be a haven. My people will ensure your safety within the borders of our new City State. Together, we will live under our own laws, and we will do so peacefully, right alongside our human friends. You have no need to fear us, but please ..." Toby's voice failed as a wave of sadness swept over him. "Please stop killing us. Any human who wishes to live peacefully among us is welcome to stay in Los Angeles. Those who continue to use violence against us do so at their own peril."

Toby stepped back. "That is all."

Sound returned as suddenly as it had faded as reporters fired questions at him. But Toby said nothing as he led his fae back up to the safety of Aghadoon.

"You know what you've done, don't you?" Orla asked.

"I've staked a claim on this land, so your people will have a place of refuge."

"Maybe. But right now, you've declared open season on all the fae living in this city. None of my people are safe here, so you'd better follow through with your promise to protect them." She reached for his shoulder, pulling him to a stop. "Because if you don't, prince or not, I will kill you myself."

Chapter Sixteen
SOPHIE-ANN

"I only want my daughter back." Sophie listened to her father's voice over the radio as she leaned back on the torn leather seat of the cab taking her to the one place she knew the man would be.

I really hope that's true, Dad.

She'd been in a gas station getting snacks with the little bit of human money Lochlan had given her when she saw Tia's brother on the news. He probably didn't even realize he'd basically declared war on the humans. There was no way the American government would allow the fae to take Los Angeles for their own without a fight.

He'd just made everything worse.

She wasn't sure why she cared so much, or what she was going to do when she faced her father, but part of her just wanted to see the relief on his face when he found out she was alive. She wanted to know he truly cared.

L.A. was the logical place for him to be after Toby's

announcement. It would become the staging ground for any further attacks on the fae. Palm trees lined the road, their shadows shielding cars from the harsh California sun. There was a familiarity here, despite the fact it had been years since she accompanied her father to the L.A. HAFS headquarters.

The largest sector of the organization was here in this city filled with fae. Unlike in New Orleans, HAFS wasn't welcome, even by other humans, so they operated under even stricter secrecy.

The cab pulled up in front of a dilapidated building on the outskirts of the city, one that held deception in every chipped cement block, every broken window. After paying the driver, she got out and stared up at the enormous structure. No one came or went through the front entrance. She remembered that, yet she knew the guards would already have caught her on camera.

So, she waited.

There were two of them. They wore plain jeans and polo shirts, no indication that they guarded the heavily fortified building. Both men had tattoos stretching up the pale skin of their arms, a language she couldn't decipher.

Lifting her chin, she met their curious gazes, choosing to ignore the handguns attached to their belts. Neither man moved to pull their weapons.

"This is a secure facility," the first one said, his tone mocking, as if a girl like her couldn't possibly understand.

"Wait." The second one put a hand on his comrade's chest to hold him back. "She look familiar to you?"

"No."

"I swear I've seen—" His eyes widened.

Sophie didn't wait for him to put it together. "I'm Sophie-Ann Devereaux. You will take me to see my father."

Second douche-bag hit the first one's arm. "Luke, we've got her. Imagine the reward. I knew she was alive."

The first, Luke, didn't speak as he stepped forward, reaching for Sophie. A meaty hand landed on her shoulder, sending a spike of pain through her that she tried to ignore. "You're coming with us." He shoved her toward the door, waiting for his friend to open it.

They entered what appeared to be an abandoned warehouse. A blank canvas of broken concrete stretched past fractured wooden chairs and abandoned desks, ending at a set of heavy steel elevator doors. The only indication that this was something other than a symbol of the past was a small keypad by the elevator.

Sophie stumbled forward with a shove from behind. The second guard walked ahead of them, entering five numbers into the keypad and then pressing his thumb to a biometric scanner below. The doors opened silently. No sound of machinery, no creaking of the metal.

It was like the suffocating air drew all noise from the room as Luke pushed her across the threshold. The second guard didn't join them before the doors closed.

By the time they reached the lower level, all manner of noises invaded her senses. Luke's heavy breathing. Chatter coming from the other side of the door. The clacking of keyboards. Somewhere, an alarm sounded before cutting off suddenly.

When the doors opened, Sophie found herself in L.A. HAFS command. Rows and rows of computers filled the large room. Giant screens spanned the back wall, where guards watched videos of various parts of the city.

"Luke," a too-familiar voice called. "Heard you captured an intruder and—" Gabe stopped in front of them, his wide eyes traveling over her face, down the length of her neck. He shook his head, as if he didn't believe what he saw.

"She says she's the Devereaux girl." Luke's hand closed

around her arm in a vice-like grip. "Nick seemed to believe her, but we all know the truth. Whether the old man will admit it or not, his daughter is dead."

"Thanks, Luke." Gabe's jaw tightened. Sophie recognized that look. Since he was a kid, he'd had problems with anger, and he was about to lose control if the other man didn't back off right now. "I'll handle the intruder from here."

Nick's grip tightened. "Like fae you will."

Sophie winced from the pain, and Gabe's eyes darkened. He stepped toward Nick. "You will take your filthy hand off her right this moment, or I will break every one of your fingers as I do it myself."

Indecision warred in Nick's eyes before he released her with a shove toward Gabe. "I don't need the trouble."

"Return to your post."

With a growl, Nick left Sophie standing alone in a sea of people with the man she was supposed to have married. Married and then left as a widower. She'd have been the perfect wife for him when she was dead. Then he could inherit everything her father had created.

Gabe didn't speak for a long moment as he stared at her. His hard eyes softened. Then, in a rush of breath, he said, "How are you here? No, you don't have to answer that. Not to me. Save the answers for your father. Soph, I thought you were dead."

"I'm supposed to be." She rubbed her arm where she was sure she'd have a bruise from the guard's grip. "I'm not."

His lips curled into a smile much kinder than any she'd seen on his face before. "That's good. I'm glad." He looked like he wanted to hug her or kiss her or just anything to prove she was really there.

Sophie reached out, gripping his hand. Whatever he'd turned into, they'd once been friends. "I have stories, Gabe. They saved me."

His smile fell, and he leaned closer. "If you're talking about who I think you are, don't say that here."

"Sophie-Ann?" Another member of the New Orleans HAFS sector recognized her, her voice way too loud. Others crowded in, some recognizable, some new to her. They repeated her name, like it couldn't possibly be true.

Gabe wrapped an arm around her as he shouted at them to stay back. No one listened to him. The noise became all she heard, the crowd all she saw. She stood frozen to the spot, unable to make any of it stop.

Not until another sweeping voice yelled above the din. "What is going on here?" The familiar admonishment in his voice gave Sophie comfort. Her father had always been a harsh man, but never unfair. Not to her or those who followed him.

He pushed his way through the crowd, coming to a stop when he'd almost reached her. There was no reaction on his face, no relief in his eyes.

Gabe released her, and for once, she wished he'd pull her back against him, protect her from the realities she'd returned to face. Drawing in the courage Gulliver told her she had, she stepped toward her father.

"Hi, Dad." She shrugged one shoulder.

"Soph." He reached out, touching a strand of her hair that had fallen forward in the squeeze of the crowd. It was smoother now, stronger than the wisps of hair left from chemo. The magic had strengthened every part of her.

"Did I miss anything?" Like a war.

As if something snapped inside him, he yanked her into a crushing hug, the kind that stole a child's fears, their doubts. Sophie let herself sink into him, soak in the safety a father's arms should represent.

"I was so afraid for you," her father whispered.

He'd also used her disappearance to further this war, but now was not the time to bring that up. "I'm okay. I promise."

"But how." He moved her out to arm's length to examine her.

"Maybe we should give my fiancée some space." Gabe led the others away to give her some privacy with her father.

Sophie cringed at the word fiancée. Everything she'd been through finally gave her the courage to do what needed to be done. Turning away from her father, she waited for Gabe to meet her gaze. "Look, I'm going to be honest. I never said yes to marrying you in the first place. I thought I was dying, so I never intended to live as your wife. Now that I'm still here, I still don't plan that. Sorry, Gabe, but the wedding is off."

She expected her father to protest, but instead, he only stared at her. "You're different."

"No, I'm still me. Just the version of myself I never got to be." The version Gullie saw. She shoved thoughts of him to the back of her mind, worried she'd never see him again. "Dad, can we speak alone?"

"That's not a good idea." An unfamiliar man walked toward them, the others giving him a wide berth. He was tall, thin, and wholly intimidating. With gray hair and crystalline eyes, there was an intensity about him.

"Honey." Her dad drew her against his side. "Meet Commander Clarkson, the leader of the worldwide HAFS. He oversees every sector."

Sophie had heard about Doctor Alec Clarkson. His name was spoken of in hushed voices. Even those in HAFS feared him, feared what he could do to them. Rumor was he had a series of institutions across the world, where he locked up those suspected of having magic so he could study them. Now, his eyes were set firmly on her.

"From what I gather, Miss Devereaux, the last time anyone

saw you, you were at death's door." A dark, bushy brow rose in question.

Sophie resisted the urge to shrink away from him. "I ..." She stood to her full height. "The fae saved my life."

Shocked voices rose around her, some angry, others merely curious.

Commander Clarkson rubbed his ridiculously groomed mustache. "So, you're saying you're one of them now?"

It didn't escape her notice how her father loosened his grip and stepped away from her. That should have hurt, but she'd deal with him later. "No, what I'm saying is that maybe there's more to them than we thought." This was what she'd come back for, what she needed to do.

"She's full of their magic," someone yelled. "You can practically smell it on her." The crowd gave her more and more space until she was an island, separated from anyone else by the angry swells. Even her father drifted from her side, refusing to meet her gaze.

Still, the doctor didn't react. His calm was calculated, dangerous. In him, Sophie recognized a ruthlessness she'd never seen before. This was a man to be careful of.

"No." She tried to raise her voice enough to be heard over the scared and vengeful HAFS members.

"Don't you remember the darkness?"

"They're going to destroy us!"

"They won't." Sophie turned, trying to find whoever said that. "The fae only want to live in peace. They helped me when they didn't have to. I met one of their queens, and they don't want a war."

It was as if none of them could hear her, or maybe they just didn't want to. "Listen to me!" she yelled. "We have to stop this. No more humans or fae have to die." Desperation flooded her as she realized what she'd refused to acknowledge before.

It was too late. These people had gone down a road none of them wanted to come back from. There were no forks, no roundabouts allowing for a quick change in direction. It was a straight line between here and a war that could destroy everything. A war they thirsted for.

Still, Commander Clarkson only watched her.

"I'm sorry, sir." Her father grabbed her arm. "My daughter is obviously still not well. She's confused."

"Dad, I'm—"

He ignored her. "I will take her somewhere to rest from her journey."

Commander Clarkson pinned those intense eyes on her father. "I expect you to deal with this."

He nodded, steering Sophie away from the crowd.

"Dad." She tried to break away from him. "What are you doing? Let me go."

"Not until you're my daughter again." He guided her down a series of hallways, never letting go. Stopping at a heavy steel door, he produced a key and unlocked it, shoving her in. "Sophie, I love you, but right now, you must decide which side you're on. I can't protect you in this. I won't."

Those final words echoed in the nearly empty concrete room long after he locked her in. She sank onto the small cot, burying her face in her hands.

I can't protect you. I won't.

If she wanted to do the right thing, she truly was alone.

Chapter Seventeen
GULLIVER

Gulliver walked across Lake Hollywood Park, lost in the wonderful discovery he'd made just this afternoon. Today would forever be an important day in his life.

The day he discovered tacos.

He'd made the trip down to the street vendor three times since lunch. The first time was an accident. He was supposed to meet a small group of fae refugees who would be staying in Aghadoon. He'd found the tacos on the way. On the trip back, he'd made them wait while he bought more tacos before he finally escorted them into Aghadoon to one of the small houses they'd set aside for the local fae who might be in danger.

A wonderful aroma had caught his attention on that first trip, and a very nice human man with a thick mustache asked him if he'd like a taco. Gulliver didn't know what a taco was, but he knew he needed to taste whatever the man had secreted away inside his restaurant on wheels. And it was the best decision of Gulliver's life.

He'd always loved human food. Cheeseburgers were his favorite, and Chinese dumplings were high on the list too. Pizza was life, but tacos? Pure ecstasy.

He'd never had anything like the crunchy shell of deliciousness filled with meats and cheeses and spicy sauces. It was sort of like the meat pies he loved from home but better. Tacos came in all kinds of flavors. There were even some with soft chewy wraps filled with fried things called shrimp and fluffy white rice and flecks of herbs and spices Gulliver couldn't place. The funny green goo was his favorite—cool, creamy, and tangy with bits of onion and lime. It cut through the heat of some of the spices.

He did not like the crunchy green peppers that made his eyes water.

Biting into his seventh or eighth taco of the afternoon, Gulliver decided he liked the carnitas the best, though he had no idea what a carnita was. Melted cheese and a burst of sour cream hit his tongue, and he groaned out loud.

"So good." He rubbed his belly as he strolled up to the pillar entrance of Aghadoon with a bag full of tacos he intended to share with his dad and maybe Toby too if there was enough, but he was already second-guessing that decision.

"Stop right there." Someone shoved Gulliver back a few paces, and he almost dropped his taco. Good for the buffoon who struck him that he managed to save the last precious few bites. But a dollop of sour cream and the green stuff splattered on the grass at his feet.

"Hey, watch it. That was the best part." Gulliver clutched the bag to his chest to keep them safe.

"What business do you have in Aghadoon?" the fae demanded.

"Business?" Gulliver scowled at the new guard. "No business of yours." He tried to sidestep the guard, but the fae lurched in front of him, a wall of chest and arms keeping him from the entrance.

"What, do you expect me to sleep in the park? I'm full from my lunch. I need a nap, and you're keeping me from it."

"Aghadoon is only open to the fae. Get out of here, boy."

"Boy?" Gulliver lifted his chin, prepared to kick this fae and run. His dark fae features were hidden in this realm, but that didn't make him any less fae.

The fae shoved him again, and Gulliver dropped his bag of tacos. The guard stepped on them, crushing the delicate shells.

"No!" Gulliver gasped. "Okay, *now*, I'm angry." He gathered up the bag, dusting off the bits of dirt and grass. "And don't think I won't eat this. I'm out of funny human money, and I lost Tia's plastic money card."

"Get lost, kid."

"No. I think you owe me three new tacos. Unbroken ones, if you please."

"I owe you a black eye if you don't get lost now."

"I've been lost most of the time I've been in the human realm. I'd like to avoid that if possible."

"Gullie, what's the trouble here?" Griffin came up behind him, whistling a tuneless song.

"This ... fae won't let me in, and I'm late for my afternoon nap." Gulliver thrust a finger into the guard's face. "And he hurt my tacos."

"Well, that's really not a good idea, young sir," Griffin said. "I can personally attest to how cranky my son gets if he misses his nap. Worse than his little sisters. And if you messed with his food, you'll never hear the end of it."

"Don't be rude, Dad. You take naps too."

"I'm old. I have excuses. Old war injuries and the like." Griffin patted his son's shoulder, and Gulliver snorted a laugh.

"Please let us through, and we'll be out of your way." Griffin gave a nod of respect to the guard.

"Get out of here. Both of you." The fae folded huge arms over a barrel chest.

"This one has the look of an ogre about him, doesn't he, Dad?" Gulliver was growing impatient. That last taco was one too many, and he needed a moment in the privy before that nap.

"No need for that tone." Griffin pulled himself up to his full height. "I'm sure you'll find our names on your list there." He pushed hair over the tip of one of his pointed, obviously fae ears.

"Sir! Sir!" One of the humans with a funny-looking stick in her hand waved to get Gulliver's attention.

"Go away." The guard barked at the woman and pointed Gulliver and Griffin back the way they came, completely ignoring Griffin's hints at his non-human heritage.

"Looks like we're going to have to sneak in," Griffin muttered as they retreated. "I don't suppose there's a back way into Aghadoon?"

"Probably, but you'd need magic to find it, and at the moment that counts both of us out." Gulliver stared up into the brilliant sunlight of a beautiful California afternoon. He'd just learned that was where Los Angeles was, in a kingdom called California. It was supposedly near an ocean, where humans liked to swim, but in Gulliver's experience, oceans meant dangerous creatures, violent storms, wicked hot temperatures along the fire plains, or freezing icy blasts along the shores of Iskalt. Humans did the oddest things for entertainment.

"Sir?" The woman waved at them again. "Care to make a statement?" She held her stick out, and Gulliver glanced at his father before they crossed the park to where she stood with the other humans behind a bright yellow stretch of tape that wouldn't keep anyone out if they really wanted to visit the park or the fae village that had landed there.

"Beautiful day we're having," Griffin said in his most endearing voice.

"Are you fae?" She spoke into her stick and then turned it back toward them.

"Yes, we are," Gulliver said warily.

"I am Prince Griffin of Iskalt and keeper of the rift in Myrkur." Griffin sank into a courtly bow. "This is my son, Lord Gulliver of Myrkur."

"Lovely to meet you," the nice lady said, her red lips curving into a friendly smile. "Can you tell us why the fae have come to our world?" She held the black stick in Griffin's face. "So many humans believe you've come to take over. Can you comment on that?"

Griffin laughed, shaking his head as he attempted to charm the young lady. "Just a few short years ago, we only had three kingdoms. Now, after a long war and some magical mishaps that hid part of our world for eons, we're up to five huge kingdoms. And here we are in the human realm now." He shrugged. "Who knows what's next?"

"I'm only here to eat," Gulliver added as the woman grew silent. "Humans make the best food."

"F-food?" she stammered, taking a step back.

"Uncle Griff!" Toby called to them from the entrance to the village. "Gullie, let's go."

"Oh, hey, Tobes." Gulliver walked away from the lady, who didn't seem so interested in talking to them anymore. "You know the new guards wouldn't let us in?"

Toby waved them through the line of local fae working security. "I added your names to the list of approved fae; he should have let you in." Toby led them up to the library at a quick pace. "Others have to answer questions first."

"They didn't even ask our names, did they, Dad?"

"No. I don't think we made it that far."

"They seemed to think we didn't belong here," Gulliver said.

"Imagine that." Toby shook his head, shooing them into the library, where Xavier and several of the local fae leaders were crowded around one of the human screen gadgets they were always staring at.

"Look, Dad." Gulliver pointed at the screen. "We're on the human feletision."

"How?" Griffin looked behind him the way they'd come. "We were just out there talking to that nice lady, and now we're on the human screen?" He leaned toward the small tablet. "Can you hear us?"

"What. Did. You. Just. Do?" Xavier growled, and Toby laid a hand on his arm, shaking his head and muttering something like, "don't bother."

"Who are the idiots?" a really scary-looking woman asked.

Toby sighed. "I've never seen these two before in my life."

Chapter Eighteen
SOPHIE-ANN

You must decide which side you're on.

Sophie stared up at the white ceiling, looking for patterns in the old stains from long ago leaks. Yesterday, she found one that held a remarkable resemblance to the Statue of Liberty, but she couldn't find it again this morning.

The game reminded her of better times. Before her mother died, and they'd visited one of the many parks near their home in the Quarter. Sophie and her mother used to lay on a blanket, looking up at the clouds for familiar shapes.

Once again, she found herself dreaming of a life where her mother never died in a blast of magic. A life where Sophie-Ann Devereaux grew up with a mother and a father who adored her, living in a world that never grew dark and had never known the touch of fae magic.

Sighing, she rolled onto her side, facing the door that had yet to open in the two days since her father had dragged her in here. Her stomach gnawed at her insides, and she tried not to think about food. They'd given her water, at least, but no amount of it filled the aching hunger inside her.

She'd lost all sense of time without a window to see the sun rise and set. Claude Devereaux wanted her to pick a side, but Sophie had a hard time aligning herself with someone who would do such a thing to his own daughter.

Staring at the shimmer of light under the door, Sophie busied herself with watching for passing feet. Only a few pairs had gone by her cell throughout the day, and none of them had stopped.

Her eyelids started to droop again, and she groaned irritably. She'd had enough sleep to last her a lifetime. The world was falling to pieces, and she needed to get out there to do her part. She sat up and rubbed her eyes, searching the tiny room for a way out. But over the last two days, she'd studied every crevice in the room, and she was stuck.

Shadows moved by the door and paused.

Sophie held her breath, hoping someone would finally open that door and tell her that her father had made a mistake. That he loved her too much to lock her up like this.

A key slid into the lock, and the knob turned slowly, as if her visitor was trying very hard not to make a noise.

"Dad?" She stood hesitantly as her father stepped into the room, a grim look of determination on his face.

"We have to get you to the doctor, Sophie-Ann." He reached for her arm, not meeting her gaze as he unceremoniously marched her from the room.

"Dad, wait." She tried to move from his grasp, but his fingers wrapped tightly around her arm, refusing to let go. "Why are you doing this?"

"It's not safe. We have to get you help." He ushered her down the empty corridor to an exit, where Gabe waited with a car.

"I'm perfectly fine," she tried to explain. "I've been hea—"

"Don't say it!" he hissed, shoving her into the back seat of a silver sedan. "Do not say those filthy words again." He slammed the door in her face and snatched the keys from Gabe.

For the first time ever, Sophie wished Gabe would come with them. She stared at the man she was supposed to marry and found sympathy there.

Gabe laid a palm on the window and mouthed the words, 'I'm sorry', before her father pulled away.

They drove in silence for a while, Sophie in the backseat and her estranged father in the front. He drove too fast, muttering to himself until she worked up the courage to speak.

"Where are we going, Dad?"

"Just be quiet, Sophie-Ann." He sounded so weary and defeated. "We are going to fix this."

"There is nothing to be fixed. Not with me."

But he refused to say any more.

They arrived at a small clinic on the outskirts of Los Angeles. Her father screeched to a halt in a parking spot by the door and was out of the front seat almost before he had the car in park.

He opened the door and reached in to lift Sophie out. Just like all the other times he'd taken her to the hospital or the many clinics they'd visited when she was at her sickest.

"I can walk on my own." She tried to twist out of his arms, but he held her tight.

"It's Saturday, but Dr. Anderson has agreed to see you. We won't have to wait long, and then we'll be back at headquarters, where you can rest."

"I don't need rest. I'm fine." She was about to get really angry if her father put her through rounds of unnecessary tests and treatments she didn't need.

"Please." He hugged her close as they stepped into the dark waiting room of the clinic. "Just be patient. We have to do this."

"Ah, there's our girl." Dr. Anderson gestured for them to follow him down a long narrow hall. "How's she feeling?"

"She's not herself," her father answered for her.

"She's fine," Sophie added. "This isn't necessary."

"Let's just start with a few scans, shall we?" Dr. Anderson stepped into a sterile room, and her father laid her on the MRI machine.

"Just relax, Sophie-Ann." The doctor flashed a light in her eyes and checked her pulse. "Nice and steady. Good." He put a stethoscope in his ears and laid the circular chest piece against her skin. "Good, good. Heart sounds perfect."

"I really don't need—"

"Sophie-Ann, just cooperate. We have to do this." Her father paced the cold white room.

"Mr. Devereaux, you'll need to wait outside while we run the scans." A technician waited behind a wall of windows to start the machine.

"You know the drill, sweetheart. Lie still, and it'll be over soon." Her dad left the room, closing the door behind him.

"Really, Doctor, this isn't necessary."

"You have Leukemia. We need to see what's going on before we can continue your treatment."

"Fine." She laid back, giving herself a minute to relax. She really hated MRIs. It felt like getting buried alive.

For the rest of the afternoon, they poked her, X-rayed her, and drew blood to run every kind of test known to man. Her father was determined to believe she was still dying of Leukemia.

Finally, the doctor came back into her room, where her father had insisted she lay on the bed like a sick patient.

"Good news and bad news." Dr. Anderson moved to sit on a

round stool by her bed. "The good news is, she isn't sick. At all. There are no signs of Leukemia."

"So, she's in remission?" Her father's voice filled with hope. "The last treatments worked?"

"No. And that's the bad news, Claude." The doctor turned to her father. "There is no sign that Sophie was ever sick. No signs of Leukemia or any other illness. Her scans show a girl who has never been sick a day in her life. She has no scars, no signs of the broken wrist she had when she was seven. There isn't a scratch on her. She's in perfect health."

"Blasted fae!" Her dad punched a fist right through the drywall.

"Dad!" Sophie scrambled out of the bed.

"I'm sorry to have to give you such news, Claude. I know it's not what you wanted to hear." Dr. Anderson laid a reassuring hand on her father's shoulder before he left the room.

"Why does it sound like you'd rather me be on death's door?" Sophie reached for her stack of clothes, ready to get out of this place.

Claude stood with his back to her, staring with unseeing eyes out the window. "I'd rather you be dead than one of them."

Sophie tugged her jeans on under her hospital gown. "I'm not one of them. They can't just make someone fae."

"You're full of their magic."

"I've been healed with their magic, but that's a good thing, Dad. It means I get to live my life. They are not the evil creatures you think they are."

A tear slid down her father's face, and he reached to wipe it away, shaking his head. "They tainted you with their magic. You belong to them now."

"I don't belong to anyone." Anger welled within her. "I'm an adult, and the only one I have to answer to is myself."

"Just get dressed. I'll take you home." Her father's shoulders slumped as he left the room.

The drive back to the HAFS headquarters was a silent one. No amount of pestering him would get her father to speak to her.

"You're not putting me back in that room. I won't go." Sophie watched the palm trees streak past her window as they neared the building. If she had to, she would run. She was a lot stronger than her father realized.

But they drove right past the giant square building.

"Where are you taking me?" She watched as the building faded behind them, and her father turned down a side street.

"I can't do it." Her father's shoulders shuddered. "I can't."

"Can't do what, Dad?" Sophie leaned over the front seat. "You have to tell me what's happening."

"It'll be okay, Sophie-Ann, sweetheart. I-I'll fix this. There has to be a way."

He turned down a tree-lined drive and pulled through automatic iron gates that swung open and closed behind them. He glanced back at her, as if he expected some reaction from her. "Are you all right?" The iron doesn't ... hurt you, does it?"

"Wait, what ... Dad, I haven't been turned into a fae." She rolled her eyes when she realized what he was asking. "They aren't vampires. I'm me. Same Sophie I've always been but healthy." She decided not to tell him that iron didn't affect the fae as he believed.

"No." He shook his head, his eyes bulging with fear. "No, that's not true." He stopped the car in front of a stucco Spanish-style mansion with a red-tiled roof. It was beautiful, but there was no way her father could afford to stay in such a place.

"Who lives here? Where have you brought me?" She refused to get out of the car when he opened the back door. With the tall iron gates around the property, running was out of the question.

"Sophie?" Gabe came jogging out the front door and down

the steps. "Is she all right?" He pushed past her father and peered into the backseat. "How are you feeling, Soph?"

"I'm fine." She moved deeper into the backseat, fully aware they could force her out the other side, but she had nowhere to hide.

"You're really, okay?" His voice squeaked with relief. "You're not dying?"

"No."

"Get her into the house." Her father barked a command and left them in the driveway as he made his way up the stairs like he owned the place.

"Who lives here?" she demanded again.

"It's a HAFS rental," Gabe explained, trying to coax her out of the backseat. "A bunch of the HAFS leaders are staying here while we deal with these fae who think they can just claim L.A. for themselves. I can't believe it. It's all over the news." He leaned into the car. "You have to come inside with me. You have a room here. A real one. I'll try to catch you up if they let me." His eyes filled with worry. "I really am so happy you're back and that you're well. It's a miracle." He reached to grasp her hand. "Even if it is a fae miracle." He squeezed her hand gently. "I'll make sure you're safe here, Soph. Your dad is just really worried about you."

He couldn't seem to stop staring at her as he helped her from the car. It was the gentlest he'd ever been with her, even compared to when she was dying in the hospital. She had no choice but to go with him.

Her eyes didn't know what to look at as they entered the beautiful home, with its curved staircase leading up from the Spanish foyer to an open upstairs landing.

Her room was beautiful. With a comfortable-looking bed and a window overlooking well-manicured gardens.

It also came with locked doors and bars obstructing the view.

Chapter Nineteen
TOBY

Toby paced the length of the Aghadoon library, trying not to remember all the times he'd seen his father and uncle do the same thing as they searched for a way to destroy Egan and save the human realm from the darkness he'd unleashed on them.

"They say a man turns into his father," he muttered. He was alone, thankfully, and able to think of his family back in Iskalt. What would Tia do if Griffin put her in the spot he'd just put all the fae in? His father, he knew, would go running to Griffin and bash his head against the pavement until his brother told him he knew what an idiot he'd been.

But violence was something Tia inherited more than Toby. He'd always been more of a talk-it-out kind of fae, which was ironic considering he found himself among the leaders of one side in a brewing war.

The time for talk was through.

Orla barged through the door, stopping when she saw Toby.

"Are you going to do something about this?" She was the leader of the Los Angeles fae, but she knew so little of the actual fae world that it would have been funny in different circumstances.

"I'm not sure what you think I can accomplish here." Toby collapsed into a high-backed, ornate wooden chair. The library had never been comfortable, looking too ancient to exist in these times.

"He's your uncle. Deal with him." The fae leader thumped a fist on the table. She looked out of place in her jeans and t-shirt, and Toby had a sudden feeling that the library was too good for the likes of her. He'd tried not to regret asking his grandfather for help in a human war, but he couldn't help feeling like none of the fae in this world belonged in a place such as this.

And Toby was through with the disrespect. He stood once again, rising to his full height, his jaw tightening.

"I am a prince of the fae realm. You currently stand in our most sacred source of knowledge, so you will treat me as such. As for my uncle, he too carries royal fae blood. He made a mistake, but it was one born of ignorance, not ill will. We will overcome the stumble, and we will do it with his help." He moved around the table until he was face to face with Orla. "Griffin O'Shea helped save your little human world from the darkness you all fear so much, and you don't even realize it. He has been through more than you could fathom, and still, he is here to help. If you don't appreciate his aid, I will send him away. Because I will not let him be disrespected by the likes of you." He bumped the woman's shoulder on the way out of the library.

A slow drizzle wet the village, casting the mood into a gloomy stupor. All they could do was wait. As news crews hounded anyone who set foot outside the village walls and the human shows ran cycle after cycle of anti-fae rhetoric, they sat here waiting for their moment.

Not knowing what that moment was.

Toby walked through the center of town, keeping his eyes on his feet to avoid meeting the distrusting gazes surrounding him. This wasn't like Iskalt, where the fae may have walked cautiously around him but still respected him. Here, they'd started treating him like the humans treated them. Ever since Griffin's mistaken words, they whispered about the full-blooded fae in their midst who didn't belong.

Maybe they were right.

Toby entered the small cottage his grandfather called home, needing to speak with the one man who wouldn't tell him he was imagining the change in the air. Brandon O'Rourke sat at a small four-person wooden table in the kitchen. Here, everything looked as it would in the fae realm, and it gave Toby a strange sort of comfort. Being in Aghadoon made him miss Iskalt in a way he hadn't been sure he would.

"Grandfather?" He hesitated in the doorway.

Brandon looked up, his reading glasses askew. He had a worn book in front of him with yellowed pages and a leather cover. "Ah, Toby. Come in, my boy." His genuine smile was like a balm to a burn Toby hadn't realized he had.

He moved into the room and took an open seat.

Brandon stood. "I'll make us some tea. You look like you could use it."

Tea. Thank the magic. In the human realm, everyone was so obsessed with coffee. It tasted too much like the Eldur brew his mother once tried to get him to fall in love with. Toby even hated the smell.

Brandon set a steaming cup of tea that held a familiar scent. Toby looked up at him. "Fargelsian tea?" Made in Fargelsi with an abundance of Gelsi berries, no fae with magic drank it for fear it would dampen their power. Only the magic-less like Toby, who normally joined the servant class, or those in Myrkur and

Lenya, whose power worked differently, got to enjoy the delicious aromas.

Brandon smiled. "I don't have much use for my magic in Aghadoon, so I don't deprive myself of the best tea on the market."

Toby inhaled deeply before taking a sip and sighing. "It tastes like home."

Brandon set his mug on the table and studied Toby in that scrutinizing way of his. "Have you talked to your sister?"

He lifted one shoulder in a shrug. "Griff no longer has the journals. I don't have a way to communicate with her."

The knowing look from his grandfather was enough for Toby to guess what the man thought about that. Toby had the strongest portal magic—his only magic—in the O'Shea family. If he wanted to see Tia, he could. With a sigh, he set his tea down. "She won't want to see me."

"And why is that?"

"Because I didn't return with Gullie. I was kind of awful to him."

"Has Gullie forgiven you?"

"Well, we haven't talked about it, but he doesn't seem mad. That's Gullie, though. He'd never hold a grudge. I just ..." He couldn't voice the words. He didn't want to see Tia's disappointment in him. And she'd be right. Because of him, the fae world was dragged into this conflict. He shouldn't be there ready to fight, neither should Gullie nor Griff. And Aghadoon ... it belonged nowhere near the human realm. But right now, it was an anchor they needed. A way to show their might without a blatant attack on the humans, but at the same time it offered a refuge for the innocent fae who needed protection.

"Ah." Brandon nodded. "I see. You're afraid she'll forgive you too."

"Why would I ..." His voice trailed off. Was that the truth?

He and Tia had once been so close it was like they were one soul in two bodies. Even their power was connected. He might not have magic other than the ability to open portals, but when her power flowed through him, he amplified it.

And then, there was last year. He could feel her from a great distance. He knew when she was okay and when she was coming home.

None of that mattered anymore when Logan died and Toby shut himself off from everyone, including his twin sister. He didn't realize it until right then, but the hole inside him wasn't only there because he'd lost the man he loved.

He'd lost his sister too.

That, at least, was his fault.

"Grandfather, how do you do that?"

"Do what?" A smirk appeared on his lips, but he tried to hide it with his mug. The man looked no older than forty, but his eyes betrayed his age with a wisdom in them few had.

"You always know what I'm feeling before I do."

"It's because I love you, kid. From the day you were born and I held your slimy body in my arms."

"Gross."

"It's life. Get over it." His smile grew. "I've always been a man with a purpose. I was raised to be the king, then I was a prisoner, and finally, the man inside Aghadoon, who had to have all the answers. I didn't choose any of it. But with the arrival of you and your siblings ... along with your cousins in Fargelsi ... being a grandfather is a greater calling than anything else. I have spent hours upon hours just watching you as a child, learning your facial expressions, your fears, and your loves. That's also how I know your sister has already forgiven you. I know her too. You need not be afraid of that forgiveness."

"What if I don't deserve it?"

"That's the thing about love, Toby. Sometimes, forgiveness comes first. It's on us to deserve it later."

Two heavy thumps on the door ended their conversation. Brandon stood to see who it was and returned a moment later with a harried-looking Orla. She was out of breath, as if she'd run all the way here.

"Toby, have you seen Xavier?" she asked, wheezing.

"No." Toby stood, sensing something wasn't right. "What happened?"

"May... she's dead."

One of Xavier's earliest allies against HAFS. "Does he know?" Alarm ravaged him, worry for the woman he'd come to care about.

Orla nodded. "He took off, and now I can't find him."

"I know where he is." Without another word, Toby raced from the house and weaved through the streets of Aghadoon. Near the back wall of the village, there was a small alcove, protected from the rain by the overhang from a nearby shop. Xavier showed it to him a few days ago. It was the one place he could go where no one could find him.

Sometimes, this crowded village became too much for Xavier, and he needed some space. But not from Toby. He'd brought him here, and that had to mean something, right?

He was almost there when he saw him. Xavier sat on the dusty cobblestone, his back leaning against the shop next door. He had his legs bent, his arms resting on his knees, and his head hanging between them. Sitting impossibly still, he didn't sob or shake.

Toby slipped under the overhang and shook water out of his hair. He looked down at his friend, at the bowed crown of his head. Leaning against the wall opposite Xavier, Toby slid down until he sat across from him, their knees bumping together in the small space.

"They're all gone," Xavier whispered, lifting his stricken face. There were no tears, but the grief was there. "Everyone I care about. My mother. My grandparents. May They've all died because of this hatred."

Toby wasn't sure what to say for a moment, so he scooted forward, pushing Xavier's knees apart so he could crouch in front of him. "Not everyone." He reached forward, tilting Xavier's chin until their eyes met. "I'm still here."

Xavier shook him off, scooting away. "But for how long? Huh, Toby? When will you leave me too? This isn't your world. Eventually, you'll go home."

Tears gathered in Toby's eyes. "Do you really not see it?" He hadn't been this close to anyone since Logan. It felt like a betrayal, but he couldn't help wanting Xavier, wanting the closeness he'd once experienced. Logan wasn't here anymore, but Toby still had a life to live.

"The day the boy I loved died," he started. "I thought I wanted to die right along with him. Until recently, I still did." He'd never talked about this with anyone. "I understand exactly how you feel, Xavier. Your friend is gone, and I'm more sorry than you know for that. Nothing we can do will bring her back. That is the cost of war, and I've experienced it too often. But we're still here. We still have to fight. We still have to live."

"I don't know if I have any more fight in me."

"You do." Toby had never seen anyone become a leader as quickly as Xavier, and that included Tia. She'd taken quite a bit of time. But him ... it was like he was meant to guide these fae to safety, bring them to peace. Toby refused to let him give up. "Do you know how I know that?"

Xavier shook his head.

"Because I have fight in me." He reached for Xavier's hand, wrapping his around it, sliding their fingers together. "Earlier tonight, I wondered if I belonged here, but it only took a single moment for me to realize I do."

"How?" Xavier shook his head. "How do you know this is your fight?"

Toby got the impression his answer mattered more than it seemed, that the words he used right now could help Xavier off this cliff or make him jump. "Because it's yours."

Xavier's eyes snapped to his, a single tear trailing down his cheek. "She's really gone, Tobes."

"I know. But you aren't alone." He pulled Xavier into his arms, tightening his embrace until Xavier relaxed into the hug. "I will never leave you, not unless you want me to." Toby didn't know where the words came from or why they didn't hurt like he expected them to. "We're in this together."

Xavier rested his chin on Toby's shoulder. "Thank you."

Xavier shouldn't have been the one thanking him, but Toby didn't say that. Instead, he looked to the sky, wondering if Logan watched over him. *I'm sorry, Logan.* He let the thought drift away into the past. *I love you, but there is more in this life for me, and I have to live it.*

Maybe his grandfather was right. That forgiveness he was sure Tia had already given him ... he could still earn it.

Chapter Twenty
SOPHIE-ANN

"Who knows what's next?"

Sophie watched the replay of Griff's interview on the news, still not able to believe he'd actually said those words. If she'd never met a fae, never seen their palaces, their thriving world, she might have taken them the same way the people around her did.

She might have thought the fae wanted to rule over the human world.

"He's such an idiot," she muttered, rubbing her eyes.

"What?" Gabe asked from his place on the couch beside her. He was today's assigned guard, the unlucky soul who had to keep the human infected with fae magic from ... Well, from what, Sophie wasn't exactly sure. What did they think she'd do?

She was lucky it was Gabe today. As much as she disliked him still, he was the only guard who let her out of her room to watch the news and catch up on everything she'd missed. "Nothing."

"You know that animal?" Gabe pointed at Griff's image on the screen.

Sophie rolled her eyes. "I was in their world for a grand total of like five seconds. I didn't meet every single fae. So, no, Gabe. I don't know him," she lied.

He seemed to relax at that. "Well, Claude and the rest are at headquarters right now, deciding how to handle things with such a blatant threat. We've been too easy on them so far."

Easy on them? Was that what he called the bombings, the massed HAFS army outside L.A.? Because that's what they'd become in her absence. HAFS wasn't just a fringe conspiracy group anymore. They'd turned into a fighting force, with the full backing of many governments and the majority of the people. It was frightening.

"What do you think they'll do?" she asked, keeping her voice soft the way he liked it. Gabe may have been the only one happy to see her when she returned, but that didn't mean he'd changed. He still wanted to force her into marriage, still wanted her to be the meek girl he'd known.

Sophie had news for him. That girl was gone.

He shrugged. "Fight, I guess. We were planning an attack, but they'll probably move up the timeline. We have to get to them before they're ready for us. HAFS may have the numbers, but the one thing we don't have is magic."

The truth sat there in front of her, a truth that would change everything for HAFS and let them know they'd win this fight.

Most of the half-fae had little magic to speak of. The ones who did only displayed weak power. Griffin was most likely the only real danger to HAFS and only at night.

Something kept her from revealing these secrets. In all their worry over whether she was turning into a fae because of the healing magic—a ridiculous notion—not a single person had thought to ask if she'd learned anything useful. They underestimated her once again, and they'd pay for it.

"What on earth is that?" She leaned forward as the news showed a flash of light and then the appearance of a medieval-looking town right inside L.A. It was old footage, not live, but it kept her entranced.

Gabe scooted closer, his arm stretched over the back of the couch. Sophie knew what he was doing, but she could only focus on the news replay.

"We're not completely sure." Gabe's fingertips grazed her shoulder, and she suppressed a cringe. "It just appeared one day, and we can't get any of our people inside."

Magic. It had to be. The news feed switched to an aerial view of the village, with an icon in the corner that told watchers it was live footage.

"I don't understand." She'd meant the words for herself, but Gabe didn't seem to realize it.

"None of us do, but what do we really know about the fae in this other world? Only that they want to destroy us, right? They're animals."

He couldn't be more wrong. She thought of Tia and her parents. Of Griffin. Gulliver. The fae were as sophisticated as any human. They used their magic the way humans used technology, and only when they had to. Their lives were not altogether different from humans. They had families, fell in love, and just wanted to survive from one day to the next.

But this ... magical village ... it was beyond anything she'd imagined. Crumbling pillars marked an entryway that looked surrounded by men and women carrying heavy weapons. The L.A. fae were said to be more militarized than others, more organized. It made sense. They had so much to protect.

Fae scampered about the village, talking in groups. The camera zoomed in on one building in particular, where fae came and went continuously. Sophie wasn't sure how long she sat there watching the feed or what she was waiting for. Not until she saw him.

A sob lodged in her throat. Gulliver. He was there. He looked to the sky, as if staring right into the camera, right into her eyes. There must have been a helicopter or drone circling the village, gathering footage, but everything stopped.

He looked like he had the day she met him in the cafe. No tail, human-looking eyes. Kind face.

Yet ... that wasn't him. In her mind, she saw a different man. One who risked everything to save her, was best friends with everyone he saw, and spoke to her through a wall just to tell her everything she'd needed to hear.

She only wished she'd had more words for him.

The man in her head wasn't human, and looking like one stole the character from him. She missed the tail that seemed to have a mind of its own, the narrow cat-like eyes that saw every part of her.

Gabe was watching Sophie, studying her, and she drew back into the couch, regretting it instantly. His arm dropped down, coming around her. She hated it with the passion of a thousand separate worlds, but she did her best not to shy away. He was the key.

If he still had feelings for her, still wanted her, he might help when the time was right.

Yet, there it was again, scrolling across the bottom of the screen as they continued to show the village. *"Who knows what's next?"*

"Gabe?" she asked, looking up at him with an innocent expression.

"Yeah?" He played with a lock of her hair.

"Do you think they meant it? That the fae truly want our world?"

He paused for a moment, his hand going still. "I don't know."

"But—"

"Xavier used to tell me rumors about the fae world."

There was a time Gabe and his half-brother didn't hate each other, a time they'd been family when neither had much of that.

Gabe continued. "He said his father knew someone who'd lived there. A woman named Enis. He spoke of kingdoms full of castles and magic, a place where war had ended."

"Do you believe him?"

"I don't know." His voice quieted, as if he was afraid of anyone else hearing. "But what I do wonder ... if the fae have such an amazing world, what would they want with ours?"

It was in the way he said it, the doubt in his voice. Sophie had never expected to find a semi-ally in Gabe, but, like her, he knew the fae weren't a threat to them.

At least now.

That was the problem, wasn't it? While Tia ruled in Iskalt and kept the other monarchs informed, she wouldn't march here and claim what she could take with a flick of her magic. But she wouldn't rule forever, and the humans couldn't protect themselves against the kind of power full-blooded fae wielded.

Magic wasn't distinctly evil, but it had no place in a world of humans. It never would.

War wasn't the solution, but then, what was?

"I'm a little tired." She pushed herself up from the couch. "I think I'll go lie down."

She didn't give him a chance to protest before sprinting up the stairs to the room she'd been given.

There was a loose board in the floor she'd found the day before, and she pried it up to pull out the journal that connected her to the one person who'd know how to end this.

Opening the book, she stared at the blank page. Tia told her anything she wrote would make it to the identical book in Tia's possession. She'd said a fae would then normally erase what they'd written with their magic, but Sophie would have to just leave it and flip to a new blank page each time.

She pulled open the drawer of the dusty desk and dug through it until she found a pen, one that didn't look like it had been used in quite some time. Testing it on the page, she started writing.

Tia,

You might want to talk to Griff.

Tia's response came almost immediately.

What did he do now?

She barely knew the queen, but she could almost imagine the affectionate sigh in her voice. There was a lot of love for her family. *Just tell him he might not want to speak to reporters and say he wants to take over the human world.*

She could picture Tia's pacing, hear the curses rolling off her tongue. Sophie couldn't help it. She liked the queen. In a different life, they could have been friends.

Finally, Tia responded.

I'll handle him. Do you have any other news for me?

Sophie didn't want to betray her father or the other humans. She only wanted peace. *I think they're going to move up any attacks. We* ... She paused, not sure how much she should say. *Human sentiment has turned against the fae. HAFS even has the government's full attention now.*

Sophie waited for Tia's response to that, but it didn't come. She wondered if she angered the queen somehow, but she couldn't worry about that right now, not when there was so much at stake.

She needed to find a way to make both sides realize they weren't so different, make them realize peace was easier than war.

Magic didn't belong here, but what about the fae without

magic? They weren't even recognizable as something other than human. She'd always imagined this world to have a place for anyone to live the kind of life they wanted. Even when corrupted by hate and bloodshed, there were corners of the planet where peace reigned.

Was that even possible anymore? Or would HAFS not rest until every single one of the fae was gone from their world?

Chapter Twenty-One
GULLIVER

"What do you mean, we're grounded?" Gulliver blinked up at Xavier from his seat at the table in the Aghadoon library.

"We took a vote," Orla said. "It was unanimous. You two aren't allowed to leave Aghadoon. We can't risk you two *accidentally* talking to a reporter again."

"We can't leave at all? Not even for tacos?" Gulliver gaped at the group of stern faces.

"I think we messed up," Griffin whisper shouted. "But I'm sure we can get someone to bring us tacos."

"Can't we send them back to their queen?" Orla growled.

"Hey, my queen sent me here to help you." Gulliver's tail twitched behind him. Others might not be able to see his Dark Fae features, but they were still there. "If it weren't for me, you wouldn't have our help right now."

"We were doing just fine without you," Orla shot back.

"That's enough." Xavier banged his fist on the table. "We

need both Gulliver and Griffin for important reasons. Griffin is one of our only magic wielders, and he's an O'Shea who can open portals."

"And Gulliver is our connection to Sophie," Toby added. "And through her, Claude Devereaux and his followers."

"That might be helpful if I knew where she was." Gulliver's tail wilted to the floor at the mention of Sophie's name. He missed her. But Tia had sent her back home like she wanted. And Gullie wasn't sure he'd ever even see her again. Maybe he was just in the way here.

As the meeting broke up and everyone went about their important tasks, Gulliver sank lower into his chair. The chair beside him moved and someone sat down. "I have a project for you, Gul," Toby said in hushed tones. "You too, Uncle Griff."

"One that doesn't involve leaving or either of us doing anything remotely useful?" Gulliver muttered.

"Actually, it could prove to be a vital tool to our mission." Toby set a human screen device in front of him.

Gulliver shoved away from the table. "No way am I touching that."

"It's not a good idea, Tobes. I've broken a few of those things, and your mother won't let me use hers anymore," Griffin said.

"It's not as difficult as it seems. Er, maybe you can just help Gullie with ideas. Mom taught me a few things on her phone, and this tablet is just like a big phone. Humans use it to research things—and play games."

"Games?" Gulliver inched forward.

"That's not important right now. We need to find Sophie, and we have no idea where she's gone since Tia sent her back home. All we know is she's not at her house in New Orleans."

"And no one else has the time to track her down," Griffin added.

"How do we use this tablet thing to find her?" Gilliver

tapped on the screen like he'd seen others do, but it didn't light up for him.

"I forget what makes it do that." Toby picked up the electronic paper and shook it.

"Don't do that." Xavier came back to the table with a stack of books and snatched the tablet from Toby. "It's an iPad. When it's dark like that, it means the power isn't on. Just push the button on the bottom."

"Oh, right." Toby took it back and tapped the button, and the screen lit up with a funny looking apple.

"I'm not so sure you should be the one teaching them to do this." Xavier nudged Toby aside and perched on the edge of his chair between Toby and Gulliver.

Gulliver listened intently as Xavier went over how to turn the iPad on, how to charge it when it lost power, and how to search for things with a button called Google. He showed them all the news apps and how to search for the latest information. And he taught them about social media. Something called Faceplace and clocktok. Xavier told them how to use hashtags and forbid them from using the camera to record anything. He even put something called a sticker over the camera so no one could see them. Gullie just wasn't sure how the human contraption could see anything.

"Just see what you can find that could be important to us. Obscure things the mainstream media isn't reporting on." Xavier quickly scribbled down a list of hashtags for them to search, and then he and Toby left them to it.

"Want to search for a taco delivery place?" Griffin moved to sit beside his son. "We're going to need sustenance."

"Let's look for news on Sophie, and then we can ask the Google guy to bring us food." Gulliver tapped on the Google button and typed in #WhereIsSophieDevereaux.

"Wow, all that is about Sophie?" Griffin leaned in to study

the list of news articles and videos about Sophie's mysterious disappearance from the hospital.

"*Fae are involved,*" read one article on a place called Feed the Buzz. "*The girl was minutes from death, according to her doctors. Then, poof! She disappears only to return the picture of health? Either Sophie Devereaux is fae herself, or she has very powerful fae friends.*

"Hey, that's you!" Griffin nudged Gulliver. "You're her powerful fae friend."

All the articles said the same thing. After returning out of the blue, in perfect health, Sophie vanished from the public eye. Her last sighting was here in Los Angeles.

"She went right back to her father," Gulliver murmured.

"That doesn't make her our enemy, son." Griffin laid a hand on his shoulder. "It just means, no matter what awful things Claude Devereaux has done in his past, his daughter still loves him."

"Yeah, but the difference between you and Claude is you turned your life around long before you found me. You did bad things in your past, but you grew up and you found your way. Claude is an evil man. Through and through."

"And if I were still an evil man, you would still love me because I'm your father," Griffin said softly. "Give her a chance to do the right thing."

Gulliver nodded and tapped on a video from the clocktik place. A young woman who called herself TheNOLASpirit came on screen, and for a second Gulliver thought she was dark fae with her bunny ears and nose with whiskers, but he suspected it was some sort of human joke he didn't get. In this realm, even if she was like him, he wouldn't have been able to see it.

"Hashtag where is Sophie Deveraux?" the girl said. "I'll tell you where she is. That father of hers has her locked up somewhere. Back when HAFS first formed in the weeks after the darkness came to New Orleans, my parents were founding members. I was in high school at the time, so I didn't get to go to the real meetings, but I knew Sophie back then. I even babysat her frequently during HAFS meetings. She was a sweet girl. Very timid and shy. When my parents realized Claude Devereaux was off his rocker, they quit the group. We never saw them again, but that man keeps a tight rein on his daughter. More people need to be asking #WhereIsSophieDevereaux because wherever she is, it isn't good. If Sophie was healed by the fae, Claude will punish her for her involvement. And lots of people go missing around that man."

Gulliver shared a look with his father. "None of the news places are reporting anything like that about Sophie."

"They've forgotten her." Gulliver tapped on another video on the FacePlace and heard more of the same. A lot of people were worried about Sophie and what her father might do to her. "Grounded or not, we have to find her, Dad."

"We will." Griffin pried the iPad out of Gulliver's hands. "But first we need tacos."

* * *

Gullie didn't have much of an appetite. After only three tacos, he turned down the fourth. "I need to talk to Toby."

The door to the library crashed open, and both Gullie and Griff flinched.

"Don't do that, Xavier," Gullie gasped. "I thought the humans were throwing their bombs at us."

"You spent forty-eight dollars on tacos?" Xavier fumed.

"What, is that bad?" Gulliver winced. "We weren't sure how to stick the money card into your tablet thing."

"You realize I'm not wealthy, right? I'm not a fae prince with loads of gold or whatever you people value."

"Xavier." Toby came in behind him, gasping for breath. "What did they do this time?"

"They charged their dinner to my account."

"We did?" Griffin's eyes widened. "I told you it wasn't free!" He turned on Gulliver.

"It never asked for money. It's not my fault." He shoved the iPad at his father.

"To be fair, it was your idea to give them your tablet." Toby didn't hide his smile.

"I didn't know they were going to clean me out."

"Here, my good lad, this should cover it." Griffin stood up and fished a few fire opals from his pocket. "That should more than cover what we spent. It was an accident, truly."

"You two have lots of food-related accidents," Xavier muttered, studying the opals. "What are these anyway? It's not like I can deposit them at my bank in *New Orleans*, seeing as how we're in Los Angeles."

"Deposit?" Griffin frowned. "I don't think there are any impure deposits in the opals. They are quite valuable, I assure you. Particularly in Lenya."

"I will make it up to you," Toby interrupted before Xavier could really explode. "I'll ask my mother to make a contribution to your accounts. She knows all about human money."

"Fine, but I'm taking my iPad. I don't need them discovering my amazon account." Xavier snatched the device and stomped from the library.

Griffin stood, studying the fading afternoon sunset. "I better go see Brea soon. She'll make it right for us.

"Make it a quick trip, Griff. We really do need you here," Toby said.

"I'll hop back after the Iskaltian sun sets." Griffin stepped outside to open his portal in the village square.

"Things would be a lot easier if more people could portal." Gulliver sighed. "I don't suppose you'd send me to Sophie?"

"I would if I knew where she was." Toby sank down onto the chair beside Gullie.

"There's no real news of her on any of these pages. But there is a lot of speculation about her location. Some believe she's with her father—that he's done something to her as punishment for her involvement with the fae. I'm afraid Tia might have sent her into the lion's den, and Sophie is so clouded by her love for her father she can't see that's the worst place she could be. I need to go find her, Tobes."

Toby heaved a sigh and ran a hand through his hair. "It was her choice to go back to him."

"I know, but I need to make sure she's okay."

"I think you would know if she wasn't," Toby said, refusing to meet his eyes.

"What do you mean?"

"Griffin doesn't have Tia's journal. The one he was supposed to give me the last time I saw him. I asked him for it so I could send my sister a message."

"So what? He left it in Iskalt?"

"Someone else has it," Toby said. "I made Griffin tell me."

"Who has it, Tobes?" Gulliver gripped the edge of the table.

"Sophie. Tia gave it to her so she could keep us informed. If she needs help, we will know."

"And no one thought I might be the best fae to keep in contact with her? That she might trust me more than a queen she's terrified of?" Gulliver flew out of his chair, his tail sweeping the books from the table to the floor. Tia had a direct line to Sophie and she'd just let him worry?

"Tia probably thought it would be too much of a distraction

for you. I agree. You need to forget about this human girl, and let Tia handle the communication."

"Oh, so you two are teaming up against me now?" Gulliver wanted to scream he was so angry.

"Your judgment isn't always the best where Sophie's concerned."

"Seriously, Toby, I could punch you right now ... but I'm scared of our crazy sister." Gulliver slumped back down in his seat, defeated.

Toby snorted a laugh. "You and me both, Gul. Tia's frustrated she can't be here in the thick of it. The spelled journals give her a way to be involved. Part of her wants us here to be her eyes and ears, but she doesn't actually want us doing anything that will get us hurt."

"But it's Sophie." Gulliver sighed. "I can't just leave her in the enemy's hands. I can't sit around and wait for Tia to get a message from Sophie when she's in Iskalt and unable to react quickly enough. Even if her father does love her, I don't trust that Gabe guy."

"How do you know we can trust her?"

"There is something good in Sophie. She's not like her father. And I need you to trust my judgment and my intuition. She's the key to everything, and I need to find her. Sooner than later."

"I trust you, Gul." Toby finally nodded. "I'll help you, but I'm just not sure I can see the good in anyone anymore."

"Not even Xavier?" Gullie teased, and Toby blushed bright red before he punched Gulliver's shoulder so hard he flipped out of his chair.

Chapter Twenty-Two
SOPHIE-ANN

Sophie was going stir crazy inside the HAFS headquarters house in Los Angeles. People came and went at all hours of the day and night, but no one paid Sophie any mind. She was just the ditzy daughter of the New Orleans leader, who'd gotten herself wrapped up with the enemy and couldn't be trusted.

Most ignored her.

Some made their hate for her painfully clear. And others wholeheartedly believed she was tainted with fae magic.

Her only source of outside information was the news that played on the main television, and Gabe. He was the only guard who would talk to her. When Gabe wasn't there, Sophie was locked in her room with nothing to do but stare at the stains on the ceiling.

But today he was here, and Sophie got to sit beside the pool with him, presumably enjoying the California sunshine, hiding behind her sunglasses and a tabloid magazine. Gabe dozed in the lounge beside her, leaving her free to study those coming and going across the lawn from the garage to the house and back.

Stern faces wore grim expressions as men and women came to receive their marching orders from the leaders of HAFS. Sophie took note when guns were involved. And there were *a lot* of guns. The garage had been converted into an armory, and trucks arrived all afternoon picking up and delivering weapons and ammunitions of all kinds.

HAFS was preparing for all-out war against the fae, and Sophie didn't know what to do with that information. She had the means of warning the fae queen of Iskalt, but she hesitated. At war with her heart and her mind. If she helped the fae, then it would most likely end badly for her father, and the loss of a great deal of human life. Innocents as well as those acting on hate.

But if she helped her father and HAFS, then she would lose her fae friends. She'd never see Gulliver again. And so many innocent fae lives would be destroyed for no good reason. It wasn't right.

Neither choice was one she was willing to make. So, she sat here day after day, collecting information that might help sway her one way or the other.

"Time to go back inside, Soph." Gabe sat up with a groan. "Fun time is over. I need to check in with my unit."

"Fun time, right." She set her magazine down, not having looked at a single page. Wrapping a towel around her waist, she gathered her things to go back inside.

"You're looking good, Sophie." Gabe threw an arm around her shoulders. "Strong and healthy. Whatever the doctors gave you at the hospital is really working for you."

"Sure is." Sophie pasted on a smile. Gabe was a lot like her father. He didn't want to see what was so clear to everyone else. Sophie was only here because of the kindness Gulliver showed when he'd risked everything to save her life.

Back inside, Sophie settled on the couch in front of the TV.

"I've got to get to work." Gabe tried to pull her back up.

"Just let me catch the afternoon reports, and then your relief can take me back to my room. It's not like I'm going anywhere." She curled up against the leather sofa, tucking her beach towel around her as she turned up the volume.

"Oh, look, it's Dad." She leaned forward, eager to hear what her father had to say to the journalist interviewing him.

"It's a war on terror." Claude Devereaux said in response to the woman's question. "The fae have repeatedly brought harm to the human world, and it's time we sent them back where they belong."

"Darn right." Gabe moved to sit on the arm of the sofa next to Sophie. She cringed at his nearness, but without Gabe, she wouldn't know what was happening beyond these walls. As much as she hated to admit it, she needed him. And he was growing on her. He was as blind as her father when it came to the fae, but the difference between Claude and Gabe and the rest of HAFS was they genuinely believed they were doing the right thing.

"The fae who mistakenly believe they can claim Los Angeles for themselves will know better once we send them packing." Her father puffed up his chest and smiled into the cameras. "We're coming for you."

"We're so glad to have you here today, Mr. Devereaux. But there is one question on everyone's mind." The woman smiled into the camera, her eyes alight with curiosity. "Just where is Sophie Devereaux?"

"Hey, look at that, you're on TV." Gabe grinned. "People want to know more about you." He winked.

"My daughter is home," Claude said firmly. "That is all anyone needs to know."

"So, what are you all planning?" Sophie asked in an absent

voice, like she hadn't spent the last hour working herself up to ask the simple question. She'd asked before, but Gabe was dying for her to trust him. She could sense it.

"Something big." Gabe patted her head and ran his hand down her hair.

"It sounds like Dad's planning a big battle."

"Oh, it's not just him. But it's nothing for you to worry about." He squeezed her hand. "We just want you focusing on yourself. Put your energy into your therapy sessions and getting back on your feet."

Sophie smiled and nodded. That was one thing neither of them could admit to themselves. Sophie didn't have cancer anymore. She was perfectly healthy, though they still treated her like she was made of glass.

"Some say she was healed by the fae. Is that true?" The woman on TV leaned in toward Claude.

"Uh-oh." Sophie flinched. That was the worst thing she could have asked her father.

His face turned bright red, and he shouted, "That is a lie! A filthy lie! My daughter is being treated by her doctors as we speak. She has not been tainted by fae magic." Spittle flew out of his mouth, and Sophie thought her dad looked like a lunatic. No one would ever take him seriously if he couldn't keep his temper in check.

"Touched by fae magic?" The woman frowned. "Are you saying if a fae performs magic on a human it ... taints them in some way?"

"My daughter is pure. She's a sweet girl, who has been through a lot in the last months. She needs peace and quiet."

"You let her out again, Gabe?" A HAFS soldier named Parker sneered at Sophie. She hated Parker, but he was one of her father's trusted men and one of her regular guards.

"I needed some exercise and sunshine, Parker." Sophie

sighed as she dropped the remote and stood to leave. "You may escort me back to my room." She gathered up her bag and tucked her beach towel around her waist as she followed Parker up the stairs.

"Don't expect me to give you any special treatment," Parker snapped.

"I wouldn't dream of it." Sophie waited for him to unlock the door before she stepped inside. That was her. Sophie Devereaux, willing prisoner.

* * *

"Your therapist is here." Parker opened the door to Sophie's prison room, and she forced herself to roll out of bed. Her *therapy* sessions were a joke. She didn't even think her doctor was a real doctor. He worked for HAFS and apparently specialized in people like her. Whatever that meant.

"Come on in, Doctor James." She moved to sit on the chair under the window, where they held their daily therapy sessions that usually consisted of James talking and her listening. Or pretending to listen.

"How are you feeling today, Sophie?" James sat in the chair opposite her, crossing his legs and taking out his iPad.

"Good."

"Getting plenty of rest?"

She let out a frustrated sigh. "Plenty. A lot more than I really need."

"You're still considered a cancer patient. You have to take care of yourself."

"I had new scans when I came to L.A. I feel great. Better than ever. When will I be allowed to get more exercise?"

"We want you to take it easy for now. Our sessions are part of your current treatment."

"Treatment for the crazy girl, who thinks the fae healed her cancer." Sophie smirked at the doctor pretending there was something wrong with her.

"Take me back to that day when the fae boy abducted you from your room at the hospital."

"We've been over this, Doctor. I was so sick I don't remember anything until I woke up."

"In the fae world."

"No." Sophie lied. She knew exactly what this therapy was about. The doctor wanted to know all her secrets, but she would not budge on her story. "When I woke up, I was in a nice hotel room somewhere in Los Angeles, and I felt better." She shrugged. "That is literally all I know."

"Then, why were you gone for so many months? Why did they keep you hostage?"

"No one kept me against my will. There was no one around when I woke up in that hotel room. When I asked at the desk, they said I was allowed to stay for as long as I needed. The room was paid for up to six months. So, I stayed."

"Why? Why didn't you return to your father?"

"I didn't want to." I twisted my hands in my lap. "I knew how he would react when I realized I wasn't sick anymore. And honestly, I really enjoyed not having HAFS in my life. But eventually, I got homesick, so I wanted to find my father and let him know I was okay. I didn't expect to be taken prisoner."

"You're not a prisoner, Sophie."

"I have a guard around the clock, my room is always locked, and I'm literally not allowed to leave the grounds. Sounds like prison to me."

"It's for your own safety and health. We still need to run some tests."

"Fine, what would you like to know that I haven't already told you a dozen times?"

"Are you willing to try hypnosis?"

"Hypnosis?" Sophie gaped at the therapist. "What will that solve?"

"Sorry, Doctor," Parker stuck his head into her room, "we need to call this visit short. It seems the president is on her way, and we have to scale down our occupants to only those who absolutely have to be here."

"The HAFS president?" James tilted his head at Parker. "That doesn't make any sense."

"Because it's *the* president. Like of the United States. She'll be here within the hour, and we have to be ready."

"I see." He turned to Sophie. "Think about what I asked, and we'll talk about it next time."

"Sure." Sophie stood, just short of shooing him out of her room so she could talk to Parker. *There is no way on this earth or any other world I'm letting that charlatan hypnotize me.*

Just as Parker was about to close the door, Sophie stuck her foot out to stop him. "What's the president coming here for?" she asked.

"None of your business."

"Right. I'm sure you wouldn't know anything anyway."

"Oh, I know things. You think Claude would let one of the grunt soldiers watch over his daughter?" He scoffed, as though she'd insulted him.

"Then, what's she want with HAFS?"

"What do you think, Sophie?" He sneered. "She's finally taking us seriously. Think about it. She's coming here, to us. That means she's ready to work with us to solve this fae problem once and for all."

Sophie frowned. "You think she's going to be on board with taking lethal action against the fae?"

"Those idiots think they can claim Los Angeles as their territory. That was an idiotic move on their part. The U.S. will not tolerate any entity on our soil who thinks they can take one of our biggest cities and we'll just sit back and let them. POTUS will take it as an act of war. Those fae creatures brought this on themselves."

"I need to see my father." She tried to push her way past Parker, but he shoved her back into the bedroom.

"He's not even here right now. He's dealing with important things. Now, be a good girl and go wash your hair or paint your fingernails."

She wanted to punch his stupid face when the click of the deadbolt sounded and she was all alone in her room again with no way of helping anyone.

Sophie paced across her room. From the big windows overlooking the pool to the bathroom and back again. There were people everywhere. HAFS people as well as the Secret Service. But Sophie couldn't think of anything other than getting to Gullie and warning him of what might be headed their way.

With the Secret Service on the grounds, now was probably not the time to try to escape. Or was it?

She peeked through the blinds of the bathroom window. Everyone was waiting for the president's arrival. They would be looking for anyone trying to sneak into the house. Not out of it.

Ever since her arrival here, she'd put off a risky attempt at escape. Her guards checked on her too often to make a go of it, and security was high during the night.

But she'd been working on a plan. If she were honest with herself, she would admit she'd just been too scared to try it. But now, she had a reason to risk it.

She could just see over the hedges to the house next door, where the landscapers were working on a new backyard. Sophie had spent hours watching them resod the backyard, adding a koi pond and a garden path from the pool to the new deck. Today, they were cleaning out the garden beds, adding new mulch, and replacing some of the wilted bushes with new flowering plants in a riot of tropical colors.

Pacing back to the bedroom, Sophie grabbed her bag. The one she kept her sunglasses and poolside reading materials in. She crouched down at the foot of her bed to retrieve Tia's journal from its hiding place under the loose floorboard and stuffed it in the bag. She hadn't written to her recently, but it was only a matter of time before she would have to.

Chewing on her bottom lip, Sophie stood in the middle of her bedroom, second-guessing herself.

"Gulliver would do it." She clutched the bag and returned to the bathroom, locking the door behind her. Climbing onto the edge of the tub, Sophie lifted the vent from the ceiling. It was a wide, industrial vent. One she'd become very familiar with over the last few weeks. At night, when everyone was sleeping, Sophie stayed up late, creeping through the vents, studying her best options for escape should it come to that.

She kept another bag in the vent with the items she'd collected to aide her escape. There was a gardening uniform she'd stolen from the basement. It looked close enough to what the landscapers next door wore that she thought she could get away with it.

After she stuffed the uniform into her bag, Sophie pulled her hair up into a hat and crawled up inside the vents, pulling it closed behind her. She shuffled her way down the hall to the second-floor laundry room. She had to psych herself up for it, but making as little noise as possible, she shimmied out of the vent, landing on top of the washing machine.

This was a mansion, and the laundry room was quite large, meant to serve as a headquarters for the maids. But HAFS didn't employ a maid service. And from what Sophie could tell, no one used the upstairs laundry room. A huge laundry chute ran down to the utility room in the basement. This was the part where she could not make any noise.

Sophie climbed feet first into the chute, letting herself slide slowly down until the shaft dropped at a sharp angle, and she lost control, landing in a heap on the concrete floor of the utility room.

And she wasn't alone. The room was full of screens showing all the security cameras on the property.

"Is that ... Sophie Devereaux?" someone asked, nudging her over with the toe of his boot. "Claude's daughter?"

Sophie looked up to find three HAFS security guards staring at her.

"I really wanted to go sit by the pool," she blurted. "Don't tell my dad."

"Come on, kid." One of the guards who couldn't have been more than a handful of years her senior pulled her up to her feet. "No one has time to deal with this right now."

"We should call Claude. He'd want to know she was trying to escape."

"She's not escaping," one of the three said. "You heard her. She just wanted to sit by the pool. Haven't you heard her guards complaining about how much she pesters them to let her out. Gabe's the only one who can control her."

"Not that I don't love hearing you all talk about me like I'm not here," Sophie gathered up her belongings and tossed her bags over her shoulder, "but either step aside and let me enjoy a few hours by the pool, or if you must, take me back to my room." She rolled her eyes and tried to pull off the spoiled dumb girl act.

"Just take her back up to Parker." The one that seemed to be in charge ordered. "I'll keep working on the cameras. Stupid Secret Service kicked us out of our own office," he muttered under his breath.

"Missing something?" The security guard marching her

down the hall seemed to be taking far too much joy in her predicament.

"Sophie?" Parker glanced at the locked door and back at her. "How did you—Where have you been?" he hissed, looking over her shoulder to make sure no one else knew of his mistake.

"She was trying to get to the pool." The guard shoved her forward. "Caught her coming out of the laundry chute."

Parker snatched his keys from his pocket and unlocked the door. "Inside, now!" He pointed to her bedroom and turned on the guard. "Not a word of this to anyone. I'll handle it."

"Yes, sir." The guard gave him a salute and headed back down the hallway.

"Don't start." Sophie wiped her eyes. "I'm absolutely miserable in here, and I just wanted some fresh air."

"While the freaking President of the United States is here?" He ran a hand through his hair. "I don't know why Gabe puts up with you."

"Just leave me alone." Her eyes brightened with tears. "You don't know what it's like being cooped up in here all day."

"Save the waterworks for someone else." Parker stomped around the bedroom, checking all the windows. "How did you get out of here anyway?" He moved into the bathroom to check the windows there.

"I climbed out of the bathroom window and shimmied down to the balcony below." Sophie blew her nose loudly, amplifying her misery. "Then, I went down the hall to the laundry chute, hoping it would lead me to the back door."

"Never again, Sophie." He glared at her. "You will never do this again. At least, not on my watch."

"Don't tell my dad." She sniffed, giving Parker her best poor-me look. If he told anyone, he'd be in way more trouble than her, and he knew it.

"Just ... behave yourself, and after the president leaves, I will take you down to the pool myself." He slammed the door closed and locked her inside.

Sophie sat back on her bed, her heart hammering a mile a minute. That was close. She couldn't risk it again. At least, not for a while. She grabbed her pool bag and dragged it across the bed to her side.

There was only one thing left to do. And she should have done it long before now.

She opened the notebook and began to write.

Tia,

I've been struggling to decide what to do. But tonight, I've decided to do the right thing. There are things you need to know. Things that will help you protect the innocents on both sides of this coming war.

Because that is what this is coming to. Get the fae out of Los Angeles. They are coming for you.

And please, keep Gulliver safe.

Sophie.

Chapter Twenty-Three
GULLIVER

"The humans are coming! The humans are coming!" Griffin stumbled out of a portal into the library during the middle of a council meeting.

"Dad, are you okay?" Gulliver moved to get him a chair.

"What is he talking about?" Orla sneered at the interruption. "And does he have to do that in here?"

"When I am speaking," Griffin sucked in a breath and dropped into the chair Gulliver slid behind him, "you will listen." He gave her his fiercest, 'I'm a prince' face.

"What news do you have, uncle?" Toby gave him his full attention.

"Tia received a message from Sophie. We don't have much time."

Gulliver shot out of his chair. "How is she? Where is she?" he demanded.

"She didn't say." Griffin gave him a sympathetic look. "But

she's witnessed the queen of this country arriving at the HAFS headquarters."

"You mean the president?" Xavier interjected. "The President of the United States made the effort to talk to HAFS? At their headquarters?"

"Isn't that the same thing as queen?" Griffin asked.

"Not important, but no, it's not the same." Orla tapped her dagger against the table. "Get on with it, Prince."

"War." Griffin leaned over the table. "They will bring war against us with their machines. Right here in Aghadoon."

Bedlam erupted around the room, but Griffin raised his voice. "Sophie believes it will begin after sunset ... tonight. We don't have time for bickering and mistrust." He talked over the frantic murmuring of Orla and her people. "We are all fae. Let's work together to protect our people. All of them."

"How do we know we can trust this Sophie girl?" Orla asked. "It could be a trap."

"Because she's good." Gulliver spoke without thinking. "Because she will never sit back and let innocents suffer, no matter what blood they carry in their veins. I'd stake my life on her word. And Tia's. Tierney O'Shea is not stupid. She would have tested the messenger to make sure the person writing in the journal was no one other than Sophie-Ann Devereaux. We would be fools to even consider this warning is any sort of trap. It's our chance to prepare, and we shouldn't waste any more time."

"Put out the call," Orla issued the command to her right hand. He gave a nod and quickly left to gather his unit.

"What call?" Toby asked, looking at Xavier for answers.

"We have to protect the fae of Los Angeles," Orla answered, holding up a hand to halt her people from leaving. "Since our arrival in Los Angeles, we've established safe houses throughout the city. Old bunkers, basements, and shelters where our fae can go to escape attacks like the one we face now. Each shelter will have magic wielders capable of erecting minor shields of protection, though our magic is nothing compared to yours."

"Grandfather?" Toby turned to Brandon. "Do we have any soldiers to spare for these shelters?"

"Come with me to Fargelsi for an hour, and we will have a team of magic wielders for each shelter. You are the only O'Shea able to accomplish such a feat in time."

Toby exchanged a look with Xavier before he nodded. "Let's go." He left with Brandon, and a moment later Gulliver saw the flash of Toby's portal through the window.

"Aghadoon will open its doors to anyone needing refuge tonight." Orla's eyes blazed with defiance, as if anyone would disagree with her.

"Of course." Griffin nodded. "As the senior royal representative of the fae world in Brandon's absence, I give you my word we will not turn away anyone with even a drop of fae blood. But when the battle is upon us, our shields will go up and our doors will be sealed. Make sure your fae know the time to act is now. Anyone within an hour's distance from the village will be welcome with open arms. Others will need to seek refuge elsewhere."

"Cal, let everyone know help is on the way," Orla said. Her soldier went to deliver the message.

"Do we know anything more?" Xavier asked. "Is that all Sophie said?"

"The humans and their leader didn't like it when Toby declared Los Angeles a safe haven for fae," Griffin said. "The human queen saw it as the fae's attempt to take territory away from this country. She took it as an act of war."

"That's not what he meant," Gulliver said. "He just wanted the fae to have a central, safe place where we could protect them."

"What we meant doesn't matter," Orla said as she stood. "And we don't have time for further discussion. Can my fae treat Aghadoon as our center of command during the fight?"

"Of course," Griffin said. "We are here to help."

"Your *help* was what got us into this mess."

"And we'll help get us all out of it." Gulliver moved to stand beside his father at the table.

"I will ask that your fae take charge of protecting Aghadoon," Orla said. "But mine will be in charge of this battle as a whole."

"Agreed." Griffin nodded. "Our soldiers and magic wielders are here to help, but outside of Aghadoon, you are in charge."

Orla scowled at Griffin. "I remember you. Weren't you the buffoon who got the media's attention in a taco outing with your son just a few days ago?"

"Yes, but I am also a Prince of Iskalt and guardian of the rift in Myrkur. When the time calls for it, I can be a ruler. It took me a long time to learn to embrace life with my family to its fullest. I prefer a life with little responsibility, but make no mistake, I am no imbecile when it comes to war."

"Noted." Orla lifted her chin, showing the first signs of respect for him.

* * *

Toby and Brandon returned within the hour with both Lenyan and Gelsi soldiers and magic wielders. Even Gulliver could understand the strategy there. No one wanted the humans to learn how their magic worked. That Iskaltians only had magic at night, while Eldurians were powerful during the day. And Myrkurians only had defensive magic.

With Fargelsians and Lenyans, there were no limitations to when they could use their magic. The Gelsi soldiers would draw their power from the ancient words of magic and from the earth itself, while Lenyans held powerful totems to direct their magic. With Brandon and Griffin in charge of the night battle, the village's vulnerabilities were safe for the moment.

"We have Eldurians and a fresh troop of Lenyans gathered in Iskalt should we need them," Toby explained when he returned with his grandfather. "I'll go back just before dawn if the fight still continues. Uncle Finn and Keir will return with me to relieve Griffin and Brandon."

Gulliver paced across the library, unsure of how much help he would be in this fight when he had no magic to speak of. Gripping the sword at his hip, he knew he could protect himself with it, but it was the only weapon he was good at.

"Why so frustrated?" Griffin found him walking the dusty aisles of the library. "Besides the obvious worry about the coming battle and that your girl is out there somewhere with the enemy."

"She's not my girl." Gulliver shrugged. "But I still worry about her. She's my friend."

"And she's a smart young lady. She can handle her father." Griffin laid a hand on Gulliver's arm. "Promise me you won't go galivanting across this topsy-turvy city tonight trying to save her?"

"I don't even know where she is." Gullie sighed, turning toward the wide windows facing the activity swarming at the center of Aghadoon. "And I'm not much good to anyone here."

"You will lead the company charged with protecting the library."

"What?" Gulliver's head snapped toward his father. "Are you *insane*? Shouldn't that responsibility fall to Brandon?"

Griffin chuckled and shook his head. "Brandon's magic will be needed elsewhere tonight. But Aghadoon is a sacred place. You know what it would mean for our people should it be destroyed."

Gulliver nodded, his tail thumping against the floor with a nervous tick.

"And if the library itself should need to be protected, that would mean the humans have breached our shields and our magic wielders have fallen."

Gulliver nodded again. "I will protect the magic of Aghadoon with my life."

"No, you will not." Griffin smiled. "You will protect it to the best of your ability, but haven't we all learned an important lesson over the years? Magic isn't everything. It's a huge part of our way of life, but we can live without it if we have to."

"You're right. I live without magic all the time, and I'm okay." Gulliver gave his father a half smirk.

"Be careful tonight, son." Griffin pulled him into his arms.

"You too, Dad. We've been through a lot, you and me. From the slums of the Myrkur palace to the happy life we had for a short time in Fela before we met Mom."

"That's when all our adventures began." Griffin laughed at the memory of those days. "I'll be helping Brandon guard the walls of the village," Griffin said as they broke apart. "If you need anything, send a messenger."

"Good luck, Dad." Gulliver slapped him on the back. "If you get hurt, Mom's going to kill you."

"Don't I know it." Griffin smiled as he left the library to take up his position for the attack.

"I still haven't seen any signs of the human army yet." Toby peeked out the windows after Griffin left.

"You'd think if they planned to attack us at sunset, they'd have their soldiers in place by now." Gulliver returned to his pacing.

"From what Orla has told me, the humans prefer the element of surprise." Toby walked in the opposite direction of Gulliver.

"We should see their funny bird planes soon."

"Helicopters," Toby supplied. "Xavier said we will be fine with our shields up." Toby fidgeted restlessly in front of the large window overlooking the park with the Hollywood sign in clear view. "I just don't know why he has to go out there without me."

"We don't have magic," Gulliver said sadly.

"Neither does he. Not much anyway." Toby sighed. "He can protect himself with basic shields, but that's as much magic as he has. But he insisted on going out to help bring his people to safety."

"Then, what are we doing here where it's safe?" Gulliver stared off across the city, wondering where Sophie was and if she would be safe tonight.

"We are doing what royals always do." Toby sighed. "We give the orders and plan the strategies our soldiers will execute because that is what they have been trained to do, and this is what we have been trained to do."

"Yeah, but I'm not royal."

Toby reached for Gulliver's hand. "You're royal adjacent. Everyone knows you belong with me and Tia."

"Thanks, Tobes." Gulliver gave his hand a squeeze.

"It's nearly sunset," Toby said. "We should probably get ready to take our positions outside." Toby was responsible for helping Gulliver protect the library that would likely never need to be protected. But Toby had to be ready to open a large enough portal to evacuate fae should the need arise.

"Send out the message to the Google man," Toby said. "Then, let's go."

"It's not Google, Toby." Gulliver sat down at the table and took Xavier's tablet in hand. "It's the ClockTok." He tapped on the icon and hit record like Xavier showed him. "Hi there, internet people. This message is for all the fae of Los Angeles and the surrounding areas." He read from the script Xavier had left for him. "Do not be alarmed. The humans have decided they don't want us to be safe here in the city. Most of you know this by now as the message has been going out to all the local fae communities since early this afternoon. The humans plan to attack us at any moment. If you have not already arrived at a safehouse, stay wherever you are. If you can get to a basement, lock up your house and seek shelter in place. Do not go outside. I repeat. No matter what you hear, do not go outside. My people and our trained soldiers and magic wielders will protect you. Stay safe, and if you are anywhere near the Hollywood Hills, no matter what you hear, stay in your homes. HashtagBeSafe."

"No, you type the hashtags, Gullie!" Toby hissed.

"Oh, right sorry. I'll hashtag you all in a minute. Be safe." Gulliver ended the video and copied all the text Xavier had written out for him before he posted the video.

Gulliver heard a deep humming noise that reverberated in his chest.

"They're coming." Toby double checked the sword at his hip.

"Let's go."

They crossed the library and exited onto the porch of the rundown building that was older than anyone would ever know. Gulliver felt an overwhelming urge to protect it and all the magical secrets it held within.

Toby took half their unit to guard the front of the building and Gulliver took the other half to the rear, where Aghadoon overlooked the Hollywood Hills. Nothing stood between him and the fast human planes flying overhead but a wide field of grass and the glow of magic sealing the village off from anything the humans might throw at them.

"All right, soldiers." Gulliver faced his troops. All eight of them. "We might not have the most dangerous task tonight, and we may very well end up with a front row seat to a quick and easy battle, but we are guarding one of the most important artifacts known to faekind. Do not take it lightly. Stay on alert, and should it come to a fight, give it your all, but when I say enough is enough, we will abandon the village if the call is given."

"Yes, sir!" The young rag-tag group of half-fae and a few young Fargelsians drew their weapons and prepared for a long night.

"Gelsi soldiers, get your shields up."

"Yes, sir!" The two magic wielders he'd been given went to work, calling out their Gelsi spells to weave a web or protective magic over the library, independent of the stronger shields over the village.

"That was so weird," Gulliver muttered to himself, wondering how on earth he'd ended up leading even these few soldiers all on his own.

A sharp whistling noise had them alert and on guard a moment later.

"What is that?" a Gelsi soldier asked, looking up to the sky for a source of the noise.

"Bombs," a half-fae from New Orleans answered. "I sure hope your magic is as strong as you all claim." His hands trembled as he lifted his weapon—a human automatic gun.

"Keep your focus soldier," one of his fellow half-fae soldiers said, her own voice shaking.

"I've seen magic shields strong enough to isolate an entire kingdom," Gulliver reassured them. But even he couldn't take his eyes away from the glaze of magic in all colors surrounding them.

"That one sounds close!" A girl from Gelsi looked at Gulliver for orders. "What do we do, My Lord?"

"Stay in place." Gulliver gripped his weapon, feeling frustrated that there wasn't an obvious enemy to fight.

The ground shook beneath them, and something exploded overhead.

"What's happening?" Gulliver crouched, throwing his hands over his head, but nothing rained down on top of them.

"It's working!" The Gelsi soldiers cheered.

"What was that?" Gulliver moved away from the protection of the building, down onto the grassy slopes behind Aghadoon. The sky was alight with bursts of colors in every shade, but nothing breached the shields.

"A bomb just exploded right freaking there." One of the half-fae soldiers moved to stand beside him. "And it just stopped in dead air. Like magic." She turned in a circle, staring up at the sky.

"That *was* magic." Gulliver let out a whoop of joy, relieved that the shields seemed to be holding. For now.

Chapter Twenty-Four
SOPHIE-ANN

"Gabe!" Sophie hammered on the door to her room, but no one came. It had been that way for hours.

"Ugh, I'm sick of this." She pushed away from the door, rubbing the side of her hand. Something was going on. Something big, and Tia was counting on her for information.

She didn't have a choice. Sophie gathered up her nerve and her bag and headed for the bathroom. She hadn't tried escaping again, but she had figured out where she could hide in the vent systems to overhear conversations.

One of those was the common room just down the hall from her bedroom. Close enough where she could get back quickly if she saw anyone coming up the stairs or heading for her room, but far enough where she could see what was going on throughout the house.

Turning on the shower to cover her absence, she pulled herself up into the vent and inched her way toward the nearest the common room. Instantly, she noticed a difference. On a normal day, HAFS members swarmed all over the house, gathering in multiple rooms to hold meetings and discussions.

Today, the house was quiet. Only a few members could be seen from her vantage point. One of them was her father and a man she didn't recognize. Seated beside the cold fireplace, they talked quietly as others came and went up and down the stairs on their various errands.

"How are her therapy sessions going with Doctor James?" the older man asked her father.

"He says she's receptive to what he has to say, but he feels her resistance whenever he brings up hypnotic therapy."

"Because it's not happening with that quack," Sophie murmured to herself. *If he's an actual doctor, I'm a super model.* She crept forward, inching toward the vent closest to the fireplace, where she could hear them better. She could also see the news on the giant television, and it caught her attention for a moment when she saw the fae village that had settled in the Hollywood Hills. Her thoughts drifted to Gulliver, and she hoped he had safely returned to Iskalt.

That thought gave her courage.

"You know what she needs," the man sitting with her father said. "You're just prolonging the inevitable."

"I want her treated right here where I can keep an eye on her," Claude insisted.

"In Sophie's situation, one-on-one therapy will only get her so far." The man leaned forward, elbows on his knees as he talked with her father. "She has a long way to go, Claude. She's been touched by fae magic. We know that for certain now."

Sophie let out a small gasp. They were talking about her cancer. She knew she was healed and cancer free, but it was still hard to believe.

"All her scans are clear. The doctors can't find a single thing wrong with her. None of the usual minor abnormalities that come up in routine MRIs. No inflammation in her abdomen from the chemotherapy. Claude, there are no signs the girl ever had cancer treatment of any kind, much less just months ago. If the clinical trial healed her like you insist, then her body would be wrecked by the drugs. She'd still be weak and struggling to recover her stamina. Whatever they did to her while she was in fae captivity, it restored her body to its fullest. She is the picture of health."

"And I'm glad for it." Claude hung his head, and his shoulders shook with silent sobs. "What does that say about me, Doctor?"

The doctor reached over to rest a hand on Claude's back. "It says you're a good father, who is grateful to have his daughter whole again. But she will always hold the taint of their magic within her. We need to take her in for the full treatment."

"I know." Her father wiped his tears away. Sophie had never seen him cry. Even at her mother's funeral, Claude Devereaux was a pillar of strength for his daughter.

"I don't want things to end for Sophie the way they did for her mother."

Claude's eyes snapped up to glare at the doctor. "I did what was expected of me. I did everything your father asked, and it didn't work."

"And my father and I both tried to help her, but she didn't want it. She was too far gone. Sophie isn't."

"I'm scared for my little girl." Claude twisted his hands in his lap, not meeting the other man's eyes.

"Sophie isn't in love with this fae boy who took her to his world. She doesn't show any of the signs her mother displayed when she came back to you."

What are they talking about? Sophie pressed her ear toward the vent, trying not to miss a word of their conversation. Nothing they'd said about her mother made any sense. She was killed in a fae attack.

"And that is a relief, but I'm still hesitant to let her go to that place. When my wife came back, she wasn't the same."

"And it was her own fault. She didn't do the work. She resisted the therapy. In the end, you had no choice but to end her life."

Sophie nearly cried out but slammed a hand over her mouth, her eyes wide with disbelief.

"It was the hardest thing I've ever done. I loved my wife. Even after she ran off with that filthy fae monster, who convinced her she didn't love me anymore."

Mom cheated? With a fae? Sophie wracked her brain, but she couldn't remember a time when her mother wasn't there. Not until after her death.

"Like mother, like daughter," the doctor said. "But it's not too late for Sophie. Not yet. I don't want to see her executed like her mother."

Sophie clamped her mouth shut, choking back her sobs as her heart broke into a thousand tiny pieces. Her mother hadn't died because of a fae attack. She'd died because she'd fallen in love with a fae. And HAFS killed her for it.

"It would kill me to see that happen to her." Claude sobbed. "I took care of her mother. It was my responsibility to see it done, but I could never end my daughter's life." He shook his head. "I'd rather die myself than see her end up like her mother."

"Then, the only choice is to let us take her, Claude. She needs our full attention. Together, we can erase the damage the fae have done to her mind and body, but we must act soon or we'll lose our chance to help her."

Claude nodded. "I will tell her tomorrow."

Good luck with that, Dad. Because I will not be here. She didn't care what it took. Tonight, while the house was quieter than usual, she was out of here. Sophie started to inch her way back toward her room when Gabe darted up the stairs into the common room.

"It's started." He grabbed the remote and turned up the volume. "Their magic is proving to be strong. We haven't been able to penetrate their shields yet, but the president has given orders to shower their strongholds with everything the air force has."

Sophie wiped her tears and turned her focus on the screen. Fires had erupted all over Los Angeles. She watched as bombs rained down on the fae village, exploding against the dome of magic the fae had erected to protect themselves.

Sophie breathed a sigh of relief that they were safe. At least, for the moment.

Her father and the doctor leapt out of their seats a moment later, blocking the screen from her. "Would you look at that?" Claude whistled, all his emotions over his daughter vanished in his excitement for the war he'd had a hand in starting. "It's cracking."

"We'll get through those shields yet." Gabe slapped Claude on the back. "Wish I could be out there fighting the good fight."

"You will, son." Claude draped an arm around him. "This is just the beginning. Before it's over with, the armed forces will be begging for HAFS soldiers. We've been fighting fae scum for more than a decade."

They moved, and Sophie caught a glimpse of the huge screen again. Chaos rained down on the fae. They'd managed to breach the shields and some of the old buildings were burning. A lone figure stood on the slopes behind the village, waving his sword toward the sky. She'd know him anywhere.

"Gullie." She gasped just before another bomb lit up the sky. The explosion broke through the barrier, and there was too much smoke and fire to see if the boy she owed her life to was still there.

"I gotta go check on Sophie. Make sure she's not up to anything." Gabe snickered as he headed toward her door.

"Crap." She shuffled back down the vent as quickly as she dared.

"Hold off on that," Claude called him back. "I need to talk to her first." Sophie couldn't hear them anymore as she dove through the vent in her bathroom, landing in the tub with a hard smack against the surface. "Ouch." She scrambled up and slammed the vent shut.

Her heart was still hammering in her chest as she leaped onto her bed and picked up a book from her bedside table just as the door opened.

"Hey." She glanced up, expecting to see her father with Gabe, but the doctor stood in the middle of the room with two guards she didn't recognize. "Oh, I'm sorry." She closed her book with trembling hands. "I was expecting Gabe."

"Hi there, Sophie. I'm Doctor Clarkson. I've been speaking with your father about your therapy." It was then she realized she'd met him before. The commander.

"I see." She dropped her gaze to the floor. She didn't trust herself not to start screaming and raging about everything she'd just overheard.

"You aren't making enough progress under Doctor James. Claude understands your health is of the utmost importance."

"And what do you suggest, Doctor?" Sophie willed herself to remain calm. She needed to agree to whatever the doctor said just to appease him enough to leave her alone for the night. She had to get out of here immediately before it was too late.

"I have a new treatment I'd like to give you tonight. It's just a mild sedative that will help you relax and open your mind." He turned to one of the guards, who handed him a pill bottle.

"Nothing scary, I promise." He gave her a fake smile and handed her two yellow pills.

"What is this for?"

"It's part of your treatment. Your father has signed off on it."

"I'm an adult. I make my own decisions for my health." She knew it sounded lame given that she was standing inside the prison cell her father had locked her in for weeks.

"Not this time, Sophie, dear. You've gone through a traumatic experience with the fae. It's important that you trust us to take care of you."

"I'm fine. Perfectly healthy." *You said so yourself, you lousy creep.*

"You're dealing with residual issues that can't always be seen on the surface."

"Is this part of some kind of hypnosis therapy? Because I've told *Doctor* James a million times I'm not doing that."

"We can talk about it." The doctor approached her.

Sophie scooted back, and the guards descended on her. One of them held her down, and the doctor swooped in and stuck something in her arm.

"Ouch!" Sophie pressed a hand over her arm as the guards eased their grip on her.

The room started to spin, and her world went dark. Her last conscious thought was that she'd left Tia's journal in the vents.

* * *

Sophie woke up with a pounding headache and stars dancing overhead.

Her vision cleared, and she realized she was seeing the actual stars. But she couldn't move. Her arms and legs were strapped down, and someone wheeled her on a gurney toward a set of double doors.

"What's happening?" Her words came out slurred, and her head felt as though it weighed a hundred pounds.

"Shh, Sophie, everything will be all right," a stranger's voice sounded just behind her. "We'll get you settled into your room in a jiffy, and you'll be able to rest soon."

"Where am I?" She blinked her eyes as the man rolled her toward those doors. "No. Stop." She tried to move, but the man kept pushing the gurney.

"No. Don't take me in there." Panic rose in her chest as she made out the sign above the door.

Welcome to the Clarkson Institute.

Epilogue

"August, where are you going?" The nurse chased after the rambunctious ten-year-old.

"I have to see." He avoided her grasp and ran for the windows. That burning sensation he got from time to time was stronger. He could feel it pulsing just under his skin. The doctor didn't like it when he talked about how powerful the sensation made him feel.

"August, stop it this instant."

"I just want to see her." He hopped up on the table at the end of the common room, pressing his face against the windows. So many times, he'd wanted to break through that glass and leave the institute behind, but he wasn't strong enough. And there was no one out there who could help him anyway. Instead, he watched as the girl on the gurney twisted and turned, trying to free herself of the restraints. He wanted to tell her that was the last thing she should do. They would just give her the yellow pills that would make her sleep all day and drool on herself.

"The girl with the blue hair," he whispered, his breath fogging up the glass. "She's real."

"Who is she?" The nurse took his arm and pulled him back down from the table. "How do you know anything about this girl, August?"

What she meant was, how could he possibly know anything about a girl he'd never seen before when he'd never set a foot outside this building in his whole life.

"She's the one I've been waiting for."

There's one more book to finish up the series! Keep reading for Fae's End!

Queens of the Fae book Twelve

FAE'S
END
HOLLYWOOD
MELISSA A. CRAVEN
M. LYNN

Chapter One
GULLIVER

Smoke filled the air as another explosion cracked against the weakening shields over Aghadoon.

"Get down!" Toby ran at Gulliver, smashing into him and sending them both to the cobblestones. The building behind them erupted, raining down rocks and rubble on their heads.

Toby covered him with his body.

Breath wheezed in Gullie's lungs as he stared up at the hole in Aghadoon's shield, a shield of magic that was supposed to be impenetrable. But this wasn't magic. At least, not in the fae sense. The human's technology had proven to be more powerful than even Tia's magic.

"You okay?" Toby yelled in his ear.

But the ringing in Gulliver's own ears drowned out his voice as Toby climbed off him.

"We have to get to cover." Gullie's voice wasn't loud enough, but he couldn't seem to yell, not amidst the chaos of the battle.

Toby yanked him to his feet, and they took off running.

"Gullie, I could use your magic." Griff waved him toward the library.

Gullie stumbled after him. "How?" No one ever needed the defensive powers of the dark fae. Except now, it was still more than what the half-fae had.

They reached the library that held every bit of magic known to fae kind. If they lost this ... well, Gullie wasn't sure if the library could be destroyed, but he didn't want to find out. He'd seen what the burning of a spell did. It no longer existed. They'd destroyed the marriage bonds that way, and now, every other power that existed in their world was at risk.

By bringing Aghadoon to the human realm as a place of refuge, they may have doomed magic itself.

"We have to protect the library." Griff lifted his hands, creating a shield between them. The moon had only barely risen in the sky, so his power would grow, but for now, it had to be enough. "I need you to focus on your magic, Gullie. Like you never have before. There's a chance we could use it to buy us more time."

Gulliver concentrated. Dark Fae magic was like a built-in armor. It was just there. But now he needed to extend that protection as far as he could. He couldn't do it on his own. His power didn't work that way. Griff had to try to pull it from him, using his own magic to turn that of the Dark Fae into something more useful.

An explosion sounded behind him, followed by Xavier screaming orders.

"Everyone down!"

Griff didn't move. "Not us, Gulliver."

"Dad." A tear leaked from his eye as he fought to strengthen Griffin's shield, to hold on to the thread of power feeding into his father. It was like nothing he'd ever felt before. The raw power of his defensive magic seared his chest, flooding his body with a strange energy.

"Hold on, Gullie." Griff shouted over the explosions from the human weapons.

But he didn't know how this worked. "I can't hold it." He grappled with the power he didn't know how to control.

"Yes, you can. You have to."

He gritted his teeth, letting loose a roar as his muscles contracted and Griff pulled the magic from him, somehow boosting his own.

Gullie had been to war before, but this time was different. When the fae battled, they were on mostly even footing. Magic against magic.

The humans had the power to wipe them from the face of their world with weapons they'd never seen. And they wanted that more than anything.

A plane came into view over the village, and Gullie could hear the half-fae leaders shouting to those who'd come to fight, but he couldn't make out what they were saying.

Someone sprinted toward them, and Gullie sensed Brandon's magic the moment he joined forces with Griffin in protecting the library. The three of them were the only ones with any kind of significant power in this village, but the village itself did its best to deflect the raining fire from the violent human weapons.

They'd barely seen any human warriors, but the humans didn't need to come out to fight when they had what Xavier called bombs and missiles.

"Keep going." Brandon's voice was calm, certain. He gave no indication that he realized he was one of the reasons magic was in danger. If anyone said that to him, he'd most likely respond with the fact that the half-fae of L.A. were also mostly still alive because the village had been there to protect them. *What's more important, Gulliver? Magic or fae?*

He'd always thought they were one and the same. A fae was nothing without the power they were meant to have. But then, he saw Tia lose it and find herself. He witnessed a kingdom where magic was scarce but hope was still alive. If this library burned up right now, their way of life would change, but they'd still have those lives.

Gulliver turned to Brandon as his father's pull on his magic waned. "We need to get everyone into the village."

He'd broken the unspoken rule of the fae once. Those with human blood were not to be taken to their world. But Myles ... Alona ... Sophie. The world hadn't ended because they broke a rule.

"Where are you going?" Griffin yelled.

Gullie looked back over his shoulder. "We're taking them to the fae realm. Prepare the village."

Griff opened his mouth likely to protest, but then seemed to think better of it. Brandon didn't hesitate to run for the village square, where he would work the ancient stones to move the village.

Orla was near the broken pillars at the front gate, shards of rock at her feet. This woman led the fae of L.A. She'd kept them safe until now. Would she agree to a retreat?

"Gullie, get back inside," she yelled, shoving him behind her as another flying death machine circled the village. Lines of half-fae took cover outside the village, aiming their weapons into the sky.

Fire erupted from the back of the machine, and it veered

toward the ground. Fae scrambled out of the way, some launching into the air as a crash shook the earth beneath their feet.

Gullie's hand shot out to grip the wall. "They need to get inside. Now."

She scowled back at him. "Are you nuts, kid? My soldiers just took a U.S. Air Force jet out of the sky. We can't stop now."

The soldiers in question neared the downed jet, weapons raised as a man crawled out, choking. He looked injured, one leg not moving. One of the soldiers closed in, shouting to him, and the man raised his arms in surrender.

Gullie tugged on Orla's arm to get her attention. "If your men and women don't get inside this village right now, they'll be left behind."

She finally turned to him. "What did you just say?"

"We're taking the village to the fae realm to regroup."

She shook her head. "Leave me alone, boy. We aren't retreating now, not when were so close to finishing this once and for all."

"You're going to finish it in a body sack." He didn't know if that was the right word, and Tia would have most likely corrected him, but right now he didn't care. He wouldn't leave them behind. "Get inside this village. Now." It was an order, one he was sure to catch hell for. "I promise you'll regret it if you don't."

She studied him for a moment before another bomb went off behind them, throwing them onto their hands and knees. Pain seared up Gulliver's arms, and blood seeped through cuts in his palms.

Orla lifted her head and pushed to her feet. "Retreat!" she screamed. "Everyone back inside these walls. Now!"

Soldiers ran toward them, and once Gullie was satisfied they'd make it, he took off for the town square. The shield was still intact over this part of the village, making it quieter than the rest.

Brandon, Griffin, Toby, and Xavier stood ready to make a move.

"It's going to transport us ... with it?" Xavier sounded like he didn't know if that would be better than facing the bombs falling from the sky.

Griff ignored him. "Where are we going?"

"Not Iskalt," Toby and Gullie said at the same time.

"We're coming back," Toby said. "That will be infinitely harder if my sister locks me in the safety of the palace."

Gullie didn't disagree with that. There was no way Tia would send them back into a war. Not like she'd sent Sophie. He'd done his best not to think of her, to wonder where she was, if she watched her father and those like him try to wipe a race of people from their world and turned away.

"Fargelsi means explaining to Neeve why the village is half destroyed." Brandon shook his head. "Eldur it is."

Queen Alona and Finn would provide them with the aid they needed and the repairs to the village without the doubt and chastisement. Without trying to prevent them from returning to protect the rest of the half-fae living in this world.

Brandon started the spell, drawing on his Fargelsian magic that didn't need the sun or the moon as he pushed stones into place. Gullie didn't know how it worked exactly, only that the stones controlled the path of the village and where it would end up.

Fire lit up the dark sky as a building nearby went up in flames. It was the home he'd once stayed in with Tia and Toby as children when they'd hidden from their parents so they wouldn't be sent away from a fight they belonged in. Now, it too was gone.

Just like so many other things.

Brandon's unintelligible words filled the air with a thickness as they simmered like a pot ready to boil over. His muscles shook as he pushed the last stone into place.

Xavier's hand slid into Toby's, and Gullie stepped closer to his father. Something wasn't right. They could all feel it.

"It's so much power," Brandon grit out, his knees collapsing. He fell to the stones. "The village, it's trying."

When he opened his eyes, they were bloodshot and hazy.

"Dad, help him." Gullie shoved Griff toward Brandon.

Griff bent down to help him up. "Take a break and try again."

Brandon shook his head. "I started the spell. I can't stop it now." He whispered a string of words in Fargelsian. "I can only give it more strength from my own magic." He struggled to get the words of magic out through gritted teeth.

Cracks formed in the stone beneath their feet. The damage wasn't from a bomb or any sort of human explosion. No, this was magic.

"Aghadoon is destroying itself." Toby yanked Xavier away from a fissure opening under them.

"Brandon." Griffin shook him. "Come on, old man. Fix this. There has to be a spell in the library to stop it. Tell me which one."

Brandon's breath came in short gasps. "I can't ... hold it."

"What can we do to help?" Toby asked. "Grandfather, tell us what to do."

"Holding the shield ... trying to transport this many people ... Aghadoon is injured. It doesn't have enough magic. The village is dying. I can feel it."

"No." Griff kneeled next to him. "Tell me the spell. I don't have Fargelsian magic, but I know the language. Maybe I can help."

Griff hadn't spoken of his knowledge of Fargelsian in years. He didn't like to think about his years as the mad queen's surrogate son. At least, that was what Gullie's mother told him.

"Me too." Toby moved to their side. "I don't have magic, but I do have Fargelsian blood."

Brandon nodded and started a strengthening spell. "*Lopeta tuho ja ota minulta voima.*"

The other's joined in, repeating the same lines over and over until a crowd formed up and everyone was chanting the Fargelsian words.

"*Lopeta tuho ja ota minulta voima.*"

The ground trembled and an earsplitting crack shrieked through the village as a line ran down the cobblestone street to the nearest building, splitting it in two.

Orla ran toward them. "Everyone is inside," she told Gullie. "You promise me, kid. We're coming back."

He nodded, hardly hearing her words as he watched his father sink lower to the ground, the weight of the village's magic around his neck. Those without magic didn't appear affected, standing straighter, their voices grew louder as they spoke the spell that seemed to give strength to the ancient words.

It was no use.

Brandon fell over and Gullie scrambled to him. "Don't stop. You can't." He wrapped his arms around the older man, willing his defensive magic to give him what he needed.

The shield above them let out a thunderous boom as another rupture ripped through it. Soon, it would be completely down, and they'd be at the mercy of the humans.

Brandon grappled to hold on to Gulliver's arm. "The village can't hold the shield and transport this many people." His gaze shot past Gullie to his grandson. "But there's another way."

Gullie looked over his shoulder to find that Toby had heard him and was in a battle of wills, his eyes not leaving Brandon's. The old man was right, of course.

It had been over ten years since Toby took an entire army through one of his portals, but he was the only fae to have ever been able to do such a thing. Most O'Sheas could only transport a handful of fae with them.

Even Griff couldn't accomplish such a feat.

But the last time Toby did, it was by force when King Egan held him prisoner.

Griffin lifted his head. "Gullie, you and Toby have to get them out. They're our people. No matter where they choose to live."

"What are they talking about?" Xavier looked from Griff and Brandon to Toby. "If the village can't move, then how ..."

"Toby's magic," Griffin gasped. "It's the only way."

Xavier backed away. "You told me you had no magic."

Toby sighed, a dejected set to his shoulders.

"He doesn't," Gullie blurted. "Well, it's not normal kind of fae magic." Yet, it was the only kind of magic that could save them now.

Chapter Two

SOPHIE

"I'd like to see my father." Sophie crossed her arms over her chest, trying not to let her fear show through the brave facade she had in place. "You know he's a leader of HAFS. He wouldn't want me here." Her words were brave, but she battled to keep her wits about her.

"You know very well your father is the one who brought you here, Sophie-Ann. You will answer my questions first before I allow you to speak with him." Doctor Clarkson pushed back from his dark ebony desk, his arms resting on the soft gray leather of his chair. He'd arrived soon after her, leaving the rest of the HAFS operations in her father's hands, along with a few other chapter leaders like him. But for what? To learn the secrets of the fae? Too bad she wouldn't tell him a thing.

Sophie didn't need a reminder that her father had betrayed her, but there was still a small part of her that couldn't believe he understood what he'd subjected his own daughter to. He was confused.

Despite everything they'd been through, despite all their disagreements and frustrations, Sophie knew her father loved her. It was the fae he hated.

But the fae had saved her life.

Gulliver O'Shea had saved her life. The boy with the kind eyes and the strange tail that she now couldn't imagine him without.

"I don't know what you're talking about." Sophie gave a weary sigh. The drugs they'd pumped into her system since her arrival at the Clarkson Institute left her mind foggy and her body weak. It took everything she had to keep her mind focused, but it was a battle she was losing.

"What magic have you been exposed to, Sophie-Ann?" His penetrating eyes seemed to stare right through her.

"Don't call me that."

"Why not? It's your name, isn't it?" His long, white fingers fluttered like butterflies around his face, but she knew that wasn't right.

Squinting again, she realized his hands were steepled under his chin as he peered at her expectantly.

"My dad calls me Sophie-Ann. Everyone else calls me Sophie."

"Fine, Sophie." He sighed. "Tell me what magic you've been exposed to? What have those fae creatures done to you?"

"Nothing," she muttered, a heavy blanket of confusion settled over her. She couldn't remember why she wanted so desperately not to tell him anything. She had a reason. A good one. It just escaped her at the moment.

"The last time your father saw you in the hospital, you were at death's door. You were missing for weeks. There was no sign of you anywhere until several high-profile fae criminals returned to the human world and brought you with them, fully restored to the picture of health. Can you explain that?"

Sophie shrugged. "They healed me in one of their kingdoms. They were kind and didn't—"

"They took you to their realm?" Doctor Clarkson interrupted her.

Crap. She hadn't meant to give that bit away.

Sophie shrugged again. "They don't want a war with humans."

"They have a funny way of showing it." He scowled. "They have nearly destroyed Los Angeles in their attempt to claim it for themselves."

Sophie ran a hand through her tangled hair. "How long have I been here?"

"Tell me what I need to know, Sophie-Ann." The doctor's voice rose in agitation. "What magic have you been exposed to?"

"I don't know." Her voice grated in equal irritation. "The healing kind." She threw her hands up in defeat.

"You're lying. We've never known them to have healing magic. Try again, Sophie. This time with the truth."

"I told you the truth already, but you don't want to hear it." Her voice came out like a whine. His questions were exhausting and all she wanted was to curl up somewhere—anywhere—and go back to sleep.

"You look like Sophie-Ann Devereaux. You sound like her." Doctor Clarkson's fist slammed down on his elegantly polished desk, making her jump to attention, all thoughts of sleep vanished with her racing heart. "But they've done something to you, haven't they? They've changed you."

"Are you trying to say I'm a changeling?" She scowled. "That's not how that works. Queen Brea was a changeling. They swapped her with Queen Alona when they were babies. To protect them."

"Queen Brea?" His jaw dropped. "You don't mean Brea Robinson?"

"No. I don't know. You're confusing me." She was too tired to answer more questions. Sophie just wanted to return to her room and escape into the arms of a blissful, dreamless sleep. That was all she seemed to want to do since she'd arrived at the institute.

"Focus, Sophie. What did they do to you?"

"They saved my life." Her hands clenched into fists as she fought to keep her wits about her. She didn't want to give anything away that might hurt Gullie or his family. The fae were kind to her. They'd kept every promise they made, and she didn't want to betray them.

"How?"

"You know very well they have magic, Doctor."

"What kind of magic?" he pressed. "We know some have magic fueled by the sun, and others with moonlight. We know those with day magic are powerless at night. We know some have magic all the time, but it is a weaker magic fueled by the earth and some ancient powerful language. And the cursed darkness we experienced comes from the evil beast-like creatures who have no magic of their own."

Sophie blinked. "You know a lot more than I do, then."

"None of them have the power to heal leukemia in its final stages!" Spittle flew from the doctor's mouth, and his eye grew wild with fury.

Sophie shrank back in her chair, desperate to escape this

nightmare she'd found herself in. "It's new magic," she blurted. "New to some of them, I guess, but it's ancient magic they don't seem to know what to do with."

"But they went to the trouble of kidnapping you from your deathbed to take you to their world? Were they experimenting on you?"

"No, of course not."

"Where did this magic come from? Where did they find it?"

"It's not that simple." She rubbed her eyes and fidgeted in her seat.

"Tell me what I want to know and you can go back to your rooms. I'll even have the nurses bring you a special meal. Something you'll enjoy."

The food at the Clarkson Institute bordered on abuse. Most days, she got bland, pasty oatmeal for breakfast, cheap bologna sandwiches for lunch, and most often, an indecipherable stew for dinner with hard rolls.

The mention of decent food had her stomach growling in anticipation.

"You like Thai food?"

Her mouth watered at the thought of her favorite curry chicken and basil fried rice with cashews and pineapple.

"Where does this healing magic come from?" Clarkson demanded.

"Lenya," Sophie whispered, hating herself for the betrayal. But it wasn't like the humans could travel there anyway.

"And where is that?"

"In their world. They've only recently discovered the people of Lenya, who lived on the other side of a place they called the fire plains. There were two small kingdoms separated from the others for thousands of years. Their magic is different from the others."

"And your fae friends took you there?"

Sophie nodded. A splash of something wet landed on her hand. It took her a moment to realize she was crying.

"How did they heal you?"

"A pool. I was moments from death, and the waters of the healing pools of Lenya saved me."

"Why you?" he demanded. "From what we know of the fae, they don't take too kindly to humans. So, why would one of them bother to help a human?"

"I don't know."

Clarkson didn't need to know how many rules Gulliver probably broke to save her the way he had.

"All I know is that they were kind to me."

"You are a naïve girl if you believe them capable of anything resembling kindness." He shook his head. "When you let them touch you with their magic, you become their creature. No longer human, but not quite fae."

"That's ludicrous. I'm still me. And for the record, they treated me far better than you have, Doctor Clarkson."

"Tell me, if you're still human, still you, then why have you turned your back on your own kind in favor of your new masters?" He leaned across the desk, his eyes boring into hers.

"They aren't my masters. And I haven't turned my back on humans. I just ... I believe there is a way we can coexist if we learn to understand each other. They have a strange perception of humans. Almost childlike."

The doctor stood from his seat, a sad look on his face. "You might be a lost cause, Sophie-Ann Devereaux, but I promised your father I would try to bring you back. And I will."

"What does that mean?" She watched him move to the door to call one of the orderlies she despised. They were the worst sort of caregivers one could imagine.

"We are done for the day." He waved two men into the

office. "Take her back to her room and see that she gets a treat for dinner. Unlike the fae, I keep my promises."

Sophie didn't try to argue with him as the two men dressed in white scrubs led her from the room. In her experience, the fae kept their promises far better than most humans.

Sophie shuffled down the hall between the orderlies. The short walk from her therapy session to her room left her exhausted. She hadn't felt this weak since before she entered the hospital for the last time, when she thought she'd never leave it.

As she sank down onto her bed, she wondered if death might find her here in this awful place. Like it was circling back around for her again after narrowly missing her the first time.

"Cooperate, Miss Devereaux," the big orderly snapped at her, yanking her hand forward and dumping several pills into it.

"I am." She pulled her hand back, giving him her best glare. She wasn't sure how scary it could be considering her eyes crossed and he went all fuzzy around the edges. "I just didn't hear you." She popped the pills in her mouth, having learned it was futile to resist the drugs they shoved down her throat—literally, when she didn't cooperate.

Somewhere in the back of her mind, she knew she was never going to get out of this mess if she didn't have her wits about her, but her head was so full of fog that she couldn't find the desire to care.

"Swallow." The orderly shoved a paper cup of water into her hand, and she gulped the pills down. At least they would send her into a dreamless sleep soon.

"Leave the poor girl alone." The nurse with the pretty lavender eyes chased the orderlies out of the tiny room that wasn't much better than a prison cell. "Idiots," she muttered under her breath as she rolled a cart into the room.

Sophie sat on the edge of her bed waiting for the nurse to take her vitals.

"I'm sorry they've been so hard on you since you got here." She took Sophie's blood pressure, temperature, and pulse. "You'd think they'd have learned by now that you get a lot further with a little kindness and a patient hand." She smoothed the dirty hair back from Sophie's face. "I bet a shower would make you feel better."

Sophie shrugged. The thought of putting forth the effort to take a shower left her even more exhausted. "Maybe tomorrow. I'm too tired tonight."

"That's what you said last night, hon." She buzzed around the room, refilling Sophie's water and fluffing her pillows. "At least tonight you get the good food." She beamed a stunning smile at Sophie, and something about her seemed familiar. But the thought was fleeting.

"Let's get you comfortable and in bed." She helped Sophie ease back onto the lumpy mattress and raised the head so she could sit up to eat dinner.

Sophie's stomach grumbled at the thought of Thai food from some local hot spot, but when the nurse pulled her tray from the cart and set it in front of her, she wanted to cry. It was Thai food, of a sort.

"It's actually not that bad," the woman said, responding to the look on Sophie's face.

It was some sort of frozen dinner of chicken curry and rice with vegetables. They even put a fortune cookie on her plate next to one of those tiny cans of Coke that contained two or three sips.

"Trust me, it's better than the beef stroganoff surprise." The nurse laughed. "The surprise is that it's not beef."

Sophie cracked a smile for the chatty lady. "What's happening out there?" She blurted the question before she thought better of it.

"In the common room? The same as always. A repeat of one

familiar movie or another. You won't miss anything important if you stay in your room tonight."

"No. Out there." She pointed toward the barred clerestory windows high above her bed.

"Nothing to worry about right now. You should eat your dinner and turn in early. You'll feel better tomorrow."

"You said that last night." Sophie sighed. She was so out of touch with what was happening between the fae and the humans. If it weren't for Clarkson's constant questions about the fae, she would probably think it was all just a figment of her imagination.

Maybe it was. Maybe she didn't travel from her home in New Orleans through a portal to a far-off fantasy land. Maybe Sophie Devereaux really was crazy.

That would make more sense than a magical race of fairies who healed her leukemia moments before her death.

"And don't forget your fortune cookie," the nurse reminded her. "That's the best part." She gave Sophie a final grin and left her to her fake Thai meal.

She ate as much of the bland food as she could stomach before she pushed her tray away. As her eyes drooped, she remembered the fortune cookie.

Sophie and her dad used to love sharing their fortunes after a meal of Thai takeout. Tears blurred her vision as she cracked open the cookie and pulled out the slip of paper to see what words of wisdom were there to cheer her up.

Don't lose hope, Sophie-Ann.

Chapter Three
GULLIVER

"Everyone, move!" Griff yelled, ushering half-fae toward the portal Toby held open.

Rock sprayed from above as another missile sailed through the night sky to find its target. Yet, those surrounding them, the ones who'd been fighting the humans and running from explosions only moments ago, now looked scared.

Toby sighed, looking at Xavier with urgency. There was a new distrust in Xavier's eyes, yet he still turned to the others. "Trust them. We have no choice."

It was then Gulliver realized the truth. The half-fae were at odds with the humans, but the fae were completely foreign to them.

At Xavier's insistence, their warriors ran toward the portal, disappearing into it. Toby's magic would guide them to the right destination. No one had more control over the O'Shea power than he did.

But Gulliver didn't want to go with them. Not when Griff was staying behind. He looked to his father, saw the blood streaking down his face, the soot dulling his auburn hair.

Griff met his gaze. "I'll meet you there."

There was no guarantee of that. The village was damaged from the constant barrage of attacks. Even now, thunderous booms shook the ground. Unlike the fae who were running out of strength, the humans and their machines could go all night. Gulliver stumbled, and a hand gripped his arm. It was Brandon, the strangest and most mysterious fae he'd ever met. Tia's and Toby's grandfather also had the answers to every question they'd ever asked.

"The humans won't have this village, Gulliver." His intense gaze was enough to burn a hole right through any magic. "Your father will be safe."

"Gullie," Toby yelled. "I can't hold it open much longer."

Gulliver glanced around, realizing he was one of the last remaining in the square. Without looking back, he stepped into the portal. The magic drew him in, a familiar feeling. Unlike the portal that dropped him in Lenya, this one didn't have any chaos about it.

Toby was not his sister. He lacked every ounce of her unpredictability, and his magic reflected that. It was a clear and peaceful route to Eldur. The ground rushed up at him and he braced for the impact—stone instead of the soft grass of the farmhouse in the human realm.

Daylight filled the portal seconds before Gulliver crashed

onto the cobblestones, his knees buckling with the impact and he staggered forward to regain his balance.

The others groaned from where they'd landed flat on their backs.

"Everyone okay?" He shielded his eyes from the overbearing sun of an Eldurian afternoon as he searched for anyone who needed help.

Xavier got up on his hands and knees, the full contents of his stomach spewing out of his mouth.

Where was Toby?

Turning, Gulliver couldn't find him, but he froze when he noticed where they were. Radur City. Toby had landed them right on the doorstep of the palace, and they weren't alone.

A crowd of Eldurians stared at them, the crescendo of their alarm ringing on the wind.

One voice rose above the rest, amplified by magic. "I seem to have lost your attention." Alona, the Queen of Eldur was giving a speech, probably from the gardens above the canyon city. She couldn't have seen their arrival from up there. "It happens. I can be very boring." When no one laughed, she went on. "Come on, that was a good joke."

Gulliver heard the influence of Brea in her voice. The two semi-sisters were close, and just hearing her sent relief flooding him. They were safe. He was home. It might not have been Iskalt or Myrkur, but Alona and Finn were family too.

"Hello?" Irritation entered her voice now. "What has trapped your attention more than my boring matters of state?"

The back of the crowd seemed to gather their wits about them and realized there were fae who needed help. The Eldurians had always been known as a welcoming people. They converged on them, and Gulliver caught the frantic looks of the half-fae.

"Xavier, where's Toby?"

Xavier heaved in a breath. "I don't know." He blinked rapidly in the sunlight. "How is it day? Have we been unconscious?" His voice cracked like he was close to panic. "What have you done to us?"

"Relax." Gulliver laid a hand on his shoulder. "There is a difference in time between our worlds. Whenever it is night in the human realm, it is day here."

"Oh." He nodded, still looking a bit stunned.

"Orla," Gulliver called on their leader. "Calm everyone down. No one here will hurt you. You're safe now." He explained the shock of daylight to her and others nearby began spreading the word.

"Forgive me, Gulliver," she said, arms crossed over her chest. "But we aren't safe anywhere. You remember the bombs back there, right? We can't go from dodging bombs at night to staring down a mob in broad daylight and feel any kind of safety." She backed away from the crowd, putting herself between the Eldurians and her fae.

New tactic. Gulliver stepped toward the crowd. "We're friends. Please stay back. They're frightened."

The crowd parted with hushed whispers as a figure rushed through the gathering, stopping when he saw Gulliver.

"Finn." Gulliver's heart hitched at the sight of someone familiar. Family. And more importantly, an adulty-adult who could handle this situation far better than he could.

"Gulliver?" He shook his head. "What have you done?" He looked past Gulliver to the half-fae, most of whom still appeared human even in the fae realm. "Humans, really?" He rubbed his eyes. "As if the girl wasn't bad enough." His voice lifted on his magic. "It's okay, Lona. Gulliver is here."

"Gulliver?" Princess Darra's magic or one of the queen's guards must have amplified her voice since she had none of her own. "What's he doing here?"

"Well, I'm not really sure, but I was just about to ask him."

"Stop talking to me then and just do it."

They seemed oblivious to the fact that the entire crowd who'd come to hear the queen now listened to their conversation.

Finn lifted an eyebrow, placing one hand on the hilt of his sword as Xavier and Orla walked up behind Gulliver. "You heard her. Care to tell me why you've brought humans to Eldur? Am I to assume Tia is behind this? It smells like her."

Worry gnawed at Gulliver. Toby still hadn't appeared. Had something happened in the village? He needed to get back to the human realm to find him, but his cousin wasn't the only one he'd left behind.

Sophie was somewhere among her father's men, the ones attacking his fae.

He shook his head. "It was Toby."

"Then, where is he?" Finn's eyes widened. "Gulliver, if you lost Brea's child..." He swallowed heavily. Toby was more than Brea's kid to Finn. He was the last part of Logan in this world. The two of them hadn't existed separately since they were fourteen years old.

"We have to go back." Xavier looked over his shoulder. "We can't abandon him."

Tears gathered in Gulliver's eyes, but he blinked them away. "The only fae who could take us back is Toby."

"What do you mean?"

"Finn." Alona spoke again. "What's happening? Give me the blow by blow."

That was a Brea phrase, and Gulliver wiped his eyes at the sound of it. "Don't tell her. Please. Not yet."

Finn lifted his voice. "Just having a nice Sunday morning chat with a friend, love."

Gulliver laughed, despite the panic building in his chest.

Xavier and Orla were arguing about something, but he paid

them no attention. It didn't matter what they thought or if they felt safe. No one here would hurt them, and Gullie had never been happier to be in the fae realm.

It hit him all at once. The battle. The race to save the half-fae from a fight they couldn't win. The near destruction of Aghadoon. Leaving his father and Brandon behind. Sophie. It was too much. Gulliver lunged forward, wrapping a surprised Finn in a hug, his hands shaking.

Finn pressed Gulliver's head into his chest. "It's okay, kid." Gulliver might have been in his twenties, but he'd never minded anyone treating him younger because it was out of affection. "Whatever happened is over now. You're here."

Gulliver could still see them. The bombs, the fire raging through the sacred village. Would Aghadoon ever be the same? He couldn't seem to stop shaking.

"Take a deep breath, Gullie. You're safe now." His voice lifted magically as he turned to the crowd of stunned half-fae. "You're all safe now." To Gulliver, he asked. "What in the five kingdoms has happened?"

"My father," he said into Finn's shirt, "he's still back there with Brandon and Toby. There was a war." He pulled away. "These aren't humans, Finn. Well, not entirely. They're half-fae."

"Finn, bring Gullie to me right this minute." Alona was starting to sound irritated, but her husband stood frozen, staring at the dozens of half-fae who'd backed as far away from the crowd as they could. They had gathered in a far corner of the road running along the edge of the river canyon. Some peered down over the railing to the lower regions of the city.

A scream echoed off the nearby shops, the very cobblestones themselves, as Darra came running through the crowd. The Eldurian heir was a beautiful young woman, only seventeen, who was also a little wild. Instead of the corseted dress that fit her position, she wore a long flowing blue skirt and tunic shirt. Her hair was down and threaded with white flowers.

She collided with Gulliver before he could even register her presence. "Tia wrote to me that you'd gone to the human realm." She leaned back, studying him. "You're too good for the likes of them, Gul. Too kind." All she knew of humans were the stories from Brea of the treatment she'd received.

"I'm okay." He attempted a smile, but the anxiety churning within him pulled it taught. "I..."

"Who opened the portal? Is Toby or Griff here?"

Tears finally escaped his eyes, and he collapsed against her, his body shaking. "I failed everyone." His father. Toby. Sophie. He was here in safety with a bunch of half-fae, who looked like they'd rather be anywhere else, while the ones he cared about fought the humans.

The blazing desert sun beat down on them, not so different from the heat they'd experienced in L.A.

"Someone tell me what's going on!" Alona was yelling now. They could tell even with magic amplifying her voice.

Darra's lips twitched. "Mom had to wear her most constricting dress today."

"Had to?" Finn asked.

"Okay, she chose it. You know how she is. Well, to get down here without a trail of guards, I had to climb, and she's just salty she couldn't do the same."

"Say it again." Gulliver sighed. "Say *salty*." It was one of Tia's favorite humanisms.

Darra's smile faded. "You'll see her soon enough now that you're back." She looped her arm through his. "We'll find Toby. I promise. And Griff. We can get word to Uncle Lochlan. I think he's in Iskalt at the moment. Probably at his hunting lodge"

It would be too late, but he didn't say that. Instead, he nodded, wishing it could be true.

The crowd started running, and Gulliver turned to see what had them sprinting back toward the palace. A bright light rent the air, almost like an explosion, the kind he'd become all too familiar with. For a moment, the air shimmered and they could see through to the human realm, to the battle of Aghadoon. Artillery fire blasted through the village, exploding through the portal and into Eldur, bullets licking up the stone face of a nearby tavern.

Screams rang out in the street, and the half-fae readied themselves to fight, even in their confusion and exhaustion.

A plane soared above Aghadoon, the likes of which the fae of Eldur had never seen. And then, it was gone, as if the opening had never been there to begin with. It left a trail of fire across the sky, and one lone figure.

Toby wobbled on his feet at the center of Radur city. The hem of his shirt was singed, but he looked unharmed. That was, until Gullie noticed the blood trickling from his ear.

Gullie ran toward him, but he wasn't fast enough. Before anyone could help him, Toby's legs crumpled beneath him and his body crashed into the street.

Chapter Four
TOBY

Ringing filled his ears where a moment ago there had been nothing but blissful silence and darkness. Fire, he remembered the fire and his grandfather being trapped by it, forcing him to close his portal to help. Then came the explosions. One after another in a symphony lighting up the night.

Griffin had made him leave. Toby tried to refuse, but Aghadoon was as good as gone. In those last moments, Griffin had forced him to leave them behind.

He almost hadn't been able to get another portal open, and the moment Toby stepped into it, an explosion tore it wide open.

It took everything he had to hold it together, to prevent it from creating another rift between the worlds. By the time his feet touched down in Eldur, he'd had nothing left.

Rough cobblestone scratched at his back, and his eyes were crusted shut, but he forced them open, one then the other. Many faces hovered over him in the hot Eldur afternoon, but there was only one he wanted to see. Darra. She was here, looking so much like her brother it both broke and healed something inside him.

She smiled down at him, that front tooth slightly crooked like Logan's had been. "Hi, stranger."

He hadn't been able to set foot in Eldur since Logan died. It was too hard, but he was ready now. Ready to do whatever he needed to for the fae living in the human realm.

"I brought some friends!" he shouted over the ringing in his ears.

She laughed, tears shining in her eyes. "I can see that. You always were one for trouble."

"I think you're confusing me with my sister." It was then he noticed the other faces. Finn wore a sad smile. Gulliver looked like he was going to throw up. And Xavier ... Toby couldn't decipher the way he looked at him now.

"You don't need to shout, Tobes, we can hear you," Darra said.

"Someone want to help me up?" He lifted a brow. "Or I can just lay here in the street and go back to sleep."

"Everyone back up," Alona yelled over Toby, walking toward them through the crowd. "Give the Iskaltian prince some space."

"Look who finally decided to make her way down." Darra rolled her eyes.

There was a rough slit cut up Alona's dress, almost like she'd ripped it herself to loosen it.

"Your Majesty!" A guard ran toward her in the traditional Eldur livery.

"What is it?" Alona stepped toward him as he stopped to catch his breath.

"Aghadoon has been set down just outside the city near the orchards."

"What'd he say about Aghadoon?" Toby shared a look with Gulliver, who was blinking away tears. "They made it?" The ringing in his ears seemed to get louder and louder. "Well, what are we waiting for?"

Gulliver reached down to help him up, and Darra grabbed him under his other arm.

"Absolutely not." Alona crossed her arms. "Toby needs to get to the healer. Gulliver, you and Finn will go to Aghadoon."

"I'm not going to the palace when my grandfather and uncle might be hurt!" Toby tried to hide his limp, but he knew he wasn't fooling anyone.

Darra looked back at her mother. "It's his choice, Mom."

"This next generation of fae royals is going to drive us all into early graves." But she didn't try to stop them again. Instead, she commandeered three horses from her guards. Toby rode with Finn, who helped keep him upright. Darra and Gulliver each got their own.

Traveling on horseback through a city with no odd magic-like electricity or giant cars felt right, and yet, Toby missed the constant energy of the human realm, the way they never seemed to stop moving. There, they didn't need fae magic to have value.

He'd left Xavier behind with Alona, who he knew would make sure everyone got the help they needed.

By the time they reached the outer city limits, they saw it. The pillars of Aghadoon were half crumbled into dust, the remaining stones sticking up like reminders of the beauty they'd once held.

The high walls bore the marks of battle. Holes in the stone that would need repairs. Black burns stretched across the surface. But it was the village within that suffered the most damage.

Two figures emerged from the dust, walking toward Radur City.

Gulliver slid from his mount, ran toward his father, and wrapped him in a long hug.

Finn helped Toby down, and he refused assistance walking toward his grandfather.

"I shouldn't have asked you to come." It was what hurt the most. As much as he wanted to help their half-fae brethren, it put the fae's most sacred place at risk.

His grandfather put a hand under his chin and tilted it up. "I knew the risk, Toby. It is my guilt to bear, not yours. I did not imagine what it would come to, but when my grandson has need of me, I will come. Always." His smile reached all the way to his tired eyes. "We were worried when that explosion hit just as your portal closed."

"I can only somewhat hear you, but I'm okay." He knew there was probably still blood on his face, he could feel it trickling from his ear, but he didn't want to worry anyone. "I promise. I'm just so relieved you both made it back in one piece."

Finn cleared his throat. "I think it's about time we learned what's going on. I'm not surprised you two are involved in this." He looked from the half-destroyed Aghadoon to Brandon and Griff.

"Yes." Darra nodded eagerly. "Why were there humans sprawled all over our street during Mom's speech?"

A group of horses galloped toward them from the city, stopping when they came close. Four guards who had most likely been sent by Alona.

The first one nudged his horse forward. "We are to escort you to the palace."

Toby rolled his eyes. He was well versed in queen behavior

from his mom and sister. They were impatient and thought they deserved all information before others.

"May as well go." Darra slipped his arm over her shoulder to help him. "You won't get out of it."

All Toby wanted was to have a bath, a hot meal, get his ears to stop ringing, and then plan how they were going to defeat the humans and help the rest of the fae and half-fae in the human realm.

Yet, he knew the routine. First, he had a queen to talk to.

The guards led them through the streets that were teeming with curious Eldurians. The half-fae were nowhere to be seen, but that didn't worry Toby. They'd be cared for here.

The Eldurian palace was a maze of halls, interspersed with courtyards that featured grand fountains and beautiful gardens. They favored anything that let them sit outside among shade trees and cool water.

Toby couldn't help thinking of the last time he'd been here. It was a visit for Logan's nineteenth name day. Tia was missing, so neither of them felt much like celebrating. Instead, they sat together under the stars, wondering if his sister looked up at the same sky.

He'd never imagined he would get his sister back but lose Logan.

They passed the entrance to the residence wing on their way to the throne room, and Toby looked away. For the past couple of months, he'd managed to push Logan's memories from tragic loss into fond remembrance. Xavier's friendship helped him want to live again. He stopped wishing he'd been taken with the man he loved.

Yet, now, he was back right where he'd started.

Almost as if he could read his mind, Brandon set a hand on Toby's back. His grandfather's presence had always been comforting, a symbol of safety. The man had been through too much for anything to scare him, and his steadiness made those around him swell with courage.

The ornate mahogany doors to the throne room stood open, and Alona sat on her wooden throne, her foot tapping anxiously. Before her, Xavier and Orla shifted uncomfortably.

Darra stopped next to Xavier, still holding Toby up.

"What are you doing here?" Toby hissed. He couldn't look at Xavier in this palace, in front of these people. Shame flooded him at the way he'd let Xavier push Alona's son further into the back of his mind.

Xavier shifted away from him, almost as if Toby frightened him now. "Orla and I are representing the half-fae."

"So, it's true?" Darra asked. "Those people out there are half-fae? They look so human."

Xavier nodded. "Some of them are fae entirely, but that is rare for those living in the human realm. Our ancestors have intermarried with humans for generations."

Alona slapped a hand on the arm of her throne. "Will someone tell me what is going on?"

Everyone was looking at Toby, even Gulliver and Griff, to explain. None of them wanted to tell Alona of Tia's plan.

He let go of Darra. "I need to sit down." A page boy quickly brought over a velvet chair, and Toby sat. "Tia started hearing rumblings of a group in the human realm targeting fae."

"Why is he shouting?" Alona darted a worried look around the room. "What's wrong with him?"

"One of the human bombs exploded in his ear. He'll be okay soon. The ringing wears off after a while." Griffin clapped him on the back.

Alona nodded. "We were aware of Tia's suspicions. Our agreement was to wait and watch."

"But it's Tia."

She sighed. "Brea's daughter through and through. What did she do?"

Gulliver's tail wrapped around his middle almost like a protective shield. "She sent me to the human realm to investigate."

"I was sent with him because she wanted me out of the palace." Toby shrugged. It was the truth. "But what we learned was worse than expected. Fae and half-fae were not only being targeted by bombings ... err ... explosions in New Orleans, but in other cities as well."

"The group is called the Human Alliance for Survival." Gulliver lifted his gaze to the queen. "They think our very existence in their world threatens theirs."

"But we do not want to harm them." Alona looked as confused as Toby had been at first.

"No, but our magic is a threat to them," Toby explained. "At least, they think it is. Most half-fae have little power to speak of. Yet, the humans would still eradicate them."

"It got worse when I sort of abducted a HAFS leader's daughter." Gulliver's voice was low, almost inaudible.

But Alona heard it because she lurched forward out of her throne. "Excuse me?"

They explained the rest to her about the healing pools, bringing Aghadoon to the human realm as a haven, the attack. And then, the portal bringing them to Eldur.

Alona, Darra, and Finn were entranced by the story and also seemingly horrified. They ended on the fact that the human realm was now at war with the fae, and it wouldn't end. At least, not right away.

The fae could no longer stay out of this fight.

When they were finished, Alona went to speak with a maid about making up rooms for their guests. Xavier approached Toby. "Camp has been set up for our people outside the city. I'm going to stay there." His eyes traveled around their opulent settings like he didn't trust any of it.

"What?" He leaned closer to Xavier. "Oh, camp? Yes! That's a good idea." Despite his raised voice, Toby kept all emotion out of his tone. Once the half-fae were gone, his shoulders drooped.

Gulliver's tail tapped his back in reassurance. "This must be hard for him. Going from the human realm to one of their fairy tales."

Toby shrugged. "Sure." He had no more energy for all things Xavier, not while he sat in Logan's home.

The palace healer insisted Toby needed rest, but he didn't want to stay in the infirmary. Gulliver and Darra promised to watch over him and they were allowed to take him to Darra's chambers as long as Griffin accompanied them.

It was like old times. They sat enjoying freshly baked bread, deep red Eldurian wine, and the sharpest Fargelsian cheese, with ripe shadow berries from Myrkur, along with smoked fish from Iskalt, and sweet iced chocoah from Lenya for dessert. A feast of the five kingdoms, Darra called it.

As hungry as Toby was, he only picked at his food. He could feel Darra, Gulliver, and Griff watching him, waiting for him to break. But he wasn't his sister. He wouldn't let the entire world into his heart to learn what contents it held. His grief was his own.

After they'd eaten in silence for a while, Griff spoke up. "I'm leaving tonight."

Toby saw Gulliver snap his eyes to his father. "You can't. I ... Dad ..."

Griff reached for his hand. "It's okay, Gul. I'm here. We all made it out of there. I'm just going to Iskalt to fetch Tia. She should be here. I'll travel to the farmhouse and then on to Iskalt. The humans won't even know I'm there."

Toby let them have their moment and focused on Griff's

words. He would bring Tia here, and there was nothing Toby needed more than his sister. For so long, he'd kept her at arm's length, maybe blaming her on some level for Logan's death. He'd treated her terribly, hadn't helped in the first year of her reign.

Yet, she would still come. Because she was Tia and he was Toby. No matter what, they'd always save each other.

Chapter Five

SOPHIE

Sophie shuffled down the wide hallway, the dingy vinyl floors a stark contrast against her cheap white slippers. Fluorescent lights flickered overhead as she passed door after door, each closed to conceal the inmate ... patient ... behind the small shatterproof windows.

She was finally free. Sort of. She'd earned the privilege to visit the dining hall and common room without escort. And she'd traded in her hospital gown for blue pajama-like scrubs and a threadbare white robe. Today was her first chance to explore, and so far, Sophie didn't like what she saw.

Since her arrival at the Clarkson Institute, she'd been heavily drugged and too incoherent to take stock of her surroundings. She was still drugged, and her mind was foggy, but she no longer felt like she was underwater.

But she was weak and confused. And she needed answers. How had her own father allowed her to be taken to such a place? Sophie stood in the doorway to the dining hall, appalled to see just how many people were housed within the creepy walls of this place. It looked like a horror show. A relic of a bygone era, where unwanted people disappeared behind the walls of an asylum never to be seen again.

Her father wouldn't do that to her, would he?

She picked up a tray from one of the friendlier orderlies passing out meals to the inmates.

Patients.

Shaking her head to clear the fog, she tried to remember she wasn't in a prison, though it felt like. She moved to sit at a table by herself.

Too many other patients looked utterly defeated as they stared blankly at the walls and ceilings, or laughed softly to themselves.

Glancing down at her breakfast tray, Sophie was pleased to see a single pancake. It was the frozen kind meant for toaster ovens, and it was mostly cold, but there was butter and syrup to go with it and what looked like a scoop of powdered eggs and a carton of apple juice. A hunk of some meat-like substance occupied one corner of the tray. It was cut to make it look like ham, but she suspected it was something else.

Her stomach rumbled angrily as she poured syrup over her pancake. It wasn't much, but it was better than the pasty plain oatmeal she'd grown accustomed to since her arrival. She wasn't even sure when that was. It seemed like just a few days, but time was a confusing thing here.

"It's about time you showed up." A little boy climbed into

the chair beside her, a carton of apple juice clutched in his hand. His eyes were hollow and sunken with dark circles and a sallow look about his complexion that said he didn't get much time outside.

"Um. Hi." Sophie glanced over her shoulder to make sure the kid was actually speaking to her. She had a fleeting thought about whether the boy was really there or if her mind was playing tricks on her.

"I thought you might have decided to stay wherever you went when you disappeared, but then I saw you in that place. Nurse said it was called California."

"What?" Sophie blinked rapidly, taking in the boy's appearance. Despite his pale skin and shadows under his eyes, he looked better than most of the other patients. His eyes were clear and bright—a golden amber color she couldn't ever remember seeing before.

"I've never been there, but Nurse says it's a pretty place. Sunny, with beaches. I don't know what a beach is, but I'd love to see one someday."

His voice pulsed in her ears, and Sophie swayed in her chair.

"Who are you?" she managed to whisper.

"Dunno." He sipped from his juice box. "I don't have a name."

She blinked again, forcing her attention on the boy when it seemed to want to focus on anything else. His dark blond hair was cut short without much thought for style. He was small, but she imagined he was probably around ten years old. There was something inherently endearing about him. An innocence Sophie found oddly familiar.

"How do you not have a name?" she finally asked.

"Never got a real one." He shrugged as though it was no big deal. "Some of the nicer nurses call me August, but that's just the month I came here. Most everyone else calls me Patient Eighty-seven."

"How long have you been here?"

"Always." He leaned toward her plate, eyeing it with interest. "Are you going to eat your ham?"

"That's not ham." Sophie wrinkled her nose, shoving her plate toward him. "Help yourself."

"I like it." He took a big bite. "The orderlies usually sneak me an extra piece when it's available, but they were short today."

This poor kid had grown up in the institute. No one had even bothered to give him a decent name, and he thought a slice of fake canned meat was a treat. Sophie felt an overwhelming impulse to protect this child.

He looked up at her with wide golden eyes that seemed to see everything about her. "Where did you go? I missed you."

Sophie frowned at him, her head tilting to get a better look at him through bleary eyes. "Do you know me?" She couldn't place him, but he seemed to believe they were friends.

"Of course. You're the girl I've been waiting for." He took another bite of the not-ham, smacking his lips. "But you left for a long time. And you were really sick, but when you got home, you were different. Healthy and ... scared, I think." He cocked his head at her. "How are you still alive?"

"Well, that's a long story." She glanced around the dining hall to see if anyone was watching their exchange. "How do you know me?"

She was missing something. Her head throbbed, and it felt ten sizes too big for her shoulders. The drugs kept her docile and confused. Something tugged at her memory. Something about this kid.

"I've always known you." He leaned close, dropping his voice to a whisper. "I dream about you all the time." He pressed a chubby finger over his lips. "But don't tell the doctor about it.

He doesn't like it when I do weird stuff. And you shouldn't tell him when you dream about me."

He thought she dreamed about him? What would make him think that?

"Are you half-fae?" Sophie asked, but the mesmerizing quality of his eyes told her that much was true. But why would a half-fae child in a mental institution dream about her?

"Dunno." He shrugged again. "What's a fae?"

"Never mind." She rubbed her eyes and almost expected him not to be there when she opened them again.

"You have to quit the pills. They mess with your head." The boy gave her an intense look, an expression far beyond his years.

"They make me take them." If she could figure out a way to avoid the medication, she would, but the orderlies were thorough.

"They make you stick out your tongue and open your mouth, but they don't check everywhere. Next time, tuck the pills between your upper gums and your cheeks before you drink anything. Once they leave, stick them under your mattress until you get a chance to flush them."

"That's what you do?" Sophie marveled at the boy's ingenuity.

"You have to pretend you're still taking them." He scooted closer to her. "Just drag your feet and mumble a lot. Act confused and slow to understand things, and they'll never know you're not taking them."

"I'll try it, thanks."

"You can't trust the doctor. He's bad."

"I've figured that much."

"Or the orderlies and most of the nurses. You can only trust me and the nurse with the pretty eyes." He slipped off the edge of the chair. "Remember that, okay? Just me and the nice nurse who changes your bed linens."

"The one with the lavender eyes?" She was the only one Sophie had met that could be considered nice.

"Yes. She's good." He started to leave.

"Wait, I have more questions." Sophie turned toward him, lowering her voice. "Can you help me get out of here?"

The boy shook his head, his eyes darkening with sadness. "There's no way out of here." He laid a hand on her shoulder and frowned. "What's your name?"

"You seem to know me, but you don't know my name?"

"I know your face, and I can tell you're good in here." He tapped a finger over his heart.

"I'm Sophie."

The boy nodded, as if her name somehow made sense to him.

"Patient Eighty-seven, you're late." A familiar voice swept across the dining hall, sending everyone into total silence.

Doctor Clarkson marched across the room and grabbed the boy's arm. "You know the punishment for being late for therapy."

Sophie lunged out of her seat. "It's my fault. I kept him with my questions."

"Go." He pointed to the doorway of the dining hall, and the boy sprinted through the double doors. The doctor turned his hateful glare on Sophie, and she winced as she returned to her seat.

"See that you don't delay my patients in the future. We run a tight schedule around here."

"Yes, sir." Sophie whimpered under his scrutiny. She kept her eyes on her lap until he left through the doors and the din of conversation returned.

"Don't trust them, Sophie." The boy's voice echoed behind her, and she turned just in time to see his pale face disappear through the doors once again.

Chapter Six
GULLIVER

"I need to get back, Tobes." Gulliver paced across the narrow infirmary room. "I'm worried about Sophie. She's surrounded by the enemy."

"What?" Toby shouted. "Gul. Speak up." He rubbed the side of his face, where the healers had bandaged his ear with a potion that reeked of the volcanic mud from Eldfal. Despite Griffin's assurance that Toby's hearing would come back to him soon, the ringing in his ears still hadn't stopped, and Alona had sent him to the infirmary.

"You're really loud." Gulliver moved closer to the bed. "Did the human magic really break your ears?"

Toby nodded. "I got too close to the Aghadoon shields when one of their bombs hit."

"That's why I need to get back." Gulliver leaned closer as he yelled. "Sophie needs me." He pointed at himself, dragging out each syllable.

"It's too dangerous, Gul. I know she's important to you. If anyone gets that, it's me. But we have to figure out our next moves first."

"She might not have time!" Gulliver dropped down onto the bed beside Toby. "She's so strong, but she can be too kind sometimes. I worry what they might do to her if they find out where she's been."

Toby touched his arm. "She'll be okay."

Gulliver turned to face him, speaking slowly so he wouldn't miss a word. "You don't know that. You, of all people, have to understand. If it was Logan back there all alone, would you let anything stop you from getting to him as fast as one of your portals could take you?"

Toby's eyes dropped to his lap. "You're right. But Logan wasn't human. Sophie is, and she's in her own world now, and her father is right there with her. You have to trust that she can take care of herself."

"I know she can." Gulliver dropped his head into his hands. "It's me that can't stand the thought of what she might be going through because of her association with me. I never should have gone looking for food at her cafe."

"You and I both know that's not how you feel. She's alive right now because of you. We'll figure this out, and we'll help you find her, but not until we have all the information we need to make our next strategic move. And then, I'll take you back to the human world myself."

"Spoken like a true prince of Iskalt." Gulliver lifted his head and managed a hesitant smile for his friend.

. . .

"Toby? Toby!" A familiar shriek echoed down the hall.

"Brace yourself, Toby. Here she comes." Gulliver moved out of the way.

Toby winced, leaning back on a settee in the royal residence, where Alona had been fussing over him since the healers finally left him alone for the day.

"Toby?" Another frantic shout reverberated down the hall.

"Someone tell her to stop shouting." Toby clutched his head. "I can hear just fine now."

Gulliver opened the door to the sitting room, and Tia came stumbling in, still calling for her brother.

Toby threw his hands up to stall her. "I'll be fine if you stop shrieking like a lunatic. You're killing my head."

"Are you okay?" Tia dropped to her knees beside him. "Griff said you collapsed when you came through your portal."

"I'm fine. I just got a little too close to the explosions and hurt my ears."

"Can you hear me?" She raised her voice, smoothing a hand over his bandages.

"No need to shout." Toby winced again.

"Give him some space, Tia." Gulliver tugged her back to her feet, and she turned her attention to him.

"Are you okay?"

"Everyone's fine." Gulliver wrapped his arms around her, and his tail stroked her shoulder.

"Gul." She threw her arms around him. "I'm so sorry for sending Sophie back to that awful place. I thought it was the right thing to do."

"It's okay. I'll find her just as soon as I get back there."

"We have much to discuss first." Now that she knew Gulliver and Toby were fine, Tia fell back into her role as queen in the span of a breath.

"Are you sure you're okay?" She sat down beside her

brother.

"Really, I'm fine. I promise." He draped an arm around her.

"Good." She punched his arm.

"Ow! What was that for?" He rubbed his shoulder where she'd hit him.

"You brought an entire village of people through a giant portal, and you didn't send a single person off course? You all ended up exactly where you meant to go? It's not fair!" She smacked him again.

"Fair?" Gulliver snorted. "I think it's only fair that you aren't good at everything, Tia."

"But I'm *really* bad at it."

"It's endearing, sweetheart." Brea came into the room, making a beeline for her son.

"I'm fine, Mom." Toby let her fuss over him.

"I heard you passed out." She checked his bandages and studied his eyes. "You might have a concussion."

"I don't know what that is, but I just have a headache."

"He could barely hear for at least a day," Gulliver offered with a smirk when Toby shot him a glare.

"I heard" Tia shook her head.

"It got better. I'm fine now. Can we talk about something else? Like what we're going to do to help the half-fae camping outside of Radur City? And the ones still suffering in the human world?"

"We're going to meet with them soon," Tia said. "We will let them know they are welcome here now that they are finally home."

"That's just it, Tia." Toby shook his head. "They aren't home. You have to understand, they don't trust us. The human world is all most of them have ever known. To them, it's their home. A home they are willing to fight for."

"He's right." Gulliver moved to sit in a chair beside Toby.

"They will never feel safe here. Most of them have very little magic, if any."

"Perhaps they will be more comfortable in Myrkur," Tia offered.

"I don't think we should force them," Brea said. "They're going to want to return to what is familiar to them."

"Are you suggesting we engage in an all-out war with the humans?" Tia's eyes widened in surprise.

"No, but we will have to do what's best for the half-fae."

"We just have to figure out what that is."

"I thought I might find you out here." Griffin jogged across the dusty Eldur road to catch up with Gulliver at the entrance to Aghadoon, just beyond the city.

"I have some people to check on." Gulliver shuffled his feet, waiting for his father to catch his breath.

"You wouldn't be trying to sneak back into the human world with a certain magic village now, would you?" Griffin tilted his head back to get a good look at his son.

"No, I don't know how to drive this thing." He let his hands fall to his sides. "But if you're offering a ride, I'll take it." They walked along the perimeter of the village where the half-fae had set up camp outside of Aghadoon. They didn't trust the village and preferred the tents Alona had provided them over the last remaining houses standing inside the walls.

"You've spent too much time in the human world." Griffin laid a hand on his shoulder as they walked. "You're starting to sound like Brea."

"Toby asked me to check on Xavier, and Xavier asked me to check on Toby, so I'm going back and forth between them like a carrier pigeon delivering messages."

As they walked through the camp, Gulliver didn't miss the

looks of scorn cast his way. Now that they were back in the five kingdoms, everyone could see Gulliver's dark fae features and they were either frightened of him or they didn't trust him.

"Here comes Xavier." Griffin nodded toward the tall young man headed their way. "I'll leave you to it. I have a meeting with Orla. She refuses to talk to the queens anymore, so I'm the envoy this time. Just don't tell her I'm technically a prince or she might refuse to talk to me too." Griffin patted Gulliver on the back and set off to find the scary warrior woman who led the half-fae camp.

Gulliver waited for Xavier to find his way through the crowd of very nervous-looking half-fae. He felt bad for them, stuck in a world they didn't understand. He knew what that was like from his time in Vondur. At least these fae had landed in a kingdom that would treat them right.

"How is he today?" Xavier's eyes were tight with worry. "I thought he was doing better, but he hasn't been down here yet."

"Toby's fine. He's just resting right now." Gulliver fell in step with Xavier, and they made their way through the haphazard camp. "His hearing wasn't great for a day or so, but it's better now."

"Sounds like a concussion. Do your doctors know how to treat such an injury?"

"They're taking good care of him. I promise."

"If he's so much better, why hasn't he visited yet? The people here trust him, and they are anxious to hear from a fae they've fought beside. Even if that fae has magic he lied about." Xavier's face clouded with anger.

Gulliver sighed, pausing to look around for a quiet place to talk. "Let's go sit in the shade." He pointed to a tall fire nut tree that had just begun to smolder. That meant the nuts were almost ripe.

"That thing looks like it's about to burst into flames at any moment," Xavier hesitated.

"It won't. And I'm ready for a snack." He rubbed his stomach and headed for the lone tree everyone else was avoiding.

"Won't it be hot over there?" Xavier reluctantly followed. "It's hotter than New Orleans in July, and that's saying something."

"Just don't touch the bark and you'll be fine." Gulliver sank down in the shade of the tree and gathered several smoking pods into a pile beside him. He searched his pocket for the carving knife he always kept with him and pried open a few of the pods for a snack.

"They grow ... toasted nuts here?" Xavier examined the contents of the pod.

"They're delicious, but they can cause really bad breath, so don't eat the unripe ones."

"I think I'll pass." Xavier set the large pod on the ground, and Gulliver shrugged, tossing several of the nuts into his mouth.

"He'll come when he's ready," Gulliver finally said.

"You mean when he's done hiding?" Xavier scowled.

"He doesn't have magic, Xavier. He never lied about that."

"I saw him open that portal. It was huge and ... so powerful." He dropped his head in his hands.

"And it's the only thing he can do. Well, that and he amplifies his sister's magic, but when it comes to what the fae here call magic, he is as powerless as I am."

"Neither of you are powerless. You have your defensive magic. What you two can do defies any magic I've ever seen."

Gulliver snorted. "Just trust me when I say what Toby and I can do amounts to cheap party tricks compared to the five kingdoms—well, four kingdoms. Myrkurians are all like me."

"Then, why isn't he here?" Xavier's anger wilted until only

sadness remained.

Gulliver looked up, gazing across the grassy plains to the desert in the distance, where the fire plains used to be. It was still hot in Eldur, but since the Vatlands failed and the land was reclaimed, the temperatures were changing. Eldur would always be a desert kingdom, but it was as though all the land was healing now. Green things grew where once there was nothing but hot sand and wiry bushes.

"Did he ever mention Logan to you?" Gulliver asked.

"No."

"I'm not surprised." Gulliver sliced into another smoking pod. "They were going to be married."

Xavier studied his hands. "I see."

"Logan was the Crown Prince of Eldur. He would have ruled here."

"Was? How did he die?"

"It was a terrible accident." Gulliver suddenly lost his appetite as he remembered the look on Logan's face when he fell after the molten hot lava struck his head. "It was less than a year ago." He dusted his hands clean and wiped the sticky residue from the pods on the grass. "Toby hasn't been back to Eldur since. He hasn't handled Logan's death. Like at all. Coming back here, seeing the people who would have been his family—seeing Darra and how much she looks like her brother—it's hard for him."

"I understand." Xavier nodded. "Can you please tell him I, um ... I miss him, but to take all the time he needs."

"Of course."

"Xavier! Get over here!"

Both men jerked their heads toward the commanding voice.

"Orla." Gulliver sighed at the look of frustration on Griffin's face as he jogged to catch up with her. "I'm guessing Dad's meeting with her didn't go well.

"Come sit in the shade, Orla," Xavier called.

"Not on your life," she shouted back. "I don't go near trees that look like that." She nodded at the smoke billowing up into the sky.

"They're supposed to smolder like that," Gulliver said.

"You aren't going to convince her." Xavier stood and dusted his jeans off. "Let's go see what she wants."

"What's happening?" Xavier asked as they crossed the distance between them.

"We have to go back." Orla crossed her arms over her chest. "And if these fae won't help us, we will find a way home on our own."

"We will help you," Griffin said, exasperated. "But you need to speak with Queen Tierney and Queen Alona."

"I don't talk to queens any more than I have to," Orla insisted. "You're an O'Shea. We know what that means." She fumed at Griffin. "We have some O'Sheas among us, you know. Their magic is strong, but not even they can open portals." She glared at him again. "So, if you please, make a portal and take us all home this instant."

"It doesn't work that way," Griffin growled at her. "First of all, it's daytime and my magic only works at night. Second of all, Toby is the only O'Shea who can make a portal powerful enough to carry you all back home at once. And right now, he's recovering from an injury. So, I'm afraid you're going to have to be patient."

"Fine. Bring Toby down to the camp as soon as he feels up to it."

"That's not going to solve the problem in the human realm," Gulliver interrupted their argument. "You're going to have to meet with the rulers at some point. You need our help, and they're the ones who are in a position to give it to you. We all want what's best for your fae."

"What if the queens and a few others come down to meet with you here in Aghadoon?" Griffin suggested.

"They can come to our camp," Orla relented. "But none of my fae are setting foot in that creepy city again."

Chapter Seven

SOPHIE

Nothing changed at the institute, making it hard to keep track of the days. Each morning, a gruff nurse woke Sophie to shove pills into her mouth. Then, she went through the day trying to appear like they affected everything she did. Dragging her feet in the halls, not speaking during meals, losing focus during the forced interrogation sessions they called therapy.

She knew what they wanted from her: the truth about everything she'd gone through. She held nothing back, knowing they would think she was lying to them, telling them a fantastical story that was too hard to believe of the creatures they hated so much.

A slamming door roused her from her half-asleep state. There was little true sleep to be had surrounded by the sterile white walls and antiseptic smell.

The man she'd come to know as Grantham stepped into her room, his large frame taking up so much space she could no longer see the door. He stared down at a tablet in his hand, not sparing a single glance for her.

"You're a lucky one today." He tapped something on the screen. "It's time to increase your meds. You'll be feeling really good soon." He finally lifted his eyes before turning to pull a cart into the room.

"You'll also start having twice daily sessions with Doctor Clarkson. He seems to think you could benefit from extra time with him." The nurse dumped pills from a tiny white cup into his hand.

Sophie couldn't see them, but she pictured them in her mind. A blue one. Two white ones. But an increase could mean anything.

He didn't wait for her to respond to him because she never did. Instead, he reached forward, gripping her jaw and yanking down. His other hand shoved the pills into her mouth and then handed her a paper cup with a few dribbles of water. "Swallow."

She did as she was told and then opened her mouth to show him it was empty, lifting her tongue, as was the routine. When he was satisfied, he gave her a single nod. "Door's unlocked today. Be careful where you go. We can see you. And don't be late for the doc."

The moment the door shut behind him, she ran her tongue up under her cheek to dislodge the pills and spit them into her palm. Lifting the corner of her mattress, she stashed them in an old Jell-O cup she'd tied to the bedframe.

With a sigh, she got out of bed. Her body ached, and her head pounded, but she couldn't stay in here all day. Not when she finally had a chance to figure out what was truly going on in this place.

If she hadn't imagined the boy entirely.

After talking to him in the dining hall, he seemed to have disappeared, as if he'd never been there at all. She tried not to worry, but now that the medications had worn off, her anxiety was at an all-time high.

Something wasn't right here. It wasn't simply a mental hospital.

Creeping out into the hall, she peered down the blank walls. A few patients moved slowly, aimlessly. Two nurses rushed past, but they paid her no mind. She wanted to yell at them that nurses were supposed to do no harm. With her illness, she'd known a lot of people in the medical industry, and they all had something in common. A deep desire to help their patients.

Here, something didn't add up.

"Library," someone whispered as they passed her in the hall.

Sophie turned to see the nurse who'd been so kind to her, the one the boy with no name trusted. It could have been a trap, but she didn't think so.

It took her asking for directions to the *library* to find the sad little metal cart half-filled with old books sitting at the back of the game room. Sophie thumbed through paperbacks, thinking there must be a note or something she was meant to find here. She lifted a copy of *Anne of Green Gables* and the cover fell off, landing at her feet.

Before she could reach for it, someone else was there, bending to retrieve the cover.

"They've seen better days." The boy looked up at her, those intense eyes holding secrets she wasn't sure he even understood.

"I don't think there's anything here that's been published in the last thirty years."

He carefully wrapped the bound book in its broken cover and placed it back on the shelf. "I wouldn't know." He dropped his gaze and his toe grazed over a cracked patch of linoleum tile.

Sophie's eyes widened. If this boy truly grew up here … "You …"

He didn't know how to read.

Shame flickered across his face. "Sometimes, I take books back to my room and stare at the letters, imagining the stories they tell of the world outside. Is it beautiful?" He looked up at Sophie with eager eyes, thirsty for knowledge of a world he'd never experienced.

That wasn't an easy question. Yes, the world itself was a beautiful creation, but those living in it … "It can be. Sometimes, living in the world means people helping one another with love and grace."

"And other times?"

She sighed, not wanting to take away the image he had of what lay beyond these walls. But he deserved honesty. "People are complicated."

It was the most universal truth. Her father, the man who killed her mother, also put her in here. Yet, she didn't want to believe it was his decision. Whatever he'd done, he loved her.

But did he love her more than he hated the fae? That was the hard question.

A hand slid into hers and squeezed. There was an odd comfort in the gesture. Despite them being strangers, it felt as though they were in this together, and always had been.

Sophie shook her head. That was a ridiculous notion. She'd only just met him, yet the little boy had already managed to steal her heart.

"Come with me," he whispered.

She didn't even need to nod. He seemed to know she wouldn't argue as he tugged her across the game room, where a few other patients sat dazed.

Out in the hall, he shoved her into a corner and peered up. Sophie followed his gaze to the cameras nearby as they oscillated.

"This is a dead spot," he whispered. "The camera can't see us. Doc doesn't want me talking to you. He says you have allied with the fae against humans, but—"

"I thought you said you didn't know what a fae was?" Sophie glanced around the corner to make sure no one could see them.

"I lied." He shrugged. "Too many listeners. The doctor doesn't know all I've seen. My earliest memories are of you, Sophie. I just didn't know your name, but I knew you would come for me eventually. I've been waiting for so long. This is the only life I know, but through you, I've seen so much more. I don't understand how, and I can't control it, but it has to mean something, right?"

Sophie didn't know what to say. "But I'm human." Even if he did have fae blood, that wouldn't explain why he saw her. Then, she remembered something he said before. "I disappeared from your dreams for a while. Why?"

He lifted one shoulder into a shrug. "One moment, you were in the hospital, and I thought for sure I was going to lose you. I was so inconsolable Doctor Clarkson locked me in my room for days. Then, you were gone. I thought you'd died until you suddenly showed up again and gave me hope."

None of it made any sense. Sophie leaned down closer to him. This kid sure knew how to tug on her heartstrings. "Why? Why do I give you hope?"

He paused. "Because ... this place is evil. If we're going to defeat it, we need each other."

"Back away." The shout came from farther down the hall.

"Keep your distance." Two guards ran for them, black batons lifted in a clear warning. There had to be a reason for the odd and completely unnecessary malicious treatment of the patients here.

With no time to think about what she was doing, Sophie readied for a fight, putting herself in front of the boy. The first guard reached them and went for her, but his arm jerked and his body slammed into the wall, hanging there for a moment before he slid to the floor.

The second launched into the air, a scream echoing down the hall as he flew backward, landing in a heap.

"Sophie, run," the boy yelled.

She tried to reach for him, to help him keep up, but when she looked back, Grantham stepped in behind him and plunged a needle into his neck.

If Sophie didn't do something, she'd be next. She took off down the hall, slamming through the swinging doors that led to a row of offices where doctors provided their version of therapy. She'd never ventured past these offices, but there was a red door that basically screamed, "Open me!"

Footsteps sounded behind her and she went for the door, finding it locked. The heavy steel was immovable. It required a keycard to enter.

She only knew one person for sure who'd have one. If this door was so secure, there was something awful behind it. She had to know what it was.

Doctor Clarkson's office was near, and she peered inside, relieved to find it empty. His lab coat was draped over the back of the chair, as if he wasn't on duty today. But she knew differently. He was always here.

Making quick work of the coat, she rummaged through various pockets until she found a card clipped to the inside of the left pocket. Bingo.

"Ms. Devereaux." His sickening voice stopped her. "You're early."

Hiding the card behind her back, she tried to think of something, anything, to say to the man she detested. Footsteps sounded out in the hall, most likely the guards she'd run from before.

"I'll just come back, then."

"Not so fast, girl." He blocked the doorway.

There was no time for this. Sophie lunged for him, driving her knee up into his groin.

"Sorry," she yelled as he doubled over, and she sprinted past him. Hurting people wasn't in her nature. All she wanted was answers.

Reaching the red door, she fumbled with the key card until she managed to press it to the pad. The guards were almost on her when the door clicked, and she shoved it open, closing it before anyone could follow.

Her feet slowed to a stop as she took in the scene before her. Bright fluorescent lights flickered overhead, illuminating a hall not unlike the one she'd left. Except, this time, there weren't only doors lining the walls. There were windows looking in on people locked inside rooms like hers, though these patients were wearing restraints. Some lay on metal tables; others were forced to stand upright.

Window after window showed the horrors of the true Clarkson Institute. The patients in her wing were a front, so the doctors could do whatever they did back here.

A symbol on the wall caught her eye, and she moved closer. It showed two ancient swords and four letters. HAFS.

This was a HAFS facility. She'd suspected it from the moment she saw Doctor Clarkson, but to see it so evident sent a shock through her system.

The people in those rooms...

Her question was answered when she was halfway down the hall. She stumbled back at the sight of a winged fae cowering under intense spotlights as someone in a white coat made notes on a tablet.

But ... how? She thought of Gulliver and the way his features weren't visible in the human realm. How had HAFS done it? They'd removed this dark fae's defensive magic.

The doctor or scientist or whatever they claimed to be jerked around, his eyes connecting with hers. There was no emotion there, only a grim determination. He stepped up to the window, still staring at her, and reached for a button on the wall.

Red lights flashed overhead as an alarm sounded. The winged fae met Sophie's eyes for a fraction of a second, but they were hazy and lifeless.

All she knew was she had to get out of here. She had to let both worlds know what was happening. Unable to go back the way she came, she ran for another door at the end of the ward, her legs tiring with each step. She kept going, despite the aches, despite the tears streaming down her face and the burning in her chest.

She'd grown up thinking the fae were evil, that they wanted to destroy humans.

Now, she knew the truth. There was nothing more evil than what she'd just witnessed in this human facility.

Before she reached the door, strong arms caught her from behind. Sophie bucked and kicked, trying to break free, but It was no use. Pain pinched her neck moments before her breathing slowed, and her body melted as she faded from the world.

Chapter Eight

TOBY

"Toby." Someone poked him in the side. Hard. It could only be one person. "Toby. Toby. Toby."

Groaning, he rolled over in the unfamiliar bed, thanking Alona once again that she'd thought to give him a room far from Logan's old quarters. "What do you want?"

"Your Majesty."

"What?"

"I'm your queen. The polite question would be, 'What can I do for you, your beautiful, smart, witty royal Majesty?'"

"Go away, your royal pain in the—"

"Hey!" Tia grabbed a pillow and smacked him upside the head.

Pain ricocheted through his skull, and he pressed a hand over his ear. "For magic's sake, T."

She sat back on her heels and bit her lip. "Sorry."

"You know, for a queen, you're quite annoying."

"For a queen, huh? Did you not see our own mother make it her life's mission to do things that made Dad growl like a wild animal?"

Toby couldn't help smiling. "I hear it every time I want to yell at someone."

"Brea Robinson Cahill O'Shea!" Tia imitated their father's voice. "What have you done now?" She fell beside him on the bed, her chest heaving with laughter.

Toby couldn't remember the last time he'd just sat with his sister and talked. It was probably before Logan died, before Toby gave up on himself and everyone around him. He'd started to believe they were all just waiting for the next tragedy, the next war. There was no escaping the constant cycle of conflict and strife.

Yet, there were also moments he wanted to believe in the good. Moments that seemed to disappear over the last year.

"I've missed you," Tia whispered. He knew she didn't just mean while he was in the human realm. Her hand found his among the cooling blankets. Eldur beds required a fabric that cooled one's skin while they slept to keep the heat from overwhelming them.

"You know I have to go back, right?" He refused to let the humans win this fight.

She sighed, snuggling closer. "Yeah, I figured. I want to go with you."

He didn't give her the permission she sought because it

wouldn't matter. Tia would always do what she wanted. "You and me, side by side again?"

"Always." A breath pushed out of her. "Before you left for New Orleans ... I thought I'd lost you. Physically, you were there, but mentally, the most important person in my life was a ghost."

He squeezed her hand, hating how he'd created the distance between them. "I'm trying, Tia. I promise you, I'm trying to be me."

"You don't have to be the same fae you were before, you know. No one is expecting that. We just ... we just don't want to lose you entirely."

"You won't. Being away from the five kingdoms, going to the human realm, and fighting for something I believe in again has reminded me of everything we've been through together. We've sacrificed a lot, but we've also done a lot of good."

There was a knock on the door, and it opened before Toby could say anything.

Gulliver stood in the doorway, staring at them with a frown on his face. "Not fair. I want to join." He bounded onto the bed like a spry fox and burrowed in next to Tia, wrapping an arm around her stomach. "This is how it's meant to be."

Toby couldn't argue with that. He, Tia, and Gulliver had a bond that was more powerful than almost anything he'd known. Yet, there was so much missing from the moment, so many fears hanging over them. He knew Gulliver thought of little else but Sophie stuck in the human realm.

She may very well have been welcomed back with open arms. Maybe she sat by and watched as they launched missiles toward Aghadoon. Her father was one of their leaders, after all. Toby wasn't quite as convinced as Gulliver that she was in trouble or that she was on the fae's side.

Then, there was the fact that the sacred fae village sat nearly destroyed outside Radur City. The half-fae didn't want to be here, and their kin were still in danger in the human realm.

"Tell me it's going to be okay," Toby said to both of them.

Gulliver reached out his arm so he was practically spread across both twins, and Tia rested her head on Toby's shoulder. Neither told him everything would work out, but they all knew they would have each other regardless.

Someone cleared a throat, and they all looked up to find Brea and Lochlan in the doorway. Lochlan only showed his amusement in the twitching of his brow. Brea, on the other hand, could never hide hers. She walked into the room slowly, her arms clasped behind her back. She looked impeccable, as always, with an ice-blue gown embedded with crystals. A grin lit up her entire face.

"Hate to break up the party."

His father grunted. "They're in bed, Brea. It's not a party, and you're not breaking anything."

Tia rolled her eyes. "It's a human expression, Dad."

Lochlan had never taken to the human speech, like every single one of his children had. His wife might have been fae, but she was raised in the human realm and it was deeply ingrained in her.

Gulliver rolled off them and sat up. Toby slid his legs over the side of the bed. "Is there a reason half the family is in my room this early in the morning? Is Griff or Kayleigh going to pop out of my wardrobe?"

"That would be fun." Tia shared a smile with their mother. There was something seriously wrong with the women in his family.

His father, seemingly of the same opinion, sighed. "A boy is in the courtyard asking for you."

Toby's entire body tensed before he forced himself to relax. He hoped his family didn't notice, but he was never that lucky.

Tia rubbed his back, and his mother's lips turned down.

"He's a man, Loch. Not a boy. Stop thinking everyone younger than you is a child." She patted his cheek. "This man says those you brought into Eldur wish to meet but will only do so in the camp that's been set up for them."

"Was that all?" Toby didn't know what he was hoping for. For Xavier to be so worried about Toby that he'd climb the terrace? For him to say they were ready to go back and fight?

His dad cleared his throat. He did that a lot. "He, uh ... has asked to speak with you."

Toby couldn't. Not yet. Not here. In Logan's palace, where they'd been so happy. Where they'd dreamed of a future amid the fountains and sandstone of Eldur. Logan would have ruled while Toby stood by his side, joining their families officially.

"I can't." His voice was barely audible, but everyone in the room heard.

"Toby." His mom's sad smile was enough to make him want to run.

He spoke louder this time. "I just can't."

His mom tried to speak again, but his dad put a hand on her arm to stop her. "Okay. We'll let him know." He practically dragged his wife from the room.

Toby slid from the bed on shaky legs. "I need to get dressed." His voice wasn't sharp, but it dismissed both Tia and Gulliver. Tia hesitated just like their mother had, but in the end, Gulliver was able to pull her away.

When the door finally shut, Toby leaned against the wall, breathing heavily. His empty stomach rumbled, but if he ate anything right now, he doubted he'd keep it down. Soon, a maid would arrive to prepare him a bath and help ready him to head to the great hall for the morning meal. He had to get out of here before they did.

Changing quickly, he pulled on a simple brown tunic and

beige trousers that had been left for him. Once he laced up his boots, he marched into the hall, not knowing exactly where he was headed.

He needed to walk around, to find one of the many open-air courtyards to clear his head. There was one that contained a wishing fountain. Yes, that sounded good.

His feet had other plans because he soon found himself in a familiar part of the palace. None of the guards stopped him as he entered the royal family's residence. Darra was an early riser, so she was most likely already training. There were no wars to fight, yet she loved to start the day by sparring with her guards.

Finn normally inspected the guards and various parts of the palace early. Toby had seen it enough times to know the exact routine.

But Alona ... when he heard soft sobs coming from a familiar sitting room, he stopped, unsure if he should intrude. The door to Logan's suite of rooms was partially open, and he wondered if they looked the same. Did he still have a painting on the wall depicting him and his sister? Had the silvery blue rug been co-opted for another use?

He had to know.

Pushing the door open wider, the first thing he saw was Alona in the sitting room, perched on the edge of a cream-colored settee. She had her face buried in her hands.

As he made his way to the Eldurian queen, Toby vaguely noted that everything was just as Logan had left it. For most of his life, he'd called her Aunt Alona, despite there being no blood relation between them. She was an important part of his life. Yet, now, they stood on opposite sides of a chasm of grief, unable to help each other.

"Hi." He glanced down, suddenly regretting his intrusion.

Alona had never looked on him with anything but kindness,

and that didn't change now. "Toby." She attempted a smile. "I haven't been in here since right after it happened."

"I heard you ... from the hall."

She patted the settee beside her. "Having you here has brought back memories." She wiped a handkerchief across her eyes. "All good memories, I promise."

He took the offered seat, not sure what to say. He went with, "I've tried to avoid feeling anything since it happened."

Her hand covered his. "That's not healthy, Toby. You should feel it all, feel it deeply. Logan is a part of your soul. If you cut him out, you lose a piece of yourself."

Tears gathered in his eyes. "For a while, I wasn't sure if I still existed without him."

"Of course you do." She smiled, the gesture small. "The man we both knew wouldn't want any of us to shut down. He was so selfless. All he'd want right now is for us to keep living our lives."

"I don't want to forget him."

She brushed a hand over his cheek. "Oh, honey, you won't. You have a big heart. It isn't supposed to remain broken forever." She paused. "I heard there was someone looking for you this morning. A human boy."

"He's half-fae."

She nodded. "Does this half-fae have a name?"

He sighed. "Xavier."

"Well, my little spy—"

"Gulliver, right?" He cursed. "That man can never keep his mouth shut."

"Not exactly." She wiped her eyes again. "From how I understand it, Gullie talked to Tia, who talked to Brea. Brea brought it to me that you spent a lot of time with this man in the human realm."

"He's a friend."

"One you care for a great deal. I can tell by the reddening of your cheeks. It's how ..." She drew in a deep breath. "It's how my Logan used to look when he talked about you."

Toby averted his eyes, unable to meet Alona' s gaze while she talked of Xavier.

"Do you love this man?"

Maybe he was wrong. His eyes snapped to hers. "What?"

"Those fae are terrified in this world that feels so strange to them. They won't come near the palace. Yet, he came."

"To deliver a message about a meeting spot."

She gave a watery laugh. "Griff had already brought that to us. Xavier braved the palace gates to see you. He even asked your father if he could speak with you, though I doubt he knew exactly who he was speaking to."

Toby could only imagine the look on Lochlan's face when that happened.

Alona squeezed his hand. "This man cares about you. You don't need my blessing to move on, to search for a new future, Toby, but just know that everyone who has ever loved Logan loves you too. All we want is for you to be happy. My son would want it too."

The weight Toby had been carrying in his heart didn't fall away, but he felt the cracks begin to form in the stone. Alona was right. He couldn't stay broken for the rest of his life.

I love you, Logan. He sent off the thought that would never really leave him. *But now I think there might be more to me than this grief.*

There had to be.

Chapter Nine
GULLIVER

Different place. Same meeting. The royals of the fae kingdoms fought about what was to be done as if they even had a say. Gulliver paced the length of the makeshift meeting room they'd created outside Aghadoon. It was open to the sky, with no real walls around it, only guards keeping all those who weren't invited away.

Alona shook her head, clutching the arms of her seat, one she'd had brought from the palace. "These human weapons ... you claim they aren't magic?"

Brea stomped her foot like she was trying not to throw scathing remarks her human sister's way. "Of course they're not.

Is anything we ... they do magic?" She pushed a hand through her dark hair, lifting her eyes to the sky. "Relax, Brea. They're trying to understand."

"Is she talking to herself?" Xavier leaned close as Gulliver stopped moving.

"She does that."

Brea turned so quickly both men fell back. "Gulliver O'Shea, if you have something to say, let's hear it."

Her stare could have pierced the iciest lake.

"Mom." Tia laid a hand on her shoulder. "He didn't mean anything by it. I think you need a moment. Let's get some space."

Brea relaxed under her daughter's touch. "Fine."

The two women walked past the crowd of those who'd come to discuss the human war and ducked around the line of guards.

Gulliver let out a breath, and Toby clapped him on the back. "Don't worry, Gul. She's snapped at each of us over the last few days."

Unlike the rest of those who lived in the fae realm, Brea had connections to the humans that ran deep. She knew what they were capable of without seeing the destruction Gulliver witnessed. For most of her young life, she'd believed she was one of them, and those ties didn't just go away.

The only other resident of the five kingdoms who could possibly understand was conspicuously quiet. Myles sat on the ground in the grass at the back of the group.

Neeve cleared her throat. "So, are we saying we wish to act on behalf of our half-fae brethren?"

"Yes," Toby said at the same time his father said, "No."

They stared at each other, both stubborn enough to wait for the other to break.

Gulliver couldn't believe they didn't see it. The kings and queens he'd fought beside. The ones he knew would protect their world from any threat. They were the ones he revered, respected, loved. And yet, at this moment, they were so unbelievably obtuse.

"Stop," he yelled. They kept talking. He looked to his father helplessly.

Griff dipped his head. "This isn't about them, Gul. You've seen it, you've been there. For once, make them listen instead of lead."

Riona slid her hand into his. "Royals are the most stubborn fae."

"She doesn't mean me." Griff winked.

Gulliver almost laughed when his mother rolled her eyes and said, "I definitely mean him. In my experience, you have to be loud. And repeat yourself. A lot."

Loud. He could do that.

Gulliver drew himself up to his full height. His tail lifted, ready for anything.

"Stop talking!" The words came out as a high-pitched screech. He hadn't meant to sound like one of his sisters when they heard the word no, but there it was.

The group fell silent, all eyes turning to him in surprise. *Great job, Gullie. Now you're in for it.*

Brea and Tia chose that exact moment to return, stopping nearby.

"What's wrong?" Tia was alert, on edge.

Alona folded her hands in her lap and said calmly, "It appears Gulliver wishes for us all to shut our mouths."

His face warmed, and he was sure it was as bright as a ripe Gelsi berry. "I didn't say that exactly. I just ..."

Tia bit back a smile, clearly enjoying this a little too much. "You just what, Gul?"

"My father says I need to make you stop trying to lead so you'll listen." He suddenly didn't know what else to say. His tail dipped and wrapped around his middle.

Brea bumped her shoulder against Griff's. "He would say that, but making any of these guys listen isn't exactly a piece of cake."

Every full-blooded fae in the room stared at her like she'd sprouted two heads.

Lochlan sighed. "I never know what it means when she suddenly starts talking about cake."

"Brea." Alona looked at her with concern. "If you're hungry, I can call for something, but I doubt we have cake at this time of day."

Gulliver ground his teeth together. The human world was burning, destroying the places the half-fae humans called home, and they wanted to speak of cake? "Can we focus?"

Alona's face sobered. "Yes, of course. You had something you wished to say, Gulliver. Go ahead."

Finn gave him an encouraging nod from his place next to his wife.

"Respectfully, none of you understand the kind of damage these humans can do. Some of their weapons fly."

"So do some of ours." Riona's wings flicked in agitation.

"Yes, but Mom, you can't blast holes through Aghadoon's protective shields in mere seconds as you fly over."

Silence followed his words before Lochlan spoke. "The shield was up when that damage occurred?"

Brandon had kept silent until now. He stepped forward. "Yes. Their ... bombs ... ripped holes in the shields, shattering the ancient magic that has protected the village for as long as it has existed. And it happened faster than any of you can imagine. Griffin and I attempted to hold the shields in place with our own magic, but it was far beyond our capabilities. We had no choice but to escape the human realm altogether. If we hadn't, Aghadoon would be nothing now but ruins for the humans to pick over. And much of our magic would be destroyed forever."

"Can we not defeat them with magic?" Kier asked. He was still new to having an unlimited amount of magic now that he could use as many fire opals as he wanted. To him, it could solve almost anything.

Gulliver shook his head. "Have any of you been listening?" He couldn't believe it was even a question. "This group, the Human Alliance for Survival, developed because of their fear of us. Survival. It's what they want. They believe we are going to enter their world and destroy everything they love to take it for ourselves."

He'd only strengthened that belief when he'd stolen the daughter of one of their leaders. Yet, no one knew where Sophie even was.

"But we don't want their world," Neeve said. "We just can't allow them to terrorize our fae who choose to live there." She ran a weary hand over her brow. "It would all be a lot easier if they'd all just come home and leave the human realm to the humans."

Gulliver sucked in a gulp of air. "All our half-fae friends want is the freedom to live their lives in their own homes, without the constant fear of discovery. Yet, you all sit here discussing how we're going to go about doing exactly what the humans expect us to do. Destroying them with a power they couldn't begin to understand."

Lochlan's brow creased. "If we cannot go to war with the humans to save the half-fae, then how are we to defeat them?"

"We don't. It's time we listen and we help however we can." Toby met Xavier's gaze, and Xavier nodded, encouraging him to continue. "It's not our fight. We need to help them, but we cannot take control. Alona, Neeve, Tia, Hector, Bronagh, our half-fae friends are not your subjects. We are simply their allies, nothing more. Why don't you let them lead us in this?" He stepped aside, letting them all see Orla clearly. "Orla, why don't you take it from here."

To her credit, she didn't hesitate to come forward. "The first thing you must understand is that HAFS does not represent all humans. They have the support of certain governments, but there are plenty of people who do not fear us."

Brea offered her a smile. "Thank you for that. It's good to remember that our war is not with the humans but with this specific group."

Orla didn't return the smile before she continued. "We know a lot about them. We have the names of their leaders, the government officials who've authorized bombings. We know the people they have inside our society. Their job is to alert HAFS to upcoming threats. They know you can travel between the worlds. There's even a way they've created to determine where you have entered the human realm. It appears the atmospheric pressure changes after a portal has been opened."

"A thinning of the veil," Brandon said. "That's what we call it."

Orla nodded. "They're tracking your movements."

Griff cursed. "That means none of our normal destinations are safe."

Tia and Brea shared a look.

Orla went on. "HAFS is dangerous because of their dedication, but also the strict punishments they enforce on their own members. It's created a culture of parents turning in their own children as suspected changelings. Wives and husbands accuse each other of fae heritage."

That was ... horrible. Gulliver couldn't imagine ever turning on someone he loved. His mother squeezed his hand, probably thinking the same thing. They'd both grown up in a place where fae did just that, where they turned on each other for scraps of food and the promise of living another day.

"There's a place ..." Xavier hesitated, his eyes flicking to Brea for a moment, as if he knew something he wasn't saying. "A center where the children suspected of fae blood are sent. We have one person on the inside, but it's locked down so tightly it's nearly impossible to communicate with her. All the employees of the institute are tracked, watched.

"It's headed by the worldwide leader of HAFS, his pet project. We don't know exactly what happens there, but we do know many of the kids sent are guilty of nothing more than misbehavior."

Gulliver looked from Xavier to Brea as her face went pale. A place for children suspected of magic ... Could it ...

"This man," Brea choked out. "What is his name?"

"Clarkson. Doctor Alec Clarkson."

She shook her head, stumbling into Lochlan. He held her up. "Clar ..." She couldn't get his full name out.

It was Griff who said what those who knew Brea's story must have been thinking. "The Clarkson Institute is a part of HAFS?"

"But we only learned about them recently." Tia's eyes didn't leave her mother, worry swimming in their depths.

"There's a story among the half-fae," Xavier's voice wavered, "of a fae child raised in the human realm and being sent to Clarkson. Many of us in the half-fae movement now are young. So many of our elders were killed over the years of fighting them. We were not around when it happened, but we know it like we know our own life stories. The Clarkson Institute was the stuff of our childhood nightmares, run by the doctor's father before him. We do not know when he started HAFS, but it has been around for a very long time."

Brea shrank in on herself. Gulliver didn't know everything she'd gone through at the institute, only that it was not a place he'd wish on his enemies.

His thoughts stuttered as he realized how much Xavier and Orla knew that they'd never told him. All Brea had to do to be sent to the Clarkson Institute time and again was exhibit tiny bits of power, to see features on people others claimed not to see, and her parents themselves handed her over.

Would another parent do the same?

He caught Tia's attention, and realization entered her gaze. Without looking at Xavier, he asked, "And what would happen to a dying woman who returned healed?"

Xavier's face went through a range of emotion, finally settling on dread. "I suppose they'd do whatever they could to find out what happened to her."

"Even if she's on their side? Even if her father is one of their leaders?" He already knew the answer to his own question.

"Especially then."

Chapter Ten

SOPHIE

Sophie. The name rang in her head, but she barely heard it beyond the pain splitting her skull. *Sophie.*

She groaned, unable to grasp a thought, to hold on to it. Her head was foggy, her limbs heavy. She pried her eyes open only to find her vision swimming before her.

She was back in her room, but this time, nothing was the same. Her entire body felt like it was wedged under a massive anvil, unable to move.

Clear your mind, Sophie.

"Wha..." She tried to speak, but her tongue stuck to the roof of her mouth.

It was a long shot. I can talk to you in my dreams, but I never should have thought it was real.

"Real?" she whispered. "Real ... it's real!" Her eyes darted around the room, looking for the source of the voice. "Where are you?" She moistened her cracked lips and pushed herself up so she was sitting. "Hello?" The words slurred coming out, but she couldn't speak any clearer.

Whoa! It's you. Sophie, can you really hear me?

"Uh, huh." She recognized the voice now. The boy she'd barely gotten to talk to the day before when they drugged her and ... images flashed through her mind. Fae, glamours removed, strapped to metal beds. Winged fae surrounded by humans in lab coats.

Slow down, the boy said. *Don't speak out loud, I'm only in your head. But think all of that again so I can catch it.*

She didn't want to. It was horrific, but she did as he asked, squeezing her eyes tightly shut.

She could almost feel him quiver, and chills raced down her spine. What was this? How was it possible?

I don't know, he answered a question she hadn't asked.

But... I'm not really fae. I don't have this kind of magic. Was it because of the water in the healing pools?

No, I've always seen you. I guess it's different now since you can hear me in your head, but maybe it's because you know of my existence now.

Why us? What are we to each other?

Another thing I've never known. You're just the girl in my dreams, and now I'm the boy in your head.

Maybe she did deserve to be here. She really was going crazy, losing her mind.

No one deserves to be here. The voice in her head quieted, replaced by images that flashed before her eyes like a movie.

A little boy sitting on his own in the dining hall, begging for something more to eat. That same boy, slightly older, tied to those metal beds she'd seen before. What had they done to him?

You've been here your entire life.

My earliest memories are of this place.

She got a flash of sadness and fear from a child who should have only ever experienced love. The only light she saw in his memories was fluorescent. No sunlight, no silver shine from the stars.

You've never... Her thoughts stuttered as tears flooded her vision. This boy had never been outside these walls. He'd never looked to the moon or made a wish on a shining star, felt a warm breeze rifling through his hair.

Don't cry for me. The words were no more than a whisper in her mind.

It was more than words and images she felt. A power buzzed along her skin, making her hairs stand on end. The only time she'd felt anything like it was... *You're fae.*

I'm not sure.

Yet, his dreams were real. He could speak in her mind. This wasn't a power she'd gleaned from the healing pools. It was his.

Did they know?

She tried to swing her legs over the side of the bed, but they didn't budge. Strong fabric straps looped around her ankles, where metal buckles pressed painfully into her skin, keeping her secured to the bed. She'd been too numb to notice.

What's wrong? the boy asked, probably sensing her distress.

My legs. I can't move. She reached for the buckles, but it was no use. Her fumbling fingers and foggy mind couldn't figure them out.

They do that sometimes. The nurses will come take them off eventually. He seemed so resigned to this life, but what had he said the night before?

You knew. She leaned back on her elbows as the realization hit her. *You said this place was evil. Did you know about the fae kept in chains?*

I've only seen fae in my head, so I don't know if I'd recognize one, but those rooms, yes. They use them for study. The group that runs this place—

HAFS.

Whatever they call themselves they don't have good intentions.

You said we could beat them together. How?

She even heard his sigh. *I said we had to try.*

Something about this boy, about his power called to her. He was important. She just didn't know how or why.

The doorknob to her room turned, and she threw herself back, closing her eyes. The boy faded from her mind and she breathed a sigh of relief. She was afraid someone might look at her and realize she had a giant secret.

When Grantham entered, he went through his routine of pouring pills into her hand, and she dutifully sat up and shoved them in her mouth. At least this time he didn't do it himself with his grubby hand.

Hiding the pills in her cheek, she opened for him.

He didn't say a word as he nodded and pushed the cart from the room, shutting and locking the door behind him.

She spit the pills into her hand, wondering if this was a cycle she'd suffer for the rest of her life.

Maybe Gullie shouldn't have saved her. Surely the death that should have been hers was better than this.

Another day at the institute. Another day she had to figure a way out. She refused to die in this place. Cancer hadn't taken her, neither would hate and fear.

First, she had to know what was happening, had to help the fae stuck in those rooms with the dark windows.

There was more security here than ever, armed guards

stationed at every door. It wouldn't be as easy as last time to get to them, but there was another way.

Don't do it. The boy's voice in her mind was the only thing keeping her grounded some days. He wanted to protect her, even though he was just a kid, but this was for him as much as for her. Something inside of her needed to help him, to get him to Gullie.

Gulliver would know what to do. She had more faith in him than she'd ever had in anyone, and she still wasn't sure why.

Two guards had their hands on her arms as they marched her toward Doctor Clarkson's office. She dragged her feet, stumbling here and there like the walk troubled her, like the drugs kept her from fully rousing herself.

Clarkson's office had military medals framed and hanging on the walls. Now, he led a group the U.S. government once considered terrorists—before they joined them.

A guard pushed Sophie down onto the couch before they left her alone, waiting for the doctor. She knew they wouldn't be far, but the space was a luxury she couldn't get used to. It allowed her to breathe, to truly consider what it was she had to do.

A few minutes later, Doctor Clarkson breezed into the room in a rustle of lab coats and heavy boots. He was young, maybe in his forties. His father started the institute, but he died many years ago. Sophie remembered her dad talking about the two Clarkson men he had to answer to. He obeyed them, listened to them.

Now, she was here because he had to prove his loyalty to them.

Doctor Alec Clarkson sat at his desk, not saying a word as he leaned back in his leather chair.

Sophie refused to look away from him, not this time. She kept her eyelids heavy, so it appeared the drugs hadn't worn off, but she studied him. The way he breathed slowly, silently, his chest barely moving at all. He sat with complete stillness, a predator waiting to strike. His eyes were bright, almost kind. An illusion.

He steepled his fingers on his desk and leaned forward. "We've had quite a struggle with you, Sophie-Ann."

She wanted to tell him not to call her that, not to say her name at all. Instead, she gave him a drooping smile. "I..." She coughed. "I'm sorry. My curiosity got the better of me."

He pressed his lips together, watching her as if he could see right into her soul. "And that curiosity... was it satisfied?"

"Oh, yes. You're doing God's work here, Doctor. My father would love to see all you've accomplished. If you'd let me call him—"

"That is not possible." He pushed his chair back and stood, rounding the desk to stop in front of her. "I want us to understand each other. HAFS is only trying to protect our people. Do you understand why you're here?"

She nodded so hard it sent pain stabbing through one eye. "When the fae abducted me, I knew returning would be hard." The word *abducted* felt like a betrayal of Gullie. It was exactly what he'd done, but now, she couldn't hate him for it. He'd saved her, and she would never be able to thank him properly, to tell him that she was wrong. About everything.

Doctor Clarkson sat next to her on the couch like they were old friends and she wasn't a prisoner he kept drugged. He put a hand on her knee, and it took everything in her not to shy away in disgust. "We need to know what they did to you."

Until now, she'd fought. She'd done everything she could to keep them from believing the truth, but maybe a different truth was more important.

She let tears well in her eyes as she thought of Gulliver and never seeing him again. "It was awful." She sniffed. "The magic they used...."

His hand tightened on her knee. "An abomination."

Now was the part where she had to give up the little freedom she had left. "I think it's still inside me. That's why I'm alive. Do we even know anything about them, really? C-can they turn us into fae?" She let her voice tremble, but she wanted to laugh at the idea. Fae weren't mythical vampires.

Clarkson nodded like she'd exposed one of his fears. "We are studying them. Learning everything we can. What you saw in those rooms ... it is us protecting our fellow humans from a future controlled by the fae and their magic. Knowledge is our greatest weapon. We've been studying them for decades right here."

She bit back a grimace and forced a smile. "Thank the Lord." Her hand found his forearm and squeezed. "I know now that you're saving us. I've been a part of the alliance my entire life. Now, I might be one of them. How can I still help HAFS if I'm the very thing they hate?" She only had to plant the idea, knowing it would grow in his mind.

He stood and started pacing in front of her. "There's a way, but I hate to subject one of our own to that sort of treatment."

She rose to her feet, facing him. "Anything. Doctor Clarkson, I want to help the cause. No matter what happened to me in the fae realm, no matter what I may be now, I will still do whatever is necessary for my people."

He gripped each of her shoulders, looking down into her eyes. He didn't seem to notice how she no longer swayed, that the haze of drugs didn't cloud her irises. Instead, he smiled. "Sophie-Ann Devereaux, your father would be proud of you."

Those words, that one sentence, once would have bolstered her. Now, they did nothing but enrage the fire already burning in her heart.

Chapter Eleven
GULLIVER

Gulliver gripped the hilt of the sword strapped around his waist, trying to make himself remember why it might be a bad idea to draw it on his best friend.

"Tia, you're the newly crowned Queen of Iskalt. You cannot leave for a jaunt through the human realm when it isn't necessary," Brea argued with her daughter.

Tia stomped her foot. "Dad did it all the time!"

"Your father never left this realm during the first few years of his reign. It's important for your people to see you're devoted to them while you establish your rule."

"That's crap. They'd never even know I left." Tia's eyes

flashed with annoyance, and Gulliver took a step away from the warring mother and daughter.

"You have a lot to learn if you think servants don't talk." Brea folded her arms across her chest. "You're not going and that's final."

"That might have worked when I was ten and not the Queen of Iskalt, Mother, but I'm an adult and I am going to help Gulliver."

Gulliver cleared his throat and prayed he'd get through to them quickly before they wasted any more time. "I don't care who comes with me, but we need to leave now. Dad," he turned to his father, "can you open a portal for us? These two can figure out who's going to follow, but I'm leaving."

"And I'm coming with you," Tia insisted.

"We're wasting time, Brea." Griffin shared a look with the former queen, his eyes pleading with her to speed this along.

"Sophie needs me." Gulliver's hands clenched into fists at his side.

"You're right," Brea relented. "Let's go, but Tia can't be gone long before people begin to talk."

"Keir will keep them happy." Tia rolled her eyes. "He can return to Iskalt to make sure the place is still standing. They like him better than me anyway."

"Not true," Brea said in a soothing tone. "They adore you, darling. Always have."

"Maybe, but my husband is better at this job. He'll cover for me."

"I'll do what now?" Keir asked as he entered Alona's study with a pile of documents that likely needed Tia's attention.

Gulliver heaved an annoyed sigh. "We're going after Sophie, and Tia's coming. You have to take care of Iskalt while we're gone, which we're doing right now." He marched through the open doors into the walled garden that overlooked Radur city.

"What he said." Tia paused to give her husband a peck on the cheek before she followed Gulliver into the garden.

"We'll be back soon." Brea tucked a pair of daggers into the belt at her waist. "If you need anything, Lochlan is with the children in the village. He'll take you back to Iskalt tonight. Er ... don't tell him if you don't have to."

"Um, okay." Keir clutched the huge stack of papers to his chest and watched in confusion as Griffin opened a portal in the moonlight. "Have fun ... I guess." He waved from the doorway as Gulliver stepped through his father's portal into the human realm yet again.

"Can't we just call a human to come get us?" Gulliver paced across the living room at the farmhouse. "We did that all the time in New Orleans."

"I'm not sure we can get an Uber out here in the middle of nowhere." Brea tapped her fingertips across the screen on the phone she kept here.

"How are we going to get to the institute?" Tia paced in the opposite direction of Gulliver, throwing her hands up in the air. "This is why we need a car."

"None of us know how to drive, Tia." Brea's thumbs flew across the screen. "I never learned."

"How did you grow up in the human realm and not learn to drive?" Gulliver asked.

"I was only Seventeen when I left, and my parents never taught me. There wasn't time with all the work we had to do around the farm and my stays at the institute. Plus, they weren't exactly parents of the year."

"Did you get in touch with Mrs. Merrick?" Griffin asked.

"That's what I'm doing now if you all will hush up and let me text."

"What's wrong with dropping by to ask for a lift? We could have walked over to the Merrick farm by now." Gulliver groaned impatiently. They'd been there for hours now, waiting for the day to wane. The sun was sitting low on the horizon, and he was desperate to find out if Clarkson had indeed taken Sophie to the institute where Brea had spent so much time as a child. He couldn't fathom what they might do to her in a place like that. He didn't like the grim look Brea wore whenever she recalled her time there.

"It's rude, and humans are accustomed to texting," Brea murmured. "She's going to come pick us up and give us a ride into the city. I've told her it's not safe for her to stick around, so we will have to find our own way back."

"Hopefully it'll be through a portal with Sophie safely with us." Gulliver picked up his pacing. "When will she be here?"

"She's on her way now. Let's get a few things straight before she gets here. We have to blend in as best we can, so we need to change into human clothes. Keep your weapons concealed, and just ... don't act like a fae."

"Nice, Mom." Tia rolled her eyes. "How do you propose we do that?"

"Just do your best." Brea sighed and went upstairs to change into her preferred jeans and t-shirt attire. "And keep your ears hidden."

With Gulliver's defensive magic, he appeared human when he was in the human realm, and he knew how to dress. He went up to Toby's room and raided the closet for jeans that were a bit too short and a t-shirt that read "If I was a JEDI, there's a hundred percent chance I'd use the force inappropriately." He didn't know what a JEDI was, but the shirt fit. He didn't care too much about hiding his sword either. Getting to Sophie was more important than keeping the humans from suspecting he was fae. As Brea had said many times before, all a human had to do was have a conversation with Gulliver to know he wasn't from earth.

Once they were finally in Mrs. Merrick's giant car speeding along toward the institute, Gulliver was able to relax. All they had to do now was figure out a way in and then back out. Easy, right?

"Good luck on your mission!" Mrs. Merrick called as she drove away. After so many years of dealing with the fae family her son had married into, she never seemed phased by their antics. The drive into Columbus took longer than Gulliver would have liked, and it was nearly dark now as they walked along the sidewalk a few blocks from their destination.

"Can you two at least try to blend in?" Brea hissed at Griffin and Tia, who were calling too much attention to themselves with their behavior on the busy street. Griffin walked too close to the curb and Tia kept falling behind, staring up at the tall buildings like a tourist seeing a big city for the first time.

"For magic's sake, you act as though you've never seen a city before," Gulliver said, urging them all to keep up. "We're not here to sight see, Tia."

"Sorry, Gul, it's just been so long since my last visit." Tia skipped along the sidewalk to catch up to her mother. "I forgot how wonderful it is here, but why are there so many cars on this little street? Are they all going to the Clarkson Institute?"

"It's rush hour, honey," Brea said. "People are just going home. I need you to act normal and keep up."

"I am normal," Tia insisted.

"Grown adult humans don't run around like hyper squirrels on vacation in a city like Columbus. Especially this close to a mental hospital."

"Gullie, move your sword to your right side and try to keep it hidden so people can't see the glint in their headlights." Brea ignored her daughter.

"Can we just hurry?" Gullie moved his sword so the hilt faced away from the fast-moving traffic.

"Griff, they won't honk at you if you stay away from the curb. And don't raise your fist!" Brea shouted, shaking her head. "Fracking fae idiots. I've a mind to leave you all at the institute for a little therapy."

"We're nearly there." Gulliver pointed across the street to the heavy stone facade of the Clarkson Institute. "We just need to find a way in through the back." He kept walking past the institute, studying the layout with the security guards posted at the entrance to the parking lot.

"I forget how to get across the street when the cars refuse to stop." Tia's eyes widened at the flow of so many cars. "It's like a raging river without a bridge."

"We use the crosswalk, Tia." Gulliver pointed to the intersection ahead. "Seriously, how long has it been since you visited a human city?"

"A few years." She sniffed irritably. "And New York has the yellow cars that take you where you want to go so you don't have to walk so much."

"Hush, both of you." Brea pulled Griffin in close as the four of them approached the crosswalk, and Gulliver pressed the button. "Thank heaven at least one of you has learned something in your time here." She gave Gulliver an appreciative nod.

"Hey, I've learned lots of stuff." Griffin sounded affronted. "I know how elevators work now, and I've actually ridden a streetcar successfully too."

"Let's just get out of this busy intersection." Brea guided them across the street like a group of nervous ducklings following their mother. "We'll take the side street and see if we can find an alley entrance somewhere that's not guarded."

Gulliver and Brea hurried down the quiet street and away

from the traffic. Griffin and Tia followed, leaving the cacophony of blaring horns and loud music behind.

They stayed on the opposite side of the street from the institute, looking for a way in that wouldn't call too much attention to them.

"Look for a loading dock," Griffin whisper-shouted. "That's how we got into the hospital in New Orleans."

"Until we got kicked out," Gulliver reminded him.

"Let's not get caught this time."

"Let's," Brea said nervously. "It will not go well for us if we're caught inside the institute. It's not like a hospital."

"I thought this was a hospital." Tia rushed to keep up. Dressed in her human clothes, she no longer looked like a queen. She looked more like his best friend than she had in months.

"It is, but it's not the type where the patients can come and go as they please. It's similar to a prison."

"We're breaking into a prison?" Griffin slowed his pace. "Is that the best plan?"

"It's the only plan." Gulliver darted across the street and ducked into an alley between the main building of the Clarkson Institute and a second darker, more menacing-looking structure tucked behind it. An enclosed bridge seemed to connect the two buildings. A long span of dark windows greeted them, and no sight of a single guard anywhere.

"Over here, Gullie!" Tia called to him in the darkness. The way the buildings were situated, a hush had fallen over them, sending the noises of the city into the distance. It was as though they had entered another world. One the humans didn't see sitting among them.

This was where bad things happened to good people. Gullie could feel it in his bones.

"Don't touch that door!" Brea hissed, rushing to her daughter's side.

"But it says it's an emergency door, and I think this counts as an emergency." Tia pointed at the big red stripe across the door, marking it as an exit only.

"It will set off an alarm if you try to go through it." Brea pulled Tia away from the door. "We need to avoid alarms."

Gulliver glanced around the shadowed alley, where weeds grew up around smelly dumpsters. "Why are humans always so gross?"

He studied the windows around the doors. They were narrow and long, and the glass looked thick, but there was already a crack. And where there was a crack, there was weakness. Gulliver raised the hilt of his sword and ignored Brea's shout of, "No!"

It took several attempts, but he shoved his way through the glass, creating an opening just big enough for him to slip through.

"Careful!" Tia cautioned him, but Gullie managed to get through without seriously injuring himself on the jagged glass. "Open the door for us."

Gulliver reached for the door just as a loud beeping sounded, making him flinch.

"Um ... Hide!" Brea shouted, dragging Tia and Griffin away from the opening.

"Mom, we have to help Gullie," Tia protested. "We have to help him save his girl."

"I think we're going to have to let him save his girl on his own."

A pang of fear shot through Gulliver as he realized Brea was right.

The beeping grew louder as he searched his surroundings. He was in a large storage room with plenty of places to hide. Ducking behind a crate of small boxes containing white gloves, he just managed to avoid being seen when a bright light burst overhead and a man in all white clothes peeked into the room from another door.

"What's going on in here?" he demanded, rushing into the room to discover the broken glass. "What in the— Someone's escaping!"

"Well, now we have to run." Gulliver just made out Brea's irritated tone.

While the man was busy searching for the escaped patient, Gulliver tiptoed around him and shot through the open door into a maze of small, sad offices with short walls and claustrophobic proportions.

"Hey, you, come back here." The man lumbered after him.

Gulliver reached for the nearest door and tumbled into a bright white hallway, gloriously empty.

He almost lost his pursuer when he reached another hall filled with dark windows displaying dark fae trapped behind the white walls of the institute.

"Stop!" The man lunged for Gulliver, grabbing his arm. "Escapee!" he shrieked, but Gulliver brought down the hilt of his sword on the man's head to shut him up.

Chapter Twelve

TOBY

"Absolutely not." Orla stood at the head of the table in the library of Aghadoon. Her gaze sparked with anger as she met Queen Alona's incredulous stare. It took some convincing, but they'd finally gotten her into the village.

Toby shifted slowly to step between them, uneasy with the tension in the room between his father, the Queen of Eldur, and the leader of the L.A. fae community. His father only just returned from a quick overnight trip to Iskalt five minutes ago and looked exhausted.

"Whyever not?" Alona asked. "This is your home. Of course,

you are all welcome here in the five kingdoms, wherever you wish to settle."

The look on Xavier's face told Toby exactly what most of the half-fae would think of the queen's offer. Kind though it was, it would not be accepted.

"And we appreciate that, your Majesty, but with all due respect, this is not our home." Orla glowered at her. "It has never been our home. You should know how that feels more than anyone else at this table."

"How so?" The Eldurian queen tilted her head in question.

"Are you not human?" Orla asked. "Can you imagine if some monarch from the human realm decided your place was among their own subjects simply because you are one of them? To have a perfect stranger decide this world was not your home?"

"I see," Alona murmured. "Yet, I do not live among a people who wish me dead simply because I am not like them. My life here is not one of strife and heartache. Would your fae not have a much better life living among others like them?"

"Alona," Toby interjected, "the half-fae do not have the powerful magic of this world. What magic they do have is frightening to the humans, but we are frightening to them. They view themselves as humans in a strange land they do not understand. A land that lacks the technology and conveniences they are accustomed to. We cannot keep them here against their will when we only brought them here in a dire moment that left us with little choice. They want to go home, and I believe it is our responsibility to send them back and do our part to help them find peace within a world they understand."

"We have to think of our own fae, son," Lochlan said. "We can't risk a war with the humans, and if we interfere, it will likely come to that. We need to consider all our options, and what might be best for the half-fae communities is to bring them all here where they can be safe."

"I agree with Loch," Alona said. "I think it's important that every member of your community feels welcome here," she addressed Orla. "They need to know their futures could be here among their own kind should they choose to stay."

Orla shook her head and slammed her fist against the table. "No. We are not like you, your Majesties. You are all so eager to embrace our fae sides and welcome us to your lands, but you forget we are more human than fae. And that makes the human realm our home. Thank you for the kind welcome and assistance we desperately needed, but we must forge our own path."

Toby moved to stand beside Orla. The fierce warrior woman was scary, but he could see the pride she held for her people. Pride and determination to do right by them.

"Maybe my son is right." Lochlan sighed, looking like he wanted this conversation to be over so he could find his bed. "And he is wise. Orla represents her people just as you represent the people of Eldur, Alona. She knows what is best for them."

"Thank you, your Majesty." Orla nodded in Lochlan's direction. "My people here in the village are scared and eager to return to their homes and their families. There are countless fae back home facing HAFS on their own. To even think of bringing them all here is foolish. There are too many. Too many families that have been separated. Some don't know where their loved ones have gone. It is for them that I fight." She laid a palm gently on the table, as if to erase an unseen mark her fist left in her earlier frustration.

"Then, I think it is clear what we need to do." Toby's voice rose with confidence. He was prepared to fight alongside Orla. Even if that went against his parents' wishes. It was time to stop talking and start acting.

"Which is?" Alona asked.

"We will offer our half-fae friends refuge here for as long as they need it, but we will actively help them get back home as safely as possible. But we will not abandon them. We will help them find peace with the humans."

"I agree with Prince Tobias," Lochlan said, a hint of pride in his voice.

"I need to return to the human realm as soon as possible," Orla said. "My people need me there. Those who wish to stay behind will be safe here under the supervision of one of my trusted soldiers. Until arrangements can be made to bring them safely home."

"At moonrise tonight, I will take you back myself," Toby offered. "I would caution you not to take everyone home at once. With a few, we can slip into L.A. unnoticed. And over time, my father and uncle and I will help transport everyone little by little."

"Of course, if that is what you want, then that is what we will do." Alona fussed with the hem of her gauzy sleeve, clearly not happy with the direction this meeting had taken. "But how do we negotiate a peace treaty with the humans when their first reaction is to come at us with explosions and ... so much hate?" Her eyes filled with a sadness and uncertainty Toby was all too familiar with.

"*We* might not be able to avoid a war with HAFS." Toby shared a look with Xavier. "And we may very well have to make a show of power against the true enemy to display our might. To show the leaders of HAFS they have no hope of defeating our collective magic. But the fae of the Five Kingdoms cannot lead that fight."

"That is not our way." Alona shook her head stubbornly. "We have had peace for so many years now. None of us want to return to the days of fighting and division we knew when we were your age, Tobias. I will not have another war on our hands."

"Then, let it rest in my hands. And in the hands of other leaders like me," Orla said softly. "We are prepared to fight. I just ask that you do not hinder us from doing what is right for our people. Our enemy is HAFS, not all of humankind. There are many who will support us. Young Toby has taken the first steps to create a real home for us in Los Angeles. A place where we can live openly and at peace alongside those humans who do not fear us."

"Perhaps it is best for the five kingdoms to take a step back from this conflict," Lochlan suggested. "Orla is right; it is not our fight."

"But there are fae who have been needlessly traumatized in this conflict," Alona argued. "I can't sit back and let that happen when there is so much Eldur can offer."

"Eldur can support our cause without fighting for us." Orla stood back with her arms clasped behind her like a soldier. "We do not need an army or weapons. We can and will fight our own battles. We just need ... friends, allies to cheer us on and help us show the humans they have nothing to fear from us as long as they stop the persecution against us. Friends who can provide refuge, if and when it is needed ... should it come to that."

"I think we can all agree that Orla's requests are perfectly reasonable and the very least we can do is aid her and her people," Finn spoke up for the first time, drawing a glare from his wife. "And the rest can't be decided this instant anyway."

"Very well," Alona relented.

They all knew it wouldn't be the end of the conversation, but it was a start.

Chapter Thirteen

SOPHIE

Leather straps bound Sophie to the cot, and all she could think was, at least it wasn't the metal tables she'd seen the others on. A rough blanket scratched her skin, and it felt like ants crawled beneath the surface.

She squirmed, but it was no use. There wasn't a way out now.

I chose this. The thought popped into her head so suddenly it surprised her, but it wasn't wrong. She put herself here, subjecting herself to whatever Doctor Clarkson and the others planned for her. And she did it to help them, the fae she once hated.

They didn't kill my mother. For so much of her life, she'd thought their power was evil because it took the kindest, warmest mother from her. Even now, she could picture her mother's smile, the way it dimmed when her father neared.

How had she never seen it?

Where are you? The boy's voice had been gone from her mind since the first morning it came to her, yet now it felt as familiar as anything. A comfort in this dark place.

I don't know, she responded, not wanting to tell him the truth of what she'd done.

Yes, you do.

She'd forgotten he could see her in his dreams. There was no lying to the kid with no name, the one who had never felt the sun on his skin yet was more intelligent than most people she knew.

Doctor Clarkson is going to try to find out what the fae did to me.

The boy didn't respond at first, but her anxiety rose, almost like he was projecting it into her head.

Whatever you did, it was a mistake.

Sophie closed her eyes, shutting out the irritating fluorescents. *I didn't have a choice.*

I know.

She knew he did. Unlike the rest of the world, he saw how truly evil this place was. That the fae weren't the enemy. Instead, the enemy was among her own people.

She pictured Gullie with his unique feline eyes, the way they seemed to see all the way to the bits of herself she tried to keep hidden. He'd have done the same as her, risked himself to fight for what he believed in. She might never see him again, but she desperately wanted to prove him right.

Others may have questioned the faith he had in her, but it didn't waver. He'd seen something before she even saw it in herself, a reason to risk the wrath of his queen. He knew she was better than HAFS, that it wasn't her destiny.

Who is that guy? the boy asked.

She stopped struggling against the straps and let her breathing calm. Who was he? To his fae, Gullie was just a friend of the queen. To her father, he was the fae who abducted her. And yet ...

The fae who saved me. Not only her life. He saved her from herself. *And the one who is going to find us.*

I hope you're right. His uncertainty simmered across the bond.

Sophie smiled, despite her predicament. It was her turn to have faith. *I am.*

The door opening jerked her from the conversation, from the thoughts that almost made her forget what was coming.

Doctor Clarkson walked in, his heavy steps echoing the sudden pounding in her head. It felt like fists striking the wall she'd erected in a single moment, a wall to keep others out.

The boy.

She had to prevent him from knowing what came next.

"Miss Devereaux, I am sorry for the restraints."

"If you're sorry," she bit out, "then release them."

He gave her a sad smile. "I'm afraid they are necessary. You agreed that we must know if the fae infected you, if their magic has changed you in a dangerous way."

Tears stung the corners of her eyes. "What are you going to do to me?"

"Only what we must."

He gestured toward what looked like a mirror. She knew it wasn't what it seemed. From that hallway, others could look in and observe what was done.

The pain in her skull intensified, but she didn't know how to lower the wall and let the kid back in, even if she wanted to. "Please don't hurt me."

The door opened again, and two others walked in wearing white coats. Between them, they pushed a large device that stood on two wheeled legs. The top of it looked like an array of solar panels, but she'd seen what this could do.

Clarkson put a hand on her arm. "Your father wanted me to tell you how proud he is. Once we are finished, you may be able to return to him."

How could she possibly go back to the man who killed her mother? The same man who would hunt down Gulliver the first chance he got. She forced a smile. "I do so wish to do right by him. He's done so much."

Clarkson looked satisfied with her answer. "Sophie, let me introduce you to Doctor Clara March. Our breakthrough device is her invention. And Doctor Nathanial Kline here is a recent hire of ours. He wishes to study the molecular makeup of our fae foes in order to determine where exactly their magic originates."

It didn't make sense, this studying of the fae. HAFS' goal was to protect human life, ensure the survival of all peoples. So, why study the fae? Why break them down and learn of their magic?

Unless ...

It couldn't be real. The followers of HAFS, the governments involved, would never approve of it.

Doctor Clarkson wished to replicate magic without a fae host. Was it possible he wanted to bring their power to the human race?

Her tears dried as she saw the man before her in an entirely new light. It was genius. Convince generations of humans to turn on those suspected of having magic while his father and now he would study and learn and prepare.

The rage that surged through her came with none of the magic he suspected her of having. It was purely human instinct. She had to get free, to warn ... someone. She wasn't even sure who'd listen to her.

Gulliver.

He wouldn't even question it. If he didn't find her, she had to get to him somehow.

Doctor Kline approached with a needle in one hand. It was connected to a long rubber tube that stopped at an empty bag. "I just need some blood."

He was asking her permission while the restraints kept her in place. It was such an odd circumstance. A laugh burst out of her.

"Take it." She turned her arm to expose a vein in the crook of her elbow. "All of it if you like. I don't care."

Doctor Clarkson frowned. "Nathanial, bring me the Fentanyl."

Sophie kept calm, despite the urge to rip each of her captor's hearts right from their chests. She was well versed in the various pain medications from her treatments, but Fentanyl was the worst of them.

Clarkson approached with a syringe. A small needle protruded from the end. "Nothing to worry about. It will relieve some of the pain and keep you calm."

"No!" She tried to yank away from him. "I don't want it. Stop." No more drugs, no more remaining calm. She screamed, the sound piercing the barrier inside her mind, crumbling it to dust. Stars swam before her vision.

Sophie! The boy yelled in her head. *What's happening?*

"No. No!" She thrashed, but it was no use. The needle pierced her arm, and the plunger descended, pushing the poison into her veins.

Her protests weakened as the doctors watched, waiting for

what, she didn't know. It only took a few minutes for the drowsiness to come. Her limbs grew heavy, immovable.

"I'm going to take some marrow." She heard Doctor Kline's voice, but it sounded far away. Somewhere else.

There was pressure on her skin, the feeling of it splitting, and then a sharp pain as a needle went into her bone. Not even the medication could take that away.

Tears fell down her cheeks, and she couldn't wipe them away.

Someone wrapped a bandage around her leg while another moved the device into place above her. It rattled as Doctor March adjusted it, tilting it so one of the solar panel-like sides pointed directly down at her.

Her head swam, and the boy never stopped talking.

What are they doing to you?

Tell me what's going on.

Sophie, please.

She couldn't respond, couldn't formulate the thoughts necessary to explain any of this. Her eyelids sank as they grew heavier.

The first sound from the machine was a low hum. All three doctors filed out of the room, but she knew they wouldn't go far. They'd watch and wait. If they didn't want to be near the device, what did it do to those without magic?

The hum intensified, vibrating through every cell in her body.

Her chest jerked as if pulled by some magnetic source, arching off the cot. Her wrists and ankles struggled against the restraints.

That lasted for what felt like hours before a blast of light erupted from the panels, slamming her back onto the bed.

A scream tore from her throat as the ache turned to pain searing down her legs. It drew every bit of calm from her until her body writhed and bucked under the agony.

"Please," she cried. "It's too much." In all her years of cancer, she'd never experienced such pain. The device drained the life from her, pulling it straight from her heart.

Is this how it removed a fae's glamour? Revealed their magic? Fat tears bridged over her nose, dropping from the end as sweat dotted her brow. She didn't have any magic to pull out of her, nothing to protect her. Yet, they wouldn't stop until she did.

Doctor Clarkson didn't believe she'd come back healed and human. That much was clear.

It's killing you, the boy yelled, tears in his voice. *Fight, Sophie. Don't stop.*

I can't, she pushed the thought to him, but she didn't know if it got there.

Her blood felt like it was boiling, building up with rage and desperation and ... something else, something unfamiliar. Except, not entirely. She'd felt it once before.

The light of the device was suddenly less intense, the pain fading away with the heat racing along her skin.

She drew the light into her body, absorbed it like a sponge, cleaning up someone else's problem. It entered every cell, finding those that were healed in Lenya.

Maybe Doctor Clarkson was right.

She hadn't come back the same.

A smile curved her lips as power that didn't belong to her curled in her gut, waiting for its moment to break free. The leather straps burned where they touched her skin, reducing them to ash.

The device sparked and sputtered, the metal frame bending. Her eyes found the mirror. On the other side were the ones responsible for every evil this place perpetrated.

A place was only as bad as the humans that controlled it.

Light burst from her every pore, filling the room with the power of the device built to reveal the fae.

Keep going! the boy yelled.

She didn't understand how his power fueled her now, but now wasn't the time to ask questions. It was time to run.

Sparks rained down on her as lightbulbs burst, spraying glass across the room.

The door opened, revealing two guards with rifles. She jumped from the cot and lifted a hand. The barrels of their guns bent upward, and they flew back into the cinderblock wall, sliding down, unconscious.

The three doctors scrambled from the room in a panic. For once, they were the scared ones. Alarms blared overhead, and a red light flashed. Soon, the hall would be awash in guards. She had to find the boy and get out of here.

There was no time to deal with these three.

"You're ..." Doctor Clarkson choked.

Sophie stopped moving, looking into his eyes. "Human."

She was still human, that much she was sure of, but she'd have time to figure it all out later.

She'd just turned away when there was a thump behind her. When she looked over her shoulder, Doctor Clarkson was slumped on the ground with a man standing over him wielding a sword.

"I used the hilt," Gulliver said. "I didn't kill him."

Doctor Clarkson's blood trickled from a gash in his head, but Sophie didn't help him.

"You're here." Her eyes met Gulliver's.

"I'm—"

She didn't wait for him to finish, stepping over the doctor's body while the other two cowered against the wall.

"You're here," she repeated, pulling Gulliver to her. When she fit her lips to his, a breath of surprise escaped him before he returned her kiss as if he'd come to an institute that tortured his kind just for this moment.

Chapter Fourteen

SOPHIE

"Run, Gullie! Don't wait for me." Sophie clutched the hospital gown they'd forced her into for these experiments and struggled to keep up with Gulliver's long strides. Her stomach heaved at the way the world whirled around her, but she stumbled forward, hoping adrenaline would kick in and chase the effects of the Fentanyl from her body.

The boy's power had given her strength for a brief moment, but it was gone now.

"I'm not leaving you. Now, how do we get out of here?" Gulliver slowed the gurney they'd thrown the unconscious Doctor Clarkson on. They neared the end of the long, dark hall, and it was up to Sophie to figure out which direction to go. It was only a matter of time before the orderlies came at them with more drugs. And then, she really would be useless. They had to get out of the institute and fast, but Sophie couldn't leave the boy.

"I don't know." She glanced behind to the armed guards pursuing them and darted past Gulliver, checking a series of wide double doors until she found one that was unlocked. It opened into another hallway just like all the others. "Let's just keep running until I see something I recognize."

"Are you okay, Sophie?" Gulliver heaved his shoulder into the gurney to get it moving again, and then they were through the doors. Sophie slammed the lock in place, leaving the guards to find another way around. "What did they do to you?"

She rushed ahead, searching for anything that looked familiar. Her vision blurred, and she was certain she was slurring her words, but she had to keep moving. She had to clear her head or they were going to find themselves in even worse trouble now that they had threatened Doctor Clarkson.

"You don't want to know what they're trying to do here, Gul." Sophie ran frantically, looking for signs that would lead them back to the halls of the patient ward. From there, she should be able to find a way out. After she located the boy.

"This way." She helped Gulliver navigate a turn in the corridor that spilled them out into a wide space lined with windows and what seemed like miles of linoleum floors. The floor sloped up in an incline that connected the building they just left with the part of the institute Sophie was most familiar with.

"I think I know where we're heading." She picked up her pace as they struggled to push the gurney up the ramp. For the moment, they'd lost the armed guards, but they had minutes at best.

The orderlies here were bad enough, but she didn't want to mess with the guards and their automatic weapons. If they got their hands on Gulliver, she shuddered to think of what their machines might do to him and his defensive magic.

"Whatever happens, Gullie, you can't let them take you." Sophie sucked in a breath. Her head swam and her legs didn't want to cooperate. "If you have to leave me to save yourself, promise me you will."

"No." Gulliver shook his head furiously. "I'm not leaving without you."

"I don't want you to get hurt because of me." Tears choked Sophie's throat, but she kept pushing the gurney, her legs like lead weighing her down. The drugs made her movements slow and her thoughts foggy.

As they reached the top of the incline, they pushed through double doors into the main institute.

Sirens suddenly blared overhead, and flashing red lights illuminated the dark hallway with an otherworldly glow. She could hear patients crying and shouting as they reacted to the disturbing alarms. They'd stumbled into the fae ward.

"How about let's not get caught? I like that plan better." Gulliver grabbed her hand and pulled her along, shoving the gurney ahead of them as they picked up their pace again.

"Should we just leave him behind?" Sophie panted. "He's slowing us down."

"We're going to need the doctor for negotiations." Gulliver slammed the gurney into another set of double doors, and they burst into a hallway Sophie recognized. It was the one with the one-way windows.

"Oh, Gullie, don't look." She didn't want him to see what Clarkson was doing to others like him.

"I've already seen it." They charged past an unconscious

orderly lying in an open doorway. "I hit that guy on the head with my sword too."

Sophie glanced down to see the blade in question sheathed at his narrow waist. Something hummed in her chest at the idea of Gulliver wielding it. She remembered him sparring with it, imagined he was better than she knew considering his father was a fae prince who was probably a master swordsman himself.

Her cheeks flushed at the thoughts rushing through her mind about the combination of Gulliver's tall, lanky physique and his adorable geeky vibe, coupled with his fae warrior side she didn't know as well. She liked the contradictory combination, but now was not the time to get caught up in such distractions. Shaking her head, she pushed those thoughts aside.

"We should let the other fae out." Gulliver slowed to a stop and rummaged through the doctor's pockets for his keys.

"Yes." Sophie grabbed the keys from Gulliver's hand and moved to unlock the nearest door, her hands trembling.

A young woman with skin that shimmered like fish scales in a thousand beautiful colors greeted her with a hiss of hatred.

"Help the others." Sophie tossed the keys at her. "And get them out of here!" She didn't have time to wait for them all to escape, but it was the best she could do for the Dark Fae the doctor had been experimenting on for who knew how long.

"What are they doing to the Dark Fae here?" Gulliver glanced back as they raced down the hallway, leaving chaos behind them as dozens of angry fae poured out of the rooms.

"We can thank the good doctor for destroying the one thing keeping them safe in this world. He's managed to strip them of their defensive magic, Gullie." Sophie panted. "That's why you cannot let them take you."

Gullie nodded. "The Asrai back there can definitely take care of herself, but if she's been out of water a long time, she'll be weak and a bit addled. You don't want to run into an Asrai having a bad day."

"When we get out of this, you'll have to tell me what an Asrai is." Sophie skidded to a halt at intersecting hallways. "Through there!" She pointed at a door marked with room numbers.

"We need an exit, Sophie." Gulliver turned in a circle. "Look, there's a red sign down that way."

"No," Sophie shouted. "I can't leave without him."

"Who?"

"There's a boy with no name. He's been helping me, and I won't leave him behind."

Something cracked in Gulliver's expression, and for some reason it gutted her, seeing such a hurt look cross his features.

"Okay." He nodded without questioning. "Let's go find your friend."

"Get in here!" The nurse with the pretty eyes opened the door to the patient wing, waving them through as though she'd been waiting for them. The boy clutched her hand as they rolled the doctor through the doorway.

"See, I told you she'd come find me." The boy tugged on the nurse's hand.

Bedlam had erupted in the ward, and terrified patients ran up and down the halls, shouting and screaming along with the wailing sirens. Orderlies chased them down, ignoring Sophie and Gulliver and the nurse who probably just saved their lives.

"Oh, you really meant a little boy." Gulliver beamed a huge smile at Sophie when she took the boy's hand.

"I'm not little. I'm ten. At least, I think I am."

"He's been helping me." Sophie was relieved to see him again. She crouched down beside him. "Are you hurt?" She checked him over.

"No, but they hurt you." He pressed his palms against her

cheeks, his eyes filled with a shadow of pain she realized he'd probably experienced right along with her.

"I'll be okay," she assured him. "And I won't let them hurt you anymore."

"You three need to go," the nurse said as she waved her key card in front of a keypad that opened the double doors to a small empty waiting room. "Take this." She thrust the card into Sophie's hands. "It'll get you through the next two doors and into the staff parking lot. You can take my car." She shoved her keys into Sophie's hands. "Just do not get caught. You have to get out of the city. These are HAFS soldiers, and they will not stop. They practically worship him." She gestured at Clarkson. "They'd do anything for him."

"Why are you helping us?" Gulliver asked, a look of confusion in his face. "I thought all humans hated us."

The nurse shook her head. "Not all of us. My grandmother was half-fae, and HAFS killed her for it. They'd kill me if they knew I had even a drop of fae blood. It's time we all work together to stop this kind of hatred." She lifted the little boy onto the gurney at Clarkson's feet. "Keep him safe."

She turned back to the patient ward as HAFS guards flooded in from all sides. "Run!" She shut the double doors behind her as gunfire erupted.

"No!" Sophie screamed as blood splattered across the narrow windows. The nurse slid to the floor and more gunfire exploded. Tears streaming down her cheeks, she reached for a tall lamp in the corner of the small waiting room, Sophie ripped off the lampshade and dashed the bulb against the floor before she shoved the slim metal rod through the door handles to slow anyone pursuing them.

"Let's get out of here, Sophie." The little boy pointed to the metal door with the big red exit sign labeled 'Employee Exit Only'.

Sophie swiped the dead nurse's card at the keypad, and they moved into another long hallway. Only one more door stood between them and freedom.

Two HAFS guards managed to get through the barrier and chased them down the hall.

"No!" Gulliver shoved Sophie toward the door and drew his sword. He leaped up onto the gurney, putting himself in front of the little boy with no name. "Take one more step, and he's dead." Gulliver flicked the sword point at Clarkson's neck, drawing a thin line of blood.

"Drop your guns on the floor," Sophie shouted, fumbling with the key card.

"You heard the lady." Gulliver pressed the blade harder against the doctor's throat. "Drop your weapons."

"You don't have the guts, you filthy fae abomination," one of the guards taunted Gulliver, refusing to lower his weapon.

"I have guts just like a human." Gulliver crouched over the doctor. "And what would it matter if I didn't? Would that make me any less of a person?"

"You're not human. That makes you filth." The first guard took a shot, but Gulliver ducked.

"Don't you dare shoot that gun at him," Sophie shrieked, wishing she had something to throw at them.

"Drop the sword, boy, before you hurt yourself."

Gulliver smiled. "You should know, I'm not afraid to use this sword. I've been training all my life, and it wouldn't be the first time I've had to fight against evil. I've seen the things your doctor has done to my people. All the worlds would be better off without him in it. Even yours."

"Come on, kid, this is over. I won't hesitate to shoot you." The other guard lifted his gun.

"No!" Sophie shouted, but she needn't have. Her jaw dropped as Gulliver leapt from the gurney, swinging his sword.

Blood splattered as his blade found purchase, and the guards screamed. Gulliver drove them back down the hallway, relieving them of their weapons until they disappeared behind another door, bleeding from their wounds.

"Gullie?" Sophie's voice came out breathless as he marched toward her, shoving his sword back in its sheath. He didn't have a scratch on him. She hurried down the hall to grab one of the guns and slung it over her shoulder.

"You have that door open yet, Soph? I'd really like to leave this place now." Gulliver grinned, his cheeks flushed with pleasure at whatever expression he found on her face.

Sophie shoved the door open and headed across the parking lot. "Let's get out of here."

She smiled back at Gulliver and the three of them—and the unconscious Doctor Clarkson—rushed out into the night.

Chapter Fifteen
GULLIVER

Gulliver would rather face a host of guards with his sword than a stone field of human automobiles. He stood too stunned to move as he scanned them in the night. It was like entering a jungle with no knowledge of what kind of creatures lay in wait.

"Which one do you think is hers?" Sophie fumbled with the keys until she gripped a tiny black box between her fingers.

"What is this place?" the boy asked, his eyes just as wide as Gulliver's.

"What?" Sophie didn't look at him as she scanned the rows.

"A parking lot. Have you never ..." She stopped speaking, and Gulliver wasn't sure why.

He'd seen parking lots in New Orleans, but one never got used to giant metal structures that could move without magic.

A beeping sound came from one of the automobiles as lights flashed.

Gulliver fought the urge the shriek and jump into Sophie's arms. "What's happening? Have they found us?"

Even in the dark, he could sense she rolled her eyes as she started walking. "No. That nurse just has good taste in cars."

She approached the sleek red car that shone in the nearby streetlight that appeared to take power directly from the moon. Where else would it come from in the middle of a parking lot?

Sophie yanked open the door before looking at both Gulliver and the boy. "Are you two coming, or would you prefer to go back to the institute?"

Both boys scrambled to lift the unconscious Doctor Clarkson into the car and then climbed in after him. As the engine rumbled, Gulliver couldn't get the image of the half-fae nurse out of his mind. He'd seen enough human weapons by now to know what they were capable of, but it was still shocking every time. How could they be scared of magic when they were so much more powerful?

Well, at least more powerful than most fae. He really wanted to see Tia and Brea take them down...

Oh crap!

"Wait!" Gulliver yelled as Sophie sped through the parking lot.

She slammed on the brakes, and they lurched forward. Gulliver's head smacked the dashboard, and he groaned. "What'd you do that for?"

"You don't yell at someone when they're driving. I thought you saw something with your fae vision that I was going to hit."

The boy leaned between the seats. "You're fae?"

"I don't have better vision just because my eyes look different. You were driving just fine. A little fast for my taste, but we're almost out."

She gripped the wheel tightly. "Then, why on earth did you yell at me?"

"Oh, that. Um ..." He rubbed his throbbing forehead. "I kind of forgot I didn't come here alone."

"How do you forget that?" Her voice rose an octave, one step away from panic.

"I saw you and ..." He shrugged. "Tia and Griff are going to kill me."

"You brought a queen and a prince to the institute and just left them?" She pressed her foot down on the gas, and the car jolted forward. "Guess we're going back in."

"Two queens. And last I saw them, they were near the side entrance. I got in that way." He pointed down a narrow street behind the building.

Sophie was quick to turn down the street. "We'll never find them this way."

She parked and jumped from the car.

Gulliver scrambled out after her. "We'll find them. She's not even your queen. Why are you so worried?"

She turned so fast he almost slammed into her. "Because they came for me. Me, a nobody. Someone whose own father wrote her off. The last person who truly cared for me died many years ago. Yet, they're risking capture to free me."

His brow creased. He didn't understand. "But ... that's what we do. We care about each other more than our own lives."

He couldn't fathom a place where that wasn't the case, where people thought of themselves before their loved ones.

Tears glistened in her dark eyes, reflecting the starlight. "We have to find them."

"We will. Come on." He took her hand and turned back briefly. "Boy. Keep an eye on the doctor. If he wakes, make sure it isn't for long." He pulled a dagger from his hip and slipped it into the boy's hands.

"We'll be right back," Sophie said. "I promise."

Gulliver knew nothing of the kid Sophie insisted on saving, nor any of her reasons, but he trusted her. More than he'd thought possible of any human.

The boy looked scared, but he nodded and watched them run off into the darkness.

Noises danced through the night, a high-pitched song. He slowed to hear it.

"Police sirens," Sophie explained. "We don't have much time."

They sprinted along the side of the building, looking at every possible entry point, but there was no sign of them. Had they been caught?

Was it really a mistake bringing the Queen of Iskalt here?

Guards poured from the side entrance into the night, running off in pairs to search their surroundings.

Gulliver pressed Sophie up against the side of the building to avoid them. His breath came heavily as two armed guards rushed by.

He could feel Sophie's every movement, her intake of air. Her chest rose against his and wide eyes lifted. Her lashes dipped down, brushing against her pale cheeks, and he couldn't move, couldn't breathe.

Just standing was a struggle.

His entire body was on fire, delicious flames licking up his spine. "Sophie," he whispered.

She placed a hand on his chest, and for a moment, he thought she'd draw him closer, that she wanted to repeat the kiss neither of them had acknowledged. Instead, she pushed him back. "They're gone."

Air rushed into his lungs. "Are you sure?"

She nodded, tucking a strand of blue-tinted hair behind one ear. "But I don't think Tia or your father are out here."

A curse escaped him. "They must have made it inside already. We can't leave without them."

"I know."

Her words held so much meaning, and he realized she did know. She felt it too. Even with her human blood, they were hers. Her people. The ones who came for her.

"Come on." He led her back toward the front, where they'd seen the guards, and drew his sword. If he had to fight his way to Tia, Griff, and Brea, he would.

Three patients ran out the door and down the steps before the guards stopped them, aiming their guns right for their chests. Gulliver had to do something. He had to help them. When the human police got there to reinforce the guards, there'd be no hope.

"Stay here," he muttered, hoping Sophie listened to him.

Yet, when he walked forward, he could sense her steps behind him.

The guard at the front turned and started yelling, his long gun aimed at Gulliver.

"Stop right there!"

Gulliver kept going. This would be so much easier if he had Tia's power.

"I said stop." There was fear in the man's voice, but with so many tortured fae now running loose, Gulliver didn't blame him.

"I'm not going to hurt you."

Bullets pierced the night, coming from three guards at once. Gulliver lunged back to cover Sophie. Something fast sailed right past his head and he sucked in a breath as he stood from his crouch.

"Well, now, I can't keep my promise." It was something Tia would have said, and he needed to channel her anger to protect Sophie. Releasing her, he whirled to face the guards before they could shoot again. The blade of his sword cut through the first like he was made of air.

The second stumbled back, but Gulliver wasted no time jumping toward him. Lessons with his father, sparring with Tia and Toby, it all came back to him now.

The third guard took off running, but Gulliver didn't chase him. He looked to the patients who were frozen in place and jerked his head toward the street. "Go."

He didn't have to tell them a second time.

"That ..." Sophie couldn't get another word out as her entire body shook.

He sheathed his sword and drew her close. "We really need to get out of here."

Heat radiated off her, and her shaking slowly calmed as her pulse beat against him.

Yelling came from the direction of the car, and they looked at each other before they took off running. Gulliver didn't know anything about the boy other than that he was a child and couldn't protect himself.

Except, he was wrong.

Sophie skidded to a halt, and Gulliver crashed into her before taking in what she saw.

"You can't have him," the boy yelled.

"Kid." It was Griff. "Hand over Doctor Clarkson, and we'll let you go on your way."

"No!" Power radiated from him, striking Griff in the chest and tossing him into the air. He sailed in an arc before slamming into the ground next to Gulliver.

Griff groaned.

"Nice of you to finally show up, Dad." Gulliver had no trouble admitting how entertaining this was, even if they didn't have time for it.

The boy let loose another bit of magic, but Brea blocked it.

Tia stormed toward Gulliver. "Where have you been?" She stopped. "Oh, Sophie. Hello. I'm glad you're not dead."

"Ringing endorsement." Sophie smiled.

"I don't know what that means." Gulliver had long since stopped asking. "But we need to go. Oy! Boy!"

The boy had a hand lifted toward Griff again. "About time you came back. These ones want the doctor."

"As much as I enjoy watching my father sail through the air, we have to go." He walked toward the car and put a hand on the boy's shoulder. "He's with us. Everyone, get in." The sirens grew louder as they piled into the car. There was no time to open a portal and get through, so it was the best they could do.

Except, when Gulliver looked at the back seat, Sophie sat smashed against the door.

"No." That meant ...

Tia slammed her foot down, and they sped through the dark city streets, whirring past cars with red flashing lights on top.

"Slow down," Griff yelled.

"Not likely." Tia sped up, and Gulliver gripped the door handle so tightly he was sure his knuckles turned white.

"Watch out!" he screamed as the side of the car scraped against another, busting off the oddly shaped looking glass in the process. Tia veered away from an oncoming car, a grin spreading across her face.

"Mom, we need these in our world."

Brea looked as green as Gulliver felt. "Not on your life, kid."

Sophie was mumbling something, but Gulliver couldn't hear her. "What?"

She didn't meet his eyes. "I'm praying."

Doctor Clarkson made a low sound, but he didn't get a chance to make another before the boy hit him on the head with the hilt of Gullie's knife, making him go still again.

There was more to this kid than met the eye. The magic, the willingness to do what it took.

Gullie would need to learn more about him if they survived this car ride.

By the time they reached the farmhouse, the car reeked of Griff's puke. Gulliver practically fell out of the door, his throat hoarse from yelling.

"I just want to go home." Brea dropped to her knees in the grass. "Where there are no cars my daughter can drive."

"Want me to open a portal?" Tia, the only one who didn't look disturbed by that ride, asked.

"*No*!" Gulliver, Griff, and Brea all yelled.

"Yeesh." She crossed her arms. "You get your friends lost in a hidden kingdom one time, and everyone suddenly thinks you can't do magic."

"Griff." Brea pushed to her feet. "Please do it before our queen here gets any ideas."

It wasn't until Griff opened the portal and Gulliver stepped through that he realized he'd done it.

Gulliver O'Shea saved the girl.

Chapter Sixteen
TOBY

"Can we be done with portals for a little while?" Sophie clutched her middle, like she was going to be sick. Toby was familiar with the feeling. Whenever he went through someone else's portal, it was a nauseating experience. He prided himself on the smooth transition of his own portals. The one magical thing he could do better than anyone else. The one magical thing he could do, period.

"Rough landing?" He offered her a hesitant smile as he stood to greet the returning special operative team. At least that was what his mother called it whenever they did anything sneaky like break someone out of a mental hospital and bring them to Eldur.

"You could say that." She lowered herself onto the nearest chair. "Is it always so infernally hot here?" She waved a hand in her face, stirring the sweaty tendrils of blue-tipped hair around her temples.

"Afraid so, but we're glad to have you back with us." Toby smiled at the way Gulliver hovered behind Sophie, like he wanted to give her the world but didn't know if she'd accept it.

"Glad to be here." She sighed, leaning her head back against the chair. "I will never get used to leaving one place at night and stepping through a doorway into daylight. It's exhausting."

"We'll find you a room soon," Gulliver murmured behind her. "And some food."

"Darra, honey." Alona studied Sophie's odd choice of clothing. "You're about the same size as Sophie. Could you go get her some clothes? She'll need a few suitable garments while she's visiting."

"No dresses." Sophie managed to lift her head. "Please," she added with a smile.

"A girl after my own heart." Darra scurried off to her rooms.

"We should get Sophie and her little friend here to the healers, Alona," Brea suggested. "I'm sure they've had an awful time at the institute."

"And who do we have here?" Alona beamed at the little boy clinging to Sophie's side.

"I don't know." He looked the queen in the eye. "Who are you?"

Alona laughed and crouched down beside him. "I'm Queen Alona of Eldur. What's your name, darling?"

"Don't have one. What's an Eldur?"

"It's a where not a what," Toby explained.

"How does he not have a name?" Alona frowned up at Brea.

"Never got one." The boy's eyes were round as saucers as he took in everything at once. "This place is pretty. I like it." He plopped down onto the floor at Sophie's feet, refusing to release her hand.

Brea shook her head at Alona. "Long story, sister."

"Dad!" Tia exclaimed when Lochlan rushed into the room with Finn. "I thought you'd gone back to Iskalt with Keir."

"I don't know. Maybe something about my wife and daughter absconding with a human they broke out of a mental hospital made me want to come right back. I thought I might need to check up on them to see if they've gone mental themselves."

Toby shared a look with his father. The two of them were always the reliable ones to Tia and their mother's impulsive streaks.

"It's my fault, Loch." Gulliver took the blame. "We had to help Sophie."

"It's good to see you safe again, Sophie. Why don't we get you and your friend settled so you can rest? Gulliver, come with me and give me the details I'm sure my wife and her daughter will intentionally leave out in their own recount of the night's events."

"It's always *her* daughter when she's done something impulsive," Brea muttered.

"Can't blame him for that, Mom." Toby laughed. "That apple didn't fall far from the tree."

"Oh, you hush." Brea laughed and pulled Toby into a hug. "Your lives would be boring without us, and you both know it."

Gulliver grasped Sophie's hand as they followed Lochlan from the room.

After they had gone, Griffin lumbered into the room, shouldering a nearly unconscious human onto an empty chair. "This one's going to need some precautionary restraints, Brea."

"On it." Brea murmured a few Fargelsian words, and the arms and legs of the chair moved like vines to wrap around the man's waist and ankles, leaving his hands free for the moment.

"Who's this guy?" Toby frowned at the oddly familiar man. He was certain he'd seen his face before. He looked at Xavier standing beside him. "Do you know this man?"

Xavier nodded. "He's the worldwide leader of HAFS. How on earth did you get your hands on him?"

"Gullie knocked him out with his sword," Tia said proudly.

Toby's eyes widened at that. Gullie was an excellent swordsman, but he abhorred violence of any kind. It wasn't like him to fight unless he'd had no other choice.

"It appears we all have a lot to discuss." Alona sank down onto her chair under a wide window overlooking the palace grounds and the canyon of Radur City far below.

"This man has a lot to answer for." Orla spoke for the first time, her eyes blazing with fury. "Many fae lives have been lost because of him and his father."

Toby stepped between Orla and the man in question. He could see it in her eyes, she was out for blood, but if he really was the leader of HAFS, then they needed this man if they ever wanted a chance of finding peace with the humans.

"I think he's coming around," Alona said. "Tia, get the man some tea and something to eat."

Tia moved to the sideboard on the other side of the room, heated water for tea, and stacked a platter high with little sandwiches and pastries. She brought enough for everyone and set it on the table in front of the strange human.

"Here. Have some tea." Tia poured hot water over a spicy Eldurian blend of black tea, with cinnamon and cardamom and plenty of sugar. "Take it easy. You've had a pretty nasty bump on the head."

She placed the teacup in his hand.

His eyes scanned the room, taking in all the fae beaming welcoming smiles at him.

"Wha ... what's happening?" He closed his eyes and groaned. "Where am I?"

"You're in Eldur," Alona said softly. "Take a moment to get your bearings."

The man's eyes opened wide with fright, followed by anger as he flung the teacup at Tia.

Quicker than a blink, she lifted her hands to block the scalding hot tea with her magic. "Hey! That was hot!" She guided the tea back into the cup and it settled down gently on the table.

"Devils!" the man spat, struggling against the bindings Brea had placed as a precaution.

"Please calm down and tell us your name." Toby raised his voice.

"It's Doctor Clarkson," Brea said softly, the restraints tightening around the human. "He looked just like his father, and I knew him all too well."

"Wicked heathens. Take me back to the institute this instant!"

"I'm afraid we can't do that," Alona apologized. "Brea, you're suffocating him. Relax."

"You will not hold me against my will!" The doctor nearly tipped the chair over in his agitation. "And you will not use your vile magic on me."

"We kind of have to if you want to go home," Toby offered. "And I will be happy to take you there just as soon as the moon rises. If you'll just speak calmly with us, I am certain we can come to an understanding."

"How dare you abduct me from my place of work. This is an act of war." Spittle flew from his mouth. "You will never take our world. I will not have it."

"We don't want it," Tia blurted. "Not that it isn't nice and all, but we have our own world to look after. And just so we're clear ... how is bringing you here any different form you all taking innocent fae into your awful asylum to experiment on?"

"You are an abomination. I will not be held captive by such wicked creatures!"

Tia shared a look with Toby, her face asking the obvious question of whether or not they were dealing with a person of sound mind.

"Doctor, we don't want to hold you captive." Toby stepped forward. "The restraints were a precaution. If you'll just calm down, I am sure we can speak civilly."

"He doesn't know how to speak with a civil tongue." Orla sneered at the man. "He only understands violence."

"Well, we will not be answering violence with violence," Alona said. "If you cannot calm down so we can negotiate a peace with you and your people, then we will never reach an end to this struggle. We want nothing of the human world. We only want the fae living among you to be treated well."

"It's not going to work, Alona." Brea moved to stand in front of the doctor. "His family has never listened to anyone they deem beneath them. And he will never see anyone with magic as a person to be treated with respect. Don't waste your breath."

"You!" The doctor looked up at Toby's mother. "You died when you were just a girl. Your parents insisted they took care of it."

Brea tilted her head, eying the doctor with wary eyes. "What do you mean my parents took care of it? They relinquished their parental rights to the institute after I accidentally used my magic on Myles."

The doctor snorted a laugh. "They did no such thing. The Robinsons were determined to fix you, even after you killed your friend."

"I didn't kill him. Myles is King Consort of Fargelsi." She crossed her arms over her chest. "See, we treat humans and half-humans here a lot better than you treat the fae in your realm."

"Your idiot parents believed they could rid you of your erratic magic. They wanted that more than anything in the world."

"My parents hated me." Brea frowned.

"Oh, they cared for you, Brea Robinson." The doctor's face broke into a menacing smile. "They cared far too much for their abomination of a daughter. When you escaped with your fae friends, they went after you. We were told they caught up with you and did the right thing."

"Which was what?" Brea demanded.

"They were supposed to have put a bullet through your brain, but I see they utterly failed."

"My parents knew I was fae? They were involved with HAFS?"

"They brought you to my father the first time you displayed signs of magic. They were worried about you, convinced you were a changeling."

"I was." Brea lifted her head defiantly. "I was the child of two very powerful fae rulers, heir to two thrones and more magic than any other fae ever born, before my daughter became even stronger. And you convinced me I was crazy." Her hands clenched into fists. "You could have told me what I was, but you made me question my own sanity."

Her voice shook with emotion, and together, Toby and Tia stepped up beside their mother to comfort her.

"It's okay, Mom." Tia took Brea's hand in hers. "It's all in the past, where it belongs."

"Griff, Xavier, I think it's time we take our guest to his rooms." Toby didn't take his eyes off the doctor. "Perhaps he will feel like discussing options for peace after a good night's rest."

"We'll take him to the dungeons." Xavier stepped forward.

"No. We won't treat him the way he has treated us. Take him to one of the guest suites, but place a guard at his door. For his protection." Toby wrapped an arm around Brea's waist. "He's done enough damage here for one day."

Chapter Seventeen
GULLIVER

Brea's eyes flashed with pain, and Gulliver couldn't seem to shake the faraway look she'd had since she laid eyes on Doctor Clarkson. Ever since he was a child, he'd known her as the warrior queen, the strong and stubborn woman who could vex Lochlan O'Shea and get away with it. The girl who once had two princes in love with her.

"Do you think she's okay?" He looked back over his shoulder as he left the sitting room with Tia by his side.

Tia sighed. "She's insisting she's fine. But it can't be easy for her."

"So you believe she'll be all right?"

"I don't know. My mom ... she had a rough childhood. I can't imagine living in a place where magic is nothing more than a curse. They hate our kind, Gul. How do we reason with people who lock up children just for being fae? For years, they let her think she was losing her mind. They let her think her parents abandoned her."

Sliding an arm around her shoulders, he hesitated before responding. "Are you so sure we can reason with HAFS?"

"I can't think like that. There has to be a way to stop all of this, to live in peace."

"If you find it, let me know." He hugged her to his side, his tail patting circles on her back.

"We will find a way and we'll do it together. All of us."

Her head dropped onto his shoulder. "Being in charge is exhausting." She pushed him away with sudden strength. "Don't just stand here talking to me, you bumbling fool."

"Whoa, talk about mood change."

She stomped her foot in a very unqueen-like way. "There is a pretty girl who you just freed an entire hospital of prisoners to save sitting in the healing ward. Doctor Clarkson isn't important right now; she is. So why are you standing here with me?"

He wasn't sure what to say to that. Leaning down, he dropped his voice. "I kissed her."

"What?" Tia's eyes lifted to his. "I didn't catch that."

"I kissed Sophie," he said louder this time. "Well, actually she kissed me, but I kissed her back." A few servants stopped in the hall for a moment when he yelled but then continued on their way.

Tia, on the other hand, grinned like she'd known all along. "Of course you did. I'd be very disappointed in you if you hadn't."

He turned away from her. "Walking away now."

"Go get 'em, tiger!"

"I'm not a tiger." He waved over his shoulder. "And all I want is her."

She said the strangest things sometimes.

Most days, walking through the Eldurian palace was a wonder with the courtyards, fountains, and bright artwork, but today the long halls and crisscrossing corridors were nothing more than the distance standing between him and Sophie.

When he finally reached the arched doorway that led to the expansive healing ward, he stopped. Sophie sat on the edge of a feather bed in a pair of Darra's black leather riding pants and a long red tunic. Her blue-tipped hair was pulled back with a white ribbon. And she was beautiful. Despite her human heritage, she fit in this world.

It was more of a feeling than any look that made her blend in. Clothes could change, even demeanor could be refined—just like Brea—but a person's soul ... that was constant. And Sophie's soul was content. He could see it in her eyes, in the way her legs swung happily, her bare toes grazing the stone floor.

Her eyes were on the high ceilings with the exposed beams and arched stone. She didn't look at him before she spoke. "This place is even cooler than Iskalt."

His brow furrowed. "It's very hot. I don't think I'd say it was cool at all."

She lowered her gaze, one eyebrow raised. "You're kind of adorable."

His face flamed at that, so he brushed it aside and walked toward her bed. The boy was nowhere to be found, and neither were the two palace healers. Even the servants seemed to have left them alone. It was a rare moment of peace among the busy kingdoms.

"How are you?" He flinched at how idiotic the question sounded. How was she? Probably not good. She'd just spent too much time in an institute where they did magic knew what to her.

She cut off his thoughts with a simple, "I'm not sure." That was fair. He wasn't exactly sure how he was either.

A piece of hair fell loose from the ribbon, and she tucked it back. "It's nice to be clean. They even took me to a room with the biggest bathtub I've ever seen. It was like a pool in the floor, and it had hot running water. I didn't know you all did indoor plumbing here."

You all. It was just another reminder that she was human and he was fae. "In Iskalt, they bring in copper tubs and magically heat the water, but it's much easier here. When I'm home, we just use the kettle and then mix the steaming water in with the cold. My mother doesn't like having servants, so we do everything ourselves."

She nodded like she was imagining it. "Much different from just turning on the shower."

"I enjoy showers in the human realm." Slowly, he took a seat beside her on the bed. "There are a lot of things there I like."

A sad smile played on her lips. "Most of it is overrated. I'd give up all human conveniences for even a sniff at what you have here with your entire family."

A sniff? "I might not try to smell my father. He's always very busy, so doesn't take as many baths as he probably should. And my sisters ... definitely keep your nose away from them."

"That's not what I ... never mind. I didn't know you had sisters. How old are they?"

"Seven and nine. And they're royal pains too."

She smiled. "You love them."

"More than anything. Just don't tell them I said that or I'll never hear the end of it."

Their voices dropped off, and they shared the silence, the sound of their breath the only noise to reach their ears.

One of the healers walked in, his steps echoing off the high ceilings. He crossed the room and exited through another door.

Gulliver released a breath. "I—"

"You kissed me back." Sophie's words were soft but clear.

"You kissed me first." He turned to look at her and found her watching him.

"I didn't expect you to come for me."

"Is that why you kissed me?"

He couldn't breathe while he waited for the answer, not sure what he wanted to hear.

After a few beats, Sophie shook her head. "No. It was because when I was locked up, I missed you. I don't think I realized how much until I saw you."

"You ... missed me? But ..." How? He wasn't like her. With his tail, his eyes ...

"Stop." She touched the side of his face, her fingers gliding across his skin. "I know what you're thinking, Gulliver O'Shea. Isn't it enough to say I thought of you? That you kept me going?"

One corner of his mouth curved up. This was it. He would get to kiss her again, to enjoy it this time and memorize every moment. His eyes flicked to her lips, watched as she released a puff of air.

And then, the whispering came. "Do you think we're interrupting them?"

"Probably. I can't tell. Why are they so close to each other?"

Gulliver closed his eyes for a moment in exasperation, and Sophie laughed. Hearing that sound was worth the interruption. It had been too rare.

He turned to Brea, who stood with a hand on the boy's shoulder.

"Sophie." The boy ran toward her and jumped onto the bed to give her a hug. "I left to explore when the healer wasn't looking, but then I couldn't find my way back." He pulled away, his voice hoarse. "I can't hear you."

"She's right here." Gulliver looked from the boy to Brea, who shrugged.

"He means in his head," Sophie explained, not taking her eyes from him. "I can't hear you either."

"It's like when you disappeared before."

A realization hit her. "When I first came to the fae realm." That was it. Their connection only worked in the human world. "Do you have your magic?"

He shook his head.

"What do you mean?" Alarm hit Gulliver. He'd seen what the boy could do when he threw Griff in the air.

"As soon as we entered the portal, I felt it leave." The boy grinned. "It felt ... like freedom. My magic has only ever caused me problems." He jumped off the bed, tears in his eyes.

Brea pulled him into a motherly hug. If there was one person this kid needed in his life, it was the Queen Mother of Iskalt. "You're safe now," she murmured. "We will protect you."

Sophie reached for Gulliver's hand, as if he could lend her strength. Their fingers intertwined. "He grew up in the institute since he was a baby."

Brea's eyes widened, and tears glistened in their depths. She'd been in and out of the institute for years as a teen but never for long. "How did his parents let that happen?"

The boy looked up at her. "I don't have any parents, ma'am."

"Oh, honey." She hugged him tighter.

"Do I have to go back there?" he asked. "Are you going to send me back to the humans since my magic doesn't work anymore?"

She put a hand under his chin and tilted his face up. "You listen to me. No one will hurt you again. Your future is now yours to choose. If you wish to stay, there is a place for you here."

Sophie leaned her head on Gulliver's shoulder. Her cheeks were damp, and he wondered if she needed someone to say that to her. Or maybe she wanted to go back and live among her kind. All he knew was, in that moment, he didn't have the courage to ask.

"First order of business." Brea patted the boy's head. "Our new friend doesn't have a name and that won't do."

He sniffed. "I think I'd like having a name. Can I have a dog too?"

A laugh burst out of Brea. "One thing at a time." She leaned down to whisper, "But yes, we may be able to find you a dog."

His grin was so large that Gulliver had to keep himself from blubbering along with Sophie.

Sophie leaned forward to pull the boy to stand in front of her. "What do you feel like? What name fits you?"

His little lips pursed as he considered her question. It was only a minute before his eyes lit up. "One of the nurses used to read to me, and we read every book in the institute's library."

"Wouldn't be hard," Sophie grumbled.

The boy shrugged. "There was one that took us ages to read. It has all sorts of stories. Then, when we finished, we read it a couple more times. I think I'd like one of the names of the superheroes in that."

Brea smiled. "Myles had a horse named Captain America once."

"That's a strange name." Gulliver would never understand humans.

Sophie pushed them forward. "So, what's this superhero's name?"

The boy stood up straighter. "Jesus."

The two women were silent, and Gulliver looked between them, unable to read their expressions.

Finally, Brea rubbed the back of her neck. "Kid, do you mean you read the *Bible* over and over?"

"Yes!" He bounced on his toes. "That was the title. Jesus had magic just like me. I always thought I was like him."

Brea tried to stifle her smile, but it didn't work as her lips curved. "I think we should go with your second choice. Jesus is a very famous man."

He shrugged. "Okay. Then ... Noah. He really liked animals. I've never been around them, but I think I'd like animals too."

There was no stopping all their smiles at that.

Gulliver stuck out a hand for him to shake. "Welcome to the fae realm, Noah. Your new home."

Chapter Eighteen
SOPHIE

The lingering effects of the drugs were finally out of her system now. Sophie stared out the window of her beautiful room in the Eldurian palace. The exotic courtyard drew her attention to the tinkling fountains and the palm fronds rustling in the dry desert breeze. Before she retired for the evening, the healers had given her a potion that had strengthened her body and restored the clarity of her mind. After a nap and a good meal, she and Noah had been given their own rooms.

It was hot, and she couldn't get comfortable as she tossed and turned, her mind whirring with too many thoughts at once. She had so many questions. Questions about her father and how her mother died. Questions about her past. Uncertainty about her future.

Shoving the thin cooling blanket aside, she rolled out of bed and reached for the robe Princess Darra had brought her. She didn't know where she was going, but she had to get out of this room and stretch her legs. Too much time in the institute had worn her down physically.

She wandered along corridors and through courtyards, getting lost and found again when she stumbled upon the doctor's room. Guards stood sentry in the hall outside.

Squaring her shoulders, she approached the fae guards. "I'd like to see Doctor Clarkson."

The male guard glanced at his female companion before they stepped aside.

"Call for assistance should you need it." The man nodded as she opened the door.

It was a simple room. Nothing as lavish as the one she'd been given, but it seemed comfortable, which was far more than he deserved.

That he and other members of HAFS couldn't see the fae's kindness baffled her.

"No need to creep around in the dark. I am awake." The doctor sat up from the bed, where he'd been lounging. "I will not rest while among the enemy."

"They aren't the enemy," Sophie said, stepping into the moonlight streaming in from the window above his bed.

"You have fallen under their influence, Sophie. I cannot help you now."

"You think you're helping anyone?" Fury heated her tone. "In your institute of horrors?"

"I do what I can to save the humans who have been tainted by their evil magic."

"They aren't evil! The fae of the five kingdoms are the

kindest souls I've ever known. They are almost childlike in their innocence and ignorance of the evils that humans perpetrate against them. The only thing they are guilty of is their overzealous desire to help, in that it often has the opposite effect."

"You have been duped, you stupid girl. Just like your mother."

"What do you know of my mother?" Sophie took a step closer to Clarkson, searching his face for the answers she needed. There was still so much she didn't know about her mother's death. She knew it was her father who pulled the trigger, but HAFS was behind it.

"She betrayed your father, and she betrayed her kind when she chose a fae abomination over her own family."

"What do mean she chose the fae?" She tilted her head, pretending to be confused. "My mother died when the darkness came."

"You think that's when HAFS began?" The doctor laughed mirthlessly. "My father gathered the first humans to our cause before I was born. The fae have been among us for generations, and they grow stronger and stronger as the years pass. They will take us over when their numbers surpass ours. They want the human world for themselves."

"No," Sophie insisted. "They just want to live in peace."

"Peace?" Clarkson snorted. "You are even more naïve than your mother was. They will breed with humans until they wipe us out completely. Even now, it is difficult to find humans completely untainted by fae blood and their unholy magic."

"What does it even matter?" Sophie threw her hands up, completely bewildered. "We're all people who want the same things in life. Who cares if they have magic we can't understand? You don't see them waging war against us because we have technology they find equally terrifying. The only thing that makes them different is their pointy ears and their truly odd sense of humor."

"You forget your friend with the tail and feline eyes. The fae with wings, horns, or scales like fish. What sort of feral creatures have their ancestors bred with? And now they want to mix with humans? No. We will not have it. I will fight until my last breath to save our world for the humans."

"And kill how many innocents along the way?"

"Innocent lives will always suffer when it comes to war."

Sophie knew she was fighting a losing battle with this man. Hate was ingrained in him. A hate his father had taught him and probably his grandfather before that. Nothing would change that kind of blind willfulness.

"How did my father become involved with HAFS? When?"

"Long before you were even born. He brought your mother into it when they married, though she remained on the outskirts of the group, refusing to take a leadership role like your father."

"And then, the darkness came, and she died."

"The darkness wasn't the harbinger of her death. Her death was her own doing."

"How? Tell me what happened."

"She was unfaithful. But your mother loved you." Clarkson met her gaze for the first time. "I believe you were the only reason she stayed in an unhappy marriage for as long as she did."

"She loved my father." Sophie knew deep in her soul that her mother had once loved Claude Devereaux. She'd watched her father mourn her mother for more than a decade. He was lost without her. Surely she must have returned that same devotion before HAFS came between them.

"She did, in the beginning. As Claude rose in rank through the years, she resisted. She wasn't happy when he became the leader of HAFS in New Orleans. But she stayed. For you."

"My father always said magic killed my mother." Tears

burned her eyes, but she refused to shed them. Not when she was so close to having the answers to so many questions.

The doctor laughed at that. "I suppose, in a way, it did."

"I remember when she died. There was a loud noise and a flash of light, like headlights. And then, she was gone. The fae killed her that night."

But it wasn't them. Maybe her father had talked about it so much she remembered his version of what happened that night.

"She got herself killed when she fell in love with an abomination."

"Love?" Sophie blinked back her tears. "She had an affair with a half-fae?" It all made sense now. Of course her father would have lost his mind over that.

The doctor nodded. "He had strange magic, even for the fae. He looked human. That's how they work their way into human lives, hiding what they are."

"And she wanted to leave?" She ignored his narrowminded waffle.

Clarkson nodded again. "She wanted to leave Claude and take you to live among the fae." He snorted a laugh, as if that was the most ridiculous thing he'd ever heard. "She lost her mind." He shook his head. "HAFS had to step in to save her, but she wouldn't hear of it. She stayed in the institute for a while, and it soon became clear she was expecting another child. A fae child."

Sophie gasped. "She had a baby?"

"She was mad for her lover and their child. He helped her escape, and they were going to run away together, the three of them. But she wouldn't leave you."

Sophie's mind reeled with this information. "And it got her killed, didn't it? HAFS killed her."

Except, it was Claude who'd done it. That was the part that never made sense to her. Since the night she'd overheard her father and the doctor talking about her mother's death, Sophie couldn't figure out how her dad had found it within himself to actually kill her mother. But jealousy? She could see it now.

"Claude took her home and kept her away from her lover. After the child was born, she tried to leave again. She took the baby and tried to pick you up from school. She was going to leave that night, though she had no car, no money, or means to travel. Her bags were packed, and it seemed as though she intended to walk out of the city with an infant and a young child."

"I remember that day." Sophie choked on her words. "The darkness had just started to creep across the city. Mom came to get me from school early." She frowned. "I don't remember the baby, but I had to be at least eight or nine years old by then. I should have remembered him."

"Your father encouraged you to forget him ... after."

She shook her head. "This doesn't make any sense."

Sophie studied the doctor's face, searching for signs of his lies.

"Claude went after her. He knew what had to be done. We never tolerate dissension among our ranks."

"And he killed her for it." Sophie shook her head again.

"It was your father's responsibility to deal with her treachery. Your mother wasn't well, Sophie. It had to be done."

"Wasn't well?" she whispered. "Because she had the audacity to fall in love with someone not quite human?"

"They are vile creatures. They must be stopped. And when a human is too far gone, there is only one answer."

"Murder?" She glared at him; her fists clenched at her sides.

"Claude loved your mother. He did what he had to do to save her soul."

"No." She stepped away from the doctor. "He was a jealous fool."

"He was a fool. He couldn't bring himself to kill her child,"

Clarkson continued, a gleam of triumph in his eye. "So, he brought the boy to the institute."

"Noah," Sophie gasped as she sank to the floor. "He's my brother."

"The boy was fae. A disgrace. He wasn't your brother. He wasn't human."

"What did you do to his magic?" She thought about the doctor's machines. The same ones that ripped through her, searching for traces of magic. What had Noah experienced in a lifetime at their hands?

"We couldn't rid him of magic, but we diminished it."

"Diminished?" What must Noah have been capable of before they tampered with his magic? "You're monsters." She scooted across the floor toward the door, unable to get her feet under her as her body trembled with so much emotion she couldn't identify all she was feeling. Anger, sadness, and so much rage. "You tried to break him."

"And we did. His magic is erratic and dangerous now. He can't be allowed to roam free. But the boy has given us valuable information on the genetic makeup of fae. Through him, we have learned to identify the markers of those with magic and those without. We will eradicate all magic from our world in one way or another. And then, we will go after every human with even a drop of fae blood until our world is pure again."

"You're disgusting. All of you are past redemption. You'll never be satisfied with peace, so why should we even try?" In that moment, Sophie set her father free. Nothing he could say or do could ever make up for the damage he'd done to their family. She'd never doubted his love, but she could never condone his actions. He would have to bear the responsibility for those actions all on his own.

Her mother had another child. A beautiful boy whose terrifying magic seemed to be tempered in the fae world. Noah was her family now, and she would do right by him.

"You're a silly child, Sophie Devereaux. HAFS will never settle for peace with the fae. We will take the world back for the humans. And anyone who stands in our way will not stand for long."

Sophie reached for the arm of a nearby chair and pulled herself up. She wiped her eyes and gave the doctor one long last look. "You will not win this war."

She turned and left him to his delusions.

Sleep would never come to her now. Searching the rooms nearest to hers, she found Noah sleeping soundly in one just across the courtyard.

She imagined any other ten-year-old would be too terrified to sleep in a strange bed in a strange land, but not her brother. She sat beside him, watching him sleep with a sweet smile on his face.

"I won't let anyone hurt you ever again." She brushed her fingertips over his forehead, smoothing back his soft curls so she could study his face for signs of their mother.

She saw her in the shape of his eyes and the curve of his mouth. In his sweet disposition and his uncanny ability to make the best out of the worst situations.

She traced a finger along his hairline, the soft dark blond curls much like their mother's.

And Sophie smiled when she noticed the subtle point of his little ears that he got from his father.

Chapter Nineteen

GULLIVER

"You'll like it, I promise." Gulliver slid a steaming mug of Eldur brew across the pub table. "Brea says it's a lot like the humans' coffee drink, but I've never been fond of the taste. It's a little too bitter for me, but it's popular among the working class in Eldur. Probably because it'll wake you up so fast you might not blink for hours."

"Says the fae who gets drunk off a few sips of wine." Tia snickered, but Gulliver kicked her under the table. He was dorky enough on his own and didn't need his best friend helping him look even more foolish in front of Sophie.

"You should try the chocoah." Tia wrinkled her nose at the

Eldur brew. "We've just started importing it from Lenya, and it's so good. We can't get enough of it at the palace. It's like human hot chocolate, but even better. It tastes like chocolate, but creamier and sweeter." She dipped her head to sip from the brimming mug in front of her. She sat back with a full chocoah mustache she wiped away with her hand.

"Can I try both?" Sophie eyed the frothing sweet drink Tia was slurping down. "I bet they'd be amazing if you mixed them. It would sweeten up the coffee with the chocolate and dial down the bitterness while making the chocoah a little less sweet."

"Oh." Tia's eyes widened. "That actually sounds delicious." She leaned over the table to get the barmaid's attention and ordered two more of each drink.

"Might be even better iced too," Sophie suggested.

"Ow. What was that for?" Gulliver gripped his shin where Tia had kicked him under the table.

"I like her. Don't screw it up."

"Stop talking, Tia," Gulliver growled

"We were hoping marriage and a crown would force her to grow up." Toby rolled his eyes. "No such luck."

"You're right, the Eldur brew stuff is a lot like coffee," Xavier admitted, clearly trying to change the subject back. "Just not as good."

"It's a little too bitter," Sophie agreed. "But it'll do in a pinch."

"My mom says that a lot," Tia said. "But as much as I love humanisms, that one has never made any sense. Who's doing the pinching? And why?"

"As lively as this conversation is, that's not what we came all the way down here to discuss." Gulliver looked over his shoulder at the other pub patrons, minding their own business. "Are you sure this is the best place to talk?"

"I used to come here a lot with Logan and Darra. The pub

owner will chase away anyone who gets too nosey." Toby nodded at the man behind the bar. "We can talk. Just keep your voices down." He looked at Tia as he spoke.

"Why do you say that like I'm the loud one?" She scowled at her brother.

"Because you *are* the loud one." Gulliver sipped his chocoah, thinking he agreed with Sophie. The sweet drink might benefit from some of the bitterness of Eldur beans.

She was better since her arrival in Eldur. More focused and decisive. She hadn't said as much, but Gulliver got the feeling she'd left a lot of her past behind her at the Clarkson Institute. She just woke up her second morning here and seemed to have a lot more determination. Most of which was directed at protecting Noah.

"Peace talks are only going to work if both parties are interested," Xavier began. "And I don't know if we have the kind of time that will take to convince Clarkson to even consider a truce."

"We don't," Sophie said. "And he won't ever consider it. That man can't be reasoned with."

"So, what do we do if one side of this situation refuses to negotiate?" Toby asked.

"It's not just fae verses human, though," Sophie said. "There are three sides here, and we're trying to reason with only one of them."

Gulliver forced himself to focus on all her words and not just the part where she lumped herself in with the fae. She thought of them as a *we*, and that made him feel all sorts of emotions he wasn't ready to think about yet. Not that he had time for such things.

"What do you mean?" Tia asked.

"She's talking about HAFS," Gulliver offered.

"I thought that's what we were talking about." Tia frowned. "Doctor Clarkson is the head of HAFS."

"He is, but he isn't the leader of all humans. Only those who believe the fae are evil magic wielders waiting to gobble up their world. Not all humans are like him."

"Unfortunately, HAFS are behind the strikes against the fae communities in our world." Xavier leaned against the table, leaving his drink forgotten.

"But now that the human government has become involved in the fight for Los Angeles, the information people are getting is filtered through the hate of HAFS," Sophie said. "It's like your everyday human has just realized HAFS was right all along, so now they're listening to everything they say, believing it must be the truth.

"We need a way to get the real truth out to the non-HAFS humans." As Sophie talked, Gullie leaned in to hang on her every word. "A way to help them see fae aren't the monsters they've been led to believe they are."

"But how can we do that?" Tia's voice sounded distant, like she was thinking deeply while she poured Eldur brew into her chocoah mug and sloshed it around before she took a hesitant sip.

"Hmmm, that is good, Soph." She lifted her mug, and Gulliver shook his head at his best friend. Maybe her thoughts weren't so deep after all.

"Focus, Tia." Gulliver slapped his hand on the table to get her attention.

"What? I am." She took another sip. "We need a way to talk directly to the human population. To get past HAFS."

"Well..." Sophie shared a look with Xavier. "We could do that."

"The media?" Xavier let out an anxious sigh. "That could go badly for us if we aren't careful."

"So, we'll be careful," Sophie said. "Find the right person to talk to, someone who won't twist your words to make it fit their agenda."

"We should talk to Orla," Toby suggested. "She might know of someone we could trust."

"She does know someone." Xavier nodded, a smile spreading across his face. "She has a cousin who is mostly human, no magic of any kind, but she's sympathetic to the fae."

"How will that help?" Gulliver asked, not seeing how a sympathetic human could help them get on the human feletision.

"She's a reporter in L.A., and people love her. Most would never know she had fae blood."

Tia chewed on her bottom lip for a moment before she spoke. "Could she get me on the televisions so I could talk to the humans?"

Chapter Twenty
TOBY

This was either a really terrible idea or the best one they'd had in a long time.

"What does this do?" Gulliver reached for a piece of equipment, and two humans simultaneously yelled for him to stop. It was too late. He stumbled, startled by their noise, and knocked into the black box on a stick in front of him.

It crashed to the floor, leaving the entire room in an air of shocked silence.

Gulliver's face went bright red. "Oops."

"Hey, Gul." Brea put a maternal hand on his back. "Let's move away from the cameras, yeah?"

He nodded sullenly and followed her.

Tia could barely contain her laughter as Orla and Xavier scrambled to right the camera and make sure it wasn't broken, issuing apologies as they did.

There were six of them who'd traveled from the fae realm. The two half-fae rebels, Brea, Tia, Gulliver, and Toby. It was too dangerous for Sophie to come all the way here, so she'd meet them at the farmhouse with Griff when all of this was done.

Toby turned to take in what Xavier had called a news studio. There was a desk behind the cameras with spots for two humans. He'd seen the news before, but this was different, more somehow. The people who worked here told the rest of the human world what was happening and what they should believe. It was a kind of power he'd never imagined.

"Kind of cool, right?" Xavier joined him, a hesitant smile on his face.

Toby hated himself for putting that hesitation there. His conflicting emotions about Logan shouldn't have made Xavier doubt himself. They were friends, of course they were. But though neither had acknowledged it, there was also something more. When Toby was with Xavier, he could hope again. Plan for a future that had felt so dark and lonely for too long.

There were still bruises on Xavier's olive skin from the battle in Aghadoon, a new scar above his left eye. Yet, he was the same man who'd seen two out-of-their-element fae in New Orleans and tried to help them.

Toby realized he hadn't responded, so he nodded. "It's very ... human."

He would never admit this to his sister or his parents, but he loved the human world. Not the evil here, but the way a person didn't need magic to have worth. Their magic was in the technology that was available to all.

He fit in here among the half-fae in a way he didn't back home.

"Is that a bad thing?" Xavier didn't sound defensive, only curious.

Toby thought for a moment. "No. Just different."

Like him.

Having no magic other than the O'Shea portal ability made him an outsider among his own people. He knew they tried not to see him as such, but it was impossible. Even Tia, who often needed him to be her amplifier, sometimes looked at him with pity.

Xavier lifted a hand, but let it drop, and Toby wanted to know what he was going to do. Give him a friendly pat on the shoulder? Touch his cheek? Take his hand?

Whatever it was, Toby wanted to lean into him. Alona had been right. Logan wouldn't want him to grieve forever. Yet, it wasn't that simple. It never was.

"I'm sorry." The words came before he realized he'd spoken them.

Xavier's brow furrowed. "You're sorry ..."

"For avoiding you, not telling you why. I've made so many mistakes."

Xavier's hand brushed the back of Toby's. "I know about Logan." He waited a beat before continuing. "I'm so sorry, Tobes. If I could give him back to you and disappear, I would."

"What if I don't want you to disappear?"

They stared at each other for a long moment, and Toby didn't breathe, couldn't breathe.

Their standoff ended when a black woman with long, beautiful curls walked out and clapped her hands. "Are we ready to change the world?"

Toby was momentarily stunned by the woman who must

have been Orla's cousin. She had a face made for the human televisions, with sparkling white teeth, a bright and genuine smile, and deep green eyes.

Orla greeted her with a kiss on each cheek before turning to the group. "Everyone, this is Stella. Her cameraman is named Bones."

"Bones?" Tia chuckled under her breath.

Orla shot her a look. "They're risking a lot for this. They've made sure the rest of their crew is away for the night and locked the doors so no one else can get in. We need to record this quickly. She'll put it on the air in the morning."

It made sense now, why they had to wait until the dead of night to come in. The other humans who worked here didn't know what was happening.

Orla walked Stella toward Tia and Brea. "These two will be going on the air."

Stella adjusted a piece of plastic that rested on her head, stretching toward her mouth. "Welcome, your Majesty." She directed the greeting to Brea.

Brea laughed. "Oh dear, I convinced my husband to get me out of that role the moment my daughter was ready. Tia here is the Iskaltian queen now."

Stella nodded, not correcting herself. "I have a friend who will air this overseas with subtitles in French, Spanish, and Chinese. Do you have preferred pronouns so we can get the introduction, right?"

Tia looked at her mother in confusion.

Toby didn't know the answer to that either. What was a pronoun? Why was it important?

Orla put a hand on Stella's shoulder. "Let's not break their fae brains. Put them down for she/her."

"Got it. I just always want to be sensitive." She walked back toward the camera to speak with Bones.

Orla rubbed her eyes. "It's hard to grasp that the fae world doesn't understand the human way of life. Do you two know what you're going to say?"

Tia shrugged. "Figured I'd wing it. That's what humans would call it, right?"

Brea rolled her eyes. "Yes, we're prepared. Ignore my daughter."

Orla nodded. "Well, we have a lot of lives riding on this."

Toby's chest tightened as their conversation finished.

"How do your mom and sister have so much faith in a president they know nothing about?" Xavier asked.

Toby couldn't take his eyes from the confidence in Tia's posture. He'd questioned so many of her decisions in life, but this was the right one. "They're both queens. They know what it is to have the well-being of an entire kingdom on their shoulders. It's less faith and more hope that the human leader has even an ounce of what they do."

"And what's that?"

"Love for their people."

Stella gestured for the two women to join her. She positioned them both in front of a giant green wall. It would look odd on camera, but Toby figured she knew what she was doing.

Toby went to Gulliver at the side of the stage to watch them. Tia stuck her tongue out at him, and he sighed.

"We're seriously putting the fate of our people in that girl's hands?" Orla shook her head. "I think we've all gone mad."

Toby's jaw clenched, but Gulliver beat him to a response.

"That *girl* is a queen. She deserves to be treated as such. And she has saved more fae than you can even fathom exist. So, yes, your fate is in her hands, and you should be darn glad it is."

Toby patted his back in solidarity. He was glad Tia had Gulliver. After Logan died, when he couldn't be there for her, she'd still had a brother. Toby had allowed his grief to swallow him whole, but it hadn't left her alone.

His pinky hooked around Xavier's, not quite handholding but almost. When Xavier didn't pull away, Toby smiled.

This would work. It had to.

Bones lifted a hand and Stella yelled, "Everyone quiet!"

One of Bones' fingers dropped, then another, until finally, he pointed the last one at the two queens.

Neither of them spoke.

Stella cursed. "That means start."

"Oh." Tia bounced on her toes like she couldn't contain her nervous energy. "Well, hello there."

Toby slapped a hand to his forehead.

"Chill, Tia." Brea took her hand.

"You chill, Mom." Tia ripped it away. "You don't get to tell me what to do anymore, remember? I'm your queen."

"You're my daughter first."

They'd had this argument more times than Toby could count. "For magic's sake, can my family just act normal for once?"

They both looked at him and straightened, taking it as a challenge. They were the same person, and it was never more evident than in that moment.

Tia turned to look at the camera, and Brea followed suit.

"Hello, humans." Tia smiled, trying to look normal, but it actually seemed like she'd lost her mind.

Brea's smile was more natural as she said, "I was one of you once. Well, I thought I was. I lived in ignorance of the fae, not even knowing of their existence. You know about us, so yay!"

Tia rolled her eyes. "My name is Tierney O'Shea. I am one of the queens of the fae, and I've come here to beg your mercy. Our people are suffering. From bombings in your cities to all-out war, we are dying. And so are humans. None of us want this. The fae have only ever wanted peace."

Brea picked up where she left off. "I spent the first seventeen years of my life in the human realm before becoming a queen of the fae. I know how terrifying it is to learn of magic and the kinds of abilities those different from you have. It probably scares you as much as technology scares my husband. You should see a fae catch sight of a car for the first time." She doubled over in laughter.

Toby coughed, trying to remind his mother to maintain some semblance of seriousness.

Brea's face sobered. "We don't want to fight. All we want is safety for those fae and half-fae who live in your world."

"For that," Tia started, "we must speak to your leader. To the queen of the United America—"

"President of the United States of America," Brea coughed.

"—and you are watching this, know that we wish to meet, ruler to ruler. We are prepared to negotiate for peace, for an end to the fighting. All we want is an end to the terrorist group known as HAFS that is destroying cities in their search for fae."

"Yes." Brea stepped closer to the camera. "Take me to your leader." Her voice sounded odd.

Tia yanked her back. "But like, in a non-terrifying way." She side-eyed their mom. "There is an address we will give to the representative of the president. Call this number." She rattled off the number Orla set up for this purpose. "We hope to hear from you." She nodded once and walked off the stage.

Brea was still laughing as she approached Toby. "I've always wanted to say that. 'Take me to your leader'." Tears danced in her eyes.

"Why are you like this, Mom?" He bit back a smile, the kind she always seemed to be able to pull out of him.

She wrapped an arm around his shoulder and guided him

toward the door. "Because, kiddo, life shouldn't be so serious all the time. Sometimes, we just have to enjoy the moment when we don't know how many more we'll get together."

As she dragged him away, he glanced back at Xavier. The other man walked with his hands deep in his pockets, his shoulders hunched.

Toby wanted to enjoy his moments too.

Chapter Twenty-One

SOPHIE

Tension filled the farmhouse. Two days ago, the message to the President aired. Sophie was the only one who hadn't believed the woman would actually come to a farmhouse in Ohio. She was the President of the United States, after all. A title that meant little to the fae. Their leaders were much more accessible, less guarded.

"Stop pacing," Tia snapped at her brother.

Toby ignored her.

There were too many people crowded into the small living room, too little space. Sophie could hardly breathe.

Xavier crossed the room, sliding his hand into Toby's and dragging him toward the hallway for a break.

She wondered if anyone else saw it. The way the two men cast glances at each other, looking away when their eyes met.

They were falling in love.

Just like she was. Minute by minute, day by day. Every touch, every smile, every time she heard Gulliver say her name in that whispery way of his.

Right now, she wasn't sure why. Gulliver and Tia had raided the fridge as soon as they ran in the door and now sat side by side in a pile of wrappers, crumbs coating their shirts. Gulliver had Nutella smeared on his lips, and Tia had dripped sauce from a hot pocket onto her pants.

In other words, they were a wreck as they waited for a call from the most influential person in the free world.

At least Kier wasn't here to watch Tia sink into her food coma. He was back in Iskalt making sure the kingdom didn't fall into the icy seas or something. Gulliver told her about a wicked storm off the coast to the north, but she hadn't completely understood what he was talking about.

Tia burped as Griff took a spot leaning against the wall beside Sophie. "I'm sorry."

That surprised her. "For what?"

"Not teaching my son how to not be gross."

A laugh escaped her. "It's okay. Certain foods here are ... addictive."

"He's going to miss them." She got the feeling he wasn't only talking about the food.

She had so many decisions to make. Was there a place for her anymore among the humans? Would her brother come back here with her?

Brother. She still hadn't gotten used to that thought, but she wished he was here with her. The only thing she knew was that it would always be her and Noah.

"What's it like?" she asked. "Having a brother?"

Griff didn't answer for a long moment before he sighed. "I spent most of my life hating Lochlan. We were raised separately, as enemies. It wasn't until I'd spent a decade in the prison realm, been forgotten by the world, and then helped them restore memories and destroy the dark king that we even got a chance to be family."

"Whoa." That was ... dark. "And now?"

"We're figuring it out still. I think we always will be. But I can now say I wouldn't want to live my life without my brother and his family. When it's good, it's a love unlike anything else."

A smile curved her lips. She couldn't wait for a lifetime getting to know Noah. "And Gullie? You two truly love each other, don't you?"

Griff wasn't his biological father, but what they had was so very different from the controlling relationship her own father created. She hadn't seen it at the time when her father was sitting beside her hospital bed for years, taking care of her.

Griff gave her a sad smile. "You could have this, Sophie."

He gestured around the room where Tia and her father were arguing. Brea was watching them like it was a soccer match. Gulliver was half asleep. She knew Griff meant not only those present, but their family who wasn't here. Kier, Gulliver's mother and sisters, the royal family she'd met in Eldur.

"I know." Tears flooded her eyes because it was true. They'd welcome her and Noah with open arms. It was who they were. But she wasn't fae. Did she belong in their world?

"Take it from me, Sophie. Sometimes, a family is made, not born." He left her with those words and approached the couch, shoving Gulliver's head to wake him up. He sat with a start and scowled at his father.

The front door banged open, and Orla sprinted in, holding a ringing phone in her hand. It was a prepaid phone she'd bought for a single purpose.

The President's call.

Tia jumped to her feet. "Answer it!"

Toby and Xavier rushed back in to join them as Orla put the phone on speaker. "Hello?" she said.

A low voice responded. "The President of the United States will arrive in five minutes."

Then, they hung up.

The room burst into chatter.

"They were supposed to call and ask where to meet!" Tia's eyes held panic.

"How did they know where we were?" Toby asked.

They didn't understand the true power of the President. They could find out anything. And now, she was on her way to a small, broken-down farmhouse in Ohio full of chaos and confusion. And a fae queen with pizza stains on her pants.

No, this wouldn't do.

Sophie pushed off the wall. "Everyone shut up!"

They kept talking.

This wasn't working. Searching the room, she found a small end table and climbed onto it. "Quiet!"

This time, they looked at her, their talk dying away. She wanted to wither under their stares, but she couldn't back down now.

"I have gone through too much at the hands of HAFS for this meeting to fail." She jumped off the table. "Xavier and Toby, make sure there's a comfortable place for her to sit. Orla, go into the kitchen and put a kettle on. Gulliver, get the crumbs off your shirt. Tia, try to act like a queen, and for Fae's sake, go change your pants!" She turned to Brea and Lochlan, the latter scowling.

"Go on, honey." Brea smiled. "I'm quite enjoying this. Don't stop when it's my husband's turn. He loves being told what to do."

Somehow, she didn't believe her. "Sir," Sophie started, trying to keep her voice from shaking, "the Secret Service will most likely come first. You should go greet them."

"What's a Secret Service?" he asked, crossing his arms.

Brea laughed. "You're going to love them, Loch. They won't make you angry at all."

"Brea, can you—"

"Take care of the President?" Brea finished.

Sophie didn't admit that was exactly what she was going to say.

Brea nodded in excitement. "This is the highlight of my little human heart."

"You don't have a human heart, Mom." Tia rolled her eyes as she practiced her posture.

"I once thought I did."

"I don't get it." Gulliver stood and shook his entire body so the crumbs fell off. His tail finished dusting off his shirt. "Why are you acting weird, Soph?"

How could he not get it? "The President is coming. Here. Like right now and there are candy wrappers everywhere!"

"So? My best friend is a queen."

They would never understand.

A heavy knock sounded on the door, and Lochlan, like an obedient man, went to open it.

Two large men in black suits pushed him aside and rushed into the room. Another was outside, circling the farmhouse.

"Clear!" one of the men yelled from another room. A few more rounds of 'clear' rang out with the men not saying a word to them. Lochlan was already fuming.

"Told you that you'd like them." Brea patted her husband's back.

The two men reappeared in the living room, one of them looking like he was talking to himself.

"Which one of you are the President?" Gulliver asked.

Neither responded.

Tia stood, her spine ramrod straight. She put on her stern queen face. "You can't just barge into the human farmhouse of a fae queen."

Sophie looked away to hide her smile. Sometimes, the fae were too adorable.

The front door opened again, and the third agent gestured to a black town car rolling down the gravel drive, dust kicking up in its wake.

Chapter Twenty-Two
GULLIVER

Gulliver stood on one side of the door, waiting with Griffin for the human queen to get out of her car. She seemed in no hurry to come inside. The men who came in first were still running around, checking every nook and cranny of the house—for what, Gulliver couldn't fathom.

"All clear for the Falcon to fly," one of the men in dark suits told his wrist.

"Humans are a strange lot, aren't they?" Griff scratched his head as he watched the woman exit the rear seat of the sleek black car. It was nicer than anything Gulliver had ever ridden in, that was for sure.

"Madame President, they are ready for you." Two more suited men escorted the woman up to the front porch. She gave the house a once over, and her delicate nose wrinkled as she removed a pair of dark glasses from their perch.

"And this is where they chose to meet?" She eyed the holes in the screen door. "Odd choice for diplomatic negotiations."

"I'm told their queen grew up in this house, ma'am."

"The queen's mother did," Gulliver shouted through the screen. "At least, one of the fae queens, I mean."

"And you are?" The human queen, president, whatever stepped into the kitchen, her suited guards leading the way.

"Gulliver, your Majesty." He bowed his head. "Er, Lord Gulliver O'Shea, I mean. Ma'am." He gave a little salute the way he'd seen the human soldiers do.

"Lord?" She arched a brow at him.

"My son, your Majesty." Griffin bowed. "Prince Griffin O'Shea of Iskalt." He offered his arm, but her guards closed in on her, not allowing the propriety.

"You have more than one ... kingdom?" she asked.

"Last count was five, your Majesty," Gulliver offered. "But they tend to crop up out of nowhere from time to time."

"I see. And each of these kingdoms has a monarch?"

"Yes, your Majesty." Gulliver bowed again.

"I am not a queen." The woman's voice was very cold and unyielding.

"Please refer to the President as either Madame President, ma'am, or President Worthington," one of her guards explained.

"Yes, ma'am." Gulliver nodded once again. "Each kingdom has a king or queen. You will meet with her Majesty Queen Tierney O'Shea of Iskalt. My sort of cousin-sister and best friend."

"Oh, dear." The President clutched a hand to her heart.

Griff cleared his throat. "What my son means is, he is

adopted and I am Tierney's natural father. I was once married to the former queen of Iskalt. But she's now married to my brother, who raised Tierney and her twin brother."

"And that's more information than President Worthington needed to know." Brea stepped into the kitchen, extending her hand to the President, but the guards wouldn't let her approach.

"Okay, then." Brea took a step back, dropping her hand. "Please come in." She stepped aside, shooing them all into the living room. "This is my home here in the human realm. I grew up here."

"Brea Robinson?" The President took slow measured steps into the overcrowded room. "I was told you lived here, yet you are not human?"

Brea raised her hand. "Changeling." She beamed a smile at the woman but didn't get a response. "Yes, I am fae. But I didn't know that until I was almost eighteen. Before that, I just thought I was crazy. Spent some time in a mental hospital to boot."

"I see." The President looked around, and Gulliver wondered if that was the only thing she could say.

"Please, come meet my daughter, the reigning Queen of Iskalt." Brea gestured to where Tia sat perched on the edge of her seat.

"Why are you no longer queen?" the President asked. "You are still young and surely more capable and mature for such an important role."

"Oh, I never wanted to be queen, though I was once heir to two kingdoms and married into a third, it was never my forte. My husband abdicated his throne when it became clear that Tia was ready. She was born to rule."

"And she's sitting right here, Mom. Stop talking about me like I can't hear you." Tia hopped up from her seat and tried to hug the human president lady, but her guards were quick to step in. "Sorry, I'm just so excited to meet with the human ruler."

Tia returned to her seat, holding out a hand for the President to take the chair beside her.

The guards moved the chair to the opposite side of the room and put themselves between their ruler and the fae.

"All right." Tia smiled. "Whatever makes you most comfortable."

"I am not the ruler of all humans. I am the elected President of the United States of America. Though I speak for my people, I do not speak for the entire world."

"Yes, Mom said something about that."

"You'll have to forgive my high school knowledge of U.S. Politics." Brea shrugged. "My school years here were quite a long time ago."

"Tea! We need Tea. The water must be hot by now." Tia looked around for anyone capable of serving them. "Gullie?"

"On it." Gulliver grabbed Xavier by his shirt collar and hauled him into the kitchen.

"Can't you handle tea?" He pulled away.

"Not if you don't want me to blow up the kitchen."

"Excuse me?" One of the guards got a little too handsy with Gulliver. "What did you say?"

"He didn't mean it like that." Xavier came to his rescue. "He just meant he doesn't know how to run the tea kettle by himself." Xavier made a show of setting teacups onto a tray.

"Thanks." Gulliver brushed the creases out of his shirt. "They're a bit testy, aren't they?"

"Serving tea," Xavier muttered. "We should be in there talking peace."

"We're the lowest ranking fae in this house, even though I'm a Lord. Everyone else is royalty. That means we get the tea." Gulliver placed tea bags into each of the cups and set the kettle onto the tray before carrying it into the living room. His hands trembled, and the teacups rattled on the tray as he set it in front of Tia.

"Oh dear, that's a dreadful-looking tea service."

"Sorry, Tia, that's all we had." Gulliver backed away as she poured hot water over the boring human tea bags.

"Sugar?" Tia asked the President, using the tongs to plop three or four cubes into her own teacup.

"Honey," the president replied absently. One of her guards took the cup and tasted it before passing it on to his queen.

Gulliver had a hard time thinking of her as anything other than the human queen when she acted more like one than any of the queens he knew, and he knew a lot of them.

President Worthington tapped a blunt fingernail against a chip in the teacup and frowned at their surroundings. "This is how a fae queen lives?"

"Not at all," Tia was quick to reply. "Not that we need all the finery and luxury of the Iskaltian palace. We do know how to live with little when we must. Should you come for a visit, we'd be happy to show you all of Iskalt, Fargelsi, and Eldur—"

"That won't be necessary." The President waved her hand to dismiss Tia's invitation. "We have much to discuss and not a great deal of time to discuss it." She set her tea aside, sat back against the worn upholstery of the chair, and crossed her legs. "I would end this struggle between the fae and humans within the borders of the United States."

"I would have it end everywhere," Tia added. "But first, we must come to some understanding."

"We cannot allow magic within our world. Humans cannot live under the threat of a power they do not possess."

"Magic is not a new thing in this world, Madame President," Brea said. "It has been here for many generations and has only now become widely known."

"My mother is right," Tia began. "Fae have been in your world for a very long time, and they have been suffering."

"Suffering?" The President sneered at the suggestion.

"Suffering," Tia insisted. "The Clarkson Institute and both the current Doctor Clarkson and his father, the senior Doctor Clarkson, have been behind HAFS since its inception decades ago."

President Worthington shook her head. "My intel tells me HAFS came together when the world went dark."

"That is when they came to the forefront of your media," Brea said.

"Are you aware that Doctor Clarkson has been conducting experiments on the fae living among you? And he has been for at least a generation?" Tia asked.

"What proof do you have?"

"I've seen it with my own eyes." Gulliver stepped forward. "I was in the institute just a few days ago to rescue my friend Sophie Devereaux—"

"The Sophie Devereaux who was abducted from her death bed in New Orleans? The daughter of HAFS Leader, Claude Devereaux?"

"Yes, ma'am." Gulliver bobbed his head. "She was taken there because HAFS believed that by taking her to the kingdom of Lenya and healing her of her illness, we somehow turned her into one of us."

"Which is not the case at all," Brea was quick to add.

"While we were there, we saw several Dark Fae locked in rooms. The doctor had somehow removed their defensive magic —the thing that hides our Dark Fae features when we are here in the human realm," Gulliver rambled. "It's the magic that makes you see me as human when, in reality, I have a very handsome tail and feline eyes that most humans would find alarming."

"A tail? You have a tail?"

"Yes, ma'am." Gulliver's tail swished behind him, but his defensive magic concealed its movement from her eyes. "I briefly met an Asrai in the institute, and her scales were bare for all to see. Even Sophie could see them."

"Scales?"

"Yes."

"Asrai are fae that most closely resemble the human mythological mermaids," Brea explained. "They have legs and arms, but they prefer the depths of the sea to land."

"I see," the President murmured.

"They experimented on Sophie," Gulliver went on. "She said it was incredibly painful. And her half-fae brother grew up there being experimented on. His magic is very erratic now because of Doctor Clarkson's meddling."

"HAFS has done a great deal of harm to my fae," Tia said in her most queenly voice. "It cannot continue. The violence you yourself have committed against the fae in your world cannot continue."

"I regret the actions we took against the fae in Los Angeles," President Worthington admitted. "At the time, it felt like the only possible action when that young man there claimed Los Angeles for the fae." She pointed across the room at Toby. "By taking the city, he declared war on the United States."

"My twin brother, Prince Tobias O'Shea did what he had to do to provide a safe place for the fae of this kingdom to take refuge."

"Country," Brea coughed.

"This country," Tia corrected before continuing. "He nor I saw that as an act of war, and I stand behind his decision. To my understanding, Los Angeles is only one city in your great nation. I would ask that you support our endeavors to make it a city for the fae and those who mean them no harm."

"I must protect my people." The President folded her hands

in her lap. "No matter what, it is my responsibility to keep them safe from magic users."

Tia leaned forward with a small smile on her face. "That's just it. The fae of this world are my people, but they are also part human, which makes them yours as well. Collectively, it is our responsibility together to keep them safe. Just as I would protect my fae of Iskalt and you would protect your humans of the United States. Surely there must be a way we can come to an agreement that suits everyone involved."

"It's not about the people, your Majesty." The President seemed to shift her perspective as she gave Tia her undivided attention. As though she saw the young queen as her equal now. "It is about the magic they possess."

"One thing at a time, Madame President." Tia nodded. "We will come to an agreement on the use of magic within the human world. But first, we must agree to peace between our people."

"Perhaps." The President returned Tia's nod. "But we will need proof of the actions of Doctor Clarkson, and currently, he is missing."

"Oh, he is visiting my aunt's palace." Tia smiled. "He is perfectly safe and confined for the moment, but I will ask my uncle, Prince Griffin, and his son, Gulliver, to retrieve him for us while we continue our negotiations."

"I would very much like to speak with Doctor Clarkson. While we wait for his return, I will issue a warrant to search the institute for evidence of this experimentation. I am very eager to see what he's been up to."

Chapter Twenty-Three

SOPHIE

If Toby sat in that farmhouse for one moment longer, listening to that human queen speak as though the fae in her world meant nothing, he was going to do something they'd all regret. He paced across the kitchen, hanging on every word spoken in the living room.

The negotiations were mostly finished, and it was clear what the President wanted: an end to magic. She knew the fae of her realm weren't powerful wielders, but they weren't the ones she was worried about.

He should have left with Gullie and Griff to get Doctor

Clarkson, but Tia hadn't let him. Now, he stared at President Worthington.

"You can't be serious." His voice was louder than he'd intended, but he didn't back down. "That's ... that's ..."

"Not a bad solution," Tia finished, though she knew very well it wasn't what her brother thought at all. The look she sent him said as much.

He shot across the room, and one of the guards in black blocked his path.

"Chillax, man." Toby stepped sideways to avoid bumping into him. "I won't hurt your queen. I just need some air."

As he hurried outside, he heard Lochlan ask Brea what in all the magic his son meant by chillax.

Even his father's disdain for stupid human words couldn't stop the ringing in his ears, the howling of his thoughts.

The President of this human kingdom wanted to close off the fae world, to prevent fae from traveling through portals to reach their lands. Was it possible?

If it was, how could they even entertain such an idea? The O'Shea magic was part of the very fabric of fae life. They may not particularly like the humans, but it didn't change the fact they were connected to them, to their world.

Toby reached the overgrown front lawn that had provided a somewhat-soft landing spot for portal travelers since he was a kid clinging to his father's arm.

He hadn't realized his legs gave out until they hit the hard earth. There was no pain in them, only a sharp ache right in the center of his chest.

His power, the only magic he had, was considered by humans to be the most dangerous threat to their well-being.

A breeze rustled through his hair, cooling the day's heat. Dusk would be upon them soon, the moon rising into the sky to remind Toby he wasn't useless. There was some purpose for him in one of these worlds.

But what if that went away?

What if it all ended? Without the ability to open portals, who was he?

"Is it possible?" a soft voice asked behind him.

Toby didn't respond to Xavier's question right away. His harsh laughter drifted into the cloudy sky. "Possible? With magic, there are nearly no limitations."

That was what scared him.

What the President asked for ... could most likely be done. They only had to find the way.

He closed his eyes, feeling for the thinness of the veil that existed right here. The portals damaged that wall between worlds, but he'd never truly considered it damage. It brought the humans and fae closer together.

Now, they would be driven further apart.

Xavier extended a hand down to him, but Toby didn't take it. He couldn't go back into that room where his sister negotiated away their ancestral right.

A sigh hissed out of Xavier, and he lowered himself to the grass in front of Toby. "You're scared."

"I'm not." He'd gone through too much in his life to fear losing the ability that caused so much of that strife. If it wasn't for his O'Shea magic, Egan wouldn't have taken him. The human wars would have stayed just that ... human.

Except, when he considered the idea that he could lose the one thing that made him valuable to any of the royals he considered family, it made him need to hit something.

He pulled at the grass, yanking it with such force it ripped out in clumps.

Xavier didn't stop him. Instead, he began pulling the tall grasses right alongside him until they were both too tired to continue. Yet, Toby couldn't stop. He needed to let out every ounce of energy his body possessed.

"Toby."

He could hardly hear him.

"Tobes."

His fingers ached as he clawed at the dirt, not so different from the ground underneath his own palace.

There was pressure on his arm before warmth blew across his lips. Xavier closed the gap between them, stopping Toby's frantic movements by freezing him in place with a kiss.

His lips were thick, warm. And for once, Toby didn't think. He let his mind go blank and the moment take over. Energy flooded his limbs, but it was more than that.

"You are more than your magic, Tobias O'Shea," Xavier whispered.

Toby pulled back. "What was that for?"

One corner of Xavier's mouth tipped up. "Sometimes, a guy has to make a moment what he wishes it to be and not what it is."

Toby gingerly touched his lips. Sure, Xavier only wanted to calm him down, to take away the panic, but he could do it that way anytime.

For the first time since Logan died, Toby wanted to be here, to continue in this life that his first love didn't get to see. Even if it meant losing part of himself in the process.

Toby curled his fingers into Xavier's shirt and yanked him forward for another bolstering kiss before shoving him back. "Tell Tia I've gone to get answers."

"Tobes—"

"No, I'm okay. I swear. But there's someone I need to speak with."

As the only fae in known history to travel by portal from one fae kingdom to the next without a stop in the human realm, maybe the solution didn't have to be giving up his power entirely. Only part of it.

He was gone before Xavier could stop him, snapping the portal shut to avoid having any followers. This was an answer he had to find without Xavier, as much as he wanted him by his side.

The moment he set foot outside Radur City, he hurried toward the somewhat-repaired pillars of Aghadoon. There was still a lot of work to do before they could attempt moving the village again, but it was coming along.

It was just past dawn in Eldur, and the day's heat was only beginning. The streets of Aghadoon had been repaired with new masonry, the brick layers working long hours. Yet, they were abandoned at the moment.

He wandered the silent village on his way to the library, but when he got there, the door was locked. Only his grandfather had the ability to open the sealed magic, but when he was awake, he always left it open.

Toby sat with his back against the door, waiting. He'd wait all day if he had to.

Lucky for him, it wasn't long before the door opened, sending him sprawling into the library.

"Thanks," he grumbled, rubbing his head where it hit the floor. "A warning would have been nice."

"Where's the fun in that?" Brandon smiled down at him. "If you're here, Toby, and not in the human realm with their queen, there must be a reason. Come. I'll send for some Eldur brew."

"Please don't. You're as bad as Mom."

He stepped over Toby and into the library. "I've developed quite a taste for the stuff. It certainly provides an energy tea cannot."

"As if you or Mom need that." His grandfather was tireless.

"Stop with that attitude, boy." Grandfather Brandon gave a

disapproving frown. "You sound like your sister. Go on, get up and come tell me what has you worried."

Toby sighed as he climbed to his feet and closed the door behind him. He sank into a chair at the long wooden table. Around him, scrolls appeared and disappeared from shelves that almost seemed to shake each time. It wasn't a place one got used to, but the familiarity was nice. The library somehow knew what it was a fae needed to know and searched its deep wells of information for anything that could be of help.

Brandon picked up a scroll from the shelf nearest him and unrolled it, his dark brows pinching together on his seemingly young face. "Ah, the veil."

"The humans want it repaired and sealed."

"Haven't we attempted that before?"

He wasn't wrong. When Egan tore through the veil in Myrkur, they did everything to try to fix it, but in the end, they just sent Griff and Riona to guard the rift.

"That was different." At least, he hoped so. "We wanted to seal just one area. Mom said it was like spot treating a carpet that was fully covered in wine stains."

Brandon rubbed the back of his neck, his lips pursed. It was an expression almost entirely reserved for Brea and her human tendencies. "I … what?"

"She says the veil has too much damage to only heal one part of it without causing further weakness. We think we cause it to thin every time we travel into the human realm."

"Interesting." His eyes sparked with curiosity. "So, in order to heal each weak point, we need to wash the entire thing?"

How did a man who rarely left Aghadoon understand Toby's mother's analogy more than he did? "I guess."

The pensive look on his face was dangerous, and Toby knew what was coming as the man took a seat across from him. "Do you know what this means?"

"Of course I do." Toby hadn't meant to snap, but his emotions were so heightened he almost couldn't control him. "Sorry, Grandfather." He needed another of Xavier's kisses to calm the panic welling in his chest.

Brandon waved off the insult. "Boy, if I took offense every time someone sassed me, I'd have thrown your sister off the highest point in Iskalt long ago."

Toby bit back a smile. He'd give anything for things to be like they once were. Before Tia took the throne, she'd have been right at his side searching scrolls and books for any way to save their family's legacy.

She had bigger responsibilities now, and he'd accepted that the moment his father set the crown on her head.

"Start with this one." Brandon slid a book across the table. "It is tales of the portal magic throughout the generations before your father was born."

The book was fascinating, and Toby wished he'd thought to research his power before now, but it held none of the answers he sought. He flipped through it, looking for shreds of information about the veil.

Next, it was a scroll that looked like it had been pulled right from the flames.

"What does this say?" He pointed to a line in Fargelsi, a language he'd never mastered.

Brandon smiled. "The blessed will rule the fae."

"Blessed ..."

"There was a time when Fargelsians thought the O'Shea magic was all that kept our world from falling apart. It's not typically believed now, but hundreds of years ago, they needed something to hold on to, even if it was a power that originated in another kingdom."

He pushed that scroll aside and began another. Then another. Book after book, scroll after scroll.

The daylight came and went. Fae brought them Eldur brew and sustenance. Toby drank the brew without tasting it, smelling it. All he cared about was that it kept him alert.

Brandon offered him a room for the night, but he chose to sleep in the library so he could wake early and begin the process again.

The magic of the library showed him everything he would ever need to know about the O'Shea magic and its history, about the veil and how it came to be.

He wasn't sure how late it was when a line caught his eye. He leaned forward and pulled a small oil lantern closer to the thick book.

There it was. The beginning of his answer.

A way to end this war with the humans.

When the door opened, spilling moonlight across the threshold, Brandon stepped in. "I think you need a break, Toby."

Toby shook his head, his eyes lifting in the glow of the lantern. "I know what we have to do."

Chapter Twenty-Four

GULLIVER

Well, that was interesting. Gulliver couldn't stop thinking of the disdain the President had for Doctor Clarkson when she looked at him that first time.

Maybe, just maybe she didn't truly hate the fae.

"What just happened?" Griff was the first person to voice what they were all wondering.

It took more than a day to retrieve the doctor, so the negotiations with the President lasted a second day. When she returned that time, they'd been more prepared.

Now, she was gone, leaving behind a group of stunned fae and half-fae.

Sophie shrugged. "I think she's been getting some very bad advice."

"What?" Brea asked.

"It's obvious she wants to do the right thing, despite her aloofness. "I voted for her, to the dismay of my father. She's our first female president and has a lot of pressure on her, but she's always seemed genuine. The battle of Aghadoon will always stain her presidency, but I don't think it was entirely her call."

Tia had been quiet since the President's departure, and Gulliver watched her, trying to gauge what she thought. "I need to talk to Kier." She sighed. "He's much better at reading people than me. He should be here and not in Iskalt."

Lochlan put a hand on her shoulder. "Someone had to run the kingdom. Don't discount yourself. You agreed to this meeting because you sensed it could do some good."

"But has it? Can we even do what she wants? Do we want to?"

"Are you serious right now?" Orla rose to her full height. "You can't really be considering not following through. This is a road to peace, to living in safety."

"You don't understand." Gulliver couldn't help speaking up. "Traveling between realms ... our connection to humans, they're asking us to give it up."

"So?" Sophie scowled at him. "The humans wish for you to give up one tiny freedom in order to save countless lives. Are you fae really this selfish?"

"Don't you speak to him that way, human." Tia jumped between Sophie and Gulliver. "Not after everything he's done for you."

"Can we all just calm down?" Brea asked.

They ignored her.

"I just don't understand," Sophie said. "What is there to think about? The half-fae and human sympathizer lives in this realm mean more than your ability to get a cheeseburger every once in a while."

Gulliver thought of all the times they'd used traveling through the veil for necessary means. Stopping Eagan. Finding the means to free everyone trapped in Myrkur. Saving Sophie in Lenya. Speedy travel to another fae kingdom. They'd saved lives, changed their world.

Inter-realm travel was so much a part of their world it was hard to imagine society without it.

Yet, all he could manage to say was, "I *really* like tacos."

That broke the tension in the room, a tension born of tough decisions like allowing the humans to take Doctor Clarkson into custody as a show of good faith. Like agreeing to seal the veil.

Tia's arm slipped around his waist. "Gul, I need you to go help Toby. Griff can take you. We all need to get out of the human realm, but I should go to Iskalt and consult with Kier. I'll search the archives there for anything that might be helpful."

As much as he wanted to be part of this decision, it wasn't his to make and he couldn't deny Tia anything. Silently, he nodded.

Sophie followed him out. "I'm sorry."

"I know." He pushed out a breath and lifted his face to the stars. One day, maybe night would only be for sleeping and not traveling through realms.

"I just don't understand how it's even something you all need to think about. Traveling through the human realm, bringing fae here, has brought you nothing but pain."

She was wrong but he couldn't voice why. Maybe he should have seen it that way too, but instead, the vision in his mind was crowding onto the couch with Tia and Toby to watch Netflix. Raiding the kitchen or devouring a pizza while laughing and telling stories.

Some of the best parts of their lives happened here.

He looked back over his shoulder to where Brea sat on the front steps surveying the grounds. Could she really agree to never again set foot in her first home?

Sophie's hand slid into his moments before Griff burst through the front door. The screen slammed shut behind him. He leaned down to say something to Brea, making her laugh.

"You're right." Gulliver squeezed her hand. "We all know you are. There is nothing more important than ending this conflict."

"I know what they're asking of you isn't easy."

They weren't only asking it of him. Sophie may not have realized it yet, but without the portals, they may never see each other again. He looked away to hide the tears in his eyes. No human would choose a world not their own unless they were Myles Merrick.

"Time to go, Gul." Griff approached with a bounce in his step that shouldn't have been there. He was an O'Shea. The ability to cross the veil was his birthright, and he was going to lose it.

"You coming, Sophie?" Griff asked.

She shook her head. It was only a precursor of the real decision that was to come. The sudden thought hit Gullie that this could be it. Would he come back before the portal was closed?

"I ..." He couldn't get the words out. *Goodbye. I don't want to leave you.*

Sophie put a hand on each side of his face, her thumbs tracing the tops of his cheekbones. "Hey ... it's okay."

"But what if—"

She kissed him, slowly this time. He didn't know what it meant, if she was trying to remember him.

"I'll make it back before the veil closes," he whispered against her lips. He had to. This couldn't be it.

Griff cleared his throat, and Gulliver pulled away, his face heating.

Sophie offered him one final smile, and he burned the image into his mind as he stepped into the gateway to Eldur and the scene faded away.

Gulliver was so used to his father's portals he barely noticed it until he slammed into the ground outside Aghadoon. His knees rattled, but he managed to stay on his feet.

"Always improving." Griff grinned.

Gulliver ignored him, heading straight for the village that now held too many nightmares. He tried not to see the vacant eyes of rebels who'd tried to fight the combined forces of HAFS and the kingdom of the United States. He tried to shrug off the chill being back here caused.

There were no choices anymore. Maybe there never had been.

He found the door to the library open, but he hadn't expected anything else. Unlike his sister, Toby had been an early riser even before Logan died. He had normally gone through the paces of a sparring workout and handled some of his princely duties before she slinked down for breakfast.

Except this time, the alertness from his eyes was gone.

"What's wrong with him?" Griff whispered, worry edging his words.

Gulliver approached slowly, rounding the table to look into Toby's dazed eyes as he hunched over a book. He grabbed the book to see what it was, but Toby snatched it back.

"I can't get him to sleep." Brandon entered, carrying a tray. "He's living on a diet of Eldur brew and cheese."

"Toby hates Eldur brew." Something was seriously wrong.

Brandon shrugged and leaned down to set the tray on the table. "Tobes, you have company."

"I know." He grunted and continued reading.

"What book is that?" Griff asked.

"I'm not sure." Brandon's brow creased. "It's not the one I left him with when I went to bed last night, but once you know what you're looking for, the library chooses the books."

Griff gestured to the door. "Why don't you show me some of the repairs."

Both men gave Gulliver a look, and he knew their repair inspection was just an excuse to leave him alone with his friend.

"Thanks," he murmured. It was all on him.

If they were to have peace with the humans, the library had to show Toby what he needed to know, and Gulliver needed to get that out of him.

He pulled out the chair beside Toby, the wooden legs scraping against the stone floor. "Hi." He sat.

"Not now, Gullie."

Gulliver nodded, folding his hands in his lap. "I can wait."

"Are you just going to stare at me?"

"Yes."

A growl ripped from his throat, but the hazy quality of his eyes cleared as he finally looked up. "We were never supposed to have this power."

"What?"

Toby's entire body quaked. "This ... the library has shown me things. Ancient scrolls that look like they haven't been opened since they were written hundreds of years ago. A book with crumbling pages."

"Toby?"

"The O'Shea magic ... it was created to destroy the veil between worlds." Toby's voice held only a hint of the agony he was likely feeling at such a revelation.

Silence was Gulliver's only response. There were no words that could accurately describe the dread churning inside him.

Toby pushed a hand roughly through his hair. "Darragh

O'Shea, my distant ancestor, he wanted to destroy the veil. A weakness in a certain location allowed him to access the human realm, a rift similar to that in Myrkur. It showed him another creature not unlike us, except in one thing. They didn't have magic. They were powerless against us. Weak creatures easily controlled."

He paused, scrubbing a hand over his face. "The humans are right to fear us. This magic I've been clinging to only had one purpose: to rip through the veil and allow the fae to control both realms. Power. That's what it always comes down to, isn't it? More power."

"But they didn't." Gulliver leaned on the table, hardly able to hold himself up. "The veil still exists."

"Because the magic he created wasn't powerful enough for the task. Each generation it's thought to have grown. He knew that one day, there would be an O'Shea capable of his goals."

"There hasn't been—" Gulliver stopped, his eyes widening.

"An O'Shea with the portal magic of two," Toby said softly.

Tia's O'Shea power was erratic, weak. With her other magic, Toby was her amplifier. What if—

"Me."

Tia's weakness made him stronger, just like his bolstered her.

"The library showed you this?" Gulliver prayed he was wrong, that there was another explanation for why the veil weakened so much at the points Toby traveled through.

Toby slid a book in front of Gulliver. "That's not everything."

"I don't read Fargelsian."

"Concentrate. There's only a few lines here or there I can't read, and the entire realm knows I couldn't speak Fargelsian if I was on fire and their words would put it out."

"*Kaefa.*"

"Need a handkerchief?"

"No, I mean that's the word you'd use to put out the fire." Gulliver knew a few basics, but beyond that, he was lost.

"Just read." Toby tapped the book.

Gulliver focused on the words until the letters swam before him, rearranging into recognizable words. "What the ..." He didn't finish the phrase because his gaze caught on a line of text that had translated to, 'All rifts in the veil must be healed to prevent it from splitting'.

He lifted his eyes.

Toby nodded. "We risk it every time we travel. Even more so when we use my portals. I don't think we're at the point yet where it's on the verge of collapsing, but we could get there soon. Especially with my power."

Gulliver continued reading, each line getting worse than the one before it. When he reached the part that must have turned Toby into the mess he was, he inhaled a sharp rush of air. "No."

Toby nodded, burying his face in his hands. "How am I going to tell Tia? My father? Your father?"

Gulliver didn't know. He reached over, pulling Toby sideways into a hug as his friend's world crashed.

Not only did they have to seal the veil entirely, but the only way to do that was to destroy what they held most dear.

Portal magic.

The O'Shea right by birth.

They couldn't just fix what they'd broken and promise not to break it again.

Their magic had to be destroyed entirely.

Chapter Twenty-Five

SOPHIE

"You want to take me to New Orleans through a portal?" Sophie blinked at Gulliver, trying to focus on his words and not on her relief at seeing him again. "The same portals that are ripping holes in the veil?"

He couldn't be that dim.

"It's faster and we're working on a way to repair the veil." Gulliver planted his feet as though preparing to argue with her for as long as it took.

"I don't want to contribute to the problem." She gave him her most stubborn look, equally ready to strengthen her point.

"It's not going to be a problem for much longer."

"I'll take a bus. It will be fine. I just need someone to watch Noah while I'm gone."

"We'll both go with you. My dad can stay with Noah while you and I go do whatever it is you have to do."

"I'm going to see my father alone." She jutted her chin out in defiance. She had a plan, and she would see it through.

"It's not safe to see him alone, Sophie." Gulliver's voice softened with sympathy. "He's still heavily involved with HAFS."

She nodded. "And he killed my mother for her involvement with the fae, and he planned to do the same to me. I have things to say to him. In private."

"At least let me go with you to the house. I'll wait outside in the sweltering heat by myself."

She threw her hands up in the air. "Fine. But we're leaving now. I already bought us bus tickets."

"Us, us? Or us, as in you and Noah?"

"I don't want him anywhere near my father. But I figured you would insist on coming with me." She was secretly glad he wanted to come. She didn't want to miss any time she had left with him.

"Dad will take good care of Noah." Gulliver nodded, as if it was all settled.

"Dad will do what now?" Griffin shuffled into the kitchen at the farmhouse, where there was no such thing as a private conversation.

"Watch Noah while we go to New Orleans so I can speak with my father." Sophie crossed her arms over her chest.

Griffin studied her for a moment and must have seen her resolve. "All right. He can go back with me to Eldur for a few days."

"Must you travel by portal?" Sophie twisted her hands together. "I hate to further contribute to the damage to the veil. Could you stay here with him?"

"I need to be in Aghadoon, and we have a lot of fae who will need to come back to the human realm before this is over. I promise, we will find a way to heal the damage done to the veil."

"Okay." Sophie nodded. "But we're taking a bus to New Orleans."

"You two need to hurry back here. Our time in this world is coming to an end, and we have to be ready to go home once the peace is settled."

"I'll be back as soon as I can," Gulliver said.

Sophie didn't want to think about the long trip back, knowing the hardest goodbye she would ever have to face loomed ahead of her.

"Take Brea's plastic money card." Griffin fished the card from his back pocket. "And trade those bus tickets in for airfare. It's nearly as fast as a portal."

"What? No! I don't like flying. If I was meant to fly, I'd have wings like Mom's. But I don't. I have a tail. And my tail and I would rather stay on the ground."

"You're afraid of an airplane, but you'll willingly step into a magic portal like it's nothing?" Sophie tried to hide her smile.

"As long as it's not Tia's portal, then yes." Gulliver clutched something to his chest. Something she couldn't quite see, but she knew it was his tail.

"It would be faster if we could fly." She cast her eyes down with a small smile just for him.

Gullie heaved a sigh. "Fine. But I don't like it."

He took the credit card from Griffin.

"Why do you have Brea's human money card?" Gulliver wore a bemused smile.

"I borrowed it to pay for cheeseburgers. She won't care if you use it to help Sophie."

"Thanks, Dad. And by that, I mean, thank Brea for me." Gullie ran upstairs to gather his things for the trip.

Sophie went to tell Noah goodbye, promising she would come get him in Eldur when it was safe. She tried to hide the smile on her face, knowing she would get to see the fae world one last time before the veil closed forever.

"Does it ever cool off in this city?" Gulliver wiped his brow as they left the airport terminal. He hated the airports almost as much as the airplane. Sophie tried not to laugh at the memory of his hand wrapped around hers as the plane took off and again when it landed.

"Not much." Sophie soaked in the NOLA atmosphere, knowing she would likely never see it again after this trip. She couldn't live in the same city as her father. She had a responsibility to keep Noah safe, and as long as Claude Devereaux had a vendetta against the fae, he would pose a threat against Noah. "But it's home and I've always loved it here."

She gazed across the line of waiting Ubers for the one she'd ordered when they landed.

"This way." She ducked into the backseat of a bright red SUV.

"You sure?" Gulliver hesitated. "It's easier than you think to accidentally get in the wrong car."

"I'm sure." She giggled at the look on his face, remembering the story he'd told her of accidentally abducting a lady thinking she drove a taxi.

"You going to the Quarter, ma'am?" the Uber driver confirmed.

"Yes, you can just drop us off at the corner of Esplanade and Burgundy."

Gulliver clutched the door handle, and his eyes shifted uneasily as they left the airport behind.

"You okay?"

"Sorry, I'm always a little uneasy with human drivers I don't know."

"Human?" The driver glanced in his rearview mirror. "You one of those fae people?"

"Nope." Gulliver shook his head furiously. "Not me, dude."

"Aw, that's too bad. Always wanted to meet a fae. The haters give them a bad rap, but I think they're kind of cool."

Gulliver's ears turned red, and Sophie could only imagine the way the very tips of his ears would look in the fae realm. Here, he looked very much human. Handsome, though not quite himself.

The driver dropped them off just a block from the house where Sophie grew up.

"You okay, Sophie?" Gulliver grabbed her arm and tugged her close.

"Not really, why?" Her voice trembled.

"You're awfully pale."

"I'm just nervous. I'll be okay."

They walked along Esplanade Avenue, and Sophie recalled some of her earliest memories walking this same path with her mother. She couldn't help but think her mom could have saved them all a lot of heartache if she hadn't fallen in love with a fae and had a child with him. In a way, she couldn't fault her father for being angry. But she would never forgive him for killing her mother. She held him responsible for everything that had happened to Noah after that horrible night when he was ripped from her arms and taken from his fae father. She had no idea what happened to Noah's father, and she might never know, but before this day was out, Claude Devereaux would no longer have a daughter.

"Are you sure you want me to stay out here?" Gulliver held her hand tightly in his. "I can come with you for moral support."

"Thanks, Gullie, but I need to do this on my own. I won't be long." She reached for the iron gate that led to her backyard. To the garden that had once been her haven from the rest of the world. She paused for a moment as memories of her father drifted through her mind in a flash. "How could a man who loved me so much be capable of such cruelty?"

"He let hate into his heart, but he always loved you. Don't let him rob you of your happy memories."

She nodded. "Wait here."

He squeezed her hand one last time before he let go, and she stepped through the gate to find her father working in her mother's garden. The sight used to make her smile. The way he lovingly tended the flowers her mother had cultivated. She used to think he did it to keep her memory alive for Sophie. But now, as she watched him, she saw the guilt weighing heavily on his shoulders.

"Dad," she whispered.

"Sophie?" Claude leapt to his feet, letting his eyes scan the grounds, looking for HAFS members. "You shouldn't be here." He jogged across the expanse of lawn that separated them, his work overalls hanging on his frame. A testament to the weight he'd lost quickly in recent weeks.

"I won't stay long." She moved to sit under the umbrella on the patio where they'd shared in countless memories.

"They said you escaped. That you killed the doctor."

Sophie snorted at that. "I didn't kill anyone. Doctor Clarkson is in U.S. custody now, waiting to stand trial for his crimes."

"Crimes?"

"Against the fae he experimented on in his house of horrors. The institute you subjected me to."

"Fae are not human. You cannot commit a crime against them."

"Is that what you tell yourself at night to make you feel better about the choices you've made?"

"They've manipulated you, honey." He sank into the wrought iron seat beside her.

"Just like they did my mother?" Sophie stared at him. "Is that why you killed her? Because you thought she had been manipulated?"

"I tried to get through to her. I tried so hard to bring her back."

"She didn't want to be with you, Dad. That was her biggest crime. She fell in love with someone else, and you couldn't deal with it, so you killed her for it and sent her son to the institute, where Clarkson performed perverse experiments on him. The poor boy never received a name. Never got to play outside in the sun. Never breathed fresh air. You did that to him. To my brother."

"He's not your brother!" Claude brought his fist down on the chair arm. "He is fae filth."

"He is part human. Part of *Mom*. All the fae of this world are mostly human. Yet, you and all your friends would condemn them for the drops of fae blood in their veins. Just because your wife chose to be with one of them instead of you."

"Shut up!" Spittle flew from his mouth, and his eyes widened in crazed anger.

"Will you kill me now too? Because I don't think the way you do? Because I've fallen in love with a fae too?"

"Sophie." His voice broke, and all the fight went out of him. "I could never harm you."

"But you turned me over to Clarkson knowing full well what he would do to me. That if given the chance, he would kill me if I proved useless to his experimentation."

"I had to let them take you. It was the only way to get you back."

"That's your problem." Sophie stood. "You hold on to the people you love so tightly that you suffocate them. You force them to your will." She let out a mirthless laugh. "You forced me to take treatments when I would have rather died. And then, when I was healed, you forced me into an institute where they tried to rip the magic from my veins. The very magic that healed me."

"I just wanted you to be safe and healthy." A whine entered Claude's voice.

"Well, you got your wish. Just not how you wanted. I am safe and healthy, but my priorities have changed now. For the rest of my life, I will think only of my brother and his happiness. I will do whatever it takes to keep him safe."

"Wait." He reached for her. "Let me explain."

"You have." She shrugged. "You did everything you could to keep me safe within the web of lies you built up around me. To keep the truth from me so in my ignorance, I would love you. But you didn't have to make the choices you made. You didn't have to kill my mother just because she wanted to leave you. You could have let her go. You could have moved on and everything would have been different. But you didn't. And now you will pay the consequences. No matter what happens from here, you will never see me again." She started to walk away.

"No, please. You have to forgive me." Claude grasped onto her hand, dropping to his knees beside her.

"I have, Dad. I can forgive you for all the lies and the way you kept me sheltered from the truth. I can even forgive you for your willful ignorance against the fae. I just can't forgive you for killing our mother." She tugged her hand away and he let her go.

"Where will you go?"

"I don't know, but it won't be here."

Chapter Twenty-Six

TOBY

"Are you sure we have to do this?" It wasn't the first time Tia asked what each of them were thinking. Did they really have to give up such a large part of their family's identity to keep their fae safe?

Toby slid his hand into hers. They sat in the Aghadoon courtyard, the very same one that had bombs raining down on it not long ago. "I wish there was another way."

On the bench beside them, Lochlan and Griff were silent. This was their legacy too, and yet, they'd decided it was up to the twins, the very fae who'd caused the weakness in the veil if the texts were to be believed.

And they were. They always were.

Nothing that came out of the Aghadoon library held falsehoods. Hidden truths, yes, but not blatant lies. It was the only knowledge that could truly be trusted.

Tia leaned her head on their father's shoulder. "Do you ever think how much better off the fae worlds would be without anyone as powerful as me and Tobes?"

He waited a beat before responding. "Different, maybe." His hand lifted to skim over the side of her head. "But not better off. Never better off."

Griff nodded in agreement. "Without you, I'd still be in that prison realm ... if Egan hadn't found a way to take over each kingdom by now."

"Keir would probably be dead," Toby put in.

His father shot him a disapproving look, one he didn't understand.

"What? It's true. All of Lenya would have been consumed by the fire plains if she hadn't messed up her portal and dropped into Keir's lap."

Tia sighed. "I guess time is up on learning how to properly control the O'Shea power."

Toby snorted. "You were never going to win that battle, T."

Griff, seated on Toby's other side, slapped him on the back of the head. "What is wrong with you, kid?"

What was wrong with him? They were about to seal off the human realm, stripping him of his only magic and preventing him from seeing any of his new friends who decided to stay there. They still didn't know if the half-fae would ever truly be safe. "Many, many things."

Lochlan sighed, a knowing quality to it. He always seemed to sense his children's problems, but he believed in letting them come to him, unlike Brea, who wanted to charge right in and fix everything.

This time, she couldn't.

"Do you remember the first time we went through a portal?" Tia asked, lifting her head to peer at Toby.

One corner of his mouth rose. That was a day he'd never forget. "Mom's birthday."

They'd been seven years old. His mother claimed she refused to take them to the human realm until they were old enough to remember it because everyone should remember their first time.

"Dad got her an ice cream cake."

Mom's favorite—ice cream. One of the more ridiculous human creations he'd miss. Uncle Myles had been there with his human family. Even Alona came through the veil, and she didn't like to visit the world that should have been hers.

Tears hung in Tia's lashes, and Toby hated that he couldn't do anything to rid her of them.

"This is the right thing." She closed her eyes.

Each of the other O'Sheas nodded.

She sniffed. "Then, why does it hurt so much? What does our family have after this? What makes us special?"

After a long silence, it was their father who answered. "Our family has us. We were never meant to wield this power. It was created to cause havoc. So, when you ask what we have, the answer will be peace. That's worth every ounce of magic the fae world possesses."

Xavier approached slowly, as if he didn't know if he was welcome. Toby stood to greet him. "Is it time?"

He looked to the darkening sky, where the stars felt absent on a night like this.

Xavier nodded. "We can't wait any longer."

Toby knew Tia wanted to come along, to have one last human adventure, but this wasn't the time. She was still the

Queen of Iskalt. Keir would arrive in the morning, and she had to be here to receive his report on her kingdom.

"Be safe, son." Lochlan touched his arm.

Griff sent him a grim smile. "You were meant for this."

They didn't know what they'd find in Los Angeles. The President promised to begin setting it up as a sanctuary city for anyone with fae blood, but that meant half-fae congregating in the open where HAFS could find them. Would they be building high walls to keep the fae in? Patrolling them with their terrifying human weapons?

"Do we have any news?" he asked Xavier as they headed for Aghadoon's front gate.

Xavier nodded. "All indications point to the humans holding up their end of the bargain. For now."

Toby couldn't help smiling.

"What?" Xavier elbowed him.

"Nothing."

"Tobes, we're about to head into magic knows what and you're smiling."

"It's just ... you're sounding more like a fae. You called them humans instead of us."

"Well ..." He rubbed the back of his neck. "When they treat you like an other, you feel like one. We aren't fae, but we're not fully human either. Our community is in a bit of an identity crisis right now."

Toby understood every word. His entire life had been one giant identity crises. "I'm an other too, I guess."

Xavier looped their arms together. "I'm starting to wonder if everyone is."

Toby was still thinking about his words when they met Orla and a handful of her most trusted fighters on the outskirts of Radur City.

"Do we know how many there will be?" he asked.

Orla shrugged. "I'm guessing quite a few. Our people have been attacked and threatened. Many won't want to stay in the human realm."

The four queens of the fae—and King Hector—offered asylum to any half-fae who wished to leave the human realm. Once the veil was healed and sealed, they'd stay on this side and begin a new life, one they could never have imagined.

"And the call went out?"

"Yes." Orla clasped her hands behind her back. "I sent the message around the world through our network. We've given them a week now. All half-fae or fae living in the human realm who wish to leave must make it to L.A. They'll be there."

The President's aides helped them find a venue to meet. It was in the human leader's best interest to encourage the fae to leave her lands.

A heaviness settled in Toby's chest at the thought of disconnecting from the community who'd stay, disconnecting from Xavier. It was like cleaving the new world he'd found in two. He kept asking the heavens what Logan would do, but this time, he received no answer.

Logan wasn't here, but Toby was.

"Okay, let's get going." Hands grasped for him, not wanting to break contact as he pulled the power from the depths of himself. It set him alight, made every part of him come alive.

He'd miss this feeling.

Moving into the light, he brought the others along, not even straining to hold the portal together. It wasn't supposed to be this easy. He knew that. Maybe it should have been a sign that he held too much power.

His concentration broke as they tumbled toward an L.A. street outside the half-fae headquarters. The pavement came up to meet him, and he rolled as he crashed into it, popping back up to his feet.

The others moaned from where they'd collapsed onto the road.

Behind them, a door opened and an unfamiliar man stuck his head out. "Thank the great Lord above." He was older with salt and pepper hair and a weathered face. He quickly went to Orla and helped her to her feet. "Y'all gave us a fright. We've been waiting."

Orla dusted herself off and started moving.

"We're here now, Robinson." She strode past him into the warehouse.

Robinson.

"Is that a first name or last?" he asked Xavier.

Xavier's wince told him everything he needed to know. He tried to walk ahead, but Toby yanked him back. "The man who raised my mother, a human, is working for you?"

Jack Robinson wasn't his grandfather. He refused to think of him as such after the stories he'd heard. The man was the reason Toby's mom ended up at the Clarkson Institute.

"Careful." Xavier looked around and dropped his voice. "He joined us after his wife was killed in a HAFS bombing."

"Why didn't you tell me?"

"Not every piece of information will help, Toby. Some only make what we have to do harder." Like working with the man who neglected Brea, allowed HAFS to have her, and then told HAFS she was dead, so they didn't keep searching for her. It was hard to separate the actions.

Xavier looked at the device on his wrist. "We need to be at the arena in an hour."

He'd called it the Staples Center, but that just sounded like random sounds put together. The President's people had apparently made a call to secure the location and provide security assistance if needed.

Jack was speaking when Toby and Xavier joined the others.

"We've received government funds to transform derelict housing to suit our needs with half-fae pouring in from around the globe. The mayor has called three times and wishes to have a meeting with you, Orla." He looked down at a list he was reading. "The protestors have been out there night and day, but so far, they haven't been violent. Some of them raise guns in the air, but they do not shoot."

"HAFS must be waiting for something." Orla bent over an inside view of the arena. "Is everything in place?"

He nodded.

She straightened. "Good. Then, we cannot wait any longer. Xavier, pull a car around back. Robinson, you're staying here."

Xavier jogged off to obey her, leaving Toby to study the warehouse. A wall of screens sat at one end with a woman behind them, typing furiously on a keyboard.

There were half-fae rushing past and even a few humans. It was like the center of the half-fae universe.

One of Orla's men opened the door for them, and they walked into the alley to find Xavier behind the wheel of a shiny yellow car. "Taxi anyone?" he asked.

Toby knew it! He'd have to tell Gulliver. They weren't wrong about the yellow cars.

It was a short drive through mostly deserted streets. Xavier had told him of humans packing up and leaving their homes. Some stayed, but the city had emptied considerably. For now. Soon, it would be teeming with half-fae.

When they stopped, a giant domed building loomed over them.

"This is a staple?" he asked.

Xavier looked sideways at him, one eyebrow lifted. "Just ... sure, Tobes." He gave him a strange look and chuckled to himself. This is what a staple looks like."

Everything looked even bigger inside. High ceilings, a long

pathway that seemed to go around in a circle. Xavier led him to an opening in the wall, and he froze. Before him stood a massive room, probably the biggest he'd ever seen. Wooden floors, odd devices hanging from the ceiling. Thousands of chairs.

And not a single half-fae.

Orla looked just as confused as he felt. "Xavier, the message we sent had clear instructions, correct?"

"I thought so."

"Well, we have to wait." They didn't have long, but the half-fae who wanted out would come. They lowered themselves into folding seats, and no one said a word.

They'd expected hundreds, maybe thousands. The fae realm was safe for them, something they couldn't one hundred percent guarantee of the human realm.

Yet, the emptiness echoed.

Footsteps sounded on the steps behind them, and Toby looked up to find a man and a woman.

The woman smiled as she approached, and he stood. "Hello, I'm Prince Tobias. You're safe now."

Her smile didn't fall, but it did change, growing more serious. When they were close, they stopped their descent. "We haven't come to go with you."

Orla cocked her head. "Then, why are you here?"

The man answered in a heavy brogue. "We traveled here from Ireland with a large group of half-fae and have come across many others making their way to the safety of Los Angeles. We came to tell you we don't know anything of your world, Prince. It does not belong to us."

The woman nodded. "We're staying here, in our own world. We won't give it up, not when we can create a haven for all those like us. The humans will learn to accept us in time. You've given us the one thing we wanted. Hope." She laid a hand on Toby's shoulder. "And that is a priceless gift."

Toby bit back a grin as these half-fae restored part of his faith. The easy path would be to go to the fae realm, but they wouldn't betray themselves or their hearts.

Finally, Orla's lips lifted. "Welcome to L.A. This is your home now."

They were words Toby expected to say to the half-fae once they returned to Eldur, yet they felt right here in this realm.

As he watched them smile and laugh, he realized giving up his portal magic meant nothing compared to everything else he stood to lose.

Chapter Twenty-Seven
SOPHIE

Sophie slammed into the ground with a thud, the coarse dry grass of Eldur scratching her face. Toby's portals were much calmer, but she still hadn't mastered the landing.

"That was a spectacular fall." Gulliver stood over her with a smile, offering her a hand. She took it, and he pulled her up, his tail brushing the grass from her clothes.

Toby had sent them back to retrieve Noah, but Sophie didn't want to think about leaving. Not so soon after their arrival.

"I will never get used to that." She stared into his feline eyes, happy to see the real Gullie again.

"Oh." He snatched his tail away. "Sorry." He seemed to wilt before her eyes. "I forget it's a shock when we come back."

"What? No, Gullie." She laughed. "I meant the portal and the hard landing. And it was night five minutes ago, and now it's a beautiful afternoon." She pried his fingers off his tail and held it like she would his hand. She wasn't sure if that was done, but she needed him to know she wasn't ... afraid of his unique features.

His face flushed pink, and he smiled as they turned toward Aghadoon. She felt a little silly for holding his tail, but she really liked the smile it put on his face.

"You won't have to worry about portaling for too much longer." His tail snaked around her wrist and the soft leaf-like tip stroked the inside of her palm.

Sophie nodded. "It's for the best, don't you think?" She chanced a glance at him.

Gullie sighed. "For the safety of our people in the human realm, it is for the best. I'll just really miss ... tacos."

"Tacos? You're going to miss tacos?" Sophie laughed. It wasn't the first time he'd made the claim.

"It's really the best food in all the worlds." He patted his flat stomach.

"I'm sure we can come up with a fae equivalent."

"We can?" He tilted his head at her like he didn't understand the concept of recipes.

"Sophie! You're back!" Noah raced through the pillars of Aghadoon and slammed right into her. "I was afraid the humans wouldn't let you leave."

His shoulders trembled as he buried his face in her side and clutched her waist like he'd never let go.

"Hey." She wrapped her arms around his small frame and held him close. "Look at me, Noah."

He tilted his head back but refused to move.

"I promise you, I will never leave you on your own. You're my family now."

"I am?"

She leaned down to his level. "Guess what I found out?"

"What?" He blinked at her with his startling golden eyes.

"*Your* mother was *my* mother." She grinned. "She's not with us anymore, but I can tell you, she loved you so much."

"Truly?" Noah's eyes filled with tears. "I get to keep you?"

"Well, you're my brother, and I have always, always wanted a little brother." She brushed the wavy curls from his face. "And I couldn't be happier that I get to keep you." She hugged him close, her heart melting when his little arms wrapped around her neck. This kid ... he was everything.

"What about your dad? He doesn't like people like me." He dropped his arms and stared at the ground.

Sophie shared a look with Gulliver. This kid just broke her heart.

"That's why I had to leave." She took Noah's hand. "I had a few things to say to my dad."

"And?" Noah mumbled.

"And he won't be part of our lives anymore." She squeezed his hand to reassure him.

"Really?"

"Really." She smiled. "It's just you and me, Noah."

A hesitant smile lit his face. "Come on, I have to show you the magic library. It's so cool!" He tugged on her hand, and she had no choice but to follow him into Aghadoon. "It's so much better than the library at the institute. And there's another library at the palace, but it's not magic like this one. It shows you what you want to read. I still can't read, but Uncle Griff started teaching me."

"Uncle Griff?" Sophie laughed at his exuberance.

"Yeah, he said I could call him that. Is that okay?"

"Of course." Sophie and Gullie followed Noah down the newly repaired street to the library.

"Welcome back." Griffin met them on the porch. The library itself remained whole, but the village was still undergoing repairs, and fae were coming and going with tools and carts, working together to rebuild.

"I need to borrow Gullie for a little while. Will you two be comfortable alone in the library?" Griffin asked, a serious look on his face.

"What's wrong now?" Gullie sighed.

"Some of our visitors in the camp can't decide if they want to stay or go home to the humans. They want to talk to you."

"Me?" Gulliver glanced around like his father might be talking to someone else.

"Yes, you. They trust you. They want to know more about Myrkur. Some of them like the idea of staying here, but they can't decide if they want to stay in Eldur. I think they'd be more comfortable in Myrkur, where we don't have so much magic. Will you talk to them?"

Gulliver nodded, turning to Sophie. "Will you be okay here for a little while? I'll be back as soon as I can."

"Sure. I think we can entertain ourselves for a bit." Sophie glanced down at her brother with a smile. "You go on and do your thing."

"Okay. I won't be long." Gullie turned to leave with his father.

"Now, don't let Noah drive away with the village while we're gone," Griffin hollered over his shoulder.

The sound of Noah's laughter caught Sophie by surprise. She'd never heard him laugh before.

"Where's your favorite place in the village besides the library?" she asked.

"The square!" Noah grabbed her hand and hauled her off

the porch and down the street. "It's really pretty, and that's where all the magic stones are. Grandpa Brandon said he'd teach me how to align the stones once I learn to read."

"He did?" Sophie shook her head. It seemed while she was away, her little brother had been busy winning over some hearts.

They arrived at a small grassy square near the center of the village. "Let's sit in the sunshine for a bit while we wait on Gullie." Sophie sank down on the lush carpet of green grass, marveling at how vibrant it was under the unforgiving Eldur sun.

"This place is so magical, isn't it?" Noah said, as if answering her thoughts.

"And so pretty," she added, studying her brother's face. He looked healthier here. His cheeks were fuller, and the shadows under his eyes had vanished.

"The healers have been giving me potions."

"Can you still read my thoughts like before? I can't hear you."

Noah shrugged. "Not really. It's different here. Quieter. I still kind of know what you're thinking, but it's not the same. I like it. You should see if you can do it, Soph. Just sit back and let all your thoughts go for a minute and try to feel what I'm thinking."

Sophie took a deep breath and tried to release all the nagging thoughts and decisions constantly swirling in the back of her mind.

"You're not very good at this. Try closing your eyes."

Sophie smiled and did as her brother suggested. Tilting her head back, she let the sun warm her face, clearing her mind.

A moment later she opened her eyes and studied her brother again. "The potions are helping you get your strength back. And you've been spending most of your time outside in the fresh air and sunshine. Queen Alona has been feeding you well too."

"Good job, Sophie. You did it."

"I think that was more you than me, kiddo." She chuckled. "You're the one with the magic."

"But not here. At least, not like I had in the human realm." He shuddered, dropping his head down to stare at the grass.

"You'll get your magic back when we go home."

"You know, there's all different kinds of magic here," Noah said. "Some is like mine, but others are more subtle. Like Gullie's defensive magic and Grandpa Brandon's Gelsi magic. I don't know what a Gelsi is, but he has to use words to make his magic work. So, he doesn't lose control like I always do. He just has to speak the right words with the right intent and things happen exactly the way he wants them to."

"You like it here, don't you?" Sophie asked carefully.

"I love it. The people here are nice. It's like a big family, and they let anyone join. I've never had that before. And they don't make you stay inside when you want to be outside. They have the best food, and when you ask for ham, you get the real stuff. Not the fake kind from a can."

"It can be like that anywhere, Noah. Not just here. When we go home, we'll find a place we like. We can settle down in Los Angeles with the other half-fae, so you'll be around people just like you. You can go to school, and I'll make all your favorite foods. We can have real ham there too, you know? We can be together there. Always."

"But I'll have magic there." Noah dropped his gaze again.

"We'll find you a teacher who can help you learn to control it."

"What if I wanted to stay here where I don't have to have that kind of magic?" He looked up at her. "Would you leave me?"

"I promised I would never leave you, and I meant it. But I don't think we can stay here, Noah. I have no way of making a home for us here. In L.A., I can get a job to pay for things." Though, she had no idea if waitressing would even bring in enough money to support everything she was promising him.

Noah nodded.

"Anyone hungry?" Gulliver called from down the street. "I brought snacks."

"I already ate before you guys came back." Noah scrambled to his feet. "I'm going to go pack my things."

Sophie thought she saw tears in his eyes just before he ran away.

"I brought all the best snacks." Gulliver laid a blanket on the ground. "I thought we'd have a picnic," he spoke so fast, Sophie couldn't get a word in. "You'll love the pastries with the cream filling." He dumped out a pile of food on the blanket before he sat down. "They aren't the same as beignets, but they're close. And the meat pies here are excellent." He passed her a pie the size of her head. "A bit spicy like some of the New Orleans foods you like."

Sophie laid her pie down on the blanket. "I'm not really hungry." She took his hand. "There's a lot on my mind right now." She ducked her head, trying to meet his gaze, but he wouldn't look at her.

"Can't you stay for a few more days?" His voice cracked as he squeezed her hand, and his tail flicked sadly behind him. "Let's not say goodbye just yet."

"I have to do what's best for Noah," she whispered, her mind still reeling with decisions she couldn't seem to commit to.

"I'll never see you again." Gullie wiped his face, trying to mask his tears. "I'm not sure I'm ready for that."

"Oh, Gulliver O'Shea," she said his name like a prayer. "I think I have to stay here."

"What?" He finally met her eyes. "What do you mean? You want to stay in Eldur?"

"Noah likes it here. He's safer in this world. I just don't know if it's the right decision." She stood, pacing to the edge of the small village square to put some distance between them. She couldn't look into his beautiful eyes and make this decision for her little family.

"You want to stay for Noah." He said it like a statement. Like it was exactly what he'd thought she'd do in the end.

"No, you big dummy." She whirled around. "It's for me too." Now, she was the one who couldn't meet his gaze. "I just don't know if that means Eldur ... or somewhere else."

Gulliver closed the distance between them. "You can go wherever you want. I'll take you to all the kingdoms, so you can decide which you like best. It'll take longer since we won't be able to portal, but I don't mind."

"You're a good man," she whispered. "But you're a little slow when it comes to the ladies. I think that's what I love most about you."

"Love?" He blinked at her, as if he still wasn't sure what she was trying to say. Maybe she was just as bad at this love stuff as he was. "I'll always look this way." He grabbed her arms, running his hands down from her shoulders to her wrists, letting his tail wind around them. "The Gullie you met in the human realm won't be here."

"The Gullie I met in the human realm was an odd sort of human. He isn't the one I fell in love with. The one who risked everything for me was this guy right here. Tail and all. And I think I'd like to stay with him."

"Yes!" Gulliver let out a whoop of joy as he hugged her tight. "I can't wait to show you Myrkur!" But his face fell. "Only, I'm technically part of Tia's council, and she may make me move to Iskalt. It's really, really cold there. Did you hate it when you were there before?"

"Hush Gullie." She laughed. "We can figure all that out later. But would you kiss me already?"

"I can do that." He grinned and leaned in close to press his lips to hers, pulling her against his chest.

Sophie let her arms snake around his neck, her fingers trailing through his hair as his tail wrapped around her arm. She sighed into his kiss, thinking she was finally home.

"Aw! Loch, can you believe it?" The hiss of Brea's voice interrupted their moment. She sounded so much like her daughter. "Gullie got the girl!" She moved from her hiding spot around the corner, tugging her husband along behind her. "I'm so proud."

"I hope you know what you're getting into," Lochlan said.

"Er ... Happiness?" Gulliver hugged Sophie to his side, his face almost the same color as the Eldur sun.

"No. I was talking to Sophie." He shook his head. "As Tia's father and Gulliver's uncle, I will tell you that life will never be dull with these two around, and I'm afraid they come as a package deal."

Chapter Twenty-Eight
GULLIVER

Someone pounded on the library door, and just like they had for the last three days, Tia, Toby, and Gulliver ignored it.

"We're nearly ready, aren't we?" Gullie asked, peeking over Tia's shoulder at the crimson Gelsi scribbles he couldn't fully understand. Though, he could pick out enough words to get the gist of what it said.

"You can't rush magic, Gullie." Tia tried to wave him away. "Especially the kind we're doing here. Mom is going to murder me for letting you two talk me into this."

"Wait, are you sure about that word there?" He pointed to

the Fargelsian word for destroy. "Should it be *springa*, or something more like *svero*. That means to cut, right? Or maybe *skera*?" But Gullie was pretty sure that was the word to sever a spell.

"Good catch, Gul." Toby scratched out the word on his copy. "It should probably be *svero*, don't you think, Tia?"

"*Eyoa*," Tia muttered, and *springa* vanished from the parchment she was working on. "He's actually right. It should be *svero*. How did I not catch that?"

"We're not exactly working under the most ideal circumstances." Toby gave her shoulder a squeeze.

"I still don't know if we're doing the right thing, Tobes. Are you sure this is going to work?"

"It has to." Gulliver paced across the library, once again wishing he could be more help to his friends with magic.

The knocking at the door grew more persistent.

"Are you three ever coming out?" Griffin shouted. "The humans are going to start getting violent again. They want a resolution, and they want it now."

"Should I tell him we need another hour?" Gulliver leaned against the rattling door to keep his father out.

"No." Tia's brow furrowed. "I think we're done. Now, we just have to see if it works." She rolled up the old parchment and tucked it into her pocket. "Time for you to go tell everyone." Tia nodded at Gulliver as she stood up from the chair she'd occupied for most of the last three days.

"Me? Why do I have to do it?"

"Because it was your hairbrained idea to begin with." She patted him on the back and steered him toward the door.

Gulliver was ready to bolt when they opened the door to an audience of impatient fae waiting in the moonlight. After three days in the library, Gullie had lost all track of time.

"Well?" Griffin demanded.

"You three better have a solution to this mess." Brea stood with her arms folded across her chest, and Lochlan glared at them along with the other royals of the five kingdoms. They even dragged Kier away from covering Iskaltian duties for Tia.

The rest of the crowd just looked scared.

Gulliver saw so many familiar faces. Ones he loved like family and ones he'd only recently met from the human realm. Yet, they were all fae. And they all needed a solution that worked.

"So, we came up with—" he began.

"*You*. You came up with the idea," Tia corrected him.

"Okay, *I* had an idea that we should ask the library to show us the original O'Shea magic. The origin spell that gave the O'Sheas the ability to portal."

"And?" Griffin urged him to continue.

"And we found it." Gulliver kicked his boot against a loose board of the library porch.

"And what have you done with it?" Brea asked, but her gaze lingered on her daughter.

"Our first thought was to destroy it. Destroy the O'Shea legacy," Tia said. "The way you destroyed the marriage magic all those years ago."

"But we came up with a better idea," Gulliver said.

"*You*. You came up with this nonsense," Tia insisted.

"Fine. I suggested we—and by we, I mean Tia—edit the origin magic. It turns out the ancient O'Sheas and O'Rourkes were in this together. The spell was written in Fargelsian and enacted with Iskaltian magic."

"We redesigned the magic," Tia interjected. She pulled the scroll from her pocket.

"Is that written in blood?" Brandon's eyes widened in alarm.

"It is." She shied away from her grandfather's gaze.

"Tia, we don't mess with that kind of magic."

"Well, I didn't make it that way; our ancestors did. And it's our responsibility to fix what they broke." She lifted her chin in defiance.

"Whose blood is it?" Brea asked softly after the crowd fell silent.

"Mine and Toby's."

Gulliver felt bad for her. She sounded like ten-year-old Tia again. The one who'd worked with her mother to bring down the barrier around Myrkur that had made it a prison world for generations. That had been risky magic then, and they were about to take an even greater risk now. And it was all his idea.

"We're dealing with two separate realms," Gulliver spoke up. "To fix the tears in the veil caused by the O'Shea magic, it has to be healed from both sides."

"But why rewrite such dangerous magic?" Brea asked. "Couldn't we find another way to heal the veil? One that doesn't involve blood magic?"

"The only other way to fix this is to destroy the original spell." Brandon sighed. "And I don't even know if that will heal the veil. It will just make it so we can't destroy it further."

"That would be the safest approach," Griffin said.

"But it would be the end of O'Shea magic. The end of portaling."

"I think we can all agree that is something we can learn to live without," Lochlan said.

"But what if we didn't have to?" Tia raised her voice over the murmurs of the crowd. "Hear me out. Portaling has become a tool we all depend on. It facilitates travel between the kingdoms. It keeps us close. It melts away the distance separating the kingdoms and makes our jobs as leaders much easier."

"But we can travel the old-fashioned way," Brea insisted. "It takes longer and more effort, sure, but we will do everything in our power to keep the families of the five kingdoms close. We are family. We will endure."

"Right, *we* will." Tia nodded. "For this generation. And maybe a few more. But without portaling, we will naturally drift apart. Our families will divide and go their own ways, and in a few generations, we will be strangers again. And in a few more, potential enemies." Tia stepped down from the porch, her eyes earnest and pleading.

"All my life, I've watched you all work *so* hard to get where we are now. Growing up, we three have watched our parents do what is right. And we have helped you create the wonderful, flourishing world that the five kingdoms has become. Time and again, we have clawed our way out of a world divided by hate and cynicism.

"Our ancestors hated each other so much they created the vatlands to keep our kingdoms apart because they couldn't find a way to be at peace with each other. Right now, we can't see ourselves ever going back to that, but the truth of the matter is, it could happen all too easily."

"She's right." Gulliver stepped forward to join her. "We're friends now, but what happens in the future when we're nothing but strangers? What happens to my people who don't have magic of their own? Persecution at best? Another prison world at worst?"

"And what happens to Lenya if, in the future, we don't maintain the kind of relationships we have now?" Tia asked. "My husband is here to see to their wellbeing now, but they are completely reliant on us to give them the crystals they need for their own magic. How easily could that support be pulled?"

"You've made your point, my Queen." Lochlan nodded his approval. "Now, what is your solution?"

"We keep portaling, but we change the rules." Gulliver

pulled a piece of paper from his pocket, where he'd drawn the solution to all their problems.

"Right now, the O'Sheas have to travel across the veil to the human realm and back again to visit another kingdom." He pointed to the line down the center of the page that represented the veil. "So, we change the direction of the magic."

"Rather than destroy the magic completely," Tia continued, "we make it so the O'Sheas can travel from one kingdom to the next without the necessity of passing through the veil first."

"And on the other side," Gulliver pointed to the circle representing the human realm, "any O'Sheas there could do the same, traveling from one place to another without the need to pass through the veil first."

They were met with silence and wide-eyed stares.

"I tried to amend the origin magic to give the ability to more than just the O'Sheas," Tia said. "But we were locked into the blood magic of the original spell. O'Shea blood binds the spell, so we were able to amend the magic to give portaling to anyone with a significant blood relation to the O'Sheas, not just a direct descendent. That was the best we could do," Tia said with a shrug. "We thought it was a good fix."

After a few moments of silence, Griffin cleared his throat. "It is, Tia. It's an extraordinary fix."

She nodded. "All right. If we're going to do it, though, we need to do it now. Time is of the essence because the longer we wait, the angrier the human leaders become."

"There's just one thing." Toby spoke for the first time, moving to stand with his sister. "To activate the magic, it has to be done from both sides." He shared a look with Tia. "That is one of the reasons Tia opened the magic to include more O'Sheas. She was hoping there would be a close enough relative on the other side of the veil to enact the magic."

"It will work best if there's an O'Shea to do it, but just in case there isn't, I added an amendment to the spell so it can be enacted without magic—hopefully. Someone just needs to take a copy of the spell written in our blood and burn the edges of the page, and then immediately submerge it in water under the light of the moon. Using moonlight, fire, and water will cause the spell to engage, and the veil will be healed and sealed off from our world forever."

"But if we had an O'Shea volunteer, it would be that much better," Toby added softly, staring right at Xavier on the edge of the crowd. "With or without magic, a direct descendent would be ideal."

"What are you saying, Toby?" Tia's voice cracked as Toby stepped down from the porch.

"I'm saying, I'll be the one to set the spell in motion from the other side."

Chapter Twenty-Nine

TOBY

"What? No!" Tia rushed down the steps to gather around Toby with Brea and Lochlan.

"You can't be serious." Brea brushed shaking fingertips across his cheeks. "You know what it would mean?"

"I could never come back." Toby had known this was going to be hard, but he'd thought long about his decision, and it was the right one. For him. That didn't make it any easier to break his sister's heart.

"You don't have to be the one to make this sacrifice, son." Lochlan said, his eyes searching Toby's for answers. "No one does. At least, not yet. We can find someone on the other side to do this."

"Let's give Toby some space." Gulliver pulled Tia away. "I think your brother is trying to make a grand gesture." He nodded toward Xavier.

"Thanks, Gul." Toby was grateful his sister would have Gulliver when he was gone. She would need him now more than ever.

"What?" She gaped at Gulliver, tears in her eyes. "He can't do this, Gullie." She let him guide her toward her husband.

"What would you do if it was Keir on the other side?" He stared into her eyes. "You have to let him move on from Logan."

That was the thing about Gulliver O'Shea. He had more empathy than anyone Toby had ever known. Of course he was the one to get what Toby was trying to do. His sister was in good hands between Kier and Gullie. Knowing that was the only thing that had given him the strength to do what his heart wanted more than anything.

His heart broke as Tia buried her head against Keir's chest as though she could keep this from happening. Keir murmured something to sooth her, and she relaxed, but she couldn't seem to stop her tears.

"What are you doing?" Xavier asked as Toby closed the distance between them and reached for his hand. "This is your home."

"It is." Toby sighed. "And almost everyone I love is here. Except for the one person I don't think I can live without."

"We're in the middle of a war," Xavier protested, searching Toby's eyes for the truth of what lay between them.

"Perhaps. Maybe it will be over soon."

"We don't have magic like you have here."

"I don't have magic at all." Toby laughed. He turned to look at his parents and siblings, raising his voice. "Imagine living in a world where everyone around you has powerful magic and all you can do is open a door. Imagine for one second how that feels. To be born a prince without magic in this land makes you completely useless."

Brea started to protest, but Toby kept talking. "Normally, a royal born without magic would have been sent into the serving class when he came of age, but I was spared that fate.

"Now, I want you all to imagine what it was like for me to travel to the human realm to find others just like me. A whole community of fae with little or no magic. For the first time in my life, I felt useful. Their cause became my cause. I felt for these fae. I fought for them. And I fell in love with one of them." He took both of Xavier's hands in his.

"If they'll have me, I will continue to fight for them. I will use my portal magic to protect them. To facilitate the same level of communication and friendship that we have here. In the coming years, I hope to see more and more fae communities spring up across the globe. And I want to be there to see it happen.

"If Xavier will have me, I can be happy there. I can have a fulfilling life with someone I love at my side. I'm not sure I can or want to have that anywhere else with anyone else."

In a breath, Xavier rushed forward and pulled Toby into his arms with a bruising kiss, to the cheers of the half-fae still waiting to return home. That kiss held the promise of the kind of life Toby hadn't been sure was in his reach. After Logan died, his heart had shriveled up and died too. Xavier brought him back to life.

"I wasn't sure how I was going to leave you." Xavier pressed his forehead to Toby's. "I didn't want to, and I've tried so hard not to love you like I do, but it's impossible. If so many fae weren't counting on me back home, I would stay here with you, but I can't."

"That is why I'm coming with you." Toby held him close, careless of the people watching them.

"But are you sure you can leave your family behind?" Xavier searched his eyes. "I can't ask you to do that for me. I won't. I love you, but I don't ever want you to resent me for a rash decision."

"It's not rash." Toby shook his head. "Since Logan died, I've been searching for something—a life of my own without him, and I couldn't find it anywhere here. Not until I found you and your people. I've made my choice, and it's you and the world you are building for fae like us. I want to be part of it all."

Xavier nodded. "I'm in it, Toby. If this is what you want, I'll be with you every step of the way. I just want you to be sure."

"I've never been more certain about anything." Toby turned to his parents. "I don't want to leave you, Mom, Dad." His voice broke, and he was suddenly in Brea's arms as she sobbed.

"It's going to be okay, Mom." He held her tight, not wanting to let go, but knowing he had to.

"I know, son." Brea pulled away, staring into his eyes. "You make me so proud to be your mom." She brushed a hand over his brow like she did when he was just a boy. "I've watched you since Logan died and you haven't been yourself. No mother wants to see her son lose everything before he's had a chance to live."

Tears swam in Toby's eyes as she let him go.

"The farmhouse is yours now. Take whatever you need. Sell it if you want. All the documents you'll need are in the safe, along with enough human money to keep you afloat for a few months. There's also a substantial bank account. Xavier will know what to do with it." Brea gave him a last hug and stepped back, wiping her tears.

"If this is what you need to do, my son, you have our support." Lochlan wrapped his long arms around Toby. "I'm so proud of the man you've become. I wish you the best of everything in your new life. I'm just sad we won't be there to see it. But I want you to remember we are always right here with you." He placed a hand over Toby's heart. "Even if you can't see us, we're with you."

All he could do was nod at his father's final words to him, and then he was fumbling through his goodbyes with Griffin.

"I know we don't speak about it, but I am proud to be your father. Lochlan is your dad, and that's the way it should be, but every now and then, I see a bit of myself in you and your sister. You made a tough decision today, and I'm proud of you for standing up and reaching for the life you want. I want you to know it's been one of the greatest joys of my life to be Uncle Griff to you and your sister."

Toby sniffed back his tears and hugged his uncle. "Please tell Riona and the girls how much I love them and I'm sorry I couldn't say goodbye."

The other royals were all there to say goodbye in a blur of activity. Uncle Myles and Aunt Neeve both had words of wisdom and a last hug for him, along with a letter for Mrs. Merrick and the rest of Myles' human family they would never get to see again.

Alona and Finn wished him well and let him know Logan would have wanted him to move on with his life wherever he could find joy. Saying goodbye to the young princess he'd always thought of as a sister was a lot harder than he imagined. Darra had been just as lost as he was when Logan died.

"You're going to make a great queen someday, little Darra. Logan would be so proud of the young woman you've become."

"He loved you so much," she whispered against his shoulder. "I know he would want this for you."

He released her with a pang of regret for what might have been.

Toby had said all his goodbyes, except for the hardest one. He turned toward Tia, his emotions raging just under the surface.

"Tobes," Tia choked out his name, twisting her hands together. "You're the best part of me. How am I supposed to do this?"

"I don't know." His voice broke. "I'm so sorry, Tia." She rushed into his arms, and they held on to each other for dear life. "I don't know if I'll be able to amplify your magic once the veil is sealed."

Tia gave a snort at that. "Tobias O'Shea, I would give up every ounce of my magic to see you happy with someone you love."

"I just hope I'm doing the right thing." He sighed into her hair, her head tucked against his shoulder. "I know it's what I want. I worry some day you might need your amplifier and I won't be here, and then you'll be in harm's way because I once made a selfish decision."

"You hush." Tia pulled away from him, wiping the tears from her eyes. "You are the most unselfish fae any of the worlds have ever known. You deserve whatever happiness you can find, and I want you to go out there and take it and never be sorry."

"Thank you, Tia." He held on to her for a little longer before turning away. "I think I'm ready." There were so many others he needed to say goodbye to—people he would miss, but there was no time. The humans were growing impatient, and the outbreak of a full-blown war rested on his ability to leave his family behind and fix the damage he and his ancestors had made in the veil.

"You have everything you need?" Gulliver asked, his shoulders hunched.

"You know I'll miss you every bit as much as Tia?"

"Really?"

"Of course. You're like a brother to me too, you know." Toby couldn't believe after all these years that Gulliver didn't know that.

"You're making the right decision. I've been with you since this whole thing started. I've seen first-hand how their fight has become yours, and how Xavier has helped you move on from Logan. But I'll miss you. You're the one fae who can talk Tia down from her highs and lows. I don't know what I'm going to do without you."

"You'll manage." Toby smiled. "Am I wrong, or have you and Sophie made some big decisions too?"

Gulliver's ears turned pink as he glanced back to the human girl with the blue hair. "She's decided to stay. With me."

"Look at that, Gullie got the girl." Toby grinned and pulled Gulliver in for a last hug. "Take care of Tia for me. And I apologize in advance. I don't think you realize you're going to have to be you and me all rolled into one fae she won't be able to do without. But at least now, she has Kier."

The blood drained from Gullie's face as he nodded. "Don't worry about Tia. You know I'll be whatever she needs me to be."

"You're a good fae, Gul." Toby let him go. He couldn't stand anymore goodbyes. It was time. Time for him—the magicless fae —to fix the damage his ancestors caused.

"Before you go." Gulliver reached into his bag for something. "I don't know if this will work on the other side, but you should take it, just in case." He handed Toby a well-worn journal.

"You think?" He tucked it into his bag full of memories he couldn't do without.

"It's worth trying. I'll see that she checks hers in a few days, once you've had time to settle down."

"Are you sure absolutely about this, Toby?" Xavier stepped up beside him, his eyes full of questions.

"It's hard to leave them all." He glanced around the streets of

Aghadoon, at his family. "I will miss them so much, but I've never been more sure about anything."

He took Xavier's hand, and together, they led their fae to the village square.

"Is everyone who wants to go home here?" Toby called across the crowd of half-fae. His family stood at the edge of the square, having said their goodbyes.

"We're all here," Orla said. "And eager to get back to L.A. and our new homes."

"Here, here!" someone in the crowd said.

"Oh! I forgot one thing." Toby searched the sea of faces, looking for his sister. "I need one last word with my queen before I leave."

Tia nodded and made her way through the throng of people. "I am here," she said, her face pale in the afternoon sunshine.

Toby moved to kneel before his sister. "My Queen, I would like to renounce my titles and my positions as Prince Tobias of Iskalt. I wish to enter my new life as just another fae."

Cool hands cupped his face and lifted his chin. "Prince Tobias O'Shea, the Ogre Killer, you could never be just another fae," she whispered. "But I will grant your request." Her voice lifted. "You will leave here as Tobias O'Shea, my brother and friend." She pulled him to his feet and flung her arms around him. "Now, go be happy." She choked and stepped back.

"I'm ready now." Toby gave a final wave to his family, wishing for one moment he could have a last look at Iskalt before he said goodbye forever.

"Let's take our fae home." Xavier held his hand and they moved to the center of the square. "Just a quick question." He leaned in to whisper, "Why did your sister just call you the Ogre Killer?"

Toby snorted a laugh at that. "Long story."

"You'll have to tell me about it sometime."

"I really hope this works," Toby whispered, checking to make sure he had his copy of the O'Shea spell.

"It will. I have confidence in you and your sister." Xavier stepped back to let Toby open a portal big enough to take them all safely to L.A.

With a deep breath, Toby called on the only magic he had, hoping he would get to keep it, but if he had to give it up, he was happy to do that. It wouldn't make him any different from the other fae in his new home. And that was a prospect that made this difficult thing so much easier.

The magic filled him, rattling his bones with the intensity of it as it burst out of him. A crack of light slashed across the clearing where he stood. As he guided his portal magic, the crack widened into a swirling mass of light, widening to create a doorway large enough for all to pass through.

He could just make out the Hollywood sign near the park where Aghadoon had stood for a short time. The sun shone through the portal, contrasting with the darkness of the Eldurian night. Toby's heart kicked up a notch as he realized he couldn't wait to get back.

One by one, the half-fae who called the human world home made their way through the portal until only Xavier remained.

"I won't hold you to it if you decide to stay. You're giving up ... everything, and I don't want you to do it just for me."

"I'm doing it for us." Toby watched as Xavier stepped through the portal.

He held it open a minute longer, waving to his family one last time. He memorized their faces, making sure every detail was emblazoned in his mind.

"I love you!" he called to them and stepped through to the other side.

* * *

The silence was what caught Toby's attention first. Los Angeles was one of the loudest and busiest human cities he'd ever visited, even this late at night. He'd been counting on the chaos of the city to keep him distracted when the portal closed forever behind him.

"Why is it so quiet?" Xavier asked.

"The humans have mostly left," a fae Toby only vaguely remembered said. "Some remained, but they are friends. Our numbers are in the tens of thousands, and more arrive every day."

"So, it's truly our city now?" Orla asked, her eyes bright with hope.

"As long as the fae with magic follow through on their promises to seal the veil, then this is our home. Forever," the lady said.

"That's Meara," Xavier leaned in to remind Toby. "She's the leader of the Hollywood Hills fae."

"Thanks." Toby moved to the middle of the park. "Could someone bring me a basin of water?" He set his bag on the ground, fishing out the scroll written in his blood.

"This isn't your kingdom, Prince," Meara said. "No one will do your fetching for you."

"He isn't a prince anymore. He's one of us," Orla snapped. "And he needs water for the magic that will heal the veil and close it from this side. Someone get the man some water and a lighter."

"Will you need anything else, Toby?" Orla asked.

"No. Just fire and water. And someone to tell me what a lighter is," he added.

"It's like the magic sticks you use to light candles at home," Xavier explained, crouching down beside him in the darkness.

"This is home now." Toby smiled to himself as he laid the spell on the grass. Written with a mixture of his and Tia's blood, this was powerful magic, the likes of which no fae he knew had ever meddled with.

With the moon shining above, his Iskalt power came alive in a way it never did during the day. Though he didn't have much magic, he was still of Iskalt, and Tia believed that was enough to ignite the spell.

Fae gathered around to watch as Xavier helped Toby light the edges of the scroll, letting the flames curl and burn the parchment. Without a word, he dropped it into the basin Meara had brought him, and the flames flickered out. Blood seeped from the page, leaving the words behind in black lettering. Toby fished it out and laid it flat on the ground, waiting for something to happen.

"It didn't work," someone said.

"Give it a minute," another replied.

Heat shot through Toby's body, lighting him up from the inside.

"Toby!" Xavier shouted as Toby collapsed to the ground.

"I'm okay." He gasped. "Look!" He pointed to the sky where a rainbow of colors moved like the Southern Lights of the snúa aftur in Eldur. He and Logan used to sneak out to watch them in the summer. Colorful light streaked like threads of magic, healing the veil where it had been destroyed by the O'Shea magic.

"It's beautiful," Xavier whispered, staring up into the heavens.

"Magic is always beautiful. Big or small." Toby stood there holding Xavier's hand as the last of his sister's magic faded from the sky.

"Did it work?" Orla asked.

"Only one way to find out." Toby moved away from the crowd and tried to open a new portal. With thoughts of Iskalt filling his mind, he reached for his magic, but it wouldn't come.

He couldn't feel his childhood home the way he always had before.

Shaking his head, he stopped trying. "It worked."

Sadness filled him as the finality of it all struck him hard. He could never go home. It was his choice, but it still hurt.

Cheers went up all across the park, and Toby wanted to celebrate with them, but a heaviness filled his heart.

"You okay?" Xavier asked.

"Yeah. It's just so ... final."

"You're allowed to be sad, Tobes."

"Thank you." He leaned into Xavier's side.

"You think you can still open portals just on this side?"

"Probably. I can still feel the O'Shea magic. It just won't let me reach across the veil."

"Give it a shot. I was thinking we could spend a night at a certain farmhouse. I think you've earned at least one quiet night before we jump into rebuilding our world together."

"I'll try." Toby reached for his magic and a familiar sensation filled his chest. The light of his magic glowed, and a swirling doorway opened to reveal the farmhouse that held wonderful memories of his family.

"There it is!" Xavier cheered. "See, Tobes, you still have a home here. It's not the end of the fae for you. It's a whole new world for us and all of our fae."

He stepped through the portal, and with a smile, Toby followed.

Chapter Thirty
SOPHIE

"This is a strange sort of contraption." Riona struggled with the yards of lacy fabric.

"It's called a veil." Sophie giggled as Riona tried to arrange the 'contraption' on her head.

"It's a silly *human* thing, isn't it?" Riona gave the veil a frightening scowl. Frightening if you didn't know the woman behind the scowl.

"It's a tradition." Sophie reached up to help her arrange the layers of pearly lace studded with silver and blue stars. "When I was sick, I used to dream of the wedding I'd never have, and I always wanted a long veil that would trail behind me."

"Well, you look beautiful."

"Thanks, Riona."

"Call me Mom." Riona busied herself with fussing over Sophie's dress, but Sophie knew the woman wasn't the sort to make grand emotional gestures. "That is, if you want." She stopped to meet Sophie's gaze in the mirror. "I don't want to take the place of your own mother. Especially today."

"I never really knew her. Not as an adult anyway." Sophie's eyes filled with tears. "And you've been like a mother to me since I met you. I'd love nothing more than to call you Mom."

"Well, don't cry." Riona wiped the tears from Sophie's cheeks. "We don't want to send you out there with puffy eyes." She smiled, moving to arrange Sophie's dress. A fairytale work of art worthy of a princess. The subtle blush fabric fell like a waterfall of silk from her waist to the floor, and the bodice sparkled with tiny stars of silver, blues, and pinks. A sheer cape of intricate flowers and vines fell from her shoulders to trail behind her, blending perfectly with the veil of her dreams. Silver brocade and iridescent pearls studded the front of her gown from neckline to hem. She couldn't have dreamed of a more perfect dress for such a special day.

"Thank you for this," Riona said softly.

"For what?" Sophie turned to face her soon-to-be mother-in-law.

"For having the wedding here in Myrkur, where Gulliver has so many memories. It's your day, and I would have thought you'd want to have the wedding in Iskalt since it's your home now."

"My home is with Gulliver, and this is where he's from, where all his family is. I couldn't imagine having *our* special day anywhere else."

"The girls are so excited to be included. I just hope they

behave themselves. I apologize in advance if they don't. You know they're a bit of a handful."

Niamh and Nora were Gulliver's eight- and ten-year-old sisters, who would be Sophie's flower girls today—another human tradition Sophie wanted to keep.

"I'm thrilled to have them stand with us today."

Gulliver's family had embraced Sophie and Noah from the moment they met, especially his little sisters. Noah and the girls had grown close over the last year, and the three were inseparable whenever they visited, and inconsolable when they had to be apart.

Sophie had heard a lot of comparisons between them and Tia, Toby, and Gullie as kids. She just hoped it would never fall to this little trio to save the world together.

"I think I'm ready," Sophie said breathlessly. She'd heard of brides having cold feet before their big day, but Sophie couldn't wait to march down that aisle and marry her best friend in all the worlds. Gulliver O'Shea was the best man she knew, and she couldn't believe she would be able to call him her husband within the hour.

"Not quite." Riona turned to retrieve a navy silk bag from the table. "Brea gave me some tips on human weddings." She reached in. "This is your something borrowed from Brea and Tia." She held up a pair of beautiful pearl earrings that matched her dress perfectly. "They each wore these at their own weddings."

Sophie was overcome that they would think of her human traditions.

"They're beautiful." She couldn't wait to thank them.

"Something new from Neeve." Riona pulled a silver bangle bracelet from her bag. "She wanted to give you something simple and elegant." She slipped the bracelet over Sophie's hand.

"It's engraved." Sophie read the inscription. "Love always finds a way. Gulliver and Sophie O'Shevereaux." She glanced up at Riona. "I thought he was joking about sharing our names?"

"He wants to take your name the way the humans do. And he wants you all to have a fresh start. You, Noah, and Gulliver are forming a little family of your own. I think it's fitting. You have a bittersweet past with your Devereaux family and Gullie had a difficult childhood before Griffin found him. And poor Noah never had a name of his own. Found families are extra special, Sophie. You three got to choose each other."

"I love it." Sophie clutched the bracelet to her heart. "Sophie-Ann O'Shevereaux." She tried out the name. "Has a nice ring to it, doesn't it?"

"It does." Riona took her hand in hers. "The something old is my gift to you." She pulled something from her bag. "It isn't much. I grew up in Myrkur when it was a prison realm, and the only things people valued were food and shelter. But this belonged to my mother, and I had it made into a hair pin for you."

It was very old. And Sophie recognized it immediately from the stories Gulliver had told her about his ferocious mother.

"It's your family crest." She shook her head. "I can't take this, Riona. It should be my something borrowed, and Brea's earrings can be my something old-slash-borrowed."

The pewter oiche blossom represented the sacred duty of Riona's family. Sophie didn't know much about that duty, other than the story of how Riona came to name the rightful ruler of Myrkur after the fall of King Eagan.

"No. I want it this way." Riona took the pin and clipped it into Sophie's hair. It blended perfectly with her veil.

"This should go to Niamh when she's older. She will likely inherit your legacy as your eldest daughter."

Riona smiled. "The sigil doesn't carry the legacy. Besides, you're my eldest daughter now."

Sophie pulled Riona in for a hug. "Thank you, Mom." She held her tight.

"Oh, I don't want to crush your veil." She pulled back. "I think we're done with the traditions, aren't we?"

"Something blue," Sophie said and both women started to giggle. "I forgot I dyed my hair with shadow berries."

"It's lovely." Riona tucked a strand of Sophie's long, vivid blue hair behind her ear. "And a perfect something blue."

"Gullie always seemed to like the blue hair, so I wanted to surprise him with it."

"You've been starting all kinds of new trends with the Myrkurian girls."

"Have I?"

"Oh, yes. I saw a girl in town the other day with blue tipped hair just like yours when you first arrived. And I imagine your beautiful human wedding will start all sorts of new traditions among fae brides. All the Myrkurian girls are fascinated with you, you know?"

"Me? Why?"

"Because you got Gulliver's attention. My son is many things, but a master with the ladies, he is not. Every girl in Myrkur has had eyes for him ever since he finally grew into his height, but he's never given them any notice. I think he was waiting for you."

"No wonder he moved so slow." Sophie shook her head and laughed.

"Are you nervous?" Riona went to fetch Sophie's bouquet of Ilmur flowers.

"Not at all. I'm excited." Sophie fidgeted in her dress, eager to get on with it.

"The last finishing touch." She handed her a bouquet of the most beautiful white blossoms Sophie had ever seen. The flowers in Myrkur were rather dark with muted colors. These flowers came from Fargelsi, and they smelled wonderful. Sophie held them up to her face to inhale the heady scent.

"Oh, don't do that." Riona pulled her back just in time. "The scent is intoxicating up close. You'll be walking down the aisle like a magic-wielding fae after too much Gelsi wine. Or Gullie after a few sips of any wine."

"Oh." Sophie held them far out in front of her.

"The scent won't affect you unless you stuff your face into your bouquet."

"Got it." Sophie beamed at her future mother-in-law and did a little dance. "I'm so excited."

"Oh, dear." She whisked the flowers from Sophie's hands. "You are human." Riona studied her face. "Ilmur blossoms might not have been the best choice. You may need a break from the flowers from time to time. Just let me know if you start feeling funny."

"Okay." Sophie giggled, feeling as though she could walk on air.

Riona laughed. "This should be a fun evening. The gardens are full of Ilmur flowers Neeve sent over for the wedding."

"Take me to my husband!" Sophie's voice rang out as Riona took her arm to escort her to the garden, where she was about to marry the best man she knew.

* * *

Someone replaced Sophie's bouquet with a lovely bundle of shadow berry blossoms, and her head cleared some, though she still felt as though she was walking on air down the aisle. Tiny flowers bloomed as she walked over the grassy lawn, all her favorite fae seated on either side of the aisle. Eleven-year-old Noah walked beside her, looking handsome in his formal fae tunic that complemented her dress.

Niamh and Nora fluttered along before them, dropping pale blue flower petals. Their wings stirred the breeze of the mild Myrkurian summer. The gardens were breathtaking, but Sophie only had eyes for the tall young man who waited for her at the end of the aisle.

Gulliver stood nervously, his tail swishing behind him until he caught sight of her. All the nerves seemed to vanish as he darted down the aisle to meet her. Laughter swept through the crowd, and Sophie heard several whispers of, "Aw."

He seemed to realize at the last moment that he should have waited on her, but she grabbed his arm and the three of them took the final steps up to the front of the garden, where the King of Myrkur waited to perform the ceremony.

The heady scent of Ilmur flowers filled the air, but Sophie's mind was clear. Taking Gulliver's hand in hers, they approached the king, but they couldn't take their eyes off each other.

They'd come a long way from that first day when Gulliver wandered into the Vieux Carré Cafe. The scent of fresh beignets had lured him in and changed her life forever. She shuddered to think of where she might have ended up if it weren't for Gulliver.

She would have been with her mother and grandmother now, resting in the family mausoleum in the cemetery she'd visited often as a child. Instead, she was getting the fairytale happily ever after she'd only allowed herself to dream of. And it came with an incredible family who loved her as one of their own.

The ceremony passed in a blur as memories flooded Sophie's mind—happy and sad ones. Part of her missed her father today, but looking at Noah beaming up at her from his place between Niamh and Nora, she knew she was home.

"I love you, Soph," Gulliver whispered as his lips brushed hers and Hector announced them as Mr. and Mrs. O'Shevereaux.

Epilogue
FIVE YEARS LATER

Gulliver stepped through the familiar portal, leaving Iskalt behind, eager to see his wife after three days without her. Sophie was his world, but sometimes work got in their way. And for them, work always meant Tia. Gulliver still served as one of Tia's most trusted advisors, but so did Sophie.

She spent a great deal of her time with Tia, teaching her all things human so when she wrote to her brother, she would have a better understanding of his life in the human world.

And that meant Sophie went wherever Tia went because

Tia was never far from her journal that served as her lifeline to Toby.

"There he is!" Sophie's voice reached him the moment he entered Fargelsi, with Griffin following right behind.

"Missed you, Soph!" Gulliver called, not caring who heard, no matter the teasing he got from the other royals. He loved his wife and didn't bother trying to hide it.

"Papa!" A gangly little boy with a tail ran across the garden, and Gulliver swept him up in his arms. "Missed you too, Fergus." He held him tight, smothering him with kisses until he shrieked with laughter.

"The festival is about to start." Sophie took his arm, and they walked down the hill to the palace gardens. It was time for the annual festival of lights—an event he looked forward to every year since he was a child.

"Where is Noah?" Gulliver scanned the crowds of children playing on the hillside.

"He's with the girls, as usual." Sophie pointed to a group of older children already dancing under the setting sun. Noah, almost sixteen now, danced with Niamh and Nora, their wings forming a cage around him to keep the other girls at bay.

"Sophie!" Tia came rushing up the lawn, clutching her skirts high. "I just got a message from Toby!" She blew the hair from her face. "Can you explain what a surrogate mother is?"

"Oh my." Sophie reached for the journal. "May I?"

Tia nodded, handing over the book she never let out of her sight.

"Oh, Tia! This is good news!" Sophie beamed. "You're going to be an aunt."

"We're going to be aunts?" She peered over Sophie's shoulder. "Where does it say that?"

Toby and Xavier had adopted a little fae girl a few years ago, but they wanted more children. It was difficult for the fae of the human realm to adopt. It wasn't yet legal for them to adopt human children, so they had mentioned trying other means.

"They've found a young fae woman to act as a surrogate for them. They just found out she's pregnant with Toby's twins. A boy and a girl."

"What? Wait? How? I'm so confused." Tia wore a scandalous look on her face. "Did my brother ... cheat on his husband with this girl?"

"No. Um." Sophie's cheeks went pink as she leaned over to whisper the details to Tia.

"Oh!" Tia leaned back. "Human magic really is remarkable! And a little bit gross." She shuddered. "But I guess that means Toby's twins will be O'Sheas?"

"Can someone explain what's happening, please?" Gulliver leaned in closer to make himself part of the conversation. "I'm going to be an uncle again?"

"Yes. They're Toby's biological children," Sophie explained. "They'll inherit the O'Shea magic."

"What does that mean?" Gulliver asked.

"Toby's legacy will live on in the human realm, and Tia's will live on here through Madison and Duncan." Tia's and Keir's four-year-old twins were miniature versions of Toby and Tia, and the apple of Iskalt's eye.

"I just hope our kids are better at portaling than me." Tia beamed and rushed off to tell her parents the news.

"What worries will you send off into the sky tonight, Pappa?" Fergus asked from his spot on Gulliver's shoulder. Gus' tail wound around Gulliver's, and his son's cat-like eyes filled with adoration.

Gulliver took Sophie's hand, and they headed toward the gathering crowd as evening settled over the Gelsi palace. "I'm not sure, son," Gulliver said. "I don't really have any worries this year. Maybe I'll write down a few hopes for the future of the fae."

A new cowritten series by Melissa and M. Lynn begins soon! Sign up to get updates here!

Thank You!

Thanks for reading Queens of the Fae!!
Want more by M. Lynn? Don't forget to check out her Six Kingdoms series.

Want more by Melissa A. Craven?
Find the Ascension of the Nine Realms series wherever you buy books

About Melissa

Melissa A. Craven is an Amazon bestselling author of Young Adult Contemporary Fiction and YA Fantasy (her Contemporary fans will know her as Ann Maree Craven). Her books focus on strong female protagonists who aren't always perfect, but they find their inner strength along the way. Melissa's novels appeal to audiences of all ages and fans of almost any genre. She believes in stories that make you think and she loves playing with foreshadowing, leaving clues and hints for the careful reader.

Melissa draws inspiration from her background in architecture and interior design to help her with the small details in world building and scene settings. (Her degree in fine art also comes in handy.) She is a diehard introvert with a wicked sense of humor and a tendency for hermit-like behavior. (Seriously, she gets cranky if she has to put on anything other than yoga pants and t-shirts!)

Melissa enjoys gardening and sitting on her porch when the weather is nice with her two dogs, Fynlee and Nahla, reading from her massive TBR pile and dreaming up new stories.

Visit Melissa at Melissaacraven.com for more information about her newest series and discover exclusive content.

Want to see more books by Melissa A. Craven? You can view them here

Join Melissa and Michelle's Facebook Group: Fantasy Book Warriors

About Michelle

Michelle MacQueen is a USA Today bestselling author of love. Yes, love. Whether it be YA romance, NA romance, or fantasy romance (Under M. Lynn), she loves to make readers swoon.

The great loves of her life to this point are two tiny blond creatures who call her "aunt" and proclaim her books to be "boring books" for their lack of pictures. Yet, somehow, she still manages to love them more than chocolate.

When she's not sharing her inexhaustible wisdom with her niece and nephew, Michelle is usually lounging in her ridiculously large bean bag chair creating worlds and characters that remind her to smile every day - even when a feisty five-year-old is telling her just how much she doesn't know.

See more from M. Lynn and sign up to receive updates and deals!

michellelynnauthor.com

Join Melissa and Michelle's Facebook Group: Fantasy Book Warriors

Follow Michelle and Melissa on TikTok

@ATaleOfTwoAuthors

Want to see more books by Michelle?

visit https://books2read.com/ap/R5my46/M-Lynn

Want More From Brea's World?

Don't miss the free prequel,
Fae's Dilemma available at

BookHip.com/VJMXVGD

www.ingramcontent.com/pod-product-compliance
Lightning Source LLC
Chambersburg PA
CBHW020347310726
48979CB00015B/2540/J

* 9 7 8 1 9 7 0 0 5 2 9 7 8 *